TWIN BLADES

Noelle Upton

ISBN: 979-8-9890779-0-8

Cover by Teri Smithberg

Author's Note

Thank you for picking up this book! As an avid reader myself, I often skim author's notes, but I wanted to include a few content warnings and information you may refer to while reading this story.

This book contains strong language, dark themes, and explicit scenes of violent and sexual nature. Death and grief are integral to this story, and there is mention of depression, self-harm, and suicidal ideation. There are also character deaths on and off page and mention of sexual assault (an accusation made by one character to another—no acts or description on or off page). My intention is not to be gratuitous with any of these but to fit this world and these characters. If any of these themes make you uncomfortable, please take care of yourself in whatever way is best for you.

I've also included a pronunciation guide at the end of the book that you may refer to as you read.

I hope you enjoy this tale that is near and dear to my heart!

To my mother, for always encouraging me to read whatever I wished.

PART ONE

THIEVES AND SHADOWS

1

The beast before me slammed a mud-colored fist into my side. My breath caught, and the pain faintly registered in the back of my mind. But my body kept moving. I silently whipped around the stumbling brute and imagined myself as a striking, countering mist. While he lumbered around the ring, trying to track me, my speed was a taunt. And my blows struck true, even as blood from an earlier swipe of the his claws clouded my vision. The crowd above whooped as the tide of the match turned.

The rules of the ring were simple: no weapons save for your body, no magic, and no killing blows. A match was over when one submitted or was unconscious. The beast had three full heads on me height-wise, at least two-hundred pounds more muscle, and hairy knuckles ending in yellowing claws.

Usually the regular attendees of these fights knew better than to bet against me. But most tonight were those that were unfamiliar, and seeing me square up against my opponent, they'd already accepted my defeat. They gulped it down with their ale and liquor and put down more money for my opponent.

When we'd faced each other at the start of the match, the beast grinned jagged teeth as I shed my jacket, my loose tunic. I tossed them just outside of the invisible barrier of the ring, out of reach. The men, women, and other creatures cackled in delight at the female in nothing but worn leather trousers and a white undergarment on her chest. The band across my breasts stretched with each breath while still clinging securely to me. They laughed at the twin braids trailing down my scalp and back.

My eyes had cut to just above and found a set of lashless eyes, black skin, and the approving twist of a mouth. I'd smirked as the waves of my opponent's and our audience's arrogance washed over me.

And then we had begun.

We said nothing to each other as we crept forward, circled like the predators that we both were. But while his power was rippling over bulging, inch-thick taupe skin, mine was much more compact. It was folded and woven through every fiber and essence of my much slighter frame, but was ready to pounce just as quickly as his. Faster than his.

So, as he had confidently wielded his fists, throwing his body behind each swipe, I let my body take some of it without a wince. But with each blow, I twisted, ducked before he could land a second. Before he could pin me down.

And when he was off balance, I struck my own. Like a coiled snake, I let out only the energy needed and quickly brought it back to my center. I let my own razor sharp nails scratch his skin. If I bled, he would bleed as well.

His blow to my side had been slightly labored, my signal that he was growing tired enough. I flicked a glance back up to the crowd above and caught the briefest of nods from my grinning friend. The patrons of the tavern stilled as I whirled around the beast, faster than many of their eyes could completely track. I felt a dark tendril of burning hunger begin to bloom in my chest and itch in request.

But I denied it with a steady exhale and swift kick to the beast's kidneys. He roared, and I could not help my lips curling back from my teeth.

Killing in the ring would result in your own death. For the invisible barrier around the ring was enchanted to strike down anyone who killed their opponent. That death was swift, before they could even register their victory. Though, I knew some still killed anyway. Wanting not to leave with gold in their pockets, but die with small glory.

When my opponent wheeled around, wheezing, I was already moving. My body rounded much faster than his, and with it, my raised heel caught his low, thick temple. I felt bones crack and laughed. He didn't have time to even lay eyes on me before they rolled in his skull, and he fell to the ground in a far meatier noise than I anticipated.

The crowd was quiet then, just for a moment, until they saw what I already knew. The beast's chest rose and fell, and I was grinning now, just as he had at the start of the match, as if he had already won. My grin was in knowing just how wrong he'd been.

Then the tavern erupted. Some shouted in disbelief, some in outrage at their money lost. But some cheered for their money won.

I felt the trembling of the barrier allow me to pass as I exited the ring, leaving the beast to wake to the coldness of his defeat, whenever that would be. His mud-colored tongue hung out of his mouth onto the blood-stained floor, and I let out a quick laugh at the comical sight.

I then grasped my jacket and tunic and headed for the wall. The weapons we discarded hung on nails or were propped up against the stone facade. My black, wide-brimmed hat was on one of those nails, and underneath it on the floor, my boots. And inside them, I had stashed my daggers. I now quickly sheathed them at my thighs and their weight was familiar, comforting.

After quickly shoving into my boots and palming my clothing in one hand, I jumped. Not bothering with the steps at the far left of the sunken ring, I grasped the lip of the tavern floor and hoisted myself up.

One of the regular fighters, my friend and mentor, Grimm, gave me a crooked grin, and his sharp, gold teeth glittered in the low lighting. He clapped a black hand that felt like sandpaper on my back, but the gesture was warm. His face was amused, knowing, and I patted my hand once on his shoulder as I pushed to an empty table on the outskirts of the crowd.

Another pair was setting up to start in the ring, judging from those now focusing their attention underneath once again. A few patrons, though, stayed where they were, engaged in raucous conversation, brooding over their drinks, or some combination of both.

I donned my thin, black tunic once again and swiped my sleeve over my brow. My own blood seeped into the fibers, but the wounds had already closed, and I felt no tenderness as I further cleared my vision. I shoved my arms through my leather jacket.

Once the new fight had begun in full swing, I rose and angled toward the bar on the opposite wall of the tavern, but as I started to meander through those in my way, a sweaty hand caught my attention. Caught my *wrist*.

I was jerked back, and the hat I grasped in the other fell to the dirty floor. The hand that snagged me did not stop at halting my movement, but pulled me until the backs of my knees were met with another's thighs.

I tipped back and landed harshly in a man's lap. My head snapped around to meet the face of my assaulter, and he was a red-faced, stocky man. His human skin was like leather, and he smelled like sweat and salt—a sailor. No, when my eyes quickly traced over him, I caught sight of the sun-bleached but well-tailored coat slung behind his chair. A wealthy sailor, a merchant.

His breath stank of arrogance and liquor as he leered at me, still grasping my wrist, and my lips pulled back from my teeth in a full-out hiss. But he was undeterred. And the men surrounding him, some of his crew, I imagined, were a chorus of laughter.

"Ah, just as feisty even though the fighting is done!" The man's accent sounded like marbles knocking between my ears, and I hissed again. "I just wanted to personally thank the young thing that made me a bit richer tonight!" I pulled against his grasp, but he only brought his other hand to my waist, pulling me to his chest. My stomach roiled as he said a drop quieter, "And perhaps if you're good, I'll let you take a few sips of *me* tonight."

I bucked against his words, but the merchant just called across the room. When I followed his gaze, I saw the familiar black, bald head. "Thanks for the tip, friend, the little one *was* a smart wager after all!" And it took everything in me not to roll my eyes. Humans were so easy to hustle.

I thrashed again, this time breaking from his hold, and the man guffawed, looking around at those with him and soaking up their approving jeers.

The one that sat slightly behind him, though, remained silent. The hooded figure clad in all-black with two short swords sheathed at their back sat silently, arms crossed and leaned back in their seat as if bored. They made no move to join in on the merchant and his crew's banter, but they sat close enough to signal that they were with them. The air around the hooded person was different from the sticky, close air of the rest of the tavern. It was still, a void.

I kissed the air at the Shadow as I pushed off of the human's lap and spun on my heel. No one made a move to grab me again, and I picked up my hat off of the dusty, stained wooden floor.

I resumed my uncompleted journey to the bar and was quickly given my winnings in a coin purse with a quick exchange of hands. Not until I shoved my way to the door and felt the crispness of the sea-kissed air did I let the sly smile start to keep its way across my lips. I dusted off the brim of my hat and set it atop my braids. The coin purse weighed proudly in my pocket, and I deposited with it the true prize I came for tonight.

The weight of the object I snatched from the merchant's coat pocket weighed heavier than the gold. My full grin was shadowed under my hat as I made my way through the streets.

~

She wrapped her arms around his broad shoulders, teasing the soft curls trailing down his neck. He moved his hands between them to the hem of her dress. His quick fingers teased the skin of her thighs underneath, and she shuddered —

I snickered as I put the small book down into the plush grass. I grasped my ceramic travel mug and took a sip of tea. The taste of chamomile warmed my throat as I looked out from the cliffside. A sharp, quick stab of nostalgia hit me square in the heart at the sight of the rolling hills, but I did my best to wash away the memories and the guilt of barely-answered letters.

The port was awakening with the pinks and oranges of dawn, and people going to and from work milled about quietly on the streets. Just a few minutes more, and I would be among them. My meeting with my current employer wasn't for another hour or so, but I'd barely slept and had hopped out of the lumpy bed before the sun rose. The lodging house I'd stayed in last night was cheap and dirty and loud—I couldn't get out of there fast enough.

I glanced to my wrist at the cuff and thought again of how I could possibly keep it. The gold gleamed and was encrusted with purple sapphires of varying sizes. The width of it was slender, but the weight of it... it was too heavy to be a simple bracelet. My lips pursed as I wondered how I could describe such a thing to my jeweler to replicate.

With a sigh, I picked up the small novel once more. My shoulders hunched in concentration over the pages as the characters backed into an alcove of a midnight garden. Just as he hiked up her skirt, lifting her against the stone facade, the faint smell of cinnamon and burning wood tickled my nostrils. My eyes stopped sweeping over the paper and stilled. The smell became stronger as something neared me from behind.

In an instant, I dropped the book to the grass once again, rising to my feet and turning toward the scent. My blades were unsheathed from my thighs and in my hands without a thought. A throbbing started at the base of my skull, but I forced my attention forward.

In the direction I faced, the sun was still working to illuminate the day. The sky there was a brightening mauve, and just a few yards before me, was the source of the scent. They moved silently, slowly toward me.

They were too close. Too close to where I had just been lounging. I cursed myself for being taken unawares.

My body hummed with the desire to act—flee or strike. To do something. But a thought floated to the forefront, reasoning that if this figure wanted to harm me, I would already be dead. Or already be fighting, that is.

I was then able to focus on the person now stopped just four paces in front of me. The smell of them was more potent and like... a roaring campfire. Their eyes were in darkness underneath the hood, but the light of the rising sun shown on a formidable jaw shadowed with hints of a needed shave. Their skin was a golden brown, just a few shades lighter than my own, but underneath seemed to glow with the burgeoning morning.

I counted five breaths as we stood facing each other, both our feet shoulder-width apart. Neither of us were fools, and we recognized the other for what they were. Though, with the fiery power radiating from them, I found myself almost second-guessing my own abilities. That and their weapons happened to be much larger than mine.

"It's a bit rude to interrupt someone while they're reading, isn't it?" I worked to make my words steady as they released into the crisp air. They said nothing, and I twirled the blades in my hands.

The Shadow reached into a pack slung on their back amidst their swords, and I stilled. However, their movements were slowed enough that I did not move to attack. When they grasped what they sought, they flung an object at me with a bored flick of their arm.

My eyes stayed on them until something rolled and nudged my brown leather boot. When I allowed my eyes to flutter down to the ground, my throat tightened, but I schooled my face into an impassive mask.

They'd lobbed a head over to me and let it roll on the bright green grass. Its sky-blue skin once resembled a clear spring day. Now it was dull, with eyes milky in death. The stringy black hair of my most recent employer was limp, and his mouth now permanently in a gray-toothed sneer.

When I looked back at the figure, I sucked my teeth and gave a quick tsk of my tongue, "Now you've cost me money. Are you going to at least show me your face? Or are all you shifty bastards cowards, too?"

A beat passed before they reached up quickly to snatch back the hood. Thick, black waves cascaded from *his* brow, and the frontmost strands were tucked behind his ears. Beside a strong nose and underneath a serious, scowling brow, were glowing eyes the color of tangerines. I stifled a flinch as the Shadow spoke through clenched teeth, "Considering that you cost *me* money, be grateful that I did not behead *you*."

I did not suppress the cackle that rose from my belly, and I bent over as it racked through me. He narrowed those haunting eyes, but was otherwise still. "And how does my petty thievery have anything to do with you, Shadow?"

Ten breaths passed, but he remained silent, eyes still narrowed. I sighed and continued, "Since you have killed my employer, where is my payment?"

He ignored my question and opted to ask another, "Who taught you how to fight?"

Another surprise. My face pinched a moment to make sense of his question. After a beat of confusion, I raised my brows in feigned incredulity, "Not used to a female holding her own?" I cocked a hip and gestured the tip of a blade to my chin, "I thought I heard there were females in your little group? Or are you all just as sexist as you are shifty?"

His eyes flared a bit—the color in them actually *brightened* for a moment. I kept the mask of defiance on, even as the cold lick of fear ran down my neck. My mind grasped for a word, a name. But the tendrils of two-hundred-year-old lessons floated and died before I could decipher them. The color in his eyes settled back to that tangerine, "Who."

This time I went for honesty, "I've had many teachers. Too many to name. Why?"

His lip curled slightly. In—in disgust, "You know techniques that you are not supposed to know. I couldn't care less about what you stole. So, I will ask again," he started moving closer. "Who. Taught. You." He stopped, leaving just a pace between us. His swords were still sheathed, but I sensed the increasing tension in him—he would attack soon. Perhaps no matter how I answered his demands, he would attack.

Would he kill me? A dark, comforting voice in the back of my mind whispered, *no*.

His head tilted slightly, and his eyes roamed my face, flaying my confidence nonetheless. I was unable to speak but did not shrink.

Never shrink. My chin stayed raised toward him.

And when I finally found my voice, it shook a bit, but I was not too arrogant to know that my fear of him was warranted, wise even. "If you are referring to me knowing Shadow techniques, I am afraid that I cannot give you the answer you seek." Though I was already a trained fighter when I'd started in the rings and taking contracts, I had to admit that the Shadow techniques had proven very helpful.

His eyebrow raised, and it was my only indication that he had had enough. I reacted without thought and moved to strike. A nick of one of the blades on his skin was all I needed, but neither made it that far. Faster than I could track, he caught both my wrists and *twisted*. Lightning pain shot up from my now-fractured limbs, and my blades fell to the grass in soft thuds.

I had no time to flinch as a hand flew to my throat. I stifled a yelp at the pain and the shockingly quick defeat.

His words were clipped with rage as he brought his face close to mine. The black of his hair was like raven's feathers, "You fight well, but I fight better. Do not continue to test me. I could not care less about what you stole, but you *will* tell me which Shadow taught you. Now. Or I will snap your neck."

I bit the words out breathlessly, "I. Don't. Know. I never got his name." The hand pressed tighter, and darkness threatened the edge of my vision. I mouthed, "I *swear*."

He made no move to release me, though. His amber eyes held me hostage. I felt mine bulging at the pressure as I futilely clawed my hands at his arms, but I did not look away. *Let him see the life leave me when he gives the final snap.*

With an annoyed suck of his teeth, he released his grasp and let me slump. I refused to crumple to the ground as the blackness in my eyes faded. My bones were vibrating, trying to make sense of how to come back together, but the throbbing pain would make picking up the blades again laughable. The throbbing in my skull was now pounding, but I swallowed, held it back. All the while he was still standing before me, watching as I tried to pull myself together.

My face was hot, and for a moment, I wished that he had succeeded at knocking me out, perhaps more. The cry I let out was ragged, outraged. And this, he was not expecting. My arms would be useless for a while, but my legs weren't. My right leg exploded as my heel shot for his gut. And this made contact.

He did not fly back like I had hoped, but fell back a step or two. I took this moment to crouch low, swiping my leg, and I made contact again. But he turned from my kick enough and almost instantly regained his footing. I scrambled back from him as I continued to suck in precious air.

My arms were trembling from the pain still radiating from my wrists. And the stomach-churning sound of shattered bones signaled a long healing ahead. I held my arms taut at my sides, lest they heal incorrectly and leave me to re-break them myself later.

My attacker made no move to come at me again. While I panted, his chest barely moved with his steady breaths. The Shadow's black fighting leathers swallowed the sunlight as much as his hair, and he just stared, head cocked, eyes narrowed. And this was worse, I realized. I was not on the ground, but I was down. There was no thrill fighting someone that could not, at least in that moment, fight back. Embarrassment was acid in my stomach, bitter on my tongue.

With my training and successes, this asshole had defeated me before I could even fight. I knew the shot to his torso was a lucky one that he recovered from without a thought. And it had taken all that I could muster in that moment. I swallowed another scream of outrage as I faced him, stiff with pain.

He gave a last sucking of his teeth and turned on his heel, deeming me unworthy of another word, another action. Unworthy of any explanation of how he'd found me or my employer.

"Where the *fuck* is my money you shifty motherfucker," I spat at him. He gave me no reaction, no uproar over my teardown.

He simply called over his shoulder as he continued to walk away, "Since you cost me my contract, I helped myself to your payment. But I'm sure with your ring winnings, you won't be left completely destitute."

And then he was gone, moving swiftly to Mother-knows-where. I glared down at where he had stood, strangling me while I did *nothing*, and I caught sight of one of those milky eyes. My toe connected with the severed head and sent it flying across the hill, my cry ringing out into the morning.

2

By the time I reached the streets of Nethras, my steps were slowed, and my underarms radiated a most awful stench. That fucker taking my payment left me a bit strapped for travel funds, and I had to ration what I had left on the two-day sail back to the mainland. My passage back to Nethras ate through most of the money I brought with me, and I didn't eat save for feeding from a willing passenger on the ship to tide me over.

The cobblestoned streets were rough under my boots, but the familiarity of it made my shoulders relax. Exhaustion crowded behind my eyes, but I had one stop to make.

My room on the small vessel from Dyna included an uncomfortable hay-filled mattress, but I avoided sleep the first night. My wrists were still healing from being broken into gravel, and one wrong turn in sleep could have set them crookedly or broken them again. The second night, my racing thoughts kept me from falling into any meaningful slumber.

The sun had set, and my small pack bounced on my hip as I stretched my hands open, closed. Though the healing was complete, it was still new, and the anxiety of some unforeseen nerve damage kept tickling the back of my mind.

The buildings in Nethras had a pleasant crowdedness, where anything one needed was surely within a few blocks' reach. Luckily, my destination was not far from the harbor, and I slipped through the streets with ease. The trading district with its myriad of foreign goods and languages gave way to the arts district, and the tinkling sounds of music and merriment almost had me veering off course. Dim, yellow lights glowed in the shop and restaurant windows, and I passed many sitting outside as they sipped on wine or laughed over their food.

But I kept on my path, taking a left, four blocks, then another right. The museums, restaurants, and storefronts gave way to inns, apartments, and finally, townhomes. The one I sought was at the end of a street lined with the yellow flowers that give it its name.

Tulip Street was a quiet one at this time, with most of its residents turning in for the night. I went round to the back door of the last unit on the right that overlooked a small grassy area. Even in the dark, I could see it littered with children's toys, most likely dropped at the ring of the supper bell.

I knocked quickly two times, paused, then once, and waited. The sound of children protesting bedtime and begging for one last piece of dessert filled my ears, and I couldn't help but smile. When the door finally opened, warm light from the kitchen filled my vision.

The female that opened the door had a frazzled look on her face, but then again, Francie always looked frazzled. Her tanned skin was flushed, and when her brain caught up, she quickly wiped her hands on the white apron still tied around her waist. Fondness filled her cerulean blue eyes as she extended her arms to me.

Chuckling, I held up a hand to stop her, "Hi Francie, I would, but I have been traveling for a few days and do *not* smell the best."

She scoffed and pulled me in anyway, "I spend all day with stinky children—your underarm rank doesn't bother me in the slightest." She gave me a good squeeze before pulling back. Her deep brown hair was plopped on top of her head in a hasty attempt at pulling it from her face. Now, it flopped about the side of her head, threatening to come undone. "Now, to what do I owe this pleasure? Please come inside! The children would love to see you."

I sighed and shook my head, "I would, but I'm in a bit of a hurry to get home and sleep for the next week," Francie laughed in that guttural way that always surprised me, and her lips pulled back enough to show her fangs, "I just came to drop off."

Her eyes were immediately glistening, as they did every time I did this. I was amazed at Francie's ability to be rendered to tears, though I'd known her for over a hundred years, so it shouldn't have really *shocked* me. But it warmed my chest the same each time. I opened the leather satchel slung over my shoulder and retrieved the velvet coin purse.

I pushed it into Francie's soft touch and closed my hand over hers, "I wanted to bring more, but hopefully this will tide you all over for a while." Francie snatched the money from our hands and flung her arms around me once again. I gave her slender back a few good pats and waited for her to pull away.

Three breaths, and she finally did, "Okay, well if you aren't staying, then I will just have to send you home with some food. You are lucky that I have a few sandwiches left from lunch." She turned deeper into the kitchen and was back in a moment, shoving a wrapped sandwich and an apple into my chest. "Please take care of yourself, Meline. And come by whenever you can. We all miss you." I nodded, smiled, and said goodbye.

As I made my way around the children's home, I deposited the food in my satchel. The walk back up Tulip Street and twenty-minute saunter was pleasant enough. Mostly, I was happy to be on steady ground again.

Nethras had been my home for the past few decades after years of trying to find somewhere to land, and it was the best mixture of everything I loved. There were enough taverns with fighting rings in the seedier districts to give me a steady flow of coin, as well as a healthy influx of contracts for blades-for-hire in the backroom dealings.

And near my apartment, there was all the good food, art, and pleasant views that I needed. A few blocks from home, I caught a lanky, well-dressed figure hunched over the handle of a shop door. Unable to resist, I sped forward and landed my hands on the person's back.

Lee yelped and whirled around, utter terror on his face. But when he focused and recognized me, he whined and rolled his eyes, "Godyx, Mel, you're an *asshole*." His pale hand fumbled through locking the doors of his bookshop for the evening, and I giggled when he almost dropped the keys onto the ground.

"It's just so *easy* with you. You really should watch your surroundings more."

Lee deposited his keys into the pocket of his tailored jacket and smoothed a hand over his crisp tunic that was tucked into close-fitting trousers. "Be that as it may, I'm about to meet my brother for drinks. Would you want to join?" A soft wind rustled the brim of my hat and Lee's coiffed dark hair.

I was already angling toward home and tossed over my shoulder, "Next time. But I'll see you tomorrow?"

He started up the street in the opposite direction and snickered, "Yes, yes, see you tomorrow."

When I finally reached my apartment building, back toward the outskirts of the arts district, I was operating on muscle-memory. The café that occupied the first floor was closed for the evening, and I rounded the side, unlocking the side door with a key that I fished out of my jacket pocket. I locked it behind me and began the ascent to the seventh floor.

My hall was short, as the building held a total of four homes on each floor, with each one taking a corner of the building, and mine faced the northeast.

When I reached my door, I unlocked it with a different key, and the pulse of an invisible barrier smelling faintly of lavender shuddered around my body as I crossed the threshold. The sticky-sweet taste of aether clung to the back of my tongue, and I swallowed to clear it from my mouth.

I stood for a moment in the dark space, listening, feeling. When I was sure that the only sounds came from myself and the noise trickling in from outside, I plopped down on the cream sofa and fished out the sandwich from my bag. My fingers worked to peel back the wax paper one-handed, and I felt a surge of satisfaction at my ability to do so. The roast chicken and cheese sandwich was a bit dry, being a few hours old, but I scarfed it down all the same while staring unseeingly at the wall of bookshelves behind me. I belatedly realized that I hadn't picked up a new trinket during this trip to add to my collection, but perhaps the next contract would prove more successful in that regard as well.

Once the paper was empty, I sunk my teeth into the apple and stood. The flesh of it was crisp and sour, and I worked my way around its core taking mindless bites and chewing quickly. I walked through a set of double doors and was met with a strong hit of my own scent.

The large bed against the far wall was neatly made. But I didn't allow myself to sit on it just yet, and instead crouched again to the floor. Holding the remainder of my apple with my teeth, I unsheathed my blades from the straps around my ankles and unbuckled those, too. I deposited both pairs in the wooden nightstand to the left of my bed while making a mental note to clean them before going out tomorrow.

When I moved into the adjoining bathing room, I nearly groaned as I turned the knobs and started the shower. Steam began filling the air, and I stripped my soiled clothing where I stood. I tossed the trousers, woolen socks, and salt-stiff tunic and undergarments into the laundry basket beside the tiled stall and the apple core into the smaller waste basket.

My shower was long as I luxuriated in the scalding droplets and aroma of my hair tonics and soap. Thoughts about the tavern, the bracelet, that damned Shadow, and my lost money floated through my mind. But I let them be carried with the other filth from my skin down to the tiled floor of the shower and to the drain. Not until I had scrubbed the entire goddess-damned trip from every surface of my body did I turn off the cooling water. I quickly dried and continued my routine by rubbing jasmine-scented cream into my skin.

Moving back into the bedroom, I retrieved an oversized tunic from my dresser and pulled it over my head. The fabric was worn from years of wear and fell nearly to my knees. I moved to the window set to the right of the bed and pulled back the opaque white curtains. The window took up most of the wall, and unobscured, the moonlight and city lights filled the bedroom. I was high enough to see the streets below, many of my neighbors just now getting their night started.

I sat cross-legged on the settee before the window with a jar of hair cream open next to me. I glided my mother's comb through sections of my hair as I worked the mint-scented cream into my kinks and curls. The process was automatic, and my fingers moved with a mind of their own as I stared out into the evening beyond my window.

I watched a street performer read from a book of poems on a street corner, and he spoke loudly enough for me to hear through the distance and the glass. He lamented a lost love, comparing them to a winter's night. It was complete drivel, but I bore witness to his efforts all the same.

After detangling, I worked the hair into two plaits on either side of my head, letting them fall over my shoulders to the middle of my back. When I finally lowered my arms and screwed the lid back on the cream, the heaviness in my shoulders caught up with me. Not a fatigue of my muscles exactly, but a lack of pure energy to fuel them. I all but crawled to my bed and flung back the thick, deep green cover. Sleep came for me so swiftly, I didn't even recall resting my head on the pillow.

3

Pounding on the front door jolted me from a dreamless sleep nearly a day later. My heart lurched in my chest, and I drew my blades from the nightstand, prowling to the door before I could form any coherent thoughts.

I blinked a few times, clearing the drowsiness, and then I registered the jubilant shouts coming from the hallway, "Open up, open up, open up!" My stance immediately relaxed, and I moved to unlock the door. Once she heard the lock ease, my friend flung the door open herself. The invisible barrier allowed her to pass, and then her arms were around me. I held *my* arms out to my sides, lest the blades I still held knick her accidentally with all of her flailing.

"Shoko," I sighed, "I thought you had a key."

My voice was crackly while hers was filled with excitement, "I do, but I didn't want to just barge in! Happy, happy birthday, my friend!" Her soft, floral scent enveloped me, and she eventually pulled away enough to plant a peck on my lips before stepping into the hallway to retrieve a suspicious amount of paper shopping bags.

I couldn't help but chuckle as she came into my home, moving about the space as if it was hers while tossing her long, black hair over her shoulder. Which, as much time as she spent here, wasn't far off.

I closed and locked the door behind her, and when I turned around, she'd already moved to the dining table, unpacking the bags she'd brought. "You know, Shoko, I could have killed you. You shouldn't wake people up from a dead sleep like that."

25

She rolled her large, cat-like eyes and huffed, "Well, how was I supposed to know you'd be sleeping? I had to come right over, so the sun has just set, obviously. And—wait. How long have you been asleep?" She waved away her question, "You've really gotten boring in your old age." She grinned up at me as she pulled something from the pocket of her black trousers.

My gaze zeroed in on the tightly rolled joint she waggled while she grinned. Shoko started the stove and brought the joint to the flame. Once it was lit, she moved soundlessly to me.

She bowed, extending it to me between two, nearly white fingers, "The beginnings of a great night for the birthday girl. My queen."

It was my turn to roll my eyes, but I took it from her all the same. She let out an excited whoop when I inhaled, held, and exhaled smoke toward the ceiling. "You know, I only smoke in the house when you're here. You're a bad influence."

She snagged the joint from me and took her own hit, "Oh please. We're both bad influences on each other." Shoko grinned from ear to ear as I laughed. "Okay, okay, I've got your real gift, but we'll open it when we get to the tavern. Oh! And I picked up that dress you wanted, and I've got my outfit as well. How was your trip?" She'd moved back again to organizing the things she'd brought, placing the garments into two neat piles on the table.

"Shit, actually. I was so tired when I got home, I slept through the whole night and day, apparently," I waved to the window. It was as if I hadn't even fallen asleep. The night sky had been out, people meandering the streets, and I'd awakened to the same sight.

The heels of my hands scrubbed at my eyes when I thought about how terribly my latest contract turned out. When the job presented itself, I jumped at the chance to get out of Nethras for a bit. I had paid Grimm some up front for his help and still owed him the rest, and I'd have to use some of my savings if I didn't get another job soon.

As I ran down the events of the past three days with Shoko; omitting what *exactly* I stole from the merchant, Grimm's name, and dropping off with Francie; she sat me down on my sofa, standing behind me and unraveling my braids.

When we first met, Shoko was absolutely fascinated with my hair, exclaiming that it was so different from her silky, thin tresses. I would run my fingers through hers, admiring the smoothness, and she'd sneer, admonishing it as limp and too fine for its own good. My hair, she remarked, had *life*, interest.

Her fingers carefully separated the waves and curls, fluffing as she went, "Damn," she drew out the word and whistled, "the fucking nerve of that male. Those Shadows always seem to just get in the way," Shoko pulled at the frontmost strands of my hair, playing with how she would style it for tonight.

I picked at my fingernails, "I really don't know what they're good for. Seems the only thing they do is take all the good contracts, and now they've outright stolen from me."

She placed her hands on my shoulders, gave a squeeze, and planted a swift kiss on my cheek, "Well, cheer up, honey. It's your birthday, and we're going out on the town! Go ahead and wash up," she leaned into my ear and whispered, "because I have been very polite about your breath, but it is growing unbearable. Then, we'll get dressed."

My hand flew to my mouth as I stood, whirling around to her, "You bitch!"

I ran to my en suite and slammed the door behind me, shutting out her cackles as I brushed my teeth and tongue. The small jar of tooth polish was nearly gone, but I managed to get enough out to adequately clean my mouth. And once I'd thoroughly scrubbed away the gunk, she and I lazily dressed. She filled me in on the week since I'd seen her, and we fussed over how she wanted to style my hair for the evening. Though she cut and styled hair for a living, Shoko couldn't ever seem to turn off her need to primp and create.

An hour and a half passed before we were dressed and ready. Shoko had opted for another pair of black trousers, though these ones were skin-tight. Her red sleeveless top was new, and it perfectly coordinated with her eyes and clung to her slim curves.

Two weeks ago, while shopping in the arts district, I had wandered into a new boutique and left without being able to get the image of one of their dresses out of my mind. I brought Shoko with me the next evening to weigh in, and the only one they had left wasn't in my size. Luckily, the saleswoman stated that they'd be getting in more in the next few weeks, and I placed my order with the support of Shoko who never disagreed with my decisions of how to spend my money. So, I more-so brought her along to help me justify the expensive purchase.

Shoko helped me slip on the deceptively simple black dress. The fit was cut close to my body, but offered a lightness and high slit that allowed me to maneuver easily. While the angular neckline was fairly modest, the back dipped to just above my tailbone. The fabric was silky with an expensive weight—it was perfect. Shoko insisted on leaving my hair down and flowing, but conceded to adding two twists to the front to pull the strands from my face. The pearl pins she anchored the twists with were my mother's.

We left my apartment and descended onto the city streets arm-in-arm. Nethras came alive in the evenings, and people of all races happily walked amongst us. Shoko and I happily greeted a stout female about half our height that worked with Shoko at the beauty parlor. Another couple with skin almost as pale as my best friend's offered us stiff but pleasant nods and waves.

Soon we reached our destination. Our favorite tavern sat just a few blocks from my home, in the heart of the arts district. The light was low, and my ears were filled with a pleasant mix of chatter and the beginnings of the full band's set. The establishment was on the smaller side with worn wooden floors and small, circular tables. A few booths with dark red upholstery lined the wall to the left of the entrance, and on the wall to the right sat the sprawling bar. In the back was a small raised stage, and the band playing now was one of my favorites.

Excited shrieks grabbed my attention, and we were waved over to a booth that contained the rest of our party. Tana and Lee were practically jumping out of their seats at our arrival. My chest warmed at the sight of them, and I gave each tight embraces as Shoko scooted into the booth. Lee complimented my ensemble with an appreciative sweep of his hand, and he cheekily winked when I praised his close-fitting blue tunic.

I slid in last, and Tana handed me a glass of wine that she'd already ordered for me. She then gave Shoko quick pecks on both her cheeks, and Lee grasped Shoko's hand tightly over the table in greeting.

"Okay, okay," Shoko shushed our chatter, "I think we need to do gifts *now* before we get too drunk." The three of us all muttered various cheerful noises of agreement.

Lee went first, and he reached a pale hand into the pocket of his jacket that hung on the back of the booth. He produced a parchment-wrapped book and placed it on the table before us. When I tore off the paper, an excited buzz started up in my chest.

The leather-bound book was light, and embossed on the cover was the title of my favorite author's newest release.

I clutched the novel to my chest and hummed appreciatively. "You sneaky fox, this wasn't supposed to be available for another two months! *How?*"

Lee ran a hand over his hair then crossed his arms, "Like I would ever reveal that. Just say thank you!"

"Thank you doesn't even begin to cover it! I will have to really scheme and plot for your birthday." Lee's brown eyes crinkled, and he grinned, fangs showing, as he ended his turn with a raising of his wine glass.

"Me, next!" Tana produced another parchment-wrapped gift and placed it on the table with her slender, brown fingers, but this one was smaller and thinner than Lee's. My cousin tried and failed spectacularly to keep her face even as her excitement threatened to bubble right over. Her tight, golden ringlets were practically vibrating as she tried to contain it. *She and Lee must have wrapped their gifts together*, I thought to myself, as the parchment looked and felt as if it were cut from the same roll.

My brow furrowed as I unveiled a small, thin box. I turned the golden case over in my hands, and the coolness of it warmed from the heat of my palms. The top had two roses etched into the metal, and when I popped the clasp, my giggle rang out for all to hear. Lined up in neat rows were six tightly rolled joints. I closed the case with a satisfying snap. Looking across the table at me, I met Tana's grinning face and sent quick kisses into the air. She returned the gesture and clasped her hands together at her chest.

A server came over and asked if we would like another round. The beautiful human woman had dark skin, and her black hair sat in a loose knot at the back of her neck. As I requested another round for our table, her eyes trailed down my neck and shoulder before returning to my face once more. My navel did a happy flicker as I responded, tossing my hair over my shoulders.

⋆

Shoko reached beside her and produced her own contribution to my birthday gifts. I recognized it as the smallest of the paper bags she'd initially brought to my apartment. Reaching inside, I found a smooth box and pulled it out. Judging from the sloshing sensation when I tilted the box this way and that, there appeared to be some sort of container with liquid in it. Quirking a questioning brow at Shoko, who just mirrored the look I gave her, I untucked the lid of the box. A familiar but full glass bottle slid carefully into the palm of my hand.

"So you can stop stealing mine," Shoko nudged my shoulder with hers and grinned. The perfume was one of my favorites, true. Coincidentally, I was already wearing the scent tonight, as was Shoko.

I snickered, "Okay, okay, I get the hint. And I love it." The bottle slid easily back into the box, and I gave Shoko a quick peck to her cheek.

Lee rolled his eyes in mock-disgust, "Ugh, can you two please stop." He furthered the act by making fake retching noises.

Shoko leaned over the table and challenged back, "Oh, I apologize. Is someone feeling a bit sorry for themselves?"

Tana smiled into her wine, "Here we go."

"Just because none of your trysts have materialized into anything long-lasting, don't take it out on us!" My finger pointed across the table at Lee as we took up this decades-old argument.

He threw his head back and huffed a laugh, "You two were honestly easier to be around when you were fucking."

And over the roar of the tavern, my best friends and I fell into a comfortable rhythm. Lee discussed his latest frustrations at the bookshop he owned with his brother a few blocks over, one I frequented more than was sensible.

Tana fussed with her strapless top and raved about the newest strain of hash that she had bred on her balcony garden, along with the other herbs she often dried or mixed into tonics and potions. "The joints all have it in there for you. Lee said it's my best yet, but you'll have to let me know what you think." After we all passed around one in celebration, Shoko promised with a smile to steal at least one more from me before the night was done.

"So, Em. What do you hope to get out of your two hundred and fortieth year?" Shoko sipped the red liquid from her glass and ran a tongue over her straight teeth.

"Oh, well, probably just what I hoped for this past year. Good times with you lot and new adventures." I shrugged.

Tana pushed a sunflower-colored curl away from her eyes, "To good times and new adventures!" She raised her glass, and the rest of us followed. We toasted to another year and clinked our glasses together.

Soon the band's set became livelier, and it reached a number ripe for writhing on the dance floor. Shoko pressed on my freckled shoulder and shoved me out of the booth. She emerged after me, grabbed my hand and pulled us to the growing sea of bodies dancing in front of the stage. Lee grabbed Tana, and the four of us reached just shy of the center of the revelry.

Shoko flung her arms over Tana's neck, and the two of them sang along to the band as they swayed together. Meanwhile, Lee's arms held my back to his chest as we moved and giggled. The smell of book pages never seemed to leave him, and it filled my nose. He pulled on one of my hands, and when I clasped mine around his, he twirled me around to the beat of the song.

I then found myself in the arms of Tana, and she embraced me tightly. We held hands and danced, her smile wide and flavored by the same high that was making my mind pleasantly fuzzy. I pulled her into a shimmying twirl, and I marveled at how similar we looked. Our fathers were brothers, but our mothers had similar enough features to the point that we'd been mistaken for sisters for most of our lives. The delicate tapering of our chins, thick brows, and wider noses were almost eerie duplicates. It was as if I was dancing with a honeyed version of myself, and I laughed loudly at the thought.

Just then, a tickling sensation trailed down my neck, and my body turned involuntarily. Rich colors of the faintly lit tavern and patrons swam happily with the music and laughter around me, but it was instinct to find the one who was watching.

That server was staring from the bar counter, arms crossed, and giving a sultry smile. Slowly, languidly, I returned it, and snaked my hips along to the music. Her eyes the color of mine locked onto the movement, and I watched hungrily as they tracked the shapes I drew with my body.

Though there was a cacophonous blend of scents in the packed room, I caught the unmistakeable flickers of her desire—the sweet smell of her, now with a warm spice that made wetness pool between my legs. My tongue teased one of my fangs, and she caught that movement, too. Lids lowered, she pivoted on a heel and sauntered down the short corridor beside the bar counter.

I disentangled my fingers from Tana's, and she spun around to dance with another Lylithan female and her group of friends. Bodies brushed against me as I made my way off of the dance floor, but I barely noticed them beneath the ramping lust in my chest. I followed the smell of the server to one of three closed doors.

My body slipped into the bathing room, and the lighting was somehow dimmer in the small but clean space than it was in the rest of the tavern. She was leaning against the counter of the sink, and I wasted no time.

She yelped then laughed when I moved too fast for her eyes, locking the door and appearing before her, hands on either side of her hips. It was an adorable vulnerability, her jumpiness, and my answering grin was flirtatious. I leaned to trail my nose along her neck, only letting my soft breath touch her skin. Her body reacted to the ghost of what I was about to do with shivers that vibrated the air between us, and her hands flew to my waist.

Arousal, mine and hers, eclipsed my senses, and it was taking all of my strength to not touch her yet, to draw out both of our pleasure for as long as possible. Her hands, though, trailed up my torso and circled my breasts, thumbs teasing the rings pierced through my nipples before running to my bare back. I couldn't help but arch into her touch that escalated my hunger, made my mouth water. Her lips were softer than the silk of my dress as she kissed and licked at my shoulder.

My moan was almost choked, and the wet warmth of her tongue made everything in me pulse in desire. The music playing outside reached another crescendo, surging at the same time my heart beat in my throat and between my legs.

I couldn't take it any longer, and while she made sure that no bit of my shoulder was untouched by her, I untied the laces of her trousers with a desperate quickness.

But even in that desperation, I took care to keep my fingers gentle and caress her soft skin. The server opened her legs wider, and I slid my right hand between her flesh and the fabric of her undergarment. The patch of hair above her warmth was soft, and the heel of my palm settled there. Honeyed wine, that's what she smelled like, and just imagining the taste of her in my mouth was almost too much. Her body trembled while my fingers hovered above where she dripped for me.

She tried to tilt her hips to feel the relief of my fingers, but I held myself still by the last strings of my control and kept her pressed into the dark stone of the counter. She whimpered into the crook of my neck at my teasing, and the gust of air with my low chuckle turned her whimpers into deep groans.

I nudged her jaw with my nose, hot skin on hot skin, and she quickly acquiesced. When she pulled back and leaned toward the mirror behind her, I gave her throat a long, slow trail of my tongue. I could taste the sticky tavern air and shea body oil and the acidic, herbaceous remnants of her perfume on her skin.

She shook against me, and the corners of my lips curled up. "Please," she breathed in frustration and lust. The want, the game, would have probably been enough to make me come, but I knew that she might melt between my fingers before then.

I met the wet trail left by my tongue with a gentle but unmistakable grazing of one of my fangs, lest she be unsure about all of my intentions. But just as I'd hoped, she tilted her head back even further and left her throat completely exposed to me.

"Fuck," I grated into her neck.

She almost came completely undone when I finally gave what she had been begging for. My two fingers slipped easily, warmly, as I circled just above her wet heat. She screamed out and bucked in my hold, and I kept my fingers moving, alternating the pattern and pressure until I settled on a rhythm that left her panting and near tears. Had she not been human, her fingernails would have broken the skin of my back with her clutching and scratching, but her intensity only spurred on my predatory instincts, my drive to consume.

Her breathing became ragged, and I pulled back my head to see her, just for a moment. Her eyes were clenched closed, ready to receive what I was bringing out of her. Her eyelashes fluttered against her smooth cheeks, and her teeth bit hard on her bottom lip.

The smell of daisies and what I was doing to her was heady, and I could no longer keep my need at bay. My mouth clamped over her neck, right on the sweet, thick vein that ran between her ear and shoulder.

Quick and painless, I pierced with my fangs, and the warmth of her blood hit my tongue the same moment she came. It was hot, vibrant, ecstasy. My eyes rolled in my head with the enthralling taste of it filling my mouth and trailing down my throat. I drank and drank.

Her fingers tangled in my hair, reaching for purchase, but I didn't pull back until I brought her to another release and shortly after sensed her energy begin to wane. The control it took to only take what I needed and leave her standing was practiced to the point of becoming another instinct. Both our breathing was now calmed, and she stayed leaning back, satiated smile spreading on her lips.

My hand withdrew from the depths of her trousers, and I brought my wet fingers to my tongue. She watched, beguiled, while I sucked the honey taste of her off of my skin.

"I heard it was your birthday," she slowly straightened and readjusted onto her feet.

I smirked, "You heard correctly."

"Well, let me give you another birthday present, then." I was about to state that she had given me plenty—her blood was already infusing with my own, and I felt the euphoric tingles of crackling life. But she settled her hands on my waist again, and I let her turn me to be the one leaning against the counter.

She was a better female than I, because she didn't torture me like I had done her. I rested one of my thighs on her willowy shoulder when she knelt before me and lifted my skirt. Her tongue was agile and generous as it worked over me, into me. Her blood and juices were still on my tongue, against the inside of my cheek, and I was already halfway there when she started.

A scream reached my ears as I felt my own crushing climax rise from my body. The band had been creating a pumping and flowing beat, and the excited shouting and singing of the other patrons were another song of their own.

But suddenly, the music crashed and stopped. There was a breath of silence before the shouts weren't in drunken joy but in fear. The haze of my high and feed and orgasm was infuriatingly difficult to disperse, but once it did, I stilled the server's head. I pulled her out from between my legs and crouched on the floor with her. Her slender, black brows pulled up in silent question, but I pressed the palm of my hand over her mouth.

The shrieking and screaming intensified, and the smell of blood and fear washed over me. I pushed away the bitter feeling of panic that caught in my throat. "Stay here." My voice was completely different from what it had just been. Harsh.

She shook her head frantically and tried to pull my hand away from her mouth. "Don't be stupid. Lock the door behind me. Stay in here, don't make a sound, and don't follow me." Her eyes stayed wide, but I felt the faint nodding of her head.

In an instant, I was in the corridor again. The initial screaming had ceased, and now, the crying and shouting was quieter, more hurried. A different kind of hunger nudged at the back of my mind. And there was a sinking despair in the depth of my chest, but I ignored both and breathed in and out, steadying my senses. My blades were already in my hand, and I moved quickly back out into the tavern.

I didn't know where to look first. To my left, I sensed a tight cluster of fear—a pair of human staff members huddled behind the bar counter. Two other bodies had already fallen at the opening that led to the space.

The stage was in complete disarray, the musicians scattered about, either running, dead, or fighting back the group that had been the cause of all this.

I scanned quickly over the twenty or so people that remained scrambling around me. I caught a flash of golden curls not ten feet to my right—

Tana.

She held off a pale female that was going for her throat. The female had Tana on her back, and their struggle threatened to tip over the table they'd landed on.

The Vyrkos's fangs were distended and snapping toward Tana's neck, and my cousin held her back by the flashing of light flaring from her palms. Tana bared her own fangs while she kicked and screamed and chanted for the aether to save her, but my cousin's magical affinities were not the fighting kind.

With barely a thought, I ran to her, leaping over bodies and plunged my blade into the Vyrkos's back. The crunch of her skin and tissues and heart made that darkness within me shiver, and rose-scented, black blood flowed over my fingers when I released her. I didn't wait for her body to still and simply grabbed her by the wheat-colored strands of her head and flung her body to the ground.

Tana scrambled to her feet, and I ran my eyes over her. Her pale, green eyes were wide with terror, and her skin was flushed. There was red blood on her face, on her hands, but it didn't smell like hers. It smelled like—

I whirled around and felt bile rise in my throat. *Where are they, where are they, where are they?*

A fuchsia-skinned male with delicately pointed ears tripped over something on the floor while running from one of the Vyrkos. Yes, I saw that all who were attacking and had laid pillage to the tavern had that pale skin and red eyes. My vision darkened while I watched what the male had stumbled on, a head, roll into the leg of a table with a thud that was barely audible amidst the chaos.

Far away, I heard my own screaming. Far away, I felt hot, wet blood on my hands and arms, and the cloying ooze of it in my mouth. Far away, I felt flesh tearing at my hand, bones breaking from my touch. It happened in an instant, and it went on and on and on until there was no one else to kill.

I swayed under the pressure that weighed on my mind. The darkness was satisfied, gone and left me disoriented and reeling from my own rage. My vision had been too sharp, hearing too honed while I had let it take control, and the change back made me rub my temples. My fists still encircled the leather hilts of my daggers, but they were slippery and covered in black.

After four breaths, I was able to focus my eyes on them, the dark beacons that I had plunged into many of the bodies that lay at my feet.

My hands were shaking slightly, and more of that black blood ran down my forearms in thick rivulets.

One of the Vyrkos that had attacked while I'd been with the

server, one of the those whose blood ran down my arm, coughed and sputtered on the floor. The face didn't look familiar, and at least there was that. But the wound in their chest was undoubtedly from the end of my dagger.

I stalked over to them, stepping over the body of a human, gray from being drained.

I stood over the male that was struggling to breathe around the black that bubbled up and spilled out of his mouth. His dark, red eyes looked up unseeingly at the ceiling, at me. He was trying to say something, maybe to ask something.

I raised my heeled boot, one that Shoko had helped me pick out for tonight, and brought it down on the male's face. My foot eclipsed his mouth and nose, and I pressed all of my weight. His bones cracked and crumbled under my heel. His flesh squelched as his skull collapsed, and I saw the moment his life left him.

The jasmine scent of his death was mouthwatering, and I inhaled it and that of the death all around me. My eyes rolled back, and my shoulders fell, relaxing.

"Meline," Tana's voice was barely a whisper and choked with tears. The darkness within me again relented, and I jerked quickly towards the sound of her voice.

She was sitting, knees bent to her chest. I sat beside her and brought her into my arms. My cousin was trembling, her teeth chattering, and I tried to shush her soft whimpers. She didn't resist as I inadvertently smeared blood on the soft gray of her top, and she leaned her cheek against my shoulder.

Tana was staring at Lee's body in front of us. I could smell that the blood on her face was his, and I kept my eyes unfocused on the floor around us. Not on his throat, torn open in a mess of flesh and bone. Not on the open cavity of his chest that was missing a heart, crimson blood staining the once-pristine tunic.

Tana and I clung to each other while the Nethran city guards finally arrived. They stomped through the space, counting the dead, searching the tavern for any other survivors. "It's just us in here and one in the toilet nearest the bar," I called out while staring at nothing. I hoped those that I had seen rushing toward the exit had escaped the attack, and I prayed that the pile of bodies I had created only consisted of the attackers. A cold bolt of fear ran down my spine at the thought of the alternative.

My cousin pulled back from my shoulder and looked at me. Her eyes were puffy and red, and her face was painted with the crusted blood of our friend.

"Leenie." My eyes itched with the impossible need to cry. Tana hadn't called me that since she was a child. I rocked the both of us like I had when I'd once pulled her from an accidental fire of her own making when she was first learning her magic, how to harness and wield the aether that was plentiful all around us. She had singed the ends of her hair and wept in shock and embarrassment.

Just as I had then, I kissed Tana's brow and pulled her head to my chest. I closed my eyes and took in her fear and her rising mourning that matched my own. Behind my eyelids, I replayed the image that had made the darkness break past my mental shields. I refused to turn to her, to the pieces of Shoko's body that I knew lay just in front of the stage and against the booth we had been sitting in.

The guards began hauling bodies away, including the attackers. One guard dressed in the light armor of their uniform looked gravely on the scene with his own blood-red eyes, his lips pressed into a firm, sorrowful line.

A few of them asked us if we knew any of the people that had died here, if we knew what happened. We both managed to give our accounts—Tana had been dancing when a group of Vyrkos walked through the front door and began killing. My stomach dropped.

The server I had fucked was being led outside by one of the guards who spoke to her in low, soothing tones. We nodded to each other on her way out, and I filled in the guard on what I had experienced. For a moment, I worried about what they would make of the blood on me, but Tana and the server's story assured them that I had fought off the attackers, killing all that were left inside.

"Would either of you need an escort home? Are you sure that you don't need any medical attention?" The guard's white hair was cut in a severe angle along her chin, and her large, sharp teeth would have been menacing, had her voice not been lilting and soft. We declined both.

As the guards continued to address the survivors and citizens outside, Tana and I remained, clinging to one another on the floor. It seemed wrong to leave while they were still here.

My cousin told me about Shoko defending her and Lee by fighting back three Vyrkos on her own before they overpowered her, and my lip trembled as I recalled the look of bitter outrage on Shoko's lifeless face and the heartbreaking fear frozen on Lee's forever.

Not until the city guards carried away our friends under white sheets did we stand and walk home.

4

I couldn't let myself tear my eyes from the window. The golden light of the sunset was usually my favorite time of day, but now, it left me feeling hollow. I watched the people below go about their evening, and the clouds were few in the sky now deepening to make way for night. A cluster of birds took off from my ledge into that sky, and I tracked their sweeping movements as they flitted to another building, then off again. Grief knotted my chest, but I tried to breathe past it. There was no other option.

The air flowed around it as I inhaled, then again as I exhaled. And with each breath, I was reminded of my friends who never would breathe again. Though the dark urge to join them boiled in my gut, I fought to not feed its heat. But to keep going felt impossible, unthinkable.

A young child, human by the look of her, dashed down the path just across the street. Her black hair was an inky trail as she sped toward wherever she was going, screaming with glee, and a dry sob racked my chest. I tried to clear memories of Shoko tossing her hair over her shoulder as she used to before setting in to listen to someone earnestly. The thought quickly turned to the last I saw her, head rolling on the floor and leaving a trail of blood.

Over and over I watched her head roll into the leg of a table, her eyes unseeing but wide, and her brow scrunched in fury. Every night for two weeks, I watched it replay in my dreams. And try as I may have to change the outcome, even for just a bit of reprieve in my own mind, the image was unflinching. I reached up my palm and let it crack against my cheek, the stinging pain like a sharp grounding.

My stomach growled, and my mind was a bit fuzzy. I tried to remember when my last full meal was and came up as empty as my stomach. Tana came by a few days ago, her eyes red from crying, and brought some bread and soup before announcing that she was going to stay with her father for a while.

Her golden curls had been dull, and watching her felt like looking at myself in a watery, distorted mirror. She apologized for some reason, but I told her it was smart to do that, to allow herself to be taken care of. I shrugged off her request for me to come with her, though. *No, no,* I'd urged her.

I had nibbled on the bread for a day and a half, the soup I made last for two. And the hunger in my stomach was easy to look past, as I had no drive to venture outside my apartment. But how long would it take before the frenzy hit? A few more days? The fact that my last feed was that night should have worried me, but I couldn't muster the feeling.

Good. Let me rot in here while I watch the world go by.

This time I would not descend into a haze of blood and intoxication and flesh. I wouldn't run and allow myself to be swept up in callous, indulgent greed. No, I would do it, painfully aware of everything. Maybe I'd reach some sort of salvation there. Maybe She'd finally fucking hear me.

But, no, I was not allowed that.

A familiar knock on the door left me groaning. And I realized that this was the first sound I had uttered since speaking with Tana. Even then, I hadn't contributed much to the conversation. Her tears and sad looks had left me wondering what to do with my hands. The pain was there, yes, but it was different. Death to her was filled with horrible charges of grief and yearning and eventually, depressed acceptance. But I knew better. Death, to me, was a different kind of labyrinth.

I called out that he was welcome to open the door, and the long, sure strides of my brother were almost as familiar as my own. He always walked like that, even when we were children. Sure of himself, eager, but also patient. Ready to reach where he was going but content to take in the journey all the while.

He crossed the living space of my home and into my bedroom. He smelled of the road, dirt and wind and leather. Underneath that, Mathieu smelled a combination of our parents. Cedar and the wind of the sea.

Without preamble, he flopped onto the settee beside me, gazing out the window, "Tana sent word about what happened." Of course she did. A flutter of irritation moved in my chest before disappearing like a puff of smoke.

When I said nothing, after a long, long time, he whispered, "I'm sorry, Em." He was looking at me now, head turned and searching my face. I let him. Though I'd not dared look in a mirror since that night, I was surely worse for wear.

A cross between a grunt and a sigh released from my lips but nothing else. There was nothing else I could give, and Mathieu didn't request anything more. He turned back to the window and we watched the sun fully descend, the moon rising to take its place.

I didn't know what made me finally speak, but I suddenly found myself asking, "How have you been?" Though we wrote letters, it had been decades since I'd seen my brother. Faint whispers of shame coursed through me.

"Busy. But otherwise fine. Did you get my gift?"

Judging from the dead flowers sitting on my table, "Yes. Thank you."

More time passed. We watched a female stake claim on one of the street corners and begin performing magic for coin. She created little flickers of light for a small boy who laughed with glee.

"You need to feed, Em." The gruff concern in his voice sent a wave of ache through my chest. Since when did he start sounding so much like our father?

He was right though. Hadn't I just been wrapping my mind around that annoying realization? Usually eating and feeding were tied to enjoyment. That sensation of a full belly or energized body was enough to motivate me to get up to the kitchen or outside to find something. But now it was just an annoyance. Another responsibility that required me to remove myself from the hollow perch I'd settled into.

"I'm fine, Mathieu. Tana brought some food."

He sighed, "You know that's not what I meant. And I doubt she brought it within the past day or two." Mathieu reached beside him, and my head snapped involuntarily to his hands as my nostrils flared.

My brother opened the leather skin he brought with him and the deep, sweet scent overtook my mind. Its depth was better than any wine, smoother than the best liquor. I reached to snatch it, but Mathieu moved it out of my grasp, "Uhuh, you're fine? You're dangerously close to the beginnings of frenzy, sister."

Baring my fangs at him wasn't completely me—a thick thread of myself was still present. The haze had just barely started to tickle the edges of my mind, I reasoned. "I'm perfectly fine," I hissed as I succeeded this time in taking the skin of blood from him. He just shook his head as I made messy work of draining what he apparently had left from his travel. The liquid hit my tongue, not hot like my body begged for it to be, but thankfully, not completely cold. I hadn't intended on drinking it all, but the second it hit my tongue, the reality of my thirst was frightening. A groan escaped as I felt my veins fill with renewed life.

Once I was done, I extended it back to him, and he accepted the empty skin with pursed lips. I hoped that he hadn't intended on having some himself, but I couldn't bring myself to be sorry if he had.

With that need taken care of, all the others came careening into the forefront. One, I was incredibly hungry. That need could be put off for a while, but I had already been so concentrated on grieving that I had pushed aside my sense of hunger.

Two, I stank. Though my brother and I had seen each other in all kinds of states, my renewed mental energy let in a bit of embarrassment at him seeing me this way.

Three, what was I supposed to do now?

When I thought about returning to finding work, my thoughts all ran to Shoko. She had been there to hear about my travel stories, weigh in on what jobs I should turn down. If things went wrong, like they had this last time, she had been there to get my mind off of it. Though she didn't live with me, she was over often enough for her presence here to be expected. For her fucking scent of hyacinth and roses and hash to linger in every room. And it was already fading. If my well hadn't dried long ago, tears would have prickled in my eyes at that realization. Perhaps even spill over. But no, my eyes had been dry for a long, long time.

Where would I even go if I left my apartment? The bookshop three streets over had been a haven for me, but could I step in there without thinking of Lee? With his throat and heart ripped out, utter terror frozen on his face? Obviously fucking not. Every street, every shop, held some memories that would inevitably lead to them, and that would in turn circle back to ruminating on that night. My birthday night.

All thought to rise and shower fizzled, and I felt deflated. Mathieu was searching my face again, and I was too tired to avert my eyes or shove him away.

If Tana and I were blurry copies, Mathieu and I were a related but distinct pair. Our hair was the same thick, coiled texture and shade of the fuzzy coat of the coconuts that grew plentiful in our mother's homeland, though he kept his cut close to his scalp. And while I inherited Maman's dark eyes, Mathieu's were like that of our father's family—a light green that reminded me of the first new grass of spring. Our mother's freckles were sprinkled on both our faces, though his were concentrated more on his upper cheeks than all over like mine. All of that with the tawny color of our skin made us look painted by the same brush, by the hand of the same artist.

"Em?" I didn't answer, but he knew he had my attention. His voice was considerate, as he had always been with me at times like this. We had both been in too many times like this.

He cleared his throat, but kept his gaze locked on mine. His hand reached out to just brush my fingers that I kept folded in my lap. "Please come back home with me."

My blank stare gave him pause. At first I was befuddled—I *was* home. But then his meaning settled. He meant to our birthplace, where he had been residing for the last two decades. He'd stopped asking me to visit a few years ago, with my letters always dodging his invitation.

Before I could begin to shake my head, he trudged on, "You can't keep on like this, Em. You will punish yourself into a frenzy and hurt someone. This city is your new home, I know. But there are now raw memories here."

"There are just as many raw memories there, if not more." My voice was raspy but steady. That was why I had left in the first place.

I hadn't been back to our home in one hundred years. What Mathieu was proposing was ludicrous.

"I know that. And I know that this idea may seem preposterous. But you need a space to heal, Meline. See what we have been rebuilding. Surround yourself with your people, with your *family*." My eyelids shut tight at the word. Family. What was left of it, he meant. "I am there, as are Uncle and Tana, and others who have missed you. Nethras will always be here for when you are ready to return." I looked frantically around my bedroom, trying to grasp for a reason to resist him. I wouldn't go back.

"I can't," my voice cracked.

The slight tightening of Mathieu's lips was the only sign of his rising frustration. His voice remained unchanged, "Meline."

The air had become tight, too close. I struggled for air through my nose, out of my mouth. He couldn't possibly understand. Back there, it wasn't just the ruins of our home, of our land. I rubbed the heel of my palm at my chest to try and calm my racing heart. My mouth was dry, so dry.

"What are you so afraid of, sister?" I flinched, for Mathieu had rested his hand on my shoulder. We were not very physically affectionate siblings, but the weight of his touch felt nice. I was able to draw in a longer breath.

"The," I licked at my bottom lip, "the memories, the people, *everything*. You don't *understand*."

The ends of his brows turned down, and I fought the urge to look away as I saw the unmistakable expression of pity on my brother's face. He pitied me, and that was somehow the worst of all. "You are right. I don't. But I want to. And I don't want to wait for decades for sparse letters this time, Em. We healed apart after The Killings. Please let us now heal side by side."

I scrubbed my fingers over my face as the memories from that time ran through my mind. The darkness, the screaming, the bodies everywhere. Then the endless haziness of flesh and blood and drugs and drink until I had settled here. Where I had found Shoko and Lee and reconnected with Tana. All the while, I had sent Mathieu little word, barely notifying him of when I had moved to the next city. I couldn't think about his own grief, his own sorrow, while I was so hell-bent on ignoring, and yet indulging, my own.

My brother, who had responded to my letters by asking how I was and expressing his care for me. Mathieu sat next to me and had never asked for much but for me to take care of myself. Together, he'd said. He wanted to help me take care of myself and do this together.

The small nod I found myself doing was the best gift I could give him. A hundred years too late, but I wanted to be there for my brother, like he had always been there for me, no matter the distance I put between us. It would at least get me out of this crypt of my own making.

To return to our home, to Versillia, was something I had resigned myself to never doing again in my lifetime. More than that, I had welcomed it. For a century, I had convinced myself that there was nothing there. Even when I read over and over Mathieu's letter that he was moving back there to rebuild. The hot lava of shame burned my cheeks.

I could do this. I would go back to Versillia, and Goddess willing, it wouldn't be the graveyard I had been avoiding all these years, but the fertile new ground for myself and my family.

~

We left for Versillia the next morning. Mathieu helped me pack all that I could manage and would be reasonably carried for the week-long journey. He had just traveled from Versillia to check on me, and now he would turn around and bring me with him. Anxiety buzzed underneath my skin, but the packing and the preparations gave me a purpose, an activity to focus my energy into.

Before exiting the city, I brought Mathieu, myself, and our horses to Tulip Street. Letting Francie know about my departure for an unforeseen amount of time was the last I had to do before going home. Home.

The sun had just turned the sky the soft color of a robin's egg, and Francie was out front and tending to the garden just beside the stone stoop. Her hair was loose and fluttering in the wind.

She turned to find the source of the clopping of hooves, and when she caught sight of me, her face warmed.

I dismounted the ochre stallion that Mathieu had purchased for me to ride back to Versillia, even with my protest about the cost. He had just snorted, stating that he would not ride all that way sharing a horse when I was a perfectly capable rider. "Besides," he had chuckled, "you packed too much for my horse to carry the two of us, my pack, and all of yours."

Before I could reach Francie, a rust-colored, bouncing blur rounded the side of the building and right into my hip. Though the force of the child's weight felt little more than a gust of wind, I feigned a grunt and an "Oof!"

"Lady Em Lady Em Lady Em!" The boy squealed into my hip. His red ringlets frizzed while he nuzzled into my side, and I brought my hand to muss them even more.

"Little Marco, it's good to see you," I giggled down at the boy who was about to burst with excitement at my unannounced visit.

Francie called over while snipping at some weeds. She wore one of her easy shift dresses and knelt barefoot in the dirt. "Marco, you were supposed to bring me some water. Did you forget?"

His emerald eyes looked up at me before turning to his caregiver, "I didn't forget! Whitley saw me get it! But... I spilled it when I smelled Lady Em coming."

Francie shook her head but could not hide her amusement. Though the children that Francie took care of were all respectful and enjoyed my visits, Marco had taken to me ever since I had seen him playing with a wooden sword and given him guidance.

I crouched so that he now stood taller than me. His tan skin was flushed almost as red as his hair, and it seemed he had lost another tooth since the last time I'd seen him. "I came to let you all know that I will be gone for a while."

Marco's lips turned down, and only then did he notice the horses and my brother behind me. He eyed the packs, and though he tried to keep his face even and brave, he was only eight years old—still practically a babe. "When will you be back?"

I reached in my jacket pocket and pulled out a coin purse. While Mathieu had set out to purchase the stallion, I had run to the Nethras bank and pulled out all of the money I could while still leaving enough in my savings for whenever I was done with this return home. I swallowed, "I'm not sure, Little Marco. This is my brother, Mathieu," I nodded behind me, "and he is bringing me home so that

I can get better."

He grabbed my shoulders and sniffed the air, "You are sick?"

"No, but I need some time to rest and be with my family." Though I spoke to Marco, I saw Francie watching us and knew that she was able to hear every word. She still smiled, but I also saw the sadness there. She'd fled Versillia just like I had.

Marco's eyes started to glisten, just a little bit, but he kept the tears from falling. "Will you write to us, Lady? While you're away?"

I swiped another pass of my hand over the curls on Marco's head, and they sprang at my touch. "Of course, I will. And I'll tell you of all my adventures. Even the small ones." And I held one of the boy's small hands and turned the palm open to the sky. I gave him the black coin purse, and his fingers, already caked in dirt from helping Francie tend to her plants, closed. They were too small to fully eclipse the purse, but he grasped it all the same.

I stood and gave Francie a tight nod that she returned. They would make the funds last, I knew. And combined with what Francie and Lydia earned at the markets and the winnings I had dropped off not too long ago, they would be set for a long while.

"Now, Little Marco, I expect you to keep up your training while I'm gone. No forgetting your daily exercises," I called over as I mounted my horse once again. The leather of the saddle was warm.

The boy nodded and stood straighter, puffing his chest out. "I won't! And I will be even taller and stronger when you come back!" He turned and ran for Francie with all of his Lylithan speed. I saw him transfer the money to Francie, and he gave an enthusiastic wave to Mathieu and I before running back to get water.

I squeezed my thighs and turned us back up the street, leading my brother and I out of Nethras and back to Versillia. To our birthplace. To our home.

To our kingdom.

5

The first thing I noticed as we inched closer and closer to the fallen kingdom of Versillia was the smell of honeysuckle. I inhaled deeply, chest expanding, and it was so sweet, so sweet. I closed my eyes and let it fill my mind. It didn't quite replace the scent of burning bodies etched in my memory during my flight those years ago. But it helped and called back to the before.

There were no gates to the main city of Versillia anymore, but the entrance was evident by the guards posted at the two giant willow trees that bordered the road. A road that was not cracked or split like I had pictured, but whole.

The cluster of guards in simple armor, weapons, and the emerald green and blush of Versillia stood at attention when they caught us nearing, but Mathieu didn't speak to them other than giving a respectful nod when they bowed. A lump caught in my throat, but I swallowed it down. The exchange seemed so casual, so familiar, but in my memories, it was Papa who they'd silenced and bowed for like that. Grief and guilt were heavy on my shoulders, and I intently inhaled that honeysuckle around us, tried to focus on the shifting muscles of the stallion under me.

I could do this. I would do this.

It wasn't long until the road led us out of the forest that preceded Versillia, and I could no longer blink. The rolling farmland hills of Versillia were lush, and the wood and brick of the homes and stables stood proud. There was livestock grazing and workers tilling the land. They bowed at my brother and me as we rode past, and soon, the rural lands gave way to tighter clusters of small but respectable homes. They varied in pastel color, and I heard the sound of laughter and chattering and life.

We continued on in silence, and we soon arrived in the city proper. It was no Nethras, but the City of Versillia was made of bright townhomes with curling iron fencing and businesses, all clustered together and bisected by winding white cobblestone. There were many Lylithans among the other beings that wandered the streets to tend to their mid-afternoon responsibilities or activities. *Children* ran in the streets, and I couldn't hide my wonder anymore.

I looked at my brother now, his pale green eyes bright like our father's, and felt such a swell of emotion that I had to blink away the dry prickling in my eyes. He had done this.

He kept his gaze on the road ahead and gave polite smiles to the people that waved greetings. Some bowed or curtsied to him and to me, though I could read a different mixture of emotions when they saw my face. Befuddlement, startled realization, and above all, a humiliating reverence.

Their stares began to weigh on me, and my shoulders grew tighter and wearier with every passing minute. Their muttered comments hit my ears like hammers, and I fought to keep my face pleasant. I could search back, recall how I had handled this as a young female, as a girl. But that had been quite different from this, hadn't it?

Mercifully, we crested another hill and reached the grounds of our family's estate. The Kingdom of Versillia wasn't a large one, and the size of our family home was smaller than other seats of power that I had seen. But where I had witnessed fire and death, there were proud, blooming magnolia trees, a deep blue pond I had splashed in countless times as a girl, and our *home*.

A few stablehands jogged out to us, and Mathieu and I handed them the reins of our horses. The front entrance of the estate had been completely rebuilt, down to the bubbling stone fountain. The black of smoke and flames had been scrubbed and painted over, and the yellow-pink of the facade and white of the window trimmings and doors were just as they were in my memories. Manicured shrubbery rustled slightly in the soft wind, and hydrangeas, roses, and rhododendrons bloomed throughout the front grounds.

I hopped off of my stallion and gave him a good pet and thanks for carrying me on this journey. He just huffed and looked around with that giant eye of his. I heard the soft thud of Mathieu hopping down from his horse while I began to unfasten the packs from my stallion's saddle.

A female opened the large front door of the estate, pushing past the golden gate that separated the sprawling front steps from the cobblestone of the front grounds. She made her way and stopped a good distance from me.

Mathieu came to stand beside us, and we both nodded to her as she straightened from her curtsy. "This is Diana. Diana, this is my sister Meline."

She lowered her eyes and held her hands demurely at her waist, "Your Highnesses."

"Diana and her family have come to work here at the estate, and she will be attending to your needs and your rooms."

I looked frantically between Diana and my brother. What would I need a personal servant for? I could keep my space clean and myself dressed just fine. But before I could object, Diana stepped forward and began worrying at the packs on my horse. "I will bring these up to your rooms, Your Highness."

Though I began to shoo her away, Diana gave me an admonishing look until I backed down. Once I did, she smiled pleasantly and began to sling the packs over her slender shoulders. Her light brown hair swayed as she walked just as easily up the steps with all of the belongings I had brought from my apartment in Nethras.

"I need to take care of a few things and properly wash the road off. Unless you would like for me to walk you to your rooms?"

I pushed away nervousness at being left alone. Of course, it was fine. Mathieu and I had been stuck together for the whole, long journey here. Some time to rest and attend to our own needs would be a good thing. "No, no, you go do what you need to do," I gave my best reassuring smile, "I remember my way around."

He returned my smile, "We shall meet for dinner this evening. There are a few people who are very excited to see you." My brother gave me a warm squeeze on my shoulder and bounded up the steps and into the estate. I had no idea what he needed to take care of, but since he had made it his mission to rebuild our family's kingdom, I didn't want to imagine all that he was responsible for now. The weight of restoring this place was no doubt a heavy one, and if Mathieu could do *that*, I could go to my rooms and be alone.

I rolled back my shoulders and filled my lungs with the perfume of the grounds. Since Diana had taken my packs, I carried nothing but my own grief and anxiety and tentative hope on my shoulders as I stepped into the house.

~

The foyer held gleaming white tile, and the grand staircase in front of me was polished just the same. The intricate crystal chandelier overhead was no longer smashed on the floor but whole and reflecting rainbows of light. I wandered further inside, and trailed my finger lightly on the walls, pristine and painted an olive color like they had been since my father's grandfather had built the estate. Portraits of our ancestors lined the corridors, as did landscapes of Versillia's farmlands and city.

The dining rooms and kitchen and offices and ballroom were just where they had always been, and though the house was quieter than it was when I was growing up, there was still ever-present noise as people moved throughout the estate, working and talking.

My feet moved along the halls that were almost cruel in how they made me keep forgetting that things were so different now. The observatory at the rear of the main house was lined with towering bookshelves on one wall, and on the other sides, walls of glass. Leather sofas and chairs were set about the room, and I trailed my fingers along those, too. They were different from the ones Papa had favored, where he'd spent countless hours reading.

Images, flashes of the past, marched through my mind. Being cuddled up next to my father with the view of the rear gardens, guest houses, and stables before us while he guided me through book after book. Once I could read strongly on my own, Papa and I would often retreat to the observatory to read, sometimes on opposite walls and in our own worlds entirely, well into the early hours of morning.

I walked to the smaller staircase at the rear of the house that also led upstairs, and my feet were heavy while I climbed. The second floor was markedly calmer, and I made my way to the eastern wing, my wing. The western had been our parents', and I didn't think I was ready to venture there. Perhaps I never would be.

Mathieu's rooms came first, and I heard the faint sound of his shower running and him walking about the space. A few doors down, I finally came upon mine. The double doors were closed, and when I grasped the golden handles and pulled them open, I sucked in a quick, shattering breath.

Like everything else here, Mathieu had rebuilt it, taken care of it. I'd loved to travel and traipse around outside, but I had loved to be in my rooms, alone with myself, most of all. The window that looked to the east and gave the view of the rising sun was the same as it always had been. And the wooden table sat with the same configuration of chairs. But after blinking a few times, I saw that it was a new table of a darker wood. The sofa of the front room was a cobalt blue and not the light color of the old one. The low table in front of it looked to be the same, though. And he had even replaced the sitting cushions that bordered the other side of it, closest to the door.

When I moved to my bedroom, a dry whimper escaped my lips into the silence. The dark wallpaper, depicting a wild green jungle, was still there. The trinkets on my bookshelves and writing desk were still there. And my adolescent sketches were still pinned to the wall above my bed.

One of the images, of Tana and I, captured Tana's eye-crinkling grin and the brooding scowl that I wore a lot during that tumultuous time with more skill than I had remembered having. She had been so *irritating* back in those days, I recalled, but I saw the care I had given to shading in her bounding curls.

There were quick sketches of those that had worked at the estate. Some, I reminded myself, that were long dead. There was a sketch of Mathieu, shoveling shit in the stables in a punishment from our father that I had been all too giddy to capture. There was another of Papa, chin resting on his hand as he bent over his desk, writing. His eyes were turned down on his paper, but I remembered sitting against the windowed wall of the observatory and drawing him while he worked.

My palm pressed to one of the larger papers that I had pinned. It was obviously one of the latter ones, as the skill was past most of the other drawings. And I'd waited until I felt most confident, hadn't I? I had practiced until I felt I could capture her as well as I could.

My mother, immortalized by my pen as she sat in the Queen's Garden. Had I colored the drawing, she would have been the same color as me, her hair the same shade as mine. That day, she'd worn it in many braids that she coiled on top of her head. She sat on a bench, with the bursting of spring all around her. I ran a fingernail over the delicate arch of her brow, the uninterrupted bow of her lip that matched Mathieu's.

Even though she was in the Versillian gardens in this rendition, she was dressed in the garb of her homeland. She wore the clothing of the High Priestess—a sleeveless, cropped top and loose, light trousers. I had filled her clothing in with the ink of my pen to convey the dark color and highlighted the golden bangles and rings she wore that day.

I squeezed my eyes shut. How had I forgotten all of these details of her? I could still hear her melodic laughter and the raspiness in her voice in the mornings. But the detail of her freckles and the charms in her braids—I had almost forgotten.

A spider-walking sensation crawled over my shoulders and down my spine. It wasn't threatening, but I had to breathe to stop myself from running from it. I had been trying to forget these raw memories for so long. But I had also shut away the cherished ones. My father's quiet kindness and my mother's regal mischievousness. Even Mathieu and Tana, who were still here—I had forgotten these moments with them.

Deep, deep guilt weighed on my back, and I let it be. I deserved it. I was a coward and not the daughter whose mother joked with her while sitting for that portrait. When news on that already horrible night that the king and queen, my *parents*, had been killed while aiding Versillians as they tended to the injured, I'd fled. I couldn't bear seeing their bodies, couldn't handle seeing the evidence that I already felt in my bones.

Empty and unseeing, I'd left. I had turned my back on the home that my father had expanded and maintained through countless nights spent at his desk. I didn't stay to see my mother's body wrapped and burned and returned to her Goddess.

Before this shrine to my childhood, to my life before The Killings,

I whispered desperate apologies to them. To Maman and Papa I asked for forgiveness, and I expressed regret to the versions of Mathieu and Tana on the wall because I still hadn't found the courage to do so in person.

And to my past self who had so eagerly recorded these memories to be looked upon for centuries, I apologized.

6

I'd managed a quick nap after the blessedly long shower in my bathing room, and after dressing in silence for supper, I went back downstairs. Diana had knocked on the door, quickly letting me know that the meal would be served shortly, and I respectfully declined her offer to escort me to the smaller dining room.

The staff members that I passed gave bows and curtsies as I passed, and I nodded jerkily at all of them, muttering greetings as steadily as I could. I smoothed a hand over my exposed navel and the long, flowing skirt that hung low on my waist. The lace-trimmed vest fastened at the front with delicate, matching cream ribbon and constricted the quick expanding of my chest. As I crossed the last few feet to the dining room, I made a mental caress at my ankles where my daggers were sheathed inside my boots and felt my shoulders relax a fraction.

I took one last stunted breath and pushed open the large door into the dining room near the observatory. Where my family had held our private, formal dinners with one another.

The room was the same color as the walls of the main corridor, and a small fireplace on the far wall crackled under the talking and laughing of those inside. The large window opposite the table set for six showed the darkened night.

Right when I crossed the threshold, I was pulled into a tight embrace. Warm, brown arms clung to me, and golden hair tickled my nose. "I missed you," Tana spoke into my own hair that spread down my back and around my shoulders. Her lavender and patchouli was a tranquil flood, and I inhaled deeply.

"I saw you just a few weeks ago," I grumbled into her, but returned her squeezing.

When we pulled back, her soft, green eyes ran a worried glance down my body and back. "Yes, but I still missed you. And I am so glad that you came." She gave me another quick hug before backing away so that I could be greeted by the next person.

"Niece," a deep and clear voice boomed from behind my cousin, "it is so good to see you once again." My uncle moved past his daughter and pulled me in, just as she had, and his embrace was almost crushing but was just as warm. I inhaled Hendrik's scent that was so much like Papa's cedar and leather. The sight of him made my eyes prickle, and the scratchiness of his beard on my temple was further reminder that I was... home.

"It's good to see you too, Uncle," I muttered into his shoulder. When he straightened, I saw that he looked just as he had all my life. His hair was golden like Tana's and my father's, and was cut short like Mathieu's. His full beard was darker and almost blended in with the light brown of his skin. His Versillian garb, a white tunic and deep green waistcoat embroidered with golden thread, was slightly rumpled, as if he'd been sitting hunched over work all day. Had he always looked this much like Papa?

"Glad to see that you've also managed to wash off the rank of the road." Mathieu called from near the fireplace where he talked with two others. The one to his left was a male who had pointed ears peeking between the strands of silver hair and dressed just as smartly as Uncle. Mathieu gestured a glass of amber liquid, "This is Ravas. He is the lead architect and planner that has been integral in our reconstruction."

The pearly gray-skinned male was lanky and taller than my brother, but his bow was graceful and swift. "It's an honor to finally meet you, Your Highness."

I blurted, "Please, call me Meline." The way Mathieu had been chuckling with Ravas suggested that they were friends. I wouldn't have a friend of my brother addressing me like a stranger and him with easy familiarity. Ravas nodded and raised his glass toward me.

Mathieu turned to the grinning one on his right, "And you remember Ajeh."

My lips turned down as I remembered the last time I had faced my brother's oldest friend and their teasing. "Always a pleasure." Ajeh was almost as tall as Ravas, but while the architect was dressed like Mat and Uncle, Ajeh was fitted in their kingdom's characteristic tight-fitting jacket adorned with crimsons and gold that only made them look more charming.

Their grin seemed to widen, and of course, they didn't bother with any formality or greetings. Their deep skin was almost shiny in its perfection and contrasted brightly against their white teeth. "Oh, always a pleasure, indeed. I'm glad to see that you're as unpleasant as always," but their taunting had no bite.

"And for what reason have you graced Versillia with your arrogance? Sjatas seen how incompetent you are, yet?" I'd fled my homeland, but I wasn't so ill-informed to have missed news of Ajeh's ascension to their kingdom's throne.

Ajeh laughed and jutted a thumb to Mathieu, "Oh, this one has put me to work. Responsibilities and all that." My brow wrinkled, but just then, the smell of food filled the room as kitchen staff brought in trays of our steaming supper.

We all sat with no one at the heads of the table and served ourselves the green beans, potatoes, roasted chicken, grilled fish, and bread. Everyone but Ravas helped themselves to the elegant decanter of blood and filled their glasses. I brought mine to my lips and found it spiced with nutmeg and clove.

The males and Ajeh launched into conversations about the journey from Nethras, the additions being made to Versillia's sport center, and which games would be played first once the construction was finished.

While they went back and forth, Tana regaled me with the update of her own long journey from Nethras where a merchant had tried to cheat her out of coin when she was trying to buy supplies. "And I put on my best impression of your scowl that means you're about to throttle someone. It was easy enough, and he backed down," she giggled into her glass, and I couldn't help but smirk when she showed me her imitation. It was surprisingly accurate.

"Is everything prepared for tomorrow?" Mathieu asked Ravas.

The male nodded, "Yes, I've gotten all the updated plans drawn up for the meeting. I've been told that the rest have arrived this evening."

"What's happening tomorrow?" I asked, and they both turned to me.

But it was Ajeh who answered, mouth full of food, "Council meeting."

"Like a city council?" Had I forgotten about a City of Versillia council? I racked my brain for a moment, and, no. Papa had run Versillia as its king and had those like Uncle Hendrik to help run the city. But there was no formal council.

Mathieu shook his head while he chewed a forkful of chicken. He swallowed, "No. One of the things we've been working on here is reestablishing the Lylithan Council."

My mouth opened, closed, opened, closed. He had never mentioned this before, not in his letters or on our way to Versillia, but everyone around me looked unsurprised by the notion.

"Whe-when did this happen?"

Uncle patted a napkin to his lips and spoke across the table to me, "For the past two years or so. It was your brother's idea, and I can't believe that I hadn't thought of it myself," he chuckled and shook his head.

The Lylithan Council had been disbanding informally a few decades before The Killings, and those massacres had dismantled it entirely. I thought back to once sneaking into a meeting where my father had just laughed at my intrusion and let me sit in his lap, practicing my reading on the map laid out on the table between him and the leaders of the kingdoms and cities that held the largest populations of our people.

Mathieu shrugged, "We've gotten through the worst of the rebuilding here in Versillia, and," he nodded to Ajeh, "as have the other kingdoms that were hardest hit by The Killings. It's time we better organize ourselves and not repeat the mistakes of the last Council."

"What do you mean?"

Now, he sighed, and gave me another one of those damned pitying looks. When had this become our dynamic? "The attack you experienced has not been the only one, sister."

I physically recoiled when his words brought forth the image of Shoko's head, rolling. I felt the prickling at my spine, not threatening, but making its presence known. Always wanting me to remember.

"There have been a rise in those Vyrkos heathens attacking Lylithans for the past few years. They were few and far between, the usual, before. But there have been more, popping up in lands where we tend to congregate, even now scattered as we are." Uncle's grim expression matched my churning guts as Mathieu spoke.

Ajeh continued, "There have even been a few in our lands as well," and the flippant tone of their voice was replaced with a steadiness that I'd never before heard them employ.

"Uncle and I had already been floating around the idea and were in the beginning stages of bringing back the Council, but the attacks made us approach it much more seriously."

I nodded through the unease that had settled in my stomach, "And what are you meeting about tomorrow?"

Did I catch a wince from Mathieu? He wiped it so quickly from his mouth, I could not be sure. "There have been... difficulties with getting some of the remaining Lylithan leaders to our cause. We're meeting to discuss how to remedy that. And share with Ajeh and the others already on the Council some of the work Ravas and his team have done."

Tana piped up now. She pressed her elbows into the wood of the table as she leaned to look at Mathieu who sat on my other side, "Who is giving you trouble?"

And there it was again—I was sure of Mathieu's wince, now. "The High Priestess of Rhaea."

My body froze, and everyone at the table seemed to turn to look at me. They were trying to get the First Goddess's High Priestess on board for the Council, but it wasn't going well. And I'd chosen to live in a city that wasn't particularly pious for a reason.

Uncle cleared his throat, throwing me a worried glance before addressing the rest of the table with strained ease, "Though I've only briefly acquainted with Isabella, this does not come as a surprise. Hopefully we can devise a way to convince her," he tried to hide yet another pitying glance to me by taking a brief drink from his glass. "How go the new sporting complex plans, Ravas?" And the rest of the table gratefully turned to the more neutral subject, but I guessed that if I hadn't been there, my family and our old friends would have continued on the topic.

My stomach was twisting in knots so badly, I lost any appetite that I may have had. My head was pounding, but I tried my best to plaster a genial smile to my unfeeling lips. After Maman's death, Isabella had ascended to High Priestess of Rhaea, and from what I'd heard, she was well-suited for the Goddess's blessing.

That wasn't the issue, though. What if she were to come to Versillia? And look at me in that judging, cutting way of hers. My choices, especially since The Killings, were my own, and after settling in Nethras, I'd sought to... atone for them. In a way. But Isabella would surely see right through that. She was the one who pulled me from my mother's womb, after all.

Tana tried to engage me in a conversation about a particularly difficult spell that she and her witch sisters had attempted earlier this week. Something about the moon cycle and a rare desert herb that they had to source from out west. But I barely heard her, just offering vague responses to feign my attention when my mind was on Councils and priestesses and a Goddess whose power I knew all too well.

7

Mathieu's and my steps clopped along the cobblestone street. My muscles felt wrung and spent after a morning of exercising in the gardens. The forms and movements were ingrained in me, but the weeks of wallowing had left me annoyingly stiff. My thighs were now trembling slightly, even though I made sure to take extra care stretching. I had taught an abbreviated, less intense sequence to Little Marco, and I knew that if he had been in the state I was in, I would have chided him for not listening to his body, for pushing himself too far.

But my lungs had heaved and my skin drenched in sweat while I pushed myself off the ground, leapt into the air, shuffled, and repeated. My knuckles were achy from striking against one of the willow trees near the observatory, even though I had thickly wrapped my hands.

My brother had found me out there, drawing out the tension in my muscles while sitting in the lush, green grass. He was freshly showered and clothed in a green and gold embroidered jacket and beige trousers when his tall and lean body jogged up to me, asking if I would indulge him in a proper tour of the new City of Versillia. I swallowed slowly but nodded. The excitement twinkling in his eyes was enough to fully stuff my anxiety to a deeper place in the back of my mind.

We had left the estate on foot, talking and updating each other on our lives with more detail than we ever had in our letters. Mathieu listened easily as I recounted my years away from our birthplace. I told him more of the life I had made for myself in Nethras, the steadiest home I had had since Versillia and Rhaestras. He laughed incredulously when I told him about the rings, about my friends that helped me maneuver the taverns, and my taking contracts when it suited me.

"I don't know why I'm surprised," he'd chuckled and shook his head.

"And how *did* you come to this wild Council idea, brother? Neither of us had much interest for it when Papa was on it, from what I recall. When it fell, I remember *you* being the one to express relief that we wouldn't have to tag along to witness the 'quarreling, pompous fools'," I did my best to mimic Mathieu's lower timbre.

He grunted, "This is true, Em. But you know that Lylithans are in need of a guiding hand. We've recovered enough to be able to think further beyond mere survival. We need to better organize ourselves and, for fuck's sake, think about the next generation. Do you know where our reproductive rates sit, sister?"

I snickered, "I can't say that I've given it any thought, to be honest."

"It's so far in the negative, that if the Vyrkos truly are uprising like they did last century, we really may go extinct," his grave words were in stark contrast to the bright spring day around us. I swallowed and smiled wanly over to him, but another pang of guilt hit me in the chest. Perhaps I was still in the beginning stages of recovery, as he'd stated, because I still felt like I was too focused on surviving to the next day while concentrating on enjoying the current one to think much ahead to the future. Let alone to the future of our entire race.

When we reached the city, Mathieu took me by the newly opened park with its large fountains and topiaries and golden benches. People of all races, dressed a bit more formally than I'd grown used to in Nethras, strolled happily and sprawled on the grounds. We walked through it and came out on the other side, where across the street, stood an ivory structure.

My steps skidded to a stop at what was undoubtedly a temple, but Mathieu just continued forward to climb the pristine steps. He'd reached the top before I forced myself to move after him. And with every step, my face pinched, each eyeful I took more damning than the last.

What—had he *done*?

The silence of this temple to the Mother's firstborn was deeply unsettling, and that whispering in the back of my mind felt irritated, almost offended.

Gauzy, white and lilac curtains hung from the ceiling, and as we walked inside, Mathieu and I didn't talk to one another. Pews made of that same ivory filled the large cella, and portraits of Rhaea lined the walls. Stained glass windows filled the room with golden light, and my eyes darted between images of Rhaea holding infants, embracing pregnant females, and healing wounded soldiers. My hands clutched at my sides as I tried to calm the swell of rage.

Mathieu sat us at the front, before a marble statue veined with gold. It was Rhaea, and Her hands were clasped demurely at Her front. The straps of Her dress were loose and hung down delicate shoulders, Her hair tied into a braided knot, away from Her face. I stared up at the depiction of the Goddess and breathed. Breathed.

Of the Mother's five children, Rhaea was said to be the most beautiful, while Zoko, the Goddess of Strategy and Combat was said to be the most striking. I hadn't set foot in a place of worship for any of the Godyxes, let alone my mother's patron Goddess, for over a century, and the too serene facade of this statue felt blasphemous.

"I had this built for Maman." If he noticed my darkened disposition, he didn't comment. This was a place of worship, of contemplation. I clenched my eyes shut, fighting to give him this. There had been no temple to Rhaea before, no temples at all in Versillia. The people here didn't hold the Godyxes particularly close, their relationship to them secular at best. And even though he had mated Rhaea's High Priestess, Papa decided not to impose this on his people when they hadn't asked for it. Maman hadn't minded, from what I could remember. Her true Temple, she'd told us, was in her homeland, where she and I traveled back to often.

I looked up to the eyes of this statue of Rhaea, and I found nothing but cold stone. I lurched up to stand, and said as calmly as I could manage, "I will meet you outside."

The temple passed by in a blur, and then I sucked in the air of the mild Versillian air, clutching at my hair piled atop my scalp. My steps were choppy, enraged, and I didn't stop until I was on the cobblestone, my back to the temple Mathieu had built. *For Maman,* he said.

He didn't make me wait long, and after the fourteenth breath that I counted, I heard Mathieu descending the steps. "What's the matter?"

I started walking further into the city. My arms shook out at my side, trying to rid myself of the feeling of that stale, *wrong* air on my skin. I hadn't set foot in a temple to Rhaea since The Killings, and all but one left me feeling this way. Sometimes, when we would travel to cities other than Rhaestras, Maman would make an appearance at the local places for worshiping her Goddess. All of them were like this, and each time I went with her, I felt this itching underneath my skin. It was *wrong.*

"Nothing," I muttered to Mathieu while we passed the pastel buildings that were unique to Versillia.

"I know it's not like in Rhaestras, but—"

"It's *fine,* Mat," I turned over my shoulder to give him a reassuring look, "I understand." And I really did. Goddess, there was a reason, that I knew more than *anyone,* why all of the temples outside Rhaestras were like this. But the feeling of those cold stone eyes on me still left my shoulders hunched and shivering.

We weaved around passing Versillians, not giving them time to greet us, but even through my stirring thoughts, I caught a few mutters and clenched my jaw. "*The Queen. She's come back,*" and, "*Protector of Innocents.*"

A cold sweat was prickling over my lip, and I had to go—I had to get *out.*

"Em!" Mathieu rounded in front of me, blocking my path, and I ran right into him. He stepped back and held my elbows, but I kept my eyes on the ground. I couldn't do this. I was already causing a scene on the goddess-damned street in front of all these people that looked up to Mathieu so much. And I truly wasn't upset with him about the temple. It just—it was *wrong,* but it was for *Maman.* But even just being in there, sitting with Mathieu and praying to that *thing…*

I pulled in a long, frantic breath, forcing it deep in my lungs to calm my panting. The darkness wasn't even swirling in me—I couldn't even blame that. No, it was just me. Weak, a coward.

Mathieu's hands squeezed gently on my elbows, "Em, look at me."

There were eyes on us, I knew. The movement of those around us seemed to have stilled. I cringed up at my brother, shoulders still drawn up to my ears, and saw worry. His brows were tilted upward, but I didn't know how to explain. There was no way for him to feel what I felt, and the fucking thing was built anyway. And despite how I felt about the actual monument, my brother had had it constructed to remember our mother. He did it with love and grief, and I would never, ever fault him for that. I knew that Maman would have accepted such a gift from him, no matter that it was *this*.

"...Is that the Warrior Queen? And her brother?" I groaned and squeezed my eyes shut with another awed whisper filtering into my brain.

"*Meline.*"

"I'm—" I swallowed and forced my eyes open, holding them wide "—I just need a little bit of time. I just—"

My brother's mouth pressed into a thin line, but he nodded quickly. I didn't want to ruin this for him. Goddess, why was this so hard? It was really nothing, just an empty building and some gossips about town. I would *not* make this any harder on Mathieu than it already was. I reached out and began wrapping my arm around one of his while turning up my lips as much as I could. It wasn't a lot, but Mathieu's shoulder's seemed to relax a bit.

He turned to my side and tucked my hand against his. I would hate myself for this later, I knew, but I let my brother steady me, walk me forward. He gave warm smiles and nods to the people that passed, quieting their side comments. And I focused on stepping, one foot at a time, and on the unblemished city around me.

Versillia was a really beautiful place. Since I had left, the images of its destruction were what I always came back to, but it was so much more. It had been this, the bright colors and activity, much more than it had been fire and blood.

Mathieu and I rounded a corner and walked past the City Hall, where those that managed the operations of Versillia worked and where Papa had had an office all those years ago. It wasn't until now, being here and walking these streets again that I remembered that it *hadn't* all been destroyed. The places that were most important to me had been, but that didn't mean the whole city had.

We continued onto the next block, my steps keeping pace with Mathieu, but the familiar pattern of magnolia trees and a wrought iron fence anchored me where I stood. My feet wouldn't keep going, and my brother's arm tugged on mine until he realized my hesitation. He had been talking cheerily about the new stables back on the estate, but quieted as he followed my gaze to our right.

My heart felt like it was going to crack through my chest and fall onto the street. I couldn't get enough air. My hand clutched at my chest, rubbing the heel of my palm in circles between my breasts. It wasn't getting to my lungs, just making it to my throat then going back out just as fast. And I felt the dark tendrils unfurl down my back, licking at my arms and legs. It was like the most delicious rippling of an endless abyss. Remembering and reminding me about what happened, and it felt like the whole realm was shaking.

The cornflower blue structure was partially obscured by young and old magnolia trees, and just to the side, there was a small garden full of fresh fruits and vegetables. Zucchini, spinach, and strawberries were labeled in large, child-like script. A woman led a line of four squealing little ones toward the rear of the building, each carrying little baskets with spoils from their harvesting. Above the door leading within, crisp letters read, *Aeras Grammar School,* named for the Godyx and Their ruling over the arts, wisdom, and love.

I could smell that each of those four children were Lylithan. And they were happy and alive and *gardening.*

Mathieu's soft whisper pushed through my halting mind, and I could tell that it wasn't his first time trying to get my attention. "We can go back home, Em. Let's get back."

But I was shaking my head so fervently that my topknot came undone. My arm slid out of Mathieu's, and I braced my hands on my thighs, all without looking away from the school. Where they had— where I had—

I barely felt Mathieu's hand moving in soothing circles on my back. I was sobbing, dryly, but sobbing at the sight of the school where I had volunteered much of my time in Versillia.

Completely restored.

It was taking all of my strength to keep the darkness back, to not let the whispers come through. The shields were cracking under the view of it all, the tender care of the garden and the swing that hung above where there had once been a pile of bodies.

And there were Lylithan children there, learning and alive and just *being*. My legs gave out, and I sat there, in the middle of the street, and looked. My brother had done this, and now that memory that haunted my dreams seemed just a bit further away.

The darkness pushed a bit further, and I couldn't resist letting it out, just a bit. I raised my hands to my brow, the movement so foreign and yet so familiar. It pushed my lips to move and mutter the names in a chant that was almost a song. I rocked and let it course through me, use me, because I could feel them. Though many of them had gone, some of the souls still clung to the grounds, and I could hear their laughter and their screams and could taste them around me.

I only distantly recognized the sun moving, cresting into the afternoon and beginning its descent while I rocked and chanted, eyelids fluttering but never closing. And the darkness wasn't at all cold. No, it was… refreshing and all-consuming at the same time. I leaned into it as I paid respect, veneration for the souls I had known. They were with Her now, but I felt the whispers of their lives and how they had once laughed and ran and learned with me, taught with me.

Flashes of that day, that evening where, in a cruel twist of fate, the children had gathered for an evening of looking at and studying the stars. We—we'd never *thought* that the more frequent Vyrkos attacks would reach Versillia. Let alone for them to target a school, to target *children*.

Francie's screams, the ripping of flesh, the overpowering rush of jasmine, and the weeping of children ran through my mind on a loop, as if my nightmares could no longer be contained to my sleeping hours.

But it wanted me to remember, to acknowledge. This *curse* that wouldn't lie, wouldn't give me *peace*, no matter how I struggled.

And the darkness reveled in being let out, forcing me to this prayer. Not until it was satisfied, folding back in and satiated, did I feel the hand on my shoulder. He was holding me steady, through it all, and I woodenly released my arms to my lap and raised my head. I inhaled, filling my lungs, and felt the throbbing in my head calmed.

Mathieu's expression was unreadable, almost blank until he twitched and gave me a wary smirk. My mouth was so dry, but my heart had slowed, my mind clearer.

Without a word, I stood and paid no mind to the staring strangers. I looped my arm around Mathieu's again, and he walked us back to the estate, continuing to speak about the improvements made and his voice its own kind of salve.

8

That evening, Mathieu came by my rooms. After we'd returned to the estate, he walked me back here upon my request, and I hadn't moved from my sofa in those hours since. Sleep descended at some point, and surrounding that, I couldn't stop thinking about the temple and the school and the city. Mathieu had built it all, honoring not only Maman and me, but every Versillian that had suffered through the massacre. He'd done all of that while I had been brawling in sticky taverns and running from the memories.

How could he even look at me? Be kind to me? When I had barely talked to him and worked to make a new family without him because I felt like ours had been too fractured, too broken. I kept flinching and cringing for it. The whole walk home, I was waiting for him to express his frustration with me, the feeling of betrayal. But it never came. He talked excitedly about how he had done all of this, about those who he worked with to accomplish all of this throughout the decades he'd been back.

His knock on my door jutted me out of my ruminating, and he again walked in on me wallowing in my own misery. I piled that shame with the rest of it, already built high in my heart so that just a little bit more was of no issue. At this point, I barely noticed.

"Are you feeling okay?" He crouched before me, brow slightly furrowed, but his face was otherwise calm. He used that fatherly tone again, and I threw some more shame onto my internal pyre.

I cleared my throat, "I'll be fine. Please don't worry anymore about me, Mat. You've already done so much."

He searched my face, jaw clenched, as if trying to decide something. And I just stared back. Eventually, he sighed and asked quietly, "Would you like to... come to the Council meeting with us? With me?"

It took me a moment to understand what he was asking. He wanted to... include me. "You'd..." my eyes traced his face wildly, searching for that pity again. Surely that's why he was asking. He wanted to get me out of this room and thought this would interest me enough to do it.

But instead, he said, "I would like your perspective on all of this. I've been wishing for it for a while, actually."

My chest hollowed, filled. Mathieu was asking for my help. "I—I —"

"You don't have to! If you're not feeling up to it today, I would understand. And if you don't want to ever help, that's perfectly fine, too!" Was my brother blathering?

"Um... I..." I sucked in a breath, let it fill my lungs, and let it go, "I would be honored to help you in any way I can, Mathieu. Just let me get changed." I didn't let myself look too long at his shocked face. He hadn't expected me to say yes, and why would he? I'd been avoiding him for a hundred years.

But my spine was a bit straighter as I walked back into my bedroom and pulled out some fresh clothes. Diana had folded my garments neatly in my old dresser and hung my dresses and skirts in the wardrobe. The frock I pulled out was a deep orange color with billowing sleeves and a full-length skirt that flowed against my hips and legs. I sheathed my blades at my thighs and tied my hair back with a ribbon. And I breathed. The heel of my hand rubbed at my chest, where my neckline dipped in a low V-shape, and I walked back out to meet Mathieu.

He wasted no time to comment further on my agreement to help, and just turned on his heel. I followed behind him, and we left my rooms, then left our wing of the estate. It was when we reached the main floor of the house that I realized that I hadn't pulled on any shoes. I was about to turn around and go back up the stairs, but Mathieu didn't make for the front door. He rounded the side of the staircase and headed up the corridor.

I hurried after him, and he guided us to one of the formal meeting rooms. Papa and Maman had often brought guests here and held all sorts of meetings. Mathieu now, too, I supposed.

The long wooden table took up most of the space, with a bookshelf along one wall and a good-sized fireplace on the other. A painting of the Versillian farmlands hung above the mantle, and there was already a bouquet of flowers and decanters of blood and liquor at the center of the table.

"The Council members are on their way, should be getting here shortly," Mathieu turned around and he looked back at me warmly. "Please let me know if this becomes too much."

It took a long moment for me to swallow the lump in my throat, but once I did, I nodded, "I will. Thank you, Mat. For—for *everything*," my voice cracked on the last word, but it was no less fervent.

Mathieu's small smile in response as he glanced at the floor was... sad? I tried to decipher why, but multiple footsteps began to approach. And the scents were familiar. I breathed and steeled my spine. I could do this for him. I would do this for him.

Uncle Hendrik led the Council members into the room, and his brows rose quickly when he caught sight of me, but clapped a hand on my back when he neared. I cringed—he wasn't expecting me to agree to be part of this, either.

Ajeh filed in after him, and wasted no time to begin complaining to Mathieu about the lack of entertainment in Versillia compared to their home in Sjatas, something they said *every* time they visited. I was glad to see that hadn't changed in the slightest.

Ravas had arrived with them, and he nodded deeply toward me. I muttered greetings to him and the final two members who arrived soon after. Edan of Trylas, a collection of villages far north of Versillia that boasted beautiful snow-capped mountains, walked easily into the room and was speaking casually to Quen from Banfas, a small desert kingdom to the west. They both nodded quickly in greeting, and we all sat.

"Thank you all for traveling. I know that joining this new Council is a heavy commitment, and I know that Hendrik, my sister, and myself appreciate it greatly." Mathieu sat at the head of the table, where our father had sat as the host of these meetings, and I felt prickling behind my eyes.

The others in the room nodded, acknowledging my brother's words, and began helping themselves to the refreshments. Quen and Edan stuck next to each other, and I tried to remember when I had last seen them. Edan, bound in a tight blue jacket that buttoned to her throat, was angled slightly toward Quen beside her, and I wondered who had agreed to be on the Council first and who inevitably followed suit. He was dressed in a traditional Banfian one-sleeved tunic that bared his right arm and that side of his chest. Though their ensembles were almost two opposite ends of a spectrum, the colors embellished on the sleeves and seams of their garments complimented each other in a way I suspected was no accident. Their scents were freshly intertwined, but there was also a depth there that signaled a longer-held alliance.

"It's good to see you again, Meline." Quen's voice held a pleasant cadence, the Banfian accent rolling smoothly off his tongue, and I couldn't help but smile back to him. A ball in Krisla to celebrate the winter solstice—that was when I had last seen Quen and Edan. And that had been... eighty or so years ago?

"Good to see you too, Quen. How is your family?"

He shrugged, and the many golden rings that lined his bronze-colored ears tinkled with the movement and brushed his black hair, "A pain in my rear sometimes, but they are well." I felt a swift twinge of envy at his words, but kept my smile steady. Quen's parents had been kind enough the few times I had met them, as had his three younger sisters.

"And you, Edan? How are things in Trylas?"

She brushed pale fingers across her brow, moving some errant strands of her short, orange hair, "Cold but beautiful, as always. You really should come visit. Though," she glanced quickly at Quen then back to me, "I am not home as much as I used to be. Either way, you are always welcome." Yes, seeing them sitting beside each other, I remembered watching them dance together at that ball. Things for many of us were quite tenuous at that time, but leave it to Krisla to be the place for us to dance and engage in decadence like we hadn't all just survived massacres.

Ajeh cut in with a roll of their eyes, "Yes, yes, everyone is so happy to see sweet Leenie after all of these years. Now, can we get this meeting over with?" I narrowed my eyes at them further down the table, but they just rolled their eyes again and leaned back in their seat.

Uncle Hendrik cleared his throat, "Yes, we are delighted to have Meline back here to aid in our efforts," he gave me a warm look, "and we have a few things on the agenda for tonight. First, Ravas, here, will share some of what he and his team have done for Versillia and what they are looking to do in the near future to further our rebuilding."

Ravas nodded to my uncle and stood. He'd walked in with a packet of papers and now began passing them out between the rest of us. After introducing himself as the chief architect of Versillia, Ravas launched into a summary of what all had been rebuilt in Versillia thus far. Many homes inside and beyond the city, the estate we sat in, the school in the city center, and countless buildings that had been destroyed in the fires at the height of The Killings.

"And, with the reconstruction of these, the Versillian people have slowly returned." I didn't miss the quick glance at me. "We have now reached a new phase where we are working to enhance the city further. Some of you have already seen the new sporting arena that we are working on, and you will find in your packets the design for the new museum and theater we are building to further citizens' access to the arts. Do any of you have any questions?"

Edan turned out to be the one with the most questions for Ravas. Trylas had been hit particularly hard during The Killings, with timely assistance difficult as reinforcements had to make the lengthy, mountainous trek. With Trylians living in a collection of towns uninterested in fully converging, Edan didn't hide her frustration in getting the leaders of each settlement to agree on most things. "I wish to further discuss this with you afterwards, Ravas. And perhaps contract you or members of your team to travel to us and present on this further."

"Of course," Ravas nodded his head deeply at her and proceeded to his seat.

"Last order of business tonight is any updates on Council recruitment. Do any of you have news?" Mathieu punctuated his question with a sip of his liquor.

"Roalld of Nethras has agreed to meet with us in a few weeks' time." My head snapped to Mathieu. No one had mentioned trying to recruit a leader from Nethras.

Uncle Hendrik nodded, pleased, "Excellent. And Quen, have you heard back from Krisla?"

"Not yet. Either he's busy and will get to my letters, or Cal is playing his usual games."

My laugh came out more as a scoff, and all heads in the room turned to me. "You know of the King of Krisla, sister?" Mathieu tilted his head slightly as he eyed me.

I didn't miss the knowing glance between Quen and Edan before I swallowed, "I do. He and I have... been acquainted. And if he hasn't responded... I would venture that he is playing his games, as Quen speculated."

"Do you think that he would respond to a correspondence from you?" Ajeh raised incredulous brows, but their eyes held that same teasing. *Shit, shit, shit.*

I sighed and allowed myself a long blink. I would do this. "He may. Though we did not part on the best of terms. But, I am willing to help in whatever way I can."

Mathieu had been listening to all of this, lips pursed, but before he could speak, Uncle Hendrik cut in, "That may be wise. Two old friends asking him to the same cause might get him to pause these games and take us seriously."

"Indeed," Ajeh's grin into their glass was serpentine, but I decided to fervently ignore them.

"Thank you, Em. I'll get with you after this, and we can draft up the letter. Anyone else have updates?"

"No, but where are you with the High Priestess?" Edan asked.

My brother's face remained calm, but the skin around his eyes tightened. He hadn't discussed further when Tana had asked last night about who had been giving the Council trouble, and I had been quite content to not ask more questions. But it would seem the other members of the Council would not let it lie as easily. "I am still waiting to hear back from her. I sent a response to her last letter yesterday."

The others around the table nodded, as if they needed no further explanation. Quen, Ajeh, and Edan were planning to stay until the end of the month, and with another meeting scheduled in five days' time, we adjourned. Quen and Edan promptly left, stating that they would be attending a show at the old theater.

Ajeh made for the door as well, and they called over their shoulder, "You can find me at that delightful little restaurant you showed me, Matty."

So then, I was alone with my brother and uncle, and my shoulders sagged a bit. The meeting hadn't been as bad as I thought, but my energy was waning nonetheless. A few hours of sleep, crumpled up on my sofa, had done more harm than good.

The two of them discussed how the meeting had gone. "Well, all things considered," stated Mathieu. He and Uncle poured more fingers of liquor into their tumblers while I fumbled in my dress's pocket.

I pulled out one of the tightly rolled joints Tana had gifted me for my birthday and leaned over the table. I lit it on one of the decorative candles beside the carafes and inhaled the hash deeply. Mathieu and Uncle Hendrik gave me wary glances but said nothing. "So, what would you like me to write to Cal?"

Mathieu stood and began to slowly pace the room with his glass in hand, "I can help you draft it, but really, we just want to ask him to be part of the Council. I'm told he is very... interesting. But the fact remains that he holds a lot of power, and Krisla has the largest urban population of Lylithans."

I held the joint between two fingers and nodded along with him. Yes, Cal was a bastard, but Mathieu was right. "I'll be happy to write to him for you."

"That will be very helpful, sister. Now Isabella..." He said this last part carefully, and I saw his previous tension echoed in Uncle's face.

I could see the clenching of his jaw, and the flash of anger in Uncle Hendrik's eyes was so unfamiliar. "She is giving us the runaround. She knows that she is one of the most important parts of this, and yet, she decides to be withholding."

"Well, good to hear that Isabella hasn't changed, either." I mumbled through an exhale of smoke. The two of them exchanged a long look but remained silent. "What?"

Mathieu cleared his throat, "Ah, well... we may need more of your help smoothing things over with her. Depending on what she says to my latest letter."

"Why? I mean, I am happy to help, but I haven't spoken with her since before I left Versillia." Unease was creeping up my back, and the pitch of my voice began to climb.

"I... may have stated in my letter that you were back home. And that you would be helping with the Council."

My jaw dropped before I quickly clicked it closed. Mathieu had said that to the High Priestess before I had actually agreed to help. To what? Bait her? I inhaled forcefully on the joint and exhaled the smoke through my nose. The nerves and pounding in my skull were a bit better, and restful sleep felt like it would be less of a fantasy now. And I didn't have the energy to be irritated or offended by his presumptuousness. If my presence could possibly sway Isabella, there, again, was another way for me to help. "And you hope that this will push her hand?"

Uncle grumbled but agreed, "Yes. She's been... quite difficult. We've both tried, as no other member knows her personally. But, you are actually the one who has spent much time with her. She may be more inclined to join us if you are part of our efforts as well."

"And why her?"

Mathieu was the one to answer, with a sigh, "Because Rhaestras remained untouched through all of this. The amount of Lylithans that call the island home is too great to ignore, as well as the number of proficient healers that temple churns out. And she is the High Priestess of Rhaea," he shrugged. "That holds more sway than we can ignore."

I stubbed my joint out inside my empty glass. The ashes mixed with the streaks of red blood, and the last tendrils curled and settled. "Like I said, I am willing to help in any way I can. If my being here and letting Isabella know so will help the Council gain traction, I have no problem with that."

They both thanked me, and we spent the next hour crafting a letter for Cal. These political movements were unfamiliar to me, but Mathieu and Uncle discussed easily, testament to all their work together thus far, about what information to include and how to word it. The letter would be in my own hand, we all agreed, and I guided them away from the total formality that they had wanted to go with.

"We were... quite close for a short period of time. He would expect a familiar tone from me." I cringed a bit at having to admit this to my relatives, but they didn't question this. Uncle coughed a bit, but encouraged me that this was very helpful. Eventually, we settled on a brief letter, in which I detailed my return to Versillia and my personal request that he consider a position on the Council as a respected Lylithan leader.

Mathieu folded the letter and sealed it with the Versillian crest, "I'll have this sent out right away. Thank you again for this, Em. You've already helped us so much." Uncle clapped my shoulder in agreement, and the three of us made our way out of the meeting room. I breathed.

Just as we made our way to the front to bid Uncle farewell, the large door opened. "Ah! I was just coming to see you!" Tana slipped through the door and pulled me into another one of her hugs. She sniffed a few times into my hair and pulled back, "*And*, you've been getting into my birthday gift. How is it?"

Her voice softened when she mentioned my birthday, and I hurried to respond, lest the sadness creep further into me, "Might be your best yet."

Uncle looked down amusedly at his daughter and stated that he would be working in the city up until the next Council meeting and that we would be able to find him at his apartment or the City Hall. Mathieu walked outside with him, calling over his shoulder that he would be spending some time at the stables for the rest of the evening.

Tana looped her arm around mine and steered us back up the corridor, "So, how did it go? How have you been?"

I shrugged, "Not as bad as I thought, actually."

My cousin grinned over at me and began filling me in about what she had been up to. There was a small community of witches in the city that she was staying with. Living with her father had lasted just a few days before it became too much, she said. But, she and Uncle had been spending a lot of time together each day, and I could feel love for her father dripping off of her words. I was happy for her, but the swell of her love for Uncle only made the concave absence of my own father press deeper.

Tana pulled us into the observatory, and the pang of loss hit me in the ribs again. There was no scent of my father here anymore. I was about fifty years too late to sense it, but I tried to imagine the particular combination of cedar and leather that was all him.

The glass walls were spotless and extended overhead, where the stars twinkled above us and the shadow of the dark moon was just barely visible.

We settled on the largest of the leather sofas, and Tana pulled out a joint from her pocket, along with a small matchbook. "My new sisters have some great stuff that I've been itching to try with you." She lit the joint and took an inhale. It smelled sweeter than the one I had smoked earlier, and when she gave it to me to take a hit, it did, indeed, taste sweeter, too.

I would surely pass out tonight, now. "I like it," I said as I passed it back to her, "though, I'm sure Papa would *not* have appreciated us smoking in here."

She giggled, "Oh, please," she waved off my statement, "Dad has told me some stories of he and Uncle Hugo and all they got up to in this house. I can guarantee that we are *not* the first to smoke hash in this room."

I threw my head back and laughed. "Yeah, Papa had told me some of those stories, too. He still probably wouldn't have liked it, though."

Tana exhaled, "Eh, maybe not. Auntie Liana would've joined us, though, I think." She gave a devious grin that I couldn't help return. Yes, Maman was much less rigid about these things, and before, she had smoked with Tana and me a few times. Much to Mathieu and Papa's chagrin.

We continued to pass the joint back and forth and reminisce on our dead parents. Tana's own mother had died in childbirth, along with the babe, a few decades before The Killings. One of the main reasons our birthing rates were so low, I knew, was how difficult it was for many to conceive, let alone give birth successfully.

Superstitious Lylithans theorized that it was the Mother keeping our numbers in check, so that our race of immortals didn't overrun the realm. Another ironic turn of fate was that the Vyrkos, who were supposedly winnowing us down, had just as difficult a time adding to their own populations, with their turning process yielding death far more often than it did a second life.

And though Tana, Uncle, and my late aunt had fallen victim to the harsh realities of our kind, my cousin spoke of her mother with nothing but joy and fondness, and once again, I couldn't help being envious of her. Perhaps it was the hash or the weariness of the day, but I told her as much.

Her face softened in that way that always made me cringe and prepare for uncomfortably sweet words, "It doesn't get easier, necessarily... but you get used to it. And, I have way more pleasant, good memories of her than the memory of how she left." Tana smiled encouragingly and held out the joint to me. "But, I imagine it is more complicated for you?" Her question was careful, quiet, but my shoulders drew up anyway. I just nodded. Complicated was a kind word, but she just smiled wryly, "We all were so jealous of you, you know?"

My head jerked back in confusion, "What do you mean?"

She shook her head, still smiling, "All of us, Mat, me, even *Cera*, for Goddess's sake. Anyone can learn magic, but you were *blessed*. Your mother and Isabella worked for their blessings, but you were *chosen*. That's hard to compete with," Tana said with a chuckle. The reality, though, was that I envied *her*. Tana used her magic to heal or make people's lives easier, better. What Rhaea had given me was closer to a curse.

She sat in silence, watching me, while I took the last drag and stubbed the joint on an empty glass from the small bar cart in the corner of the room. "I just... it has been a lot. Seeing all that Mat has done and all that I missed and all the memories."

Tana was nodding and twirling a finger around one of her curls, "Yeah, it's still a lot for me." She bit her bottom lip and scooted closer on the couch. I couldn't help my slow flinch away, but she was not deterred. She grabbed my hands, "I know you're doing things for my dad and Mathieu while you're here, but I was wondering if you would like to spend some time with me as well?"

I frowned down at our joined hands and shook my head, "Why would I not want to?"

She let out a large exhale, "I don't know! I was trying to give you some space once you got here, and I didn't know if you needed some more before I dragged you into the city!"

I scoffed and rolled my eyes, "You think I want to spend all my time with Mathieu or wallowing in my room?" Her widened eyes told me that, yes, she did, and I rolled my eyes again. "I would love nothing more than to spend my days scheming with your dad and Mat while also watching you and your witch sisters dry herbs."

Her howling laughter rang through the room. "Okay, okay, asshole, well I'm coming to get you tomorrow morning. But you'll have to go through a trial period before we let you help in our important work of just *drying herbs*." She kicked her bare foot out to jostle my arm, and soon, I was cackling and kicking at her, too.

9

The next three weeks passed in an increasingly easy blur. Walking the halls of the estate became less and less haunting, and I tried to focus on the words Tana had said that night in the observatory. It was a thought I hadn't put much credence toward when it had flitted into my mind, but Tana saying it out loud, and with the evidence of how *she* had adopted it into her life made it seem... doable?

When I walked the Queen's Garden at the end of my first week back, I fought off the rising panic and focused on all of the times I had seen Maman smile while she walked barefoot amongst her flowers. I started spending more and more time reading in the observatory, and one night, I even sat at Papa's desk.

The urge to sketch came over me after meeting with Uncle and Mathieu about Cal's lack of response to my letter, and I left the observatory with a rough drawing of the view—the rear grounds that held the staff quarters and more of the carefully groomed greenery.

I tacked the sketch up next to my childhood sketches, and over the following days, I managed to add a new drawing of Tana, smiling with her dirty hands wrapped around the roots of an aloe plant, and one of Quen and Edan, holding hands while they left the estate following one of the more informal Council gatherings.

My mornings were spent exercising and stretching outside before heading into the city to spend the afternoon with Tana and her witch sisters. The witch community in Versillia was smaller than Nethras, of course, but there were about twenty who lived in one of the western neighborhoods of the city. When Tana had casually introduced me, we both cringed when each of them bowed or knelt in some way.

One particularly unnerving interaction involved a young witchling staring at me as soon as I had entered one of the small shops Tana frequented for supplies. "Mother, Rhaea, bless me, I never thought I would ever meet the Queen Protector," and she bowed, hands at her brow.

I gaped at her like an idiot, but Tana swiftly waved off the witch's reverence, "Oh, no need for formalities, Yeva. This is my cousin, and you can just call her Meline." But she continued to gaze at me, wide eyed and disbelieving. I thanked her through my teeth when I insisted she let me pay for a stack of rolling papers and some tea.

As we continued down the street to a café for lunch, Tana huffed an exasperated sigh, "Sorry about that. A hundred years pass, and you're still a celebrity, it seems."

My own sigh was shakier, and I lifted the satchel of chamomile to my nose and inhaled, "Seems so."

The nights were filled with either more time with Tana and exploring or with Mathieu. And often, the tree of us would meet at the estate or one of the restaurants in the city. It was encouraging to see my brother relax with us and offer his own memories of our childhoods together. His eyes glinted and smile brightened as we joked, and he even let us in a bit more about his life here in Versillia.

"So, how is your love life, brother? You never talk about such things," I asked one evening when we got particularly inebriated in my sitting room.

It wasn't the alcohol that made the redness creep up his cheeks and neck, and Tana and I waggled our brows at him. Neither of us had missed the various scents he would come to our gatherings with, but we hadn't pressed him until now. He rubbed a hand at the back of his head and threw back the rest of the blood in his glass, "Ah, it's fine. Been a bit busy, so I haven't... had anything serious in a while."

I waved this away quickly, "Gah, who has patience for serious shit anyway. Though, I wouldn't have guessed that you and Ajeh were still fucking after all of these years—"

"Leen!" Tana giggled and fell over to flop on the floor.

Mathieu's face had somehow grown redder, but his twitching smile toward Tana wasn't offended. "It's... uh..."

"Oh, Mat, you know I tease. Ajeh is a little shit, but I know you two have love for one another."

He scrubbed his face and snatched the joint from my hand. He sputtered and coughed after taking a hit, but once he was able to suck in a deep breath, he chuckled. "Don't count on us becoming *mates* or anything, sister," he shrugged. "We do what we want, and it's nice having them here." I tried to picture my brother swearing vows to someone like Ajeh, mating marks then appearing on their skin for all to see.

Tana and I spared my brother more embarrassment and moved on to a new topic, but I couldn't help notice the ease with which my brother spoke. Though I would never understand how he tolerated Ajeh as he did, I could see how comfortable Mathieu was around them. How the tension in my brother's jaw eased whenever Ajeh entered the room.

It would be nice to see him relaxed, with someone to comfort him after long nights of working, but I also knew that my brother and I were much alike. Though Mat was more responsible than I, we were both headstrong and favored doing what we wanted, even if it went against what may be expected. We'd butted heads fiercely when we were children, but now that we were adults, it felt so much easier between us.

These weeks of accompanying my brother and Tana to their various tasks and responsibilities furthered my appreciation and respect for Mathieu and all that he was doing. He worked from early in the morning until later in the night, meeting with city planners, sending our correspondences to other leaders within the realm, and all the while making time to include me whenever he was able. But it was in these moments that I felt that those versions of our former selves, the ones that hung on my bedroom wall, weren't completely lost at all.

On my twenty-seventh day back in Versillia, the Council met again. This time, we congregated in one of the conference rooms in City Hall, and it was somehow one I had never been in before. It was undoubtedly less cozy than the meeting rooms at the estate, but I made an effort to settle into my seat at the table nonetheless.

This time, my brother and I were the last to arrive, while Uncle, Ajeh, Quen, and Edan were already in the midst of discussing the progress made over the past month. The three visiting members would be leaving in the next few days, and Uncle continued to lead talks of the immediate goals moving forward.

Quen brought up the importance of continuing to spread the word about the Council, and I gave a distracted nod along with the others' words of agreement.

They then launched into the long-debated task of enforcing the Council's governance once the members were established. When the first Council had been whole, it had not only led our people, but enforced rules and regulations all Lylithans were expected to follow to keep us all safe. Part of the reason the Council had disbanded was due to a growing number resenting these rules. The resentment soon reached the members themselves, and it had all went downhill from there.

Edan then brought up the topic of term limits, which weren't included in the previous Council's bylaws, and Uncle theorized, contributed greatly to its downfall. "One-hundred years seems a fair enough appointment to make progress while also allowing new voices to be heard," and no one voiced disagreement at this becoming a standing regulation.

My mind had been wandering, as it tended to once these meetings got going. But Ajeh's mention of Vyrkos attacks, with word of another just outside of Sjatas, I felt a quickening of my heart and a twist in my stomach. I worried at my bottom lip with my teeth, deciding on whether to speak the question that had been blossoming in my head since hearing of the new Council.

"Um," I brought a hand to my chest and continued, "have you thought about seeking out members of the Vyrkos community? To perhaps talk with and... negotiate with maybe?" And it was like I had stood and began speaking in tongues. The attack in Nethras had been an anomaly in a city where our two races lived in relative peace. Through a century of traveling, I knew that, though The Killings had been awful, Lylithans weren't completely innocent.

But Mathieu's face was lined with confusion and worry at my suggestion, Uncle's with barely-contained horror. Ajeh looked half-amused, half-baffled, and Quen and Edan looked downright insulted at my idea.

I began to try to remedy my apparent misstep, but a soft knock on the door broke the rising tension my words created, and Ravas entered carrying a letter. "Just came in from Rhaestras," he extended it to my uncle who gladly directed his attention on the architect and opened it. He scanned the letter quickly before thrusting it to my brother.

Mathieu's mouth moved silently as he read. His nostrils flared, and a vein at his temple pulsed more and more with every word before he flung the letter down on the table. It made its rounds to everyone else, while I sat on the edge of my seat. Mathieu and Uncle were passing something between their crossed arms and tensed looks toward each other, but neither said anything.

Quen, sitting to my right, passed the letter to me.

I recognized Isabella's hand immediately, and the strong scent of my mother's homeland wafting from the paper was enough to make my stomach churn. Her words were short, and my heart rate increased with each one. I read it thrice more before meeting my brother's eyes across from me.

The exhaustion and frustration and hope in his eyes were mirrored almost exactly in Uncle Hendrik's, and I closed mine for a breath and swallowed. I could, I would. "I'll do it."

Uncle stared at me incredulously, "Y-you're sure?"

"Em, you don't have to," but I saw the hope spark further in Mat and Uncle's eyes as my words settled into the room.

I shook my head slowly and took another deep breath. "You all have been trying to get an in with Isabella, and here's your chance. I will do this."

Edan leaned back in her seat and scoffed, "We would be fools to reject or counter this offer. The High Priestess requests her," she gestured to me, "so to Rhaestras she'll go."

I gave Edan a wan but grateful smile and turned back to them. "I told you that I was happy to help in whatever way I can. I am sure."

Mathieu let loose a breath that he'd been holding and looked at our Uncle who, after searching my face for regret or hesitation, did the same. "We again appreciate your willingness to help, niece. We shall prepare for your departure at once."

And so the room launched into planning how I would be the one to travel and to convince Isabella to join the Council. In her letter, she all but demanded that she would not entertain any more discussion of our cause unless I would be the one to talk with her. In person, and in Rhaestras. My hand rubbed at my chest whilst I nodded along to the itinerary being made.

Another place I hadn't had the courage to return to, but I was done hiding. If everyone here was willing to make sacrifices and work hard, I would do the same. For Mathieu, for our parents, and for Shoko and Lee. If doing this would honor them, I would try. I had to.

"And of course, we'll send word immediately about her escort," Uncle added, and Mathieu nodded as he wrote down this note for the meeting's minutes.

"Escort?"

"Yes, we'll commission an escort for you so that your safety will be ensured throughout the journey and negotiation. Now—"

"I don't need an escort, Uncle," my lip curled at the notion.

His mouth thinned into a flat line, but it was Mathieu who countered, "It'll just be to make sure you stay safe. After what happened in Nethras, we can't be too careful, Em."

I leaned forward, "I am perfectly capable of keeping myself safe. Besides, I assumed one of you would come with me?" My assumption came out more like a question as I took in their expressions of frustration and concern.

"No, Em. I'll be leaving in a few days to speak with other kingdoms and territories to spread word about the new Council, and Uncle will be doing the same..." And—they had mentioned that hadn't they? Fuck me, when I wasn't paying attention, they had launched into talking about their next moves, which included traveling to a few more Lylithan hubs while waiting for Isabella and Cal to respond. That's why Mathieu was looking at me like that, wasn't it?

"Well, I can go on my own. I am not a child, and I don't need an escort if you don't!" My voice was rising higher and higher, but I couldn't stop it. Meeting with Isabella with a stranger at my heels was even worse than going alone.

Ajeh pointed a finger at me, "You think they're expecting you to do something they wouldn't? If you had been paying attention, you'd know that your brother and uncle will be traveling with their own escorts as well. Wouldn't want any of you to go and get yourselves fucking killed when we're finally making progress."

I barked a laugh, "Well, Ajeh, you may be irresponsible and unprepared enough to need a babysitter, spoiled monarch that you are, but I am not. I will be going on my own."

Instead of shooting back at me, they turned pointedly to my brother and waited. I also turned to him, and my breath quickened. He shook his head, "I'm sorry, Em. But you're not going without someone," he bent back down to his notes and began to add more, "We'll send word to The Shadows tonight to send two more—"

"*The fucking Shadows Mathieu*? There's no way! You know that they did nothing—*nothing* when we were being fucking *slaughtered!*"

Both he and Uncle were shaking their heads before I even finished. "No, Em. And this council has allied itself with The Shadows in our efforts. They're a powerful Lylithan group, and they are on board to help us all. Besides, they are already sending one each to accompany your brother and I on our travels, so it only makes sense, niece." Hendrik spoke slowly as if he was talking down a child throwing a tantrum.

My fists clenched atop the table, and my nails dug into my palm. "I'm not going anywhere with a fucking Shadow, let alone two."

Mathieu sighed, "Can you all give us a moment?" He glanced at everyone else in the room, including our uncle, and I winced as they all warily complied.

Once it was just my brother and I, he scrubbed a hand over his face, "Look, Em. I know that you can take care of yourself, all right? Even before you—started doing the work you do."

"Then why don't you trust me?" I thrusted my hands towards him, all but pleading.

"It's not that I don't trust you! And Uncle and I aren't too proud to travel without our own protection."

"You think that I'm too *prideful*? Just send me with some of the guards if you're so keen on seeing me as a defenseless maiden!"

His eyes flashed, "You know I don't think that about you—"

"Yes, you do! I know that I've fucked up Mat, but I'm trying to do better! I *am* doing better! You don't have to treat me like I'm going to fucking break!"

Mathieu groaned, "Come on, now. I don't! And besides, I can't spare any of the few guards we have. Uncle and I won't leave Versillia without any of its defenses, and the rest of our Council has our backs in this."

My mind raced. No, no, I could do this but not with one of *them*. "What—what about Quen or Edan? Or even Tana! I don't need to go alone but—"

He was already shaking his head. "None of them are able to help should there be danger. And Quen and Edan have to get back to do their own work."

I clenched my eyes shut and ran my hands over my plaited hair. My chest was heaving, and I couldn't, not—not—

"Em, if you're going to do this, going to Rhaestras, we need you to do it this way. I won't accept you going without someone to watch your back. If you can't do that, that's fine. We'll send word to Isabella that it's not going to work." I flinched as if he'd struck me. And just as I was about to shoot up from the table and storm out, take back my whole damn offer, I saw the weariness, the practiced resignation. He could sense my rearing up to flee, and he was ready to accept it. Just as he had been doing for all these years. And maybe Uncle was right to talk to me like a child. Fuck, even Ajeh, too. I hadn't even been paying attention for half of this meeting, and even when I had offered to do the bare minimum because there was no other option, I still couldn't comply.

My body had been coiling to shoot up from my seat, but instead, I sagged back in my chair as if I were a puppet and someone had cut my strings. I—I said I would do this. That I would help in any way I could. And that meant doing things I didn't want to do, didn't it?

I heaved a long breath, and I saw confusion cross Mathieu's face and saw him just... bracing himself. "I... I'll...take the escort. I can do it."

His eyes went wide, but he didn't risk asking any questions. "Ah —I'll send word for two more Shadows, right away."

I bit at my bottom lip and nodded.

10

I tried my best to keep a positive attitude over the next three days, but with each hour, it seemed despair was inching closer and closer.

Tana tried valiantly to busy me with helping her harvest and, indeed, dry herbs. She guided me in mixing together salves for cuts and other injuries in the bright, spacious kitchen of one of her witch sisters. The process was one I was familiar with, but I let her guide me all the same. The rituals were soothing, and Tana's steady enthusiasm and companionship were grounding.

But my thoughts often returned to what I was about to do, where I was about to go. Multiple times, Tana had caught me lost in my thoughts and offered to travel with me. But each time, I shook off the offer with a weak laugh, "No, you have enough to do here. Plus, I won't be able to concentrate with you pressuring me to spend most of our time lounging on the beach." And this, at least, she couldn't argue with.

On the fourth day, *the* day, I awoke with a weight pressing in my chest. Despite pushing myself to the absolute edge with my morning exercises, I couldn't keep my mind from anxious churning about what I would say to Isabella after all this time and what the fuck was I going to do with *them*. I still hadn't gone into my professional issues with The Shadows, and why bother? When I had tried to convince Uncle Hendrik the day after that meeting to change his mind about the whole thing, he just rotely refused, all the while falling back to that it was already *decided*.

Later that afternoon, though, I had gone to Mathieu, and found him brushing the mane of one of the stables' many horses. "So, Mat, I was thinking... perhaps we could save our kingdom the coin, and I just take one Shadow with me, not two."

I braced myself for an argument and had readied my other points before finding him down there, but he just shrugged his shoulders and kept brushing, "It's not a matter of coin—The Shadows are doing this at no cost. And I had already decided to send only one with you. It is already done."

He looked up, and his conspiratorial smirk was so much like Maman's that it made my breath hitch. "And—does Uncle know that?"

He shrugged again, "Just gave me hell for it, but he hasn't seen you with those," he jutted his chin toward my daggers sheathed on my thighs. And that time, I didn't feign my grin at him, the easing of my shoulders.

Now, though, the nerves had begun creeping up my back again. I hadn't been able to eat after showering and dressing for the day. I snapped not one, but two combs while trying to detangle my hair before giving up and just using my fingers, breaking enough strands of hair that should have been worrisome. I smoked a joint with shaky fingers in lieu of eating before leaving my rooms.

Downstairs, I found Mathieu and Uncle in the observatory, but to Mathieu's left, however, was someone new. I hadn't scented him in my approach, and it was that fucking Shadow magic. He was noticeably shorter than my brother, but his blank stare as I entered the room was menacing in its stillness.

"Ah. Em, you and Uncle's Shadows are on their way, but Master Jones arrived a bit earlier than them and will be accompanying me as I travel to Vharas down south." I jerked my head in some vague form of acknowledgement at the pale Shadow. His head and jaw had obviously been shaved a few days prior, with the suggestion of dark hair beginning to grow back. He stood slightly behind my brother with a sword sheathed at his hip. And in true Shadow fashion, he dressed in close-fitting, black clothing and even black leather gloves.

"You're sure that you're ready to do this, niece?"

I scoffed and threw my hair over my shoulder, and thank the Mother that my voice came out far steadier than I felt, "Yes, Uncle. Quit worrying."

His lips thinned, "Well... you can select from the two Shadows arriving soon, and I will also be leaving tomorrow with the other. Do you wish to go over anything before we all part ways?" He spoke gently, as if he felt a bit regretful for our recent conversations.

I fought and barely won the battle with my eyes just itching to roll at both him and Mat's worrying at me like I was an explosion waiting to happen. But I was fucking in it now. I walked to the bar cart stocked with a fresh carafe of blood and filled a tumbler. "Not unless it would make you all feel better. It's all I've been able to think about since the others left."

And they seemed to take this embarrassing admission for the peace offering it was. I wanted them to know that I was taking this seriously, wanted them to fully entrust me with this task.

Neither deigned to say anything else as I sipped from my glass and eyed this Master Jones. I had never learned the name of any of The Shadows I'd previously encountered, and finding that The Shadows used such formalities was curious, indeed. All my encounters with them had been in... less savory places, and none that I had met dressed so formally either. Though I loathed them, I couldn't help pass an appreciating glance over the expert tailoring of Master Jones's ensemble.

"They are approaching," his low, gravelly voice was barely a whisper but loud enough for us all to hear. His accent was surprisingly familiar—a native of Krisla or its neighboring towns, perhaps?

"We'll go greet them and bring them here," Uncle grumbled, and though Mathieu passed him an uncertain glance, he followed him out of the room. And Master Jones walked out behind them, trailing after my brother, just like a shadow.

I crossed my arms and perched on one of the leather chairs in the room. My fingers rubbed at my temples, and I groaned internally, irritated with myself that I didn't bring another joint with me.

Even another sip from my glass wouldn't calm the jitteriness in my bones. And for a second, I considered backing out. Maybe it wasn't too late. I'd told Mathieu that I would help, but he couldn't really do anything if I wanted to rescind, could he?

But that track of thought was quickly halted as I thought of the shame that would be brought on my brother and uncle should I back out. The shame from Quen, Edan, and Ajeh would barely be a love tap against my beaten-down pride, but I couldn't do that to Mathieu or Uncle. And I remembered that they'd already sent word to Isabella. That she would be expecting me. I was almost embarrassed to say that this was what scared me most of all. Knowing that she would be even more disappointed in me, even with miles and miles separating us, made me want to vomit.

No, I would see this through. If for anything, my brother. I had turned my back on my position, my responsibilities by birth. And I had turned my back on him. Not all at once, but my actions had left him to do this alone. This was the least that I could offer.

I threw back the rest of the blood in my glass and set it on a small side table. Just then, my ears picked up on footsteps coming toward me. They were slightly muffled on the runner spanning the entire length of the corridor, one I had run up and down many times as a child.

I could still pick out the distinct owners. One set was assuredly Mathieu's, that same sure stride was relaxed and at home in this place. My uncle's was louder, heavier, but just as relaxed in his childhood home. The one slightly behind them was presumably Master Jones. And with theirs were two strangers that actually walked in time to Master Jones.

They all rounded the corner and filed into the room. And by the Mother, did they swallow the space. One Shadow, and it was concentrated in the area they occupied. An eerie feeling to be around, but not this room-consuming presence with the three of them.

My heart instantly quickened.

The first Shadow to enter was a slender female, dressed in a form-fitting black. At the rear was Uncle and Mathieu with Master Jones, and between the three of them—I felt the phantom pain of my broken arms.

I heard the sound of my bones snapping. The wet gritting of them shattered under my skin. And with those memories, the smell of cinnamon and flames and oak. My jaw clenched so hard, I almost chipped a tooth. My palms itched for my blades, but I held myself back.

If my brother or uncle noticed the change of my mood to one even more sour, they didn't outwardly acknowledge it. "Sister, these are the Master Shadows that we had requested for you. Pick one." Always straight to the point, Mathieu gestured a hand toward the two Shadows standing before me.

I almost choked when they both kneeled, at the same time as if their bodies were connected by some invisible tether. His frame towered over hers, but they moved with the same fluid swiftness. My anger and fear was replaced with a wash of confusion and discomfort. The bows of the Versillians were bad enough. But actually kneeling?

My panicked glance at Mathieu must have conveyed just this, but his face betrayed nothing. Had his Shadow done this, too?

I must have been dumbly staring at them, heads slightly bowed to the floor and right fist to their chests. Uncle cleared his throat, while Mathieu's lips remained in a flat line. Uncle looked to them and then back to me. *Oh.*

"You may rise," I crossed my arms over my chest and hoped my words were steadier than I felt.

The two Shadows rose as one and stood. They clasped their hands behind their backs, mirroring exactly how Master Jones was standing behind my brother. And they both stared forward, waiting for my assessment, for my choice.

Call me a coward, but I ignored the male on the left and walked slowly to the female on the right, my footsteps nearly silent. The minuscule noises ever present in quiet spaces such as this seemed to be dimmed at this moment. Though I knew my heart was racing and that these damn Shadows could hear it, all I heard was the blood rushing in my ears.

I stopped with just a few feet between us, stepping into her line of sight. She gave a deliberate tilt of her chin, "Your Highness." Now in her orbit, I felt icy power radiating from her body. No, I wouldn't want to be on the other side of her in the rings.

Though she only wore a single sword sheathed at her hip, I knew that she probably had a multitude of hidden weapons on her person. Her jacket had delicate black embroidery that swirled around the small buttons running down the front. Her trousers and boots were just as black, just as simple, and just as exquisite. I had never seen a Shadow dressed in anything but fighting leathers before, and I wondered if this was what they all wore otherwise or if this was a special occasion. The latter made me feel nauseated.

"What is your name?" The boredness of my tone, I hoped, was that of royalty that was used to this sort of thing. She smelled of pine and a cold sky, and—the barest hint of cinnamon. *Interesting.*

"Master Noruh, Your Highness."

"Hm. And I suppose being a 'Master,' you are quite good with that sword?" I lazily gestured to her large weapon.

Along with wishing I had brought that joint into the observatory, I regretted sheathing my blades inside my boots. Had they been at my thighs like I preferred, perhaps Master Noruh and I could have easily compared and discussed weapons. Because, to my delight, her cold facade cracked for a moment, giving a brazen smirk, "I am *excellent* with this sword, Your Highness." Her aquamarine eyes flared with amusement for just a breath before settling into indifference again.

She offered nothing else, staring forward and awaiting my next interaction. But I could think of nothing else for her. So there was no choice. I had to move to the other one. I fought to settle the same distance from him as I had with Master Noruh.

But here, I had to tilt my head up to meet his face. He—he was already looking at me.

Whereas Master Noruh's power was icy, his was scorching. Had I not been expecting it, I would have been unable to keep from taking a few steps back from him. But some random hill in Dyna was neutral ground. Here, in my family's home, we were in my territory.

I straightened my spine and appraised him like I was supposed to.

For the most part, he wore the Shadow mask of indifference, but just behind it, I saw... irritation? There was a set to his jaw, just ever so slightly, that echoed the all-out disgust he showed on that hill.

Because I was on the other side of the contract, now. I'd competed against a number of Shadows for higher-paying work and lost out every time. Their skills were coveted, their reputation frightening, and I knew that to him, I was a lowly thief that brawled in taverns. At least, until this moment.

"And you? What is your name?" Thank the Mother, my question came out clear and identical to when I had asked his sister Shadow.

"Master Elián," his voice was deep, almost echoing, and it rattled my spine. I thought that he was done, but after a beat, he added with a brow raised in challenge and a barely hidden sneer, "My queen." I heard Mathieu suck in a quick breath, up until now having watched this whole process in total silence. Ah, someone had warned them. And the bastard had said it anyway.

"Hm." My lips pursed as I looked him up and down. Slowly. His longer, black hair was much more kempt than our first encounter, the waves calmly rolling over his head. His jacket matched Master Noruh's in quality, the fit just as impeccable. However, the embroidery on his was more like Master Jones's, with its severe lines that spanned his entire broad chest. He wore a lone sword on his hip as well.

"And are you," I angled my head toward Master Noruh then back to him, "*excellent* with the single sword as well? Or do you prefer dual blades?"

All I had to go on was the slight flaring of his nostrils, but my shot had landed its mark. Master Elián said nothing, but there was no doubt in my mind that he recognized me the second he walked in the room, perhaps picking up my scent in the corridor. And his non-answer and clear annoyance was all the confirmation that I didn't need.

This Shadow had killed my employer.

More than that, he had stolen the payment that I was owed for successfully fulfilling my contract. And even more than that, he had left me to heal, rather painfully, the whole goddess-dammed trip back to Nethras. Without any explanation other than that *I* had somehow fucked with *his* contract. I had rivaled with some of the Shadows during my career, but Master Elián had been the first to literally steal from me.

Suddenly, the anxiety, the dread, and the trepidation I had been feeling for nearly a week vanished. *Oh, yes*, the dark excitement flowering in my chest swelled. This might just be fun.

I spun on my heel to face my brother and uncle, who were now looking at me warily. They'd finally caught on that something was happening, and their green eyes held a similar suspiciousness. Mathieu probably saw me about to say something for *statement's sake*, as Maman used to chide.

I jerked my thumb to the brute in front of me, "I pick him."

Not the target for this particular statement, Mathieu exhaled, relieved. "Very well, sister. Master Elián, you will accompany my sister as she travels to convince the remaining potential Council members to our cause. Master Noruh, you will be accompanying Hendrik, here."

I turned to her, "And I look forward to meeting again. I would like to see you wield that sword someday."

I was a bit disappointed in her formality when she bent deeply at the waist, but before she turned to take her place with Uncle Hendrik, Master Noruh's voice was lighter as she said, "I look forward to that, Your Highness. And perhaps the Warrior Queen will show me how excellent she is with her blades." She then gave Uncle a deep nod, which he returned, and stood behind him.

A genuine, deep chuckle racked my chest, and my brother let out another relieved exhale.

And that sobered me in an instant—had he expected me to behave that badly? Though he had visibly relaxed, Mathieu's shoulders were still tensed. My triumph and amusement were squandered as shame rolled over me. My own resolve bowed a bit to the weight of it, but I kept my own shoulders steady.

"Is that all, Mathieu? Uncle?"

Uncle nodded, and Mathieu said, "Yes. You leave tomorrow morning for the port and are scheduled to reach Rhaestras in almost five days' time. Your supplies for the journey are being prepared as we speak." He stepped to me now, placing a warm hand on my shoulder. "Rest up, sister. And thank you for agreeing to this." Uncle was smiling encouragingly beside Mathieu, and I didn't expect to hear the undertone of thick emotion in my brother's direct instructions. He was leading this, but he needed me. And he and Uncle hadn't thought I would be an option until now. The petulant sister who returned when our home was already repaired.

I could barely look at them. Couldn't form a response without snapping at Mat or my voice cracking with an incoherent apology. So I just gave a curt nod and disentangled from his touch. I would have liked to say that I didn't flee, but that's exactly what I did.

My footsteps were less muffled on the runner as I stomped out of the room. Had I let myself be totally consumed by the cacophony of insecurity and embarrassment and sorrow, I wouldn't have noticed the silent presence following me. *Fuck.*

The trek back to my room was a blur, the path to it so ingrained in my soul that even after one-hundred years, I still didn't need to think about where I was going. I ascended to the higher parts of the estate, where my brother's and my wing of the house was. Or, rather, we did.

I all but tumbled into my rooms, and in a blur of movement, my Shadow rushed into the space. He moved, almost too fast to track, throughout the sitting room, into my bedroom, and then my bathing room. He settled behind me, as if he had—been checking my rooms for an intruder *lying in wait?*

My brother and uncle had truly left me with a guard dog for at least the next few weeks, and I would never be alone throughout that time. Hell, I shuddered, maybe even longer than that, depending on how long I stuck around helping with this whole council business. Goddess, what had I agreed to? And it was *him.* Was it too late to ask for Master Noruh instead?

He was standing at my back, I knew. And—why was I letting him at my back like this? I spun to face this Master Elián.

His arms were crossed at his chest, and the mask of the dutiful subject had dropped completely. *Good,* I thought to myself.

We stood like this for a while, jaws set and bodies tensed for one of us to make some sort of move. He wouldn't kill me in my family's home, I knew. The Council was his employer, I supposed. And by extension, as I was the one he was guarding, I was his employer, too. He would be at the mercy of my beck and call. Tasked with laying down his life for me if the situation called for it. A small smile crept over my face as the realities of how this arrangement must surely be tormenting him settled over me. The dark amusement inched back in again, and the walls seemed to stop closing in around me.

While my lips curled up, his turned down. I sucked my teeth, "Well isn't this a delight."

He said nothing, so I continued, "I would introduce myself, but because we've already met, I feel it's unnecessary."

Master Elián stood, eyes locked on me, and remained silent. *Oh yes,* the mischievous part of me relished, *this has turned oh so interesting.*

Neither of us broke our stare-down, and Rhaea take me, I didn't know why I said what I did next. But I blurted, brows raised, "I had no idea that you Shadows fuck each other. Figures, though."

Suddenly, Master Elián was standing right in front of me. He didn't touch me, but his body crowded over mine as he bent slightly so that I could see every hard line of his face, every frightening stir in his irises. They were blazing again like when he'd shattered my bones.

"The Shadows had heard of the Warrior Queen. Protector of Innocents who fought back nearly a whole army by herself." I was biting the inside of my cheek so hard I drew blood. "We came here not because we are bound to any ruler. But because we respect what this Council is trying to do. We do not want to see any more of our people slaughtered. And I respected this Warrior Queen." His eyes trailed down my body then back up again. "What a waste."

He pulled back and was instantly perched on the wall beside the door. Arms still crossed at his chest, he looked off into the distance, dismissing me entirely.

At my sides, my fists clenched, unclenched, clenched. What a waste, indeed.

And again, I fled.

I left my Shadow to his post at the wall and retreated into my bedroom and slammed the door.

PART TWO

THE MAMBA AND THE NIGHT

11

I lay on my bed for some time, staring at the ceiling and trying to contain the violent vibrations racking my body. I was so infuriated. I thought picking him would be the delicious revenge for his blatant disrespect the first time we met. Then, he hadn't thought me worthy of an explanation or the common fucking decency to not attack me. So, being at the mercy of my whims seemed like humorous retribution when the opportunity fell in my lap.

Yet, his words cut deeper than I wanted to admit to myself. Ah, yes, the Warrior Queen who now made her living as a pickpocket for hire. While Mathieu had been rebuilding our family's kingdom, giving Versillians a home to be proud of again, I was stealing and brawling and slitting the occasional throat when the pay was good enough.

But dammit, who was *he* to judge me? The Shadows were an ancient, feared group, but they whored themselves out just like I did. True that they had a bit more bargaining power in their contracts and could afford to be choosier than I could, but at least when the Vyrkos were at our throats, I had stood for something. These shifty pricks had just stood by and done nothing. Now they wanted to come in and be part of our people's recovery? We were both jumping on the back of Mathieu's efforts and trying to claim noble intentions. At least I could admit to myself that it wasn't that so much as it was guilt.

As I ran through the past few days, my mind started creeping back to unpleasant places. Heads rolling, friends and family lost, a

Goddess that hadn't answered in a long, long time. I needed to do something.

My body shot up from the bed, and I began to pack. It was infuriatingly quick work since half of my things were still in the bags I had brought from Nethras. Mathieu's tailors had made some formal, royal-looking clothes that I folded carefully. I didn't have much besides fighting and casual outfits, and it seemed my brother had anticipated this when I agreed to help. Or maybe he had these clothes made a while ago. I was too afraid to ask.

The handful of staff working in my family's home would probably be annoyed with me packing my own bags, but I was finished in under an hour. Though I was sure there would be a multitude of wrinkles and that I would surely forget something.

I stuffed a few books from my old bookshelf into one of the bags as well. The flowery romances that I read as an adolescent weren't far off from what I read now as an adult, and hopefully enough time had passed for me to find the stories entertaining once more. All the more reason to limit Master Elián's opportunities to hit me with his cutting assessments. And to limit my inevitable breakdown or attack.

I still wasn't sure which way I would land. While flitting between tasks, I had been oscillating between the two ends of the spectrum. Though, with not having spilled blood for any reason other than nourishment in over a month, I had a suspicion that I would lean towards attacking him. And that would surely not end well for me, even being confident that I could get a few good swipes in. Maybe the poison on my blades would incapacitate him enough to where I could do some real damage.

I was daydreaming about burying a dagger into Master Elián's side as I wandered back into the living space of my rooms. While I was packing, a servant had brought up a tray of food and a decanter of blood, and I couldn't stall any longer. By the sprawling window, my table had been set and a fresh vase of yellow roses from the garden stood in the center. When I called this space my home, I had hardly ever taken a meal here, usually opting to eat in one of the dining rooms with my family or on the go to wherever.

My supper being laid out here was weirdly formal, but I shrugged the apprehension away when I caught sight of one of my favorite dishes. My appetite seemed to have come back in full force.

Trying not to drool, I made a beeline to the table and sat at the placement facing the door. Two place settings had been prepared, though my companion seemed to have not moved while I was closed up in my bedroom.

I poured some blood into a wine glass and started filling my plate. The spread was simple but plenty. Spring vegetables from the gardens, fresh baked bread, and the familiar smoked meats of the region. I added a healthy drizzle of herbaceous sauce over every morsel.

The moan I gave when I tasted the first bite was less than ladylike. Nor was me wolfing down the entire meal in a matter of seconds the decorum of a queen. But the food was hot and rich and bright. I didn't think I was ever going to get over tasting the flavors of my home after having been away for so long.

When I couldn't take another bite for fear of bursting, I took to sipping my glass. It was spiced in the way that my father had enjoyed, nutmeg and sage. Warmth bloomed in my chest, and I relaxed further into my seat.

"Too good to eat with me?" I asked as I gazed out of the window onto the eastern courtyard below. The fountain was giving its usual pleasant burbling.

I flicked my eyes to my Shadow, still standing at that wall, expecting for his eyes to be off in the distance as they were before. But his immediately locked to mine, as if he had been watching me all this time.

The few times I had taken contracts to guard people, I had found the whole process mind numbingly dull. Though my experience was certainly more limited than Master Elián's in this field, I found that most who contracted people like myself had an overinflated sense of self importance. These jobs had involved standing at doors like my Shadow was doing now, walking behind wealthy people peacocking for those they saw inferior, and staring at the ceiling. Or perhaps I just missed all the action.

Master Elián held his head cocked to the side as he stared unflinchingly. I was too full, appetite too satisfied to care, and stayed lounging behind my empty plate. I took another sip from my glass, refusing to break whatever was happening right now.

He made no attempt to hide as he took in my hair, undoubtedly an unruly, frizzy mane at this point in the day. I followed as his narrow-eyed evaluation tracked over my shoulder, down to the leg I had draped over the arm of my chair, and back to my face. He said nothing.

"You have already broken my bones and insulted me multiple times. Must you continue to disrespect me by refusing to break bread? Or is eating with your charge not allowed?" I waved a hand at the other half of the spread left in the serving dishes, his plate still clean and untouched.

He remained standing, arms crossed, and I scoffed. *Fine*, I mouthed into my glass as I took another sip and looked out the window. I wouldn't beg to have a supper companion. Especially when I was finished eating anyway.

The soft sound of wooden chair legs pulling over the cream colored rug snapped me to attention. Master Elián sat with a grace that took me aback, and I watched, gaze narrowed, while he settled into the seat opposite mine. He unabashedly emptied the rest of the food onto his plate, not bothering to parcel out the bread and opting to just take the whole basket. His pour from the decanter was equally as heavy-handed and nearly filled his glass to the brim.

I wagged a finger between him and the closed door of my rooms, "Shouldn't you not have your back facing the door like that?"

Not until he had started on the vegetables and broken off a piece of warm bread did he respond gruffly, "If you question my abilities to do my job, then by all means, relieve me of my duties, Your Highness." His eyebrow raised in that challenging way again.

"And give you the thing you so obviously crave? No, I don't think I will. Besides, I'm more than capable of protecting myself." Anger flared in my chest like a wildfire when he let out a quick, unbelieving breath through his nose.

I shifted in my seat to reach into my pocket and retrieved the joint I found while preparing my things. I lit it on the flame of the lone candle on the table, and the first inhale burned a little in the best way. I exhaled to the ceiling. The smoke hit the ivory tiles and spread before dissipating and filling the space. I tapped ashes on my empty plate and settled the joint between two fingers.

Master Elián looked at me like I'd grown another nose, his

forehead furrowed as if he was trying to figure out why I'd suddenly started barking like a dog. But I stared right back, taking in his expression of distaste and letting it roll over my shoulders. His hair was tucked behind his ears, and there were multiple piercing holes that were punched through both.

I extended the joint toward him and was not surprised when he quickly shook his head. He started tearing into the meat he'd heaped next to a lake of sauce. While I had spread the stuff over my food, he seemed to opt for dipping his into the green and brown condiment. He chewed angrily, though silently, jaw seeming to work overtime between each swallow. Was it because he was irritated with me or did it always do that?

"You said it yourself that I fight well. Yes, you may be better, but that's beside the point. I will not have you scurrying behind me for weeks on end."

His head snapped up at that. He swallowed his food and retorted, "I do not scurry. And you agreed to have a Shadow. You chose me. I will do my job as I see fit."

"As—what did you call me? Ah, yes, your *queen*. As your queen, I believe that I can command you to serve me in whatever way that *I* see fit." He kissed his teeth but said nothing.

I took another long drag from the joint warming my fingers.

He eyed the motion with bewilderment, but made no comment on it. Master Elián finished his meal and emptied the bread basket. His nose wrinkled slightly as he raised his glass to his lips. He took a small sip and set it back down on the table.

"Do you not like it?" He raised that brow again, but this time it looked like a question.

I gestured to his glass as I took a deep gulp, draining mine. He ignored my question entirely, "What is your command, then, Your Highness?"

I stubbed out the burning end of the joint on the ceramic plate and let it fall amongst the ashes. What was my command? I was out of practice giving orders beyond requesting food or directions to where my brother was at the moment. What were the limits of what I could expect from Master Elián?

"Well, first, I don't want you standing behind me, breathing down my neck all of the time. Can you agree to that?"

He crossed his arms, "Is that an order? Or are you asking?"

I sputtered for a moment. My Shadow was a fucking asshole. "It's an order." He didn't say anything, just continued to look at me, head tilted slightly to the side.

My throat cleared as I continued, "And I expect you to treat me as an equal, not some tender flower that needs protecting."

"My job is to protect," he countered. "Perhaps if you told me who taught you Shadow techniques instead of *lying* as you did, I may be inclined to follow these orders."

I groaned, "Are you still stuck on this?" I rubbed my temples, trying to quell the burgeoning headache from just five minutes of trying to talk to my new companion. This was going to be a long journey, and he wasn't going to make it easy. "I'm tired of this conversation," I pushed my chair from the table and stood.

He just sat back and watched, and I felt his eyes on me as I crossed the space back to my bedroom. At least in here he seemed to not feel the need to follow. Or was he following my less-than-confident order all ready? No, if I had gathered anything from my Shadow so far, it was that he may half-heartedly feign respect for me as an heir to Versillia and his charge, but he didn't, really.

The bathing room connected to my bedroom was lavish compared to the one in my apartment back in Nethras, and I decided to take full advantage of it tonight. To Isabella, we would be traveling nearly a week on the road and sea. There would be few and far between opportunities to wash ourselves off, let alone bathe and perfume in the way that I liked.

Mathieu, now living in the palace full-time, had thankfully repaired the running water in our family's sprawling estate. Goddess, I wonder how long that had taken.

The large porcelain tub could fit at least three people, and I filled it all the way with water so hot, the room quickly started to fill with steam. I dropped lavender and bergamot oils into the water, and the scents intertwined with the steam curling around me. My shoulders relaxed fully now, and I shrugged out of my clothes, leaving them in a messy heap. Once I crept into the scalding water, my muscles melted.

I worked a bar of citrus scented soap into a crisp, new washing cloth. As I dragged it over my skin, I imagined washing off this exhausting day. I rubbed away the careful planning of my brother and those that had already agreed to be part of this Council. Down my shoulder, over my arms, and off my fingertips. My legs carried the ghosts of walking through these halls once again. I ran the cloth over my thighs, my calves. The fabric tickled my toes as I worked off standing barefoot in the Queen's Garden, my mother's garden.

The staff my brother employed had seen to it that the garden was well-tended, and the surge of emotion I had felt standing amongst the pale pinks and oranges and violets of the flowers had almost been too much. A soft breeze smelling of ocean air had stirred my hair in a familiar way when that surge had reached an almost incapacitating peak. I had taken off my shoes. Feeling the small stones that lined the path and that breeze grounded me for however long I stood there.

It had been a mistake to avoid this place for so long.

The admission sliced again through my heart, and my mind raced to try to defend my actions. When The Killings had happened, I was so broken, the only option to keep from dying myself was to run. I did not regret this; it was what I needed to do at that time. What Mathieu and I both needed to do. But to stay away for a century? It was a catastrophic blow to my ego to fully admit that there was no excuse for it.

I rubbed more soap into the cloth and set to cleaning my torso. I scrubbed soft circles at my chest, over and around my breasts and down my stomach. With what happened to Lee and Shoko and returning to Versillia, I hadn't thought much of my first encounter with Master Elián, but my brother's and uncle's insistence of me having a security detail had let the memories start to creep back in.

The chances of *him* being the one of those hired were slim. I wasn't sure exactly how many were in their ranks, but I imagined that there were enough to make this turn of events a twisted hand of fate. Or that of an amused Goddess that loved seeing me suffer.

Why had I chosen Master Elián?

In the moment, it felt like a joke—you attack me and steal my money, I put you in a position you will no doubt hate. I now imagined lounging in the sitting room with Master Noruh instead. She seemed like a much more amenable person. Perhaps she would like to discuss fighting techniques instead of hounding me to discover where I'd learned mine, or maybe she liked to read? With Lee gone, I was desperately wishing for someone to talk to about books. Or really, anything remotely interesting that didn't consist of death or rebuilding.

I submerged myself in the bath, letting the hot water rinse away the suds that clung to my upper body.

Pushing back up into the air, I reached for the hair tonic resting on the small table with the other bathing tools and supplies, and I worked a lather at my scalp, moaning as tingles trickled down my spine.

Yes, that was part of why I had stayed away from this place, wasn't it? As one of two heirs, I would have been tasked endlessly with responsibilities. And large, arduous ones. Building up a kingdom from wreckage and ash was no small feat, and one that took decades, centuries. I had already been subjected to being the daughter of rulers, where so many of my days and nights were not my own. I had to sneak moments, pockets of time where I could act as I wished without wondering how that would reflect on my family, on our kingdom.

When I left after The Killings, there was a freedom I had never known. I walked off the edge of a high cliff of grief, and instead of plummeting to my own end, I had found wings. Shoddy ones that didn't necessarily let me soar, but they still opened me up to possibilities that had never been available to me before.

I submerged myself again, working out the cleanser from my thick hair. When I reemerged, I stopped just at my neck, and reclined my head on the lip of the tub. I sighed. If I had to sacrifice a measure of the freedom that had now filled half of my years in this realm, that was okay.

If not, why had I done it? The reason so many referred to me as the Warrior Queen. What was the point of it if I were still going to let our people suffer? For so long, I had contented myself on what I had done as being enough. For that and the intermittent volunteering I did to make up for my grave sins. But I now knew for certain that there was more to do.

I stayed in my bathtub long enough for the water to turn cool. And when I removed myself, pulling the plug to let it drain, I warmed in a large, soft towel. While I smoothed moisturizing creams over my hair and skin and dressed for bed, I planned.

I did not leave my bedroom to check on Master Elián. He could busy himself by standing at the wall, sleeping, or fucking choking, for all I cared.

Once in bed, I sat, knees propped up while I read a book that was on my old shelf. It was a tale of young love and adventure, like most of the novels I devoured as a child. The short-lived romances that I found as a girl paled to what were in these stories. And few in my adult years had given me what these books did.

At the time, I had just started learning my bite, learning that I could be anything other than a demure little thing. And though I would still return to these tales of young females finding their prince, I eventually realized that that would never be what I wanted. After my mother finally let me start training, I realized that I wanted the adventure, the fighting, the bloodshed. And I would not wait around for some grand love to do it.

But these stories gave me a sense of confounding comfort. Some of the writing was downright questionable, but I could feel the echoes of my former self come alive when I read these books. So I kept on. And I fell asleep like that, sitting up, book in hand, as I let the silly little story fill my mind.

12

Diana was annoyed with me, as I suspected she would be. Before the sun had risen, she knocked on my bedroom door. I answered quickly, as I was already awake and dressing, much to her dismay. She riffled through the packs I had prepared, correcting the folding I had done, checking over what I had included. If she smelled what was in the golden box in one of the bags, she didn't comment on it.

I left her to flit to and fro in the large room as I climbed into my leathers.

"Your Highness, I had an outfit hung in the closet for your journey," she heaved a heavy sigh as she took in my choice of travel garments. I just shrugged and made no move to the closet. She shook her head and continued her repacking.

The smart, maroon trousers and matching top she had packed for me were not only completely impractical, but too well made, also. We would be traveling covertly, as myself and the Council had decided, and that meant not drawing attention to ourselves. Master Elián and I would be better off as two anonymous travelers who looked just hardened enough to intimidate would-be thieves and petty assailants. Not a female that looked like she had money and her scowling guard dog.

And I was used to traveling in my leathers anyway.

The set I donned this morning was the color of chocolate. Broken into my body from many wears, the leather was soft and flexible with built-in sheaths for my blades. I laced up my matching boots and tucked a pair of knives at my ankles.

Diana gave the room a last once-over before turning to me, hand on a hip and arm extended. I took my hat from her and ran the pads of my fingers over the emerald-colored inner lining. Smooth silk that was put in especially for me, it was a past birthday gift from Shoko. The black, wide brimmed hat had become another part of my uniform, and I fit it comfortably over the two braids running on my head.

Ready for my journey to meet Isabella, Diana and I grabbed my packs and made our way to the front room. A tray of eggs and bacon and fruit sat at the table by the window, as did Master Elián. Even with the large meal just a few hours earlier, my stomach growled.

We deposited the packs just out into the hallway, ready for them to be brought down to affix to the horses. Diana gave me a tight nod and curtsy before continuing down the hallway to continue the preparations.

Not being able to resist the smell wafting from the breakfast any longer, I made my way to the table. I plopped down in my seat from last night and poured myself a cup of chamomile tea. With one hand, I gave my cup a dollop of honey, and with the other, I shoved a strip of bacon into my mouth.

The salt and fat was intoxicating, and I tossed three more strips onto my plate. Eggs, I liked less, but I piled them onto my plate nonetheless. Food on the road was disgusting most of the time, and the protein would tide me over for a long while.

Mouth full of scrambled eggs, I finally looked up at my Shadow. He looked out onto the rising sun with an expression that I tried and failed to decipher. His eyes, the color of apricots today, glowed in the low light. I had encountered very few creatures with eyes anything like his. And never another Lylithan.

I filed my question away for a time he may be more inclined to answer. Considering he may daydream about burying a blade in my skin the way I did him, it was wise to keep my curiosities to myself for now.

Delightfully, though, I saw a small book resting next to his plate. Unable to stop myself, I asked, "What are you reading?" I wiped my cloth napkin at my mouth and tried to keep my tone even.

Slowly, he dragged his eyes away from the window to meet mine. "A book," he brought a strip of bacon to his mouth and took a bite.

Not letting myself become deterred, I shrugged and grabbed my teacup, "Well, I love books if you ever want to discuss what you're reading. We'll be stuck together for a while, and it seems that we at least have one thing in common." I took a gulp of my tea.

He just gave a noncommittal grunt and gazed back out the window. I looked out of it myself, trying to see what was so interesting. As many years as I had seen, sunrises were beautiful, yes, but I had witnessed enough to where they weren't *that* interesting. The attention he gave this one made me wonder if something special was happening outside. As I scanned the horizon and the grounds below, I found nothing. No, nothing special, he was just dismissing me again.

I ate a bit more, as did he, and with only a few bites of eggs left on my plate, I cleared my throat. "Did you sleep well?"

His head snapped to face me, "What?"

"Did you sleep well?"

He ran his eyes quickly over my body, stopping at my hat, then at the upper part of my leathers. "What are you wearing?"

My brow furrowed, "Clothes."

Master Elián scoffed as he put his fork, knife, and napkin on his empty plate. He rose from the table, grabbed his book, and took his post by the door.

He stuffed the book in a hidden pocket in his own, black leathers. His twin swords were back, as well. He did not lean on the wall this time, just crossed his arms, waiting. And seeing him, stance eerily similar to the first time we spoke, my appetite shriveled and died. I threw my napkin down and downed the rest of my tea. It burned a bit going down my throat, but I barely noticed.

When I rose and crossed to the door, Master Elián made no attempt to hide his perusal of my body. Not a perusal of sexual interest, but one of a predator sizing up another. Or, actually, perhaps as a predator sizing up potential prey.

That wouldn't do.

I stopped just two feet in front of him, mimicking his stance and tilting my head to look into his eyes from under the brim of my hat. His face was stoney, all hard lines, while he glared down his nose at me. I grinned.

"I think we will have fun, you and I."

His nostrils flared at my bravado, "We will most certainly not."

And because he had decided he could touch me without my leave those weeks ago, I gave his chest a quick pat as I turned away from him. It was hard and warm under my touch. I left quickly, but not so quickly that I didn't feel him tense.

We moved through my family's palace in silence and headed to the stables. My father had always cursed my ability to sneak around corners as a child, and although Lylithans were able to move quickly and quietly, I seemed to have mastered this ability a bit more than most. But Master Elián quite literally moved silently. Unnerved, I finally realized how my father felt all those years ago. A warm smirk flashed across my face as we hit the wall of horse shit and hay smell.

Mathieu and Uncle were standing outside, albeit further apart than they usually did, checking with the stablehands that prepared our transport. Masters Jones and Noruh were standing behind them, and when they eyed Master Elián and myself, they gave their fellow Shadow a fist to their chest. Master Elián returned the gesture.

"I see you've learned to pack light, sister," Mathieu petted the auburn hair of a roan horse that stood already saddled. She was to be mine, then.

An adolescent with white hair and tan skin held the reins of a black horse and led it next to the roan one. Master Elián reached for the reins, realizing as I had which horse would go to whom. The boy didn't meet any of our eyes, but spoke steadily, "This here is Noxe, and her highness will be riding Bhrila."

Master Elián gave the boy a quick nod, and Mathieu said, "Thank you, Hyvan." I smiled as the boy gave my brother a bow and retreated. He gave me one as well before he disappeared into the depths of the stable.

Uncle snorted to himself then looked between the mare and me, "These horses seem quite fitting for their riders," I frowned, and he continued, "Thank you again for doing this, niece. I know that we have asked a lot of you." I grabbed the reins of the mare from Mathieu and petted her neck softly. Her eyes were the same deep brown as mine.

The dawn air was crisp, and anticipation curled in my stomach. We had a long journey ahead of us, and I still wasn't quite sure how to sit with my choice of companion. And seeing Rhaestras and

Isabella after all of this time was going to be... something.

Hopefully something that brought good news for the Council.

"This is the least I can do. Thank you both for all you have done and are still doing. I'm just trying to catch up." And to my surprise, Mathieu reached down and brought me into a tight embrace. He smelled like cedar and chamomile and ocean waves, and I brought my arms to circle his back.

Two breaths, and he released me with his hands on my shoulders. He ran a questioning look over my body, seemingly taking me in for the first time, *"What* are you wearing?"

I heard a soft chortle, just a quick exhale, and I whipped my head around, "Oh, you shut the fuck up."

Master Elián's eyes widened a fraction at the viciousness of my outburst, but Mathieu just chuckled, "I didn't mean it in a bad way. I've just," he shook his head, "I've never seen you dressed like this before."

Just as I was about to crack a snide remark at him, the earthy scent of Tana made its way to me. "Oh, good!" She sounded slightly out of breath, and when I frowned over to where she approached, I saw the very slight flush of her cheeks. Had she run all the way here? "I was worried I was going to miss you! *Someone*"—she shot a narrow look at Uncle—"let me fall back asleep after telling me he was leaving for the estate."

Without warning, my cousin pulled me in for a hug, much tighter than my brother's, and she swayed with me locked in her arms. I hesitated before giving her back gentle pats and cleared my throat, "I'll make sure to send you a letter or two, cousin. And—thank you. For all your help these past weeks."

Tana jerked back, and, yes, there was an unmistakable shimmering at the edges of her eyes, "No need to *thank* me, Leenie. I've had so much fun, and," she swallowed, "I think we *both* needed a bit of fun."

She raised her chin and planted a swift, warm kiss to my brow. My eyes rolled very, very far into my skull as I smiled back at her.

I turned to my horse. Sticking one foot in her stirrup, I hoisted myself up, swinging the other leg over her saddle. I seated easily atop her and ran a mental hand over the bags strapped to the saddle. Master Elián did the same, mounting his black mare absolutely silently. How did he do that?

Master Noruh called from behind Uncle, now clad in her own black leathers, "I think you may regret choosing this one over me, Your Highness."

I flicked my braids over my shoulders and frowned, "Yes, I have been wondering that since I uttered the words. But, I am not one to go back on a decision made." I would just think about it.

Master Noruh's shoulders rose and fell a bit in a silent laugh, but as her eyes looked to my Shadow beside me, her face broke into an all-out grin.

The blonde hair fixed in a singular plait down her back was almost white in the warming morning, and somehow, the black of her leathers didn't dull the shine. I looked over my shoulder to Master Elián who was, unsurprisingly, frowning. Just slightly, but he was definitely frowning as he and Master Noruh shared some sort of silent conversation through that connection of theirs. Were they lovers? They had definitely fucked before I had chosen between the two of them. At breakfast this morning, I could still pick up the barest hint of pine when he shifted in the air.

My mind conjured up images of lying with the two of them. Her pale face between my legs as he took her from behind. Those fiery, raging eyes of his locked on mine through every thrust. I imagined his skin smooth and rippling with centuries of well-hewn muscles. Her blonde hair loose and sprawling wantonly between my legs as her tongue swirled and licked and pulsed with each slam of his hips. I thought of me running my fangs over the milky curve of her shoulder while we fucked each other with our fingers as he watched, pumping his fist over himself.

I quickly brought my hand to my forehead and rubbed a knuckle between my brows. It had been weeks since I had been fucked properly, and now I had further reason to not trust my mind from wandering to unsavory places. *Goddess, this is going to be a long trip.*

Never one to give long speeches, my uncle called over, "Travel safely. And come back with good news, niece." I noticed the stiffness in his shoulders and chilled air between him and Mat, but my other worries quickly reoccupied my thoughts.

I nodded to Uncle, Mathieu, and Tana, then to Masters Jones and Noruh, and squeezed my calves. Bhrila started forward, and Master

Elián commanded Noxe to do the same.

We brought our horses to a comfortable trot and set out on the road toward the port. The four of us traveled on the worn, dirt road for hours with the sound of only the horses' hooves and breathing, the forest surrounding us, and the shifting of our packs. Thankfully, spring had not shown the flashes of summer yet, and we were gifted a brisk morning that turned into a mild and bright day.

Almost half the day had passed, and we slowed to a walk as we neared a stream. We were making good time, the sun still having more hours to give us. I called to Master Elián that we should let Bhrila and Noxe have a rest before we picked back up again. He said nothing, but slowed Noxe to stay abreast with me and Bhrila.

We dismounted and led the two mares to the stream. They both drank happily as I stretched my arms over my head, twisting my body this way and that. I bent and straightened my legs and rotated my ankles to combat the stiffness that would inevitably creep in at some point in all this traveling. We could cover a lot of ground on foot, even run faster than the horses for a while, but for the longer distance we had to go, and the bags we had to carry, horses were the best option. And they needed breaks.

Master Elián stood, arms clasped behind his back as he raised his face to the sky. He stood with eyes closed, breathing deeply. The deep tan of his skin was rich and almost luminous under the soft morning light. And his shoulders seemed to relax a fraction, even with the deadly swords strapped to his back. His leathers were pristine but well-worn like mine.

I did not know how much time had passed, and I hadn't realized that I was staring until he spoke softly, eyes still closed, "You're staring."

I stuck my third finger at him in a human gesture that I had learned a few decades back, "You look rather peaceful when you aren't being a complete asshole, is all."

His head snapped instantly to me, eyes flying open. A few strands of his hair became untucked from behind his ears and fell in his face. "An asshole?"

"Yes, an asshole. Like where shit comes out of."

His face pinched in disgust, "You have a wicked mouth."

"What—no 'Your Highness'?" He just shrugged and continued to sun himself like a cat. "Well, if you aren't going to use my title, then I won't use yours. Elián."

Instead of moving his head this time, his lids opened slowly, and his eyes moved to meet mine. Still some distance away, he looked down his nose at me. I raised both of my brows, waiting for him to spit something else, or tell me not to address him by just his name. But he said nothing, just looked at me. "Now you're the one staring."

He again said nothing.

I threw my hands in the air, exasperation taking hold, "I don't want to be your enemy and this bickering is growing tiresome. Can we just make some sort of truce? This whole thing is taxing enough. I don't need me and my travel companion to be at each other's throats on top of all that I have to do."

"You are the one who started with me. I wanted no business with you, let alone to be subject to this squabbling."

Swiftly, I crossed to him. I didn't stop until my feet were almost touching his, my shoulders just rising to his breastbone. I wanted to punch him squarely there, where the air would whoosh out of him, maybe make his heart stutter. My mouth spat venom as I looked up at his confounded face, "What the fuck do you mean I started all this? *You* attacked *me*."

He now shifted his posture, no longer preening toward the sun. No, he curled in, eclipsing it. I was on the slighter side, and he took advantage of his height and loomed over me.

And Elián matched me toe-to-toe in spitting venom, "You started this by costing me my contract. I did you a favor by sparing your miserable life." The rhythm of his words had begun taking a different tilt, the vowels deeper, and the consonants rolling smoother off of his tongue. "And when you had the chance to pick Master Noruh instead of me, you acted like the brat that you are and decided to make a statement. And now the consequences of that choice are taxing you? You really are the arrogant—"

And I struck him. Before he could utter another fucking word, I stepped back and struck him in his sternum.

Like I had been taught, quick like a viper. And just as I had fantasized, I heard the air leave his lungs in a strangled whoosh. He bent over, supporting himself on his knees as he sucked in air. He coughed as his body worked to repair whatever I had dislodged. If only I had managed to land such a blow the first time we'd met.

Unfortunately for me, though, his strangled breaths subsided very quickly and turned to calming, deep ones. And within seconds, he stood as if nothing had happened.

The fingers of my right hand curled, and my nails dug into my palm. I had packed a lot behind that punch, and he recovered faster than should have been possible.

And now he glared at me with fury. If I had thought he looked at me with rage before, I realized now that, compared to this, that had been longing. "Going to fight me back, Elián? Break my arms again?"

Eyes never leaving mine, face never relaxing into anything other than a promise of death, he stepped slowly toward me. He didn't stop until I almost felt the brush of his chest, but I refused to be moved. To be intimidated. I wanted a reason to brawl.

But he didn't give it to me. He just stopped, glaring downwards, and we stood that way for seven breaths.

Before breath eight could begin, he turned toward the horses who had behaved and stayed right where we had left them at the stream. He mounted Noxe and turned her around. They moved past me, not sparing a single word or glance, and waited at the dirt road.

Shouting in my mind every curse word in every language I knew, I mounted Bhrila. She walked merrily toward her sister, and the four of us continued on the road without another word. The only amicable ones between us would be the animals, it seemed.

13

A few hours after night fell, we came upon the inn that signaled the end of the first day of our travels. The two-floor building was set just beyond the road amongst a copse of mature trees. Smoke churned from the chimney and twined with the night air. A few travelers milled about, and the noises of supper being served grew louder as we neared. The thatched roof looked black in the moonlight, and the windows emitted soft light with the activity of evening. The small inn hadn't changed at all.

As we approached, two stablehands came to take our reins. The way they hastened after looking at our faces, well, particularly Elián's, indicated that they would not mess with our horses.

Elián and I unstrapped our packs from Bhrila and Noxe in silence, and I gave one of the stablehands a silver to give the mares extra food and sugar cubes tonight. My request was met with swift nods and muttered assurances.

We rounded the facade and squeezed into the inn. The air was immediately warmer inside, and the smell of stew and ale and sweat won out against the pleasant earthiness of the road. I strode to the counter at the left of the entrance, Elián silent and brooding beside me. At least he had heeded my command about standing behind me.

"We would like one room with two beds, please."

The stout female behind the counter checked a ledger. She muttered, "Not sure we've got any left with two beds," and my jaw clenched. Her pink skin was flushed with the heat of the room, and she pushed some of her frizzy gray hair out of her face. "Ah, here, we do have one that was just made available. I'll show you up there." I passed her one night's fee in a tinkle of coin that she quickly pocketed with a nod. Though visibly older, the woman moved steadily and quickly toward the set of stairs at the back of the large room. She maneuvered deftly around patrons and staff alike, and Elián and I kept just a pace behind her. When we climbed the stairs, she led us down the left side of a short corridor. Thankfully, ours was the last room on the right.

She produced a key from her apron pocket and unlocked the door. Our room for the night smelled first of soap, signaling that the staff still changed the sheets between guests. But under that, I couldn't help detect the odor of the patrons before us. Even with two beds, whoever was here last had left the smell of sex and sweat and —something else unpleasant that I couldn't place.

The room was small, but otherwise neat. Two beds sat facing the door with a small wooden table separating them. A wobbly looking lamp stood in the corner, and a circular window hung above the beds. There was a dresser set near the door, but I shuddered at the thought of putting my clothes in it.

The female handed me the key with a word about the bathing rooms at the other end of the corridor and went back to her post, leaving us to it. As the sound of her quick footsteps descended the stairs, Elián was a blur of movement as he checked under the beds, behind every bit of furniture, and tested the latch on the windows. Our last conversation made me almost forget what he was traveling with me for. When he finished, he stopped, still as a statue, in the center of the room.

Sighing, I dropped my packs on the bed furthest from the door and removed my hat. I began to walk in a slow perimeter around our room as I brought my fingers to the plaits on my head. Tightly fixed to my scalp all day, my head stung with the tension I instilled in the braids last night. My fingers flew to undo them, and I could have wept at the release I felt.

Once free, I shook my fingers in my hair, fluffing about my head and letting the curls and waves fall down my shoulders and back. I would have to redo the braids before I went to bed, but the tightness leaving my scalp for a few hours was worth it.

I turned to Elián, question at my lips, but he was already watching me with his brows low over his eyes. He had been busying himself with checking our packs, but his hands were stilled as they reached inside one of his.

"What? Do I have something in my hair?" I pawed at the strands that seemed to already be growing in volume just by being released into the air. I was no stranger to debris getting ensnared in the kinks and coils.

He just pursed his lips and focused himself back on his things. Seemingly satisfied, he closed the pack he had been inspecting and straightened. He stood with his hands clasped behind his back in a stance I realized was his resting position.

"I would like to get some food—is that all right with you?" To answer my question, he strolled toward the door, opened it, and went out of the room.

I sighed again and moved out into the corridor, locked our door behind us, and made my way back downstairs. The common space of the inn was filled with small tables and the odd booth for patrons to sit and eat. A warm fire was roaring on one of the far walls to combat the chill that now hung in the air outside. Elián stayed just behind me as I crossed to a table that was tucked into the furthest corner that I could find.

Just a few moments after we sat down, a young female, the spitting image of the older one who showed us our rooms, walked quickly to our table. Her mousy brown hair was pulled into a tight bun at the back of her head, and her hands wiped on an apron identical to the older female's. She took our order with the efficiency of one who had worked here all of her life. Only another few moments passed before she returned with two pints of ale that she deposited wordlessly on the scarred wooden table that sat between Elián and me.

I picked up my mug, but Elián snatched it out of my hand, and before I could protest, took a sniff and matter-of-fact sip. He handed it back to me, and I tentatively brought the frothy liquid to my lips. Taking a long swig, the yeasty taste hit my throat in a pleasant fizz.

A further realization hit me—he was not only to follow me and to check each new room I entered, but my Shadow was tasked to check my food for *poison*. And—he must have done that with the food back in Versillia, too. Elián took a somber drink of his ale and set it back down on the table. A few hours of riding, and he didn't look at me with the same degree of fury as he had after I punched him. But it wasn't a pleasant look, either.

I sighed and spoke softly, "Elián, I don't want this animosity between us." As much as I was itching for a fight, I knew that we were getting nowhere. And this would be much easier with things at least neutral between us. Or as near neutral as we could get them. "I apologize for hitting you earlier."

He raised a disbelieving brow and took another sip of his ale, but didn't retort. He obviously didn't trust my apology, but that was his problem. He didn't try to reciprocate it either. But nevertheless, I decided that I would make an effort to treat him as I would anyone else that I was on pleasant terms with. Like I would had I chosen Master Noruh instead of him.

As he took another sip from his glass, I said with a completely innocent tone, "You know, I think if we hadn't gotten started on bad terms, I still would have picked you. I trust you're good at what you do. And if you weren't looking at me like you wanted to kill me all of the time, I might be inclined to see if you'd want to fuck me." And just as I had hoped, Elián choked on the ale that was traveling down his throat.

He sputtered and coughed and wiped at the little bit that spilled down his chin. I tipped my head back and cackled. This was the first response he'd shown that wasn't contemptuous, and I was going to savor it.

Once he got a rein on himself, he muttered into his mug, "You are a menace," and took a long swig.

I let out another laugh into the noisy common area, "And there he is!" I jostled his shoulder, and he grumbled. But he didn't say anything else, and his eyes didn't shift into fiery fury. I would take this as progress, I decided.

We sat in a less tense silence over our drinks, and before we could finish them, the female set down two bowls of stew in front of us. Steam rose from each of them, and I didn't hesitate to dig in after my Shadow checked those, too. A bit bland, but piping hot. It was just the same as it had always been. The carrots had a pleasant mush and the meat just slightly overdone.

Elián finished his bowl quickly and pushed it to the edge of our table. I emptied mine a minute or so after him and did the same. Now with full bellies, we had a whole stagnant evening ahead of us.

"Elián?" He turned to look at me with a questioning brow raised. His body was relaxed in his seat, and he had an arm propped on the table.

"If I brought someone back to our room, what is your protocol?" Halfway joking, I was truly curious as to what he was supposed to do. Turn his back and just stand there? Stuff cloth in his ears to block the noise? Or watch to make sure that in the throws of ecstasy I didn't get my throat slit?

I thought that the question would leave him glaring or snapping or turning away from me completely, but he just sighed. He closed his eyes and rubbed two fingers at the bridge of his nose, "I would have to stand in the room and feel sorry for the poor soul who let your wicked mouth on theirs."

I couldn't stop the grin from breaking out on my face. I shoved his leg under the table with my foot, "Hey, that was funny! See, I told you that we would have some fun."

"No, we will not." His tone had less rage in it, and I knew that he accepted my apology and had seen my reasoning. We would both grow too tired if we kept on as we had. Better to be cordial, maybe even work toward being friendly eventually.

My eyes scanned over our fellow patrons. Most were dirty, unattractive. The two males who had handled our horses were the best looking out of everyone that I had seen so far, but I doubted they would let their trousers down with Elián glaring at them, arms crossed, from the corner of the room. The glimpse I got of their strong hands was enough to intrigue me, though. If anything to just spark something to think about later.

"I'm going to go outside to smoke," I made to slide out of the booth.

Elián stood and let me pass by. He followed me out the door we had entered not too long ago. Though some eyed Elián with curiosity—it was those damn swords on his back—most paid us no mind at all. There was a variety of attire worn here. Some were dressed in common, casual clothing, some in light armor, and a few in leathers like us. The staff of the inn were easy to spot in their cream-colored aprons, and they flitted about the space, eyes focused.

I sauntered round the facade of the building to the back where the stables were. I eyed Bhrila and Noxe munching on hay amongst the other horses and leaned against a wall. Elián joined me and stood as my silent shadow.

One of the stablehands sat on a bench near us. He dug into an apple as he called to the other one who was somewhere deeper inside. His body seemed formidable enough, tall with strong arms from his work. His hair was the same color as my leathers, and though he smelled like a horse's ass, he wasn't unattractive.

It took him a surprisingly long time to look my way. It always amused me how unaware of their surroundings most people were, let alone humans. I had been staring at him for at least a minute and hadn't been trying to hide it. When he finally noticed, he gave a very male smirk. My lips pulled into a grin, showing my fangs. Heat passed over his gaze, and I touched my tongue to one of the sharp teeth.

The stablehand just then noticed the male standing beside me. His face fell. He dropped the apple to the ground, rose quickly, and retreated back into the stables. Pity.

I reached into my pocket and fished out the joint I had stashed there. Holding it in my lips, I retrieved a small matchbook from my other pocket. Once it was lit, I flicked the spent match onto the ground.

The faint crackling of the rolling paper further soothed me as I inhaled. The cherry at its end flared brightly for a second, and I pulled the joint from my lips. The smoke mingled with the night air, and I felt the calming fingers of the hash tickle my mind and loosen my headache.

I took another drag, and while I did, Elián almost made me jump. He was looking down at me smoking and suddenly asked, "Why do you do that?"

"Do what?"

He nodded toward the joint and looked back at me expectantly. My lips turned down, and just as I was about to snap at him for asking, I thought better of it. His question mostly sounded of pure curiosity, and I had decided to play nice. My chest tightened, though, as I thought of how to explain the need, the habit. I just shrugged.

"It's a disgusting habit," he muttered. So much for our temporary camaraderie.

I didn't feel like bickering, so I just smoked and people watched with him silent beside me. Once the joint was spent, I crushed it under my boot.

Though the night was still, as Elián and I stood arms crossed and leaning against the inn, a breeze shifted the air around me. The unusually warm air tickled my ear and shifted the hair around it. The breeze conjured the smell of hyacinths and hash, and my heavy heart clenched.

I glanced nervously to Elián to see if he had noticed. Mercifully, he wasn't looking at me, though. He was just staring forward into the night, eyes narrowed. He didn't even react as the breeze curled around him, too, rustling those hairs that he kept tucked behind his ears. They fell in front of his face, and he pushed them back absently with a brush of his fingers.

His head tilted to the side as he stared out into the woods. I turned mine to follow his gaze and let my eyes take in the expanse of trees. The breeze and the smells it conjured had distracted me, but just as quickly as it had appeared, it vanished.

Fear. I smelled the acrid tinge of fear out there. A few more seconds ticked by as we both stood still, trying to interpret what was causing such an overpowering stench. I pushed my back off the wall, readying my stance. It was no forest-dwelling animal that was emitting this scent. With the fear, there was a meaty earthiness that was distinctly human.

I felt a primal nudging in the back of my mind, urging me to move toward that fear. Not to help, but to potentially add to it. I ignored the urge easily, as I had been doing since I was a girl, but my body snapped further to attention. I took a deliberate sniff of the air, and just under the overwhelming fear, I smelled... others. My eyes closed as I sorted through the cacophony, and yes, the fear, I realized, was twined with humanness and some sort of spice.

My eyes snapped open, and I took a step forward, only to be pulled back. My head whipped around to see Elián's gloved hand on my shoulder, holding me from proceeding. Outrage filled me, and I tried to shrug him off. He didn't budge, and when I looked up to him, his face was in that Shadow mask of indifference. Barely moving at all, he shook his head.

Too soft for the few humans milling about out here to detect, a pained cry made its way to us, coming from the direction of that stench. Another instinct snapped at me underneath my skin like a whip. I acted.

I shoved Elián's hand off of me and moved quickly and as quietly as I could in the direction of that cry. Almost instantly, I was moving forward through the trees and brush, crouched and blades in hand. The light from the inn dimmed as I moved further and further into the forest. There was no evident path, and my movements were slowed as I worked to remain undetected through the growth.

This was a different kind of focus than that I felt in the rings, facing an opponent just before a good brawl. This was the stalk, the hunt. My heart rate was calm, my senses on high alert. And as the human fear almost overpowered everything else, the others who smelled of roses also neared.

Far enough that the inn was just a golden flicker in the darkness, a small clearing opened up before me. As I crept closer, I was able to parse out the nuances of the scents—two humans. The softness of the earthiness revealed them as human women, most likely. Part of the humans' fear was probably due to their limited visibility out here. But I could see through the overgrown thickets and brush two sets of males that held each of them.

They were pale and dressed in clothing that looked worse for wear. There were two closest to me, and they stood over one of the women. She cowered on the forest floor, trying to scramble backwards and away from her assailants. Her back made contact with a fallen tree that blocked her path, and I could see the tears falling down her face. Her skirt had been torn, and with a quick scan of the clearing, I saw some fabric discarded a few feet away.

The other woman was being held against another tree, two other males holding her upright as they fed from her. One at her neck, the other kneeling before her with his lips at the vein in her inner thigh. She whimpered, and though her words weren't coherent, it seemed that she called out to the other woman.

I didn't let the rage take over the calm I had settled into, but it still rang softly. The human on the ground kicked her leg out, no other options with her blocked path but to fight. The male closing in on her caught her ankle and threw his head back, shuddering with hunger. I saw one of the long distended fangs in his mouth.

This was the one I attacked first. The other two already draining the other woman would hopefully be too far in the throes of bloodlust to react as quickly as these. In a blink, I was crouched behind the Vyrkos male and plunged my blade into his back. My arm wrapped around his neck as I felt the blade pierce his skin, tissues, spine. That dark nudging pushed at the edges of my mind, but I shook my head, shoving it away.

The human on the ground screamed as she realized that something was happening, but she remained on the ground. Her body had taken her from fleeing to fighting, and now she froze.

So did the other Vyrkos that leaned over her. I pounced on him next, taking him from the front. The male on the ground was not dead, but the poison on my blades would make quick work spreading throughout his body with that stab to his heart.

The second male had no time to react as I slashed his torso through his clothing. His scream of outrage was quickly cut by my blade piercing his heart through his chest. These males were not used to those that could defend themselves, that was certain. His breastbone cracked in the most delicious of ways, and when I pulled my blade out, he dropped, clutching his chest.

The woman on the ground was frantically searching the dark, squinting her eyes and failing to see what was happening.

A cracking pain ran down my spine as my neck was snapped back at angle that almost knocked me unconscious. I felt fire as my hair was gripped and pulled, some strands ripping out all together. The force made me topple backward, and I dangled over the ground as a cold hand fisted my hair.

14

Quickly, I brought up my blades and sliced at the arm that held my hair. My assailant dropped me with a wrathful hiss, and I landed on my back. Before I could get to my feet, a heavy, flailing body was on top of me. Another male that hadn't been with the other four—how had I missed him? His red eyes seemed to glow, even in the blackness of the night, and his fangs were out.

Blades still in hand, I struggled to get purchase, to strike. He hissed and spat in rage and pain and bloodlust, and he was getting dangerously close to my throat with his thrashing. I managed to get a swipe at his side, but he kept coming. And with each lurch, the arm I held him away with inched closer and closer. His eyes widened, his mouth going slack, and he came at me again, putting all his weight on me.

I gave yet another push to get him off, and this time, he rolled away with ease. Before I could question what had happened, I jumped to my feet, ready for him to come at me again.

But he lay on the ground, unmoving. His head was face-down, a few feet away.

Sparing a glance around the clearing, the other woman was slumped against the tree. A moment to listen, to sense, and I could hear the faint panting of her breathing. Still alive.

Next to her, lay the body of the male that had been at her legs. His head was also gone, rolled away just at the perimeter of the clearing. Behind the tree, I saw where the other male had gone.

He held the Vyrkos with one arm clamped around his chest, and the other holding his head tilted to the side, baring his throat. Elián pressed his mouth to the neck of the male that had been doing the same to the woman just a few seconds ago. His black hair was untucked behind his ears, covering half of his face. My Shadow fed, eyes locked on me in an intense glare that burned in the darkness.

The woman on the ground had begun to crawl to her companion during the ordeal, almost having reached her now, even with her limited sight. Shaking out my hair that was no doubt a tangled mess, I moved slowly to her. She stiffened as my deliberately loud steps met her ears and started crying again.

I crouched beside her and placed a gentle hand on her shoulder, brushing her tangled blonde hair. She whirled around, going rabid and trying to scratch at me with no strategy or direction. I grabbed her wrists, and she bucked against my hold.

With the most soothing voice I could muster, I urged her to calm. After a few more weak attempts to throw me, I saw my words finally reach her. Perhaps it was the obvious femininity to my voice that won her trust, but she finally absorbed my urging for her to check her companion. From the smell of the unconscious woman, she had lost quite a bit of blood, was most likely in shock, but would most likely be okay.

With my steering her a bit in the right direction, the crawling woman made the rest of the way and began rubbing the other with familiar tenderness. I picked up the scrap of fabric that had been tossed on the ground and ripped it into two. Giving one wad to the first woman along with instructions of where to put pressure, I pressed the bundle in my hand to the other's neck. The cloth wasn't immediately drenched, which was a good sign.

The bleeding woman was silent at this point, but the one staunching the bleeding with me kept speaking soft words, trying to coax the woman out of whatever stupor she had fallen into. I brought my thumb to a fang and punctured the skin. My own blood beaded on my fingertip, and I removed the cloth at her neck. I rubbed my thumb over the bite mark at her throat and worked my own blood over the wound. Explaining what I was about to do, I did the same to the wound on her leg.

"She will be okay. Were you both staying at the inn?"

The woman shook her head, stating that they lived in a small home near here. They had been dragged into the forest by the males when they had opened the door to what they thought were weary travelers.

"Would you like for us to take you back to your home?" And at first, the human paused and nudged the other woman who did not stir. I smelled the panic radiate from her, so I said gently, "She is okay. Feel her pulse. She's just passed out for a bit. She will be feeling better after a night's sleep."

After a moment of checking her companion's skin and pulse herself, she looked in my direction. A bit off, looking too far to the left, but she nodded.

I raised my head to Elián who hadn't been doing a damn thing to help these women, just standing over the three of us with his after supper dessert.

"Are you going to help us, or not?" I shot at him.

He narrowed his eyes and dropped the drained male with a meaty thud. He didn't bother wiping the black blood that dripped down his chin, "I did help you." Elián waved a hand lazily over the bodies nearest us. The woman stiffened at Elián's deep voice above her, eyes darting around before settling back to soothing the woman on the ground. In my own struggle with the Vyrkos going for my throat, I hadn't noticed Elián taking care of the rest, hadn't realized it was him saving my life until it was well over and done with.

"Well, you can help a little bit more, and help me get these two to their home."

He sighed as if this was inconveniencing his nonexistent plans for the evening and crouched beside the three of us. Though still gruff, he evoked a sprinkle of tenderness in his voice that sounded so foreign to my ears, I felt my face contort in horror. "Are you able to walk? Or do you need to be carried?"

And the human who had tried to go for my throat not moments after the Vyrkos male had relaxed at the sound of Elián's voice. She looked in his direction, still not quite landing on him, and said shyly, "If you wouldn't mind—"

Elián scooped her up in his arms and stood, unencumbered. The woman yelped a bit into the quiet at the suddenness of his movements. Her arms wrapped around his neck, and he looked down at me expectantly. Carefully moving my own arms under the unconscious human, I brought her close and stood. The scent of her blood set my mouth to watering, but I just breathed through it, let it settle over me. Had I not found them, she would have been dead in a matter of minutes with those two feeding from her.

We trudged through the forest with the two humans in our arms. I described our surroundings out loud, and the conscious woman gave us directions based on what we saw. After what seemed like endless darkness, a soft light shown up ahead as the forest began to break. The women lived in the opposite direction of the inn, and a narrow path seemed to divert off of the main road to their little cottage.

A dog barked from inside the house at our approach. We stepped up to the front door, and Elián let the woman down. Not stepping back until she showed that she could stand on her own, Elián moved to stand by me.

The woman opened the door, and the small, black dog jumped at her happily. Throwing a look at us over her shoulder, she waved us inside.

Their home was essentially one large room with another two shooting off of it on the right side. The corner to our left contained two worn but comfortable-looking chairs, a low wooden table, and a basket of blankets. A larger table set with a burning candle and two chairs stood between the main area and the small kitchen with a wood-burning stove. Wildflowers and small jars and herb bundles and trinkets lined most of the available unnecessary surfaces in the home, giving it a sweetness that made my heart clench a bit.

"Can you lay her down in here?" The woman moved to one of the rooms and opened the door. I followed her and deposited the curly-headed woman in my arms on their bed. A candle still burned on one of the bedside tables, presumably from earlier this evening before the women had been taken. The bedroom was small and simple like the rest of the home. Wildflowers sat in here too, along the windowsill above the bed. The woman piled what appeared to be handmade blankets on top of her companion and perched beside her.

"Is there anything else we can help you with?" The woman stroked a soft curl on the other's brow, petting her with an affection that left me shifting uncomfortably on my feet. I kept my eyes on the dog that had jumped on the foot of the bed. He looked at me curiously, tail wagging.

She shook her head, a tired smile on her lips, "No. You've already saved us. Thank you." The woman looked up at me now and furrowed her brow. Her eyes glazed over for a moment, and another wave of discomfort moved through me. Two breaths and I watched her eyes focus on the present once again. She looked at me now with something akin to recognition. She dipped her chin in a deep nod, "Thank you again."

I gave her a much quicker nod and spun on my heel, brushing past Elián who had returned to standing behind me and breathing down my neck. We made our way out of the warm home back into the wilderness. The trip back to the clearing seemed much shorter now that we knew the way, and we walked in silence. I hadn't experienced the same bloodlust as the Vyrkos had while they fed, but I felt the come-down of a different kind as we went. The emotions that racked through me this morning and the journey on the road were catching up to me.

Wordlessly, we began to gather the bodies and heads into a pile. We cleared the area around it of debris, branches, and fallen trees until there was just a ring of barren dirt around the corpses. Somehow one of the heads had rolled further away under a bush, and Elián held it by the hair as he brought it over.

The sight of it, skin even paler in second death, made my stomach lurch with grief, but noticeably fainter than a month ago. Despite my complicated feelings toward the Vyrkos, the males here had preyed on innocent, kind women. Their deaths had been justified.

Once all the body parts had been gathered, I took a match from my pocket and struck it on the tiny matchbook. I let it fly from my hand, and watched it land at the peak of our little pile. The bodies went up instantly in blue and red flames as Elián and I bore witness.

"You couldn't have saved me any?" I asked flatly over the flames, though I'd probably gorged myself on Vyrkos blood through the years, enough for even an immortal's lifetime. The various memories of their warm, treacly taste made me turn even more somber, but my Shadow didn't seem to notice.

I heard the soft squeaking of leather—he shrugged. "I needed to feed more than you." I recalled his all but turning his nose up at the blood that was served with our supper last night.

"Vyrkos better than the spiced human blood?" Another shudder of leather, but this time, no words followed. The fire was dying down now, the bodies almost reduced totally to ash. I took a stick that sat at my feet and stirred the flames. One of the skulls collapsed on itself with a crack and hiss, sending a puff of smoke up like an exhale.

Once the fire was out, I used the stick to spread the ashes and make sure all parts of them were burned. Satisfied, I turned back the way I'd crept when I had been following the scent of fear with no knowledge of what I would find. Elián was as silent as his profession described, though I could feel the heat of his body behind me. I sighed, we would have to talk about that again.

The forest opened up back to the inn, and we walked out as if nothing had occurred and made our way toward the entrance. Some of the humans that still hung around outside, visibly drunk, snickered as we passed.

One of them called out, slurring, "Fuugh 'er good ere mate?" He tried to elbow his friend in jest, but he missed by a good foot and stumbled.

Faster than a blink, Elián had him by the throat, pressed up against the side of the inn. Elián still hadn't wiped the black blood from his face, and he looked like death itself. His face was a neutral mask as the man stuttered and blubbered for Elián to let him go. His friend just stood there, mouth agape like a fish at the male in black leathers that had his friend by the throat.

Elián's eyes slid to me while he faced the man who now had a dark patch of fabric spreading over his crotch. The foul smell of human urine assaulted my senses.

Elián quirked an eyebrow at me, and I was so disgusted by the man and his words that it took me a moment to realize that my Shadow was awaiting my command. Did protecting me extend past just the physical and to my perceived honor, too?

Arms crossed, I walked up to the man and breathed shallowly to avoid as much of the foul smell of him as I could. His terrified eyes swiveled to me, and though he was taller than me, he appeared weak and small at the mercy of Elián. I snapped my teeth at him, and he flinched, whimpering.

I let him cower for seven breaths, letting Elián's and my silence be punishment enough for his slimy remark. The two of us had emerged from the brush with a good shoulder-width between us that held nothing but weary neutrality. And he was just a small, drunk man trying to get a rise out of us and win approving remarks from his friend.

"Let him go," I said with a smirk, and Elián dropped his hand to his side. The man crumpled to the ground, clutching his throat with angry, embarrassed tears sliding down his face. We didn't spare him or his friend another glance and made our way back inside and up the stairs.

The faint smell of us mingled with the stale air of our room when we returned, and the cinnamon and oak that clung to Elián twined with my scent in a way that gave me pause. He closed the door behind us and did another quick search before I sat at the edge of my bed. I began to work at my hair, regretting having taken it down earlier this evening. My fingers removed a few leaves and twigs that had hitched a ride in the coils. I collected them in a small pile beside me and rebraided.

Elián eyed the movement with no expression at all until I moved to the other side of my head. He then unbuckled the sheaths at his back and settled his swords on his bed. His shoulders circled a few times, and then he plopped down next to the blades. The large frame of his body took up most of the mattress, his feet hanging off the end.

My Shadow lounged with his eyes closed while thoughts of the two women in that cottage in the middle of the forest floated through my mind. I hoped that no more travelers with nefarious motives knocked on their door. And that they would be ready should it happen again.

"I had them, you know," I called over my shoulder as I gathered the pile of debris into my hand. Though the tightness was now returned to my scalp with the fresh plaits running down and ending at the middle of my back, I felt calmer. Leaving my hair down had almost allowed that male I hadn't accounted for a swipe at my throat. Maybe worse, but I was confident that I could have rebounded from any strike he may have landed.

I pressed the latch of the window with my free hand and opened it just enough to toss out the leaves and twigs that I had removed during my braiding. A long, hot bath would be in order once we got to Rhaestras, but I had no desire to use the communal bathing room tonight. My Shadow, it seemed, also felt the same. He was settled and lying back, gloved hands resting under his head.

"Considering that you didn't notice the male that had stepped away until he had you, you did not." He said without opening his eyes.

Whipping around, I stared at him incredulously, "Had you been following me the whole time? You let him grab me?"

He shrugged up at the ceiling, "The fact that you didn't realize I had been following is furthering my point. And if you are as confident in your abilities as you state, him getting a hold of you should have been of no issue."

I scoffed and turned to riffle through one of my bags. I retrieved a book. After removing my boots and setting them at the foot of the bed, I sat cross-legged against the pillows. A not entirely-uncomfortable silence filled the space as I read for a while with Elián beside me. Though I couldn't hear his breaths, when I snuck irritated glances his way, his chest moved in a rhythm not relaxed enough for sleep.

An urge to break his relaxation asked for permission against my better senses, and I acted on it without thought. I hadn't really been paying attention to what I had been reading anyway. The two women and the Vyrkos male snapping at my throat and my brother were running through my thoughts on a loop. Perhaps Mathieu had been right to send someone with me, a part of me thought. But another, louder part argued back that I had come out of every altercation in my life alive and standing. Even when the odds were insurmountable.

Yes, I was right. I could have taken all of those half-frenzied males. Deep down, I knew that I wouldn't have ventured into the dark wood without feeling confident enough to face whatever I would have found.

I threw my book at Elián's head in the quickest snap of my arm that I could muster. The humans we had encountered today, who occupied most of the inn tonight, wouldn't have been able to track the movement at all. And our beds were so close, the hit should have been instantaneous. But his gloved hand snatched the book from the air before it could connect with his face. He held it there for a breath then opened his eyes. His face remained flat, save for that cursed brow that he raised when he looked over at me. I scowled and crossed my arms over my chest.

Instead of lobbing the book back or throwing it to the floor, Elián brought it in front of his face and read the cover. He began to flip through the pages.

Remembering what the book was about, I started to reach my hands out for it back.

Before I could get a word out, he turned his head to look at me again. His other brow had raised to join the other, but he didn't comment on what he read. In a huff, I reached over the gap between us and snatched the book from his hands. He let me and just settled back in that same lounging position he had been in before.

I felt traitorous blood rush to my cheeks. And this time, I settled onto my side, giving Elián my back. The rest of our night passed in silence as I read my book to prove some point, and Elián lounging as if he didn't have a care in the world.

15

The next afternoon, we reached the port without issue and boarded a small ship scheduled to stop at Rhaestras and then continue south. Some of the crew and passengers gave us curious looks, but no one bothered us during the entire three-day sail to our destination.

Elián descended into an even grouchier version of himself while we were on the ship. After a few attempts to rile him into speaking, I gave up and ran through all of the books I had brought with me for the entire journey. Most of our time was either spent in our cabin or on the deck amongst the waves and sea spray. I wasn't sure which my Shadow hated more.

In the small room my brother had booked for the voyage, Elián paced back and forth, despite my requests for him to fucking relax. He would just pause, glare, and resume the pacing. Remembering he seemed to enjoy the feeling of sun on his face, I requested that we walk on the deck. I stood at the railing of the ship, taking in the expanse of sea and sky. The nothingness and everythingness of it never grew dull, and my eyes traced over each and every wave and splash of the creatures that dwelled within or above it. Elián, though, gripped the railing so hard that I thought he might split the knuckles of his gloves.

On the second day, when we stood side by side looking out, I spoke without turning to him, "You know, as a child, I would get very seasick on these sails to Rhaestras. Mathieu used to take me up here, and it would ease. Seeing the reason for the rocking helps the mind."

Elián just grumbled in response, gripping the railing all the same. I tried to hide my smile and failed.

As soon as the ship docked, we disembarked on Rhaestras Island.

The crew quickly brought Bhrila and Noxe to us, who looked as relieved as Elián to be on steady ground. Only a handful of other passengers got off on the island, all of them on foot and heading in the direction of the main city with us.

With the ever-changing winds of the ocean constantly flowing over the sprawling island, the air held a pleasant saltiness, even as we traveled inland. The wildness of the sea seemed to follow you wherever you went, and as we rode toward the main city, I inhaled deeply. The soil was softer here, and Brihla and Noxe walked a bit more slowly with the terrain being different from what they were used to. Though the road to the main gates wasn't paved, it was the only one that led into the protected city and was worn with thousands of years of travelers.

The towering, pale wall soon came into view. Quartz was mixed with whatever stone they used to construct the barrier when the city was established, and the wall shimmered in golds and purples in the light of the late morning. Guards patrolled the perimeter, and their sleek, golden colored armor matched the wall they watched. A few armed with large bows walked above, eyes always scanning for an assault they would need to strike down. The few that patrolled on the ground were armed with swords and shields.

We approached one of these guards who stood behind a wooden podium, checking a log and travelers as they entered the main city. The Lylithan female held a pen in hand and wrote down the name and reason for visiting of all requesting entry into the city. Three other guards stood beside her and checked the bags of each one, admitted or not.

As we filed behind those already in line, I dismounted Bhrila and led her forward by her reins. Elián remained mounted on Noxe as we progressed.

"Name and reason for visiting?" The guard wore no helmet, and her pale pink hair stirred softly in the salty breeze. The deep tan of her skin resembled Elián's, actually.

"Meline of Versillia," the guard's head snapped up, "and we are here at the behest of High Priestess Isabella of Rhaestras." I tried to keep my voice low, but the way the guards stilled made some of our fellow travelers turn to us in confusion.

The guard that had been rather short with all those that preceded us in the line brought the first three fingers of her hands together, held them steepled at her brow, and nodded her head deeply, "We are honored to have you."

I returned the gesture, "We are honored to be here. I have with me Master Elián of The Shadows." When the guard straightened, she quickly wrote our names in the ledger and proceeded to check our bags with the rest of the guards that kept trying to sneak glances at me. My few days of anonymity were slipping through my fingers like the sand that seemed to be fucking everywhere on this island.

After the guards checked our packs and stepped back, the pink-haired one returned to the podium and stated, "We would be honored to have one of us escort you throughout the city, Your Highness."

I was already shaking my head before she finished, "That won't be necessary, um?"

She searched my face in confusion before realizing what I was asking. She gave the Salute of Rhaea again, "Justinia, First Guard of Rhaestras, Your Highness."

"Right, Justinia. Thank you for the offer, but I remember my way around. We will be on our way."

She gave a quick nod in acceptance and turned to her sisters in arms who resumed their positions to check those behind us. I mounted Bhrila and brought us through the stone door that welcomed us into my mother's homeland.

~

The city looked the same and also different. The roads were paved with the same mix of stone and quartz as the wall, giving the ground we walked on a glittering quality. As a girl, I had run these streets barefoot, slapping against the warm stones. Now, I traversed them as a grown female, weary with thoughts far away from skipping carefree through the streets.

A fairly small place, Rhaestras severely limited the amount of outsiders within the city walls at any given time, and those that were not from here stuck out considerably from those that called the island home. My leathers suddenly felt hot, too constricting, as I enviously looked down to the Rhaestrans that milled about in their airy clothing. They bared much of their skin to be kissed by the sun and salty air.

"Let's go drop our things and the horses off. And I need to bathe," I didn't look to see if Elián agreed, but he didn't voice any disagreement.

The city held businesses and homes in even squares like Nethras, but whereas the buildings of the city I now called home were quite tall and clustered together, the structures in Rhaestras were no more than two or three stories high and were often surrounded by courtyards for people to sun and lounge. The weather here was typically a consistently warm temperature with a few months of storminess being the only variation in the seasons.

I stopped us as we came upon the lodging house my family had always stayed at when we visited. Three staff members dressed in the gauzy fabric customary to Rhaestrans rushed out of the entrance to greet us. They were elven, evident by their slim stature and elongated limbs. I gave Bhrila's reins to the one with loose, dark blonde hair and dismounted. She grasped them and reached for Noxe's, "We are honored to have you stay with us, Your Highness. Your rooms have already been prepared, and Kiava here will show you to them. My name is Erat, and Verot here will take care of your bags as well."

Elián dismounted and let the male named Verot shoulder our packs. He looked ridiculous, lithe arms swallowed by all of our luggage, but he moved as if they weighed nothing. Kiava's dark brown skin was the same color as her short hair, but her eyes were the dark gray of storm clouds. She beckoned us to follow her, and though she was shorter and stouter than the other two, she was clearly the one in charge. "As Erat said, we are honored to have you with us, Your Highness and Master Elián of The Shadows."

We walked behind Kiava and Verot as they led us into the grand entrance of the lodging house. There were no windows or walls, just gauzy curtains and pillars that separated the establishment from the city surrounding. Four sets of cane lounge chairs and small tables sat at the right side of the space, facing a courtyard that was visible through the lilac curtains that had been tied back for the day. A small pool had been built into the stone floor, and I could see a cluster of colorful fish swimming lazily in the water. Deep blue tiles lined the pool and its perimeter, giving the illusion that it was a slice of the sea.

Kiava continued to explain the meal schedule for the lodging house and let us know that a staff member would be by our rooms to clean it each afternoon unless we declined.

We followed her and Verot up a grand polished staircase made up of that same stone mixture. It glinted under our feet as we ascended to the second floor.

The lodging house was fairly small, only ten rooms made up the entire establishment, and only three of which were on the second floor.

There was one corridor on this floor, and the stairs flowed directly into it. On either side, ornately railed landings looked onto the main floor and contained two more sets of seating.

Kiava led us to the end of the corridor, past lush, potted plants that were native to the island and paintings depicting the city, Rhaea, and the sea. She produced two keys from the pocket of her wide, flowing trousers, and used one to unlock our door. Once it was open, she handed both of us a key and pushed back the door.

Elián disappeared from my side into the room and flitted in a blur of movement throughout the space and behind each closed door. Kiava watched, brows raised, and I sighed. He quickly returned to stand beside me, arms behind his back, and nodded. Verot carefully let our bags down just inside beside the door and stepped back to Kiava.

"Ah, well, we hope these rooms are to your liking. As Master Elián has seen, your bedrooms are there to the left," she waved a hand toward two closed doors, "and they have an adjoining bathing room. Please don't hesitate to let us know if you need anything during your stay."

I thanked them both. We gave each other the Salute of Rhaea before they turned and left us, closing the door behind them.

A deep breath left me and my shoulders relaxed. The room was decorated in the purples, creams, and gold of Rhaea, as was pretty much everything in this city. An expensive looking cream sofa sat opposite two armchairs of the same color in the middle of the room, a light colored wooden table between them. A lavender settee sat before a large window to the right that was hidden behind sheer curtains. Plush rugs in mixtures of violet, green, blue, and gold were interspersed throughout the rooms to warm one's feet against the cool stone floor. Tall plants with blooming orange flowers relaxed beside the window.

"Do you mind if I bathe first?" Elián shook his head twice and wandered to the window. He pulled back a bit of the curtain and peered outside as I picked up my packs and headed toward the room furthest from the door. My room was almost bigger than our main sitting area, and decorated in the same way. The bed was plush and smelled clean, and I could have cried after enduring the lumpy mattress on the ship from the mainland.

The bathing room between mine and Elián's rooms was no less extravagant, and I audibly moaned at the sight of the large shower tiled in that same dark blue color as the pools downstairs. A bath the size of mine back in Versillia was nestled under a curtained window. Bright green, trailing plants sat on the windowsill and dipped toward the lip of the tub.

I stripped faster than I thought possible and stepped into the shower, promising myself that I would try the bath when we returned tonight. The golden knobs were cool to the touch, and I cranked the one for hot water as far as it would go. The water pressure was heavenly, and the temperature just the right amount of scalding. Though I brought my own soaps, tonics, and creams, a small shelf built into the shower held various jars and bars to be used. One of which smelled of jasmine, and I decided to use it instead of my own.

Though I scrubbed and washed and combed out my hair for an obscene amount of time, the temperature of the water never wavered. Rubbed raw to the point that my brown skin was flushed, I turned off the water and exited the stall.

I massaged their provided lotions, also smelling of jasmine, into my skin and combed my own mint-scented cream through my hair with my fingers. Though I didn't have any clothing in the gauzy Rhaestran fabric, I had packed a few pairs of trousers in airy cotton and some tops of the same fabric. I chose a light green pair of trousers and a matching top that exposed my midriff in the common Rhaestran style and left my hair loose to dry. With no sheaths built into the trousers, I buckled a belt with its own sheaths at my waist. My blades slid into the leather like butter.

I found Elián leaning against the wall just beside the window, eyes staring at nothing and everything at the same time. As I made my way through the room, they focused and gave my body a quick assessment before meeting mine.

"Have you been here before?" I walked over to the window and pulled back the curtains. While I wished for it to be open like the airy main space downstairs, I understood that it wouldn't be wise for our private rooms. Beyond our window, we could see the rear of the lodging house that held a lush garden and another, albeit larger, pool in the same style as the one inside. This one did not contain fish, however, and there were two other guests lounging on the cane furniture dotted around the pool. The sky was clear and blue like the water that surrounded the island.

"No."

I sat and reclined on the settee, stretching my now-clean body. If we hadn't had things to do, I might have taken a nap. "That surprises me. I expected you to be well-traveled given your profession."

"Well-traveled, yes. But you know that Rhaestras is selective about who gets let in its walls."

"Sure. We have only a short while before we're due at the Temple. You should go bathe."

He eyed me with little else than contempt, and peeled himself off of the wall. He called over his shoulder, "Don't let anyone in."

I turned in my seat and spat back, "Do you really think I am that helpless and idiotic?"

Elián didn't close his bedroom door, but as he crossed the threshold into his room that looked identical to mine, he shot over his shoulder, "I do. Don't let anyone in." I heard the bathing room door shut and the shower start.

Huffing, I turned back to the window. We had made it. The sun seemed to shine brighter here, on Rhaestras. The last time I had been here, I was celebrating my one-hundred and thirty-fifth birthday.

Before returning to Versillia for the formal celebrations of the kingdom and my family, I lounged nude on the white sand beaches just beyond the city before parading the streets in a drunken marathon that lasted days. The sun deepened my skin, and I took in as much blood and food and flesh that I could to ring in Rhaea's milestone. The streets had rung its bells to commemorate the exact time the High Priestess's daughter had been born one hundred and thirty-five years prior.

The same structures were here, but some of the business were changed. The people looked the same, but the faces were different. So much had been washed away in a century, but in the same token, the island would always be this way. It would always hold these memories and also wash them away out to sea. The knot of anxiety that twisted in my chest somehow pulled tighter. I tried to steady myself, breathing in my nose and out of my mouth. Again, slowly.

What would Isabella say when she saw me? How would she take the message I brought her? If she was going to agree, why had she refused to give an affirmation to the letters Mathieu sent? Why had she demanded to speak to me? There were too many questions, and I was out of practice at handling these bullshit maneuverings. My life back in Nethras was simpler. If a job was too much of a hassle to be worth it, I just didn't take it. If the odds weren't good in the rings, I just didn't fight. At worst, there was coin lost, and I would have to make it up elsewhere. There were always other jobs, always other fights.

But with this? There was no other option. Mathieu needed the guards of Rhaestras, the whole holy island, on board with this. We needed this, and I couldn't afford to fuck up.

"Are you ready to venture out toward the Temple, my queen?" My chest leapt as Elián startled me out of fucking nowhere.

I shot to my feet and straightened my top that had become slightly wrinkled during my reclining. Cursed fabric was light but it took creases too damn easily.

"Don't call me that," and now I was the one grumbling. Accepting that pulling the wrinkles out was futile, I straightened. "Uh," I looked at Elián, standing closer to me than I realized. Or perhaps he had stepped closer after he had startled me from my brooding. His hair was wet like mine, an inky black that was combed away from his face and curling slightly at the ends at the base of his neck. He didn't smell like the provided jasmine soap that I had used. He smelled like... eucalyptus? Was that what it was? Had the bastard brought his own soap? "Uh, you look clean."

He looked at me as if I truly was an idiot, "Yes, that was the point of bathing. Are you ready to go?" He had traded his leathers for another version of the Shadow uniform. He wore a pair of fingerless leather gloves, and his black tunic was buttoned to the neck and full-sleeved, his trousers the same color to match. The fabric was similar to mine—a light cotton that would breathe a lot more easily than was customary where we were from. Or, I realized, where I was from. I had no idea where The Shadows lived or if they all lived together at all.

"Aren't you going to get too warm in all of that black?" I asked instead of the many questions that were flowering in my mind. Hours and hours traveling with this person, and I knew nothing about him.

"No."

"Where are you from, anyway? I never asked you that." He didn't answer me and just walked to the door, opening it and stepping out into the corridor. Resigning to his caginess, I let him lead us out into the city.

~

The main city of Rhaestras during the middle of the day was the epitome of relaxed, island living. With the increased activity in the mornings and evenings, the middle of the days were often a lull time where people went inside to work, sleep, or pray away the hottest hours. The familiar, humid warmth of the streets left my muscles loose.

My hair rose with each passing moment, trying to decide between drying in the heat or remaining damp due to the moisture in the air. My top began to stick to my body, clinging to every shift I made, and as we made our way deeper, I pulled it off in frustration. The damn thing was wrinkled beyond presentability anyway.

The white undergarment that wrapped around my chest was already stuck to my skin with a layer of sweat that had started under the fabric. I turned to Elián, certain that he would be pouring sweat by now dressed the way he was. Other than his hair curling away from his head, slightly frizzier than normal, he seemed comfortable. No sweat shone on his skin at all. I wanted to kick him.

Unlike Nethras, Rhaestras wasn't organized into separate districts. Businesses and homes were mixed together, with a few certain clusters. The main market was at the center of the city, and as we walked through it, many sellers had closed their carts and gone inside to escape the heat of the early afternoon. Only a few people with nowhere to go in the down time or desperate for the money stayed open during these hours.

Elián and I walked through the middle of the market toward the prize of the city. The reason why it was so protected.

After leaving behind the market, the glinting road became more and more embellished. We came upon a large garden, larger than any in Versillia or Nethras. Or rather, an almost-untouched jungle sat within the walls of the stone city.

Though the streets were adorned with palms, the gardens that surrounded the Temple were wild. The sprawling grounds held every shade of emerald and chartreuse and were dotted by the crimson and ivory of the native flowers. The main road bottomed out here, and a much thinner pathway led into the gardens that blocked all view of what was within. The stone that paved the way in was encrusted with not only quartz, but gold veins and violet jewels.

More Rhaestran guards were posted here, and I knew there were more hidden from view within the gardens. They nodded at us as we approached, surely already been made aware of our arrival.

I bent at the waist and unbuckled my sandals. "You need to remove your shoes before we go any further." I didn't check to make sure he had heard me and continued forward.

The unevenness under my feet massaged my skin, and we were soon shaded by the canopy of the gardens. The animals that called this part of the city home moved all around us, unbothered by the beings walking through their territory.

I counted the twenty breaths, in and out, that it took for the Temple to finally appear. Veined with the same gold as the path we walked, The Temple of Rhaea stood as black as night.

Six towering pillars stood equidistant at the front of the Temple, reflecting not only the Mother and her Godyxes but the powers of Rhaea herself. The onyx of Rhaea's figurative home swallowed as well as reflected the sun's light. My body hummed in a way that made me stumble as we reached the steps leading to the entrance.

A warm, leather hand caught my elbow and steadied me through the vibrations, and I closed my eyes, breathed slowly. The aroma of jasmine here wasn't the perfumed mockery in toiletry jars—it was raw and otherworldly and all-consuming. My chest was heaving, trying to suck all of it in.

Many, many breaths passed before I was able to calm the thrumming. This place, it called to every fiber of myself, and my body answered. Loudly.

I looked to the hand that still held me, up the arm of my Shadow, to his face. His black brow was furrowed, but his eyes showed nothing but indifference. How could he manage all and no expression at the same time?

Wrenching my arm away from his fingers, I rolled my shoulders back, raised my chin. Sandals in one hand, I proceeded up the steps and into the cavern that was Rhaea's true home in this realm. At the top of the steps, back aways, held a door that led to the inside. Priestesses in lavender and gold garb milled about chatting, laughing, or walking silently to wherever they had to go. No guards stood at the golden doors leading to the inside of Rhaea's Temple. And why would there be?

Elián and I moved forward, paying the staring priestesses no mind as I pushed inside.

Cool air hit us and instantly dried all the sweat that had clung to my skin the minute we left the lodging house. While outside was warm and sticky and alive, in here, it was cool and consuming and quiet. There were no windows in this part of the Temple, but golden framed mirrors clustered in motifs of the sun, the moon, and the stars sat on the three other walls that bordered the inner shrine. Candles that burned forever in different configurations based on who lit them stood on a raised dais at the back of the room. Black stone benches lined the center aisle we walked down, and a few priestesses were hunched in prayer and worship.

The altar of Rhaea was a simple thing. An onyx statue stood over all of us in the likeness of the first Godyx, the oldest daughter of The Mother. She stood, barefoot and arms open as if receiving a gift. Her first three fingers on both hands were extended, the others curled in toward her palm. Though this rendition of her was hooded, her bountiful curls sprouted from underneath the shroud and framed her smooth face.

I kneeled, dropping my shoes beside me. I brought my hands to my brow, three fingers steepled. In my periphery, I saw Elián kneel as well, though he simply brought his fist to his chest, in the same way he did for me back in Versillia. I wondered which Godyx he belonged to, if any at all, but when I stood, he followed. At Rhaea's braceleted feet stood hundreds of black candles lit by priestesses and followers alike. Finding one that stood unlit, I palmed one of the candles that already held a flame and raised it to the statue before me. I touched the wick to the unlit one, and a golden spark popped before a yellow flame bloomed. I kneeled once again and sat back on my haunches, closing my eyes.

In the bracing, stagnant air of the Temple, I felt a warm breeze caress my brow, twine my shoulders. This time, it carried the scent of jasmine and chamomile tea and ocean waves. I hugged my arms to my chest as my head leaned into my left shoulder. A lifetime passed as I let this breeze warm me, fill me. Unlike the trembling I felt at the entrance of the Temple, this presence left me feeling safe, whole. Not until I felt my mind calm, my bones soothed, did the breeze thin and disappear.

The coolness of the altar room crept back in over my skin, but my body remained warm. I got to my feet and looked down at my candle, lit by a piece of the eternal flame that had burned here since the Temple's construction when Rhaea still walked this realm.

A deep voice spoke softly behind me, barely a whisper, "I have never seen a temple to Rhaea like this."

"Oh?"

"She is... quite different everywhere else." Like in Versillia. Like in Nethras and everywhere else she had followers. Though built for my mother, Mathieu had constructed a temple for Rhaea that was a copy of the ones that the Goddess had throughout the realm. Everywhere else but here.

I knew what Elián had been expecting—white stone like the rest of the city, bright purples and gold that sang of purity and healing. Benevolent, blushing priestesses that traipsed around in white robes and sang lilting hymns. Looking around this, the first and true Temple of the first Godyx, though, the black swallowed the light like the skin of the Mother. The priestesses dressed not unlike me.

A smirk broke out on my face as I turned to him. His eyes searched the altar in fascinated uncertainty. And if I hadn't grown up with a priestess of Rhaea for a mother, who was birthed in these Temple halls, I would have felt the same way.

"Well, what's life but an extension of true oblivion?" I jutted my chin toward the statue, "She is the Goddess of New Beginnings after all." His eyes narrowed as he searched the face of Rhaea. If he heard me, he didn't remark on what I had said, and for reasons that escaped me, I blurted, "They're the color of papayas today."

He turned to me, brow raised, "Are you sure you didn't slip and hit your head in the shower?"

A soft chuckle sounded from the entrance to the altar room, and my back stiffened, all tranquility I had achieved in the past few minutes erased.

Soft steps made their way toward us, and I clenched my eyes shut, screwing my face as hard as I could while my back was turned to the approaching source of that chuckle. Before she was on me, I smoothed it completely, to be as neutral and unfeeling as the statue and the Shadow beside me.

"Cera."

16

"Meline." I turned and found her looking exactly the same as the last time I had seen her. Her copper skin was flushed, signaling that she had been outside for some time before finding me. Her long, black hair was almost blue, and it hung in a thick braid that flowed over one of her shoulders. The color of her loose top and trousers was different from the other priestesses, signaling her station. She was dressed in black.

I counted ten breaths as we stared at each other. I pretended to be Elián, face an impenetrable mask while still letting her in on the contempt I felt. She, however, let her amusement and dislike for me show clearly in the smirk and dark light in her hazel eyes. She shifted her stare to Elián, and her mouth curled into a full, conspiratorial grin.

"Not going to introduce us, Meline?"

Flatly, I looked from my Shadow to her, "This is Master Elián. This is Cera."

She chuckled and slithered to Elián, "Apologies for how rude this one is. Seems she still has some maturing to do." He looked down at her, hands clasped behind his back. I could almost feel smoke come out of my nose as I watched him eye her, not with rage or annoyance, but with curiosity. He remained silent, and she smiled wider.

"Is she ready to see me?" I had to break their stare-down. She wasn't hiding her silent undressing of my Shadow or her blatant ignoring of me.

She craned her long neck back to me, and said sweetly, "Who?" My fingers twitched, and her eyes caught the movement. I saw her take in the daggers at my waist, and her smile somehow grew. "Oh, sweet, sweet, Meline. No."

"What?"

She traded the smile for a sneer and pivoted to fully face me, "Are you deaf? I said no."

I gritted through my teeth, "Then what are you doing here?"

"Meeting with you, of course." She sounded like a parent explaining something to a child for the tenth time that they still weren't understanding. I felt that thrumming in my veins again and took a deep breath to swallow it down. I knew that she was trying to provoke me, and I wasn't confident that I wouldn't take the bait if I let this continue. I scanned the room quickly as I tried to collect myself and saw that the other priestesses in the altar room were making no secret of their eavesdropping. Again, my anonymity was gone, and they eyed Cera and I with extreme interest.

"We're leaving," I didn't address the intention to Elián, but I saw him move in my periphery as I shot past Cera. We walked quickly back up the aisle, and I pushed the door open. The smack of humid air hit me, and I sucked it down. Isabella didn't want to see me and had sent that fucking bitch. In all the worst case scenarios that I had conjured during our journey, this hadn't been one of them. In all the images that I created of her rejecting Mathieu's and my offer, she had at least agreed to speak with me first.

Fine, if she didn't want to see me, I didn't want to see her. Elián strode beside me as I neared the steps leading down to the garden pathway. He didn't ask what was going on, thankfully, but when I spared a glance his way, he was looking at me, held tilted.

I skidded to a stop before colliding with Cera. She appeared instantly, blocking my path.

Pushing around her, I seethed, "Get out of my way."

She was in front of me again, face serious this time, "I said that she wasn't ready to see you, not that she didn't intend to."

I narrowed my eyes, "Then when will she be ready?"

She shrugged, "She hasn't told me. You know how she is. Or have you forgotten since you've been doing Goddess-knows-what all these years? She sent me in the meantime."

I crossed my arms, "You're her errand girl now, is that it?"

"Being the protégé of the High Priestess does have its responsibilities. For the time being, that is entertaining you." She said the word 'protégé' as if it meant nothing, and in that, I knew it was everything. In my other worst case scenarios of our Rhaestras trip, I hadn't foreseen Cera of all people being the right hand of Isabella.

"I don't need to be entertained. I need to talk to her." I tried my best to keep my voice level.

"Regardless, she sent me until she becomes available," she cocked her head and pouted, "or would you rather me report back that you treated our hospitality so disrespectfully?"

I knew the mask on my face had cracked completely at this point. I was also growing past the point of caring. "Then how are you going to *entertain* me?"

Her eyes flicked to Elián and back to me, "Oh, you know, a tour, talking about pleasant memories. Perhaps we could spar like we used to as blushing girls." I would rather have Elián break my arms again. And I almost told her so, but an image of Mathieu and Tana and Uncle waiting for me back in Versillia flashed through my mind. Isabella had asked for me specifically, most likely due to my connections to this place. Though we had the same father and mother, Mathieu wasn't tied to our mother's birthplace like I was. And despite the fact that I never became a priestess and made my lack of interest in such known from a young age, Rhaestras had been my second home for the first half of my life.

I scoffed and flicked a hand at her, "Okay, very well then, Cera. Do your errand girl duties and show us around."

My nonchalant attitude landed the blow I'd intended. Not a large one, judging from how quickly the flare of annoyance settled back to that taunting smirk, but I caught it. "Follow me," she softened her gaze, "both of you."

I wanted to gag.

~

Cera started with walking us around the perimeter of the Temple, explaining the native flora that made up the surrounding gardens.

They were their own ecosystems entirely, and they animals lived off the land just as the priestesses did. Not much tending needed to be done, she explained. The Temple had been constructed before the city itself, and had been placed in the middle of the jungle, where Rhaea supposedly took her first steps into the realm after reaching maturity. She lived here on this island, Cera explained, for her entire stay in our world. Even as she traveled, experiencing new lands, the island was always home. The Temple had been built by her first followers to represent her power, her graciousness. And I'd heard this speech a million times before. The heat and her rehearsed presentation were lulling me to sleep.

"I'm sorry, Meline, am I boring you?"

I blinked a few times, "Of course you are. You know that I know all of this."

Arms crossed, she walked us up the western steps of the Temple. Rolling her eyes, "Yes, but your guest does not know any of this." She turned to Elián, "You've never been to Rhaestras, have you?"

He looked at her with that shade of curiosity in his eye again, but answered simply, "No."

She shot to me, "See? You're being terribly rude."

I rolled my eyes.

We were blessed with the shade of the Temple roof again, and we moved toward a door built into the onyx facade. Before she could reach for the gold handle, a priestess with delicate features and dressed in a lilac set matching Cera's black one strolled up to us. She was even shorter than me, and her skin was a curious shade of periwinkle. Her hair was a shimmering auburn pulled into a knot at the crown of her skull.

The blue female gave Cera the salute of Rhaea, "I've prepared the space you requested. Is there anything else that I can do for you?"

Cera shook her head then gestured to me, "No, Jesyn, that was all. This is Meline and her Shadow, Master Elián, by the way."

Jesyn straightened at the sound of my name. Goddess, was that going to happen every time? I gave my most polite smile and bowed, giving her Rhaea's salute. Jesyn hastily returned it and scurried off.

Our host for the afternoon just shrugged and pulled on the golden handle. The stone moved smoothly over the floor as Cera pulled it open with ease. I knew, however, that the extremely heavy door only opened for her because it recognized her as a priestess of Rhaea.

Cera continued our tour, taking us through the more private halls of the Temple that included meeting offices, the dining hall, and pointing out the wing where the priestesses resided. The jasmine and mint scent of the Temple hit something in the back of my mind that made me settle. At one moment, I felt I could curl up on one of the benches that intermittently lined the halls and get the best sleep I'd had in decades. And at another, I felt more alive than I had ever been. The stone floor wasn't cold under my feet. Quite the contrary, it felt as if it were warming me to my very core, through my very soul.

Fuck, this was not good.

Through Cera's speeches, I tried and was failing to shield against what this place was doing to me. Trying to entice me, draw me in to put roots down again. I focused on the annoying swishing of Cera's braid. The way she would wait only until I had started paying attention to what she was saying to then look at Elián earnestly.

This farce of a tour was to annoy the shit out of me, I was sure. Isabella may have told Cera to show us what had been added since I was last here (improvements to the entertainment rooms, new artwork in nearly every corridor, an extension to the priestess wing), but she was giving the full tourist treatment. Perhaps she was just eager to have newcomers that were trusted enough to take this look behind Rhaea's lilac-colored curtains, but I had the feeling it was to rile me up. And to see if Elián was susceptible to her charms.

He strolled beside me, hands clasped behind his back as always. With his clothing and swords strapped to his body, he wasn't the most out of place person to have ever walked these halls. But the Temple of Rhaea saw very few males. Even Mathieu, who had been welcomed with open arms when we were children, had told me that he felt a bit out of place here. As we grew older, he stayed in Versillia with our father more and more. When our whole family was on the island, he and my father would enjoy the city and beaches, happily leaving my mother and I to the haven within the city's jungle.

Elián, tall and unamused as he was, drew many excited stares as we followed Cera. He didn't return any of the gawking—he acted as if he didn't even notice.

The priestesses here were free to come and go as they pleased, and I knew firsthand just how regular an occurrence it was for them to change out of their garb once the sun set and partake in the pleasures beyond the jungle gardens. But a male in their own halls? That would surely be talked about for at least a decade.

After what felt like an eternity, we were led back outside, this time at the rear of the labyrinthine Temple. Down the steps, the stone was replaced with a gravel walkway that weaved amongst the rear, floral gardens. It spread so far, you had to squint to see the edges of it, and each patch was filled with any and every plant that enjoyed the heat and humidity. Birds of paradise, orchids of every shape and color, morning glories, prickly pear, cacti of various kinds. One year when my mother and I escaped the Versillian winter for Rhaestras, she had tasked me with identifying and memorizing the name of each of the plants that grew on these grounds. I was fairly confident I could identify most of them, even now.

The gravel scraped and poked at the soles of my feet, massaging the skin and calluses. Cera led us to one of the lounging areas set amongst the flowers and gestured for us to sit under a large, white parasol veined with black. The cane furniture was also black, and I settled into one of the low lounge chairs, legs extended. Elián did not sit in the one next to me but moved to stand at my back.

Cera's lips trembled as she tried to suppress a laugh and sat in the seat across from me. The sound of gravel crunching became louder and louder as a set of priestesses made their way toward us. There were three of them, and they bowed to Cera and then to me. One held a tray that contained overflowing bowls of chopped pineapple and banana. Three glasses and a pitcher of water sweating next to the fruit, and my mouth began to water. The priestesses snuck glances at Elián and quickly looked away.

The one with the tray set it on the low table between Cera and I, but before I could reach for a glass and spear one of the small forks through a chunk of pineapple, Elián swooped in. He quickly plucked pineapple and banana with his long fingers and sniffed before popping them into his mouth. He swallowed, and I saw the profile of his jaw ticking as he worked out the taste of the fruit. He poured water into one of the glasses and took a sip. His eyes didn't meet mine as he handed the glass to me and pulled back to his post behind my chair.

"Well, you have your guard dog well trained, don't you?" Cera snickered as she slipped a round slice of banana into her mouth, not looking offended in the slightest at the implication that she may have been trying to poison me. The other priestesses gave us bemused stares, but remained silent.

I took a forceful gulp of my water which made Cera snicker again.

She extended her hand and crooked her first two fingers towards herself, beckoning toward the silent priestesses. The two who had come with the one carrying the tray stepped forward and split. One stopped beside Cera, and the other beside me.

They both extended their arms toward us, offering, and Cera grabbed her priestess's pale wrist with both of her slender hands. Her dark lashes lowered as she gave a quick, precise bite into the vein that ran just under the palm. She drank deeply, casually.

I reached for the dark wrist in front of my own face, but Elián pulled it over my shoulder and toward himself. He bit and took a pull from the priestess before releasing his hold. He stepped back, satisfied that the blood wasn't poisoned. The priestess looked at him with wide eyes but said nothing. I could smell the soft scent of her arousal clear as day, and I had to suppress a chuckle.

The spiced blood that had been served during my last night in Versillia was long out of my system, and I hadn't fed since then. The blood proffered to me now tasted of grapefruit and coconut as I drank.

It always felt a bit of an incestuous practice, Lylithan priestesses feeding from their own sisters. But each time I had partaken or witnessed this, the humans that offered themselves were nothing but willing and casual about the whole ordeal. The life essence I pulled from her fueled my own, and I felt my mental capacities reinforce, my body's power swell to its fullest potential.

After a few minutes, I pulled away as I detected that the priestess was reaching that edge where her energy began to deplete. It was a balance young Lylithans had to learn to walk. To take what you needed and make it a painless ritual, one that the being you fed from was able to walk away from afterwards. After centuries of practice, I easily let the wrist go, and before I could let it drop, I watched as the two small puncture wounds I'd made begin to close over. This human was a strong healer, then.

The priestesses that fed Cera and I stepped back in line with the third one, and they all stood demurely beside their superior. The heat of the day was starting to wane, and a gentle wind rustled the flowers around us and twirled the parasol overhead. Cera sat cross legged and picked through the fruit, sipped her water. I did the same as she asked me about our journey and about Versillia.

My answers were clipped, but held less of a bite to them. Even with my best efforts, I was relaxing into this place. Or at least, relaxing into the idea of being back here for a short period of time. The gardens, the Temple halls, the city, and the beaches held far more pleasant memories than negative ones, and my younger self relished in feeling the salt on my tongue and the sun on my skin. Nethras was a beautiful, bustling city, but the temperament of this island called to me on a baser level.

"What have you been occupying yourself with for all these decades, Mamba?"

"Don't call me that," I grumbled. The name didn't invoke the same dread as the title my imposed reputation brought. It did, however, make me feel like a petulant adolescent all over again.

She laughed into the air and tossed a slice of pineapple into her mouth. She chewed it noisily, swallowed. "The Cobra and Mamba walk the Temple halls together again!" She pointed to me, a spark in her eye, "Care to give them a show?"

My laugh was more of a bark, "You itching to fight, Cera?"

"Spar, yes. Isabella still hasn't sent word that she's ready to see you, and now is your turn to entertain me."

I waved a sarcastic hand toward my Shadow, "This one might object to you coming at me with your daggers."

As soon as it left my mouth, I wish that I hadn't said it. Cera pounced on my words, "You have started answering to males, I see."

I bit the inside of my cheek so hard that I tasted blood. I shot up from my seat, balling my fists, "Fine. You want a fight, you've got one." I whipped around to look at Elián, "You alright with that?"

He looked blankly at me, "Are you asking me or telling me?" I almost launched myself at him. This whole tour, his only reactions were breathing down my neck or saying 'no'. Now he had chosen to speak, and his words were just fanning Cera's flames? It was hard for me to not think he'd done it on purpose.

Cera stood, still chuckling, "Well, let's go then." She didn't bother feigning the energetic guide anymore. The six of us walked further into the gardens, to the training ring.

17

I was grateful for the outfit I had chosen earlier today. The sun was well on its descent as I rolled my ankles, my wrists. Somehow in the few minutes it took to walk to the rings, word had gotten out about my and Cera's impending match. Another thing about the Temple of Rhaea that used to annoy the fuck out of me—the ears everywhere.

The slightly raised platform of the garden training ring was the white and lavender stone of the city, and it almost glowed in the late afternoon light. I borrowed a ribbon from the priestess that had served us earlier and tied my hair at the base of my neck. Our audience had taken to standing a few feet aways, whispering about the impending spectacle. Elián stood between them and the ring, seemingly relaxed, but I knew that he would be ready should it look like Cera might actually hurt me.

My muscles hummed with anticipation as I unsheathed my blades. The hilts were warm, and the metal shined, reflecting the light around us. I twirled them in my hands, readying.

Across from me, Cera removed her cropped top, and her black undergarment almost reached her navel. She unsheathed the blades she had hanging at her waist. They were impressive daggers that ended in slightly curved points.

On opposite ends of the ring, I faced my very first opponent once again.

Cera had been dropped at the Temple of Rhaea as a babe in the wee hours of the morning. Presumably a child of a parent that couldn't take care of her and thought that she would have a better chance at the Temple. This happened sometimes, though orphans were not as common on the little island as they were in bigger cities like Nethras or Krisla. Most of the time, the babes were cared for by the priestesses and adopted by Rhaestran families at some point down the line. However, some like Cera, decided to commit themselves, their lives, to Rhaea.

I remembered meeting the young, snide girl that was the same age as me. At the time, we weren't acolytes or priestesses amongst a sea of them that lived at the Temple. I was a quiet thing, all but clutching the fabric of my mother's trousers as she moved through the Temple in the only way one can in the safety of their true home.

As High Priestess, she was revered. As a high priestess who had mated an outsider and sometimes resided with him in a foreign land made her a curiosity.

There weren't many children living in the Temple at the time, and when Cera had found me, curled up with a book in these very floral gardens, I had thought I'd found a friend. And for those hours, she excitedly talked with me about what I was reading and the land I came from where it sometimes snowed. I asked her about what it was like at the Temple, and she told me about her ambitions of being a priestess herself one day.

And then my mother had found me. That day, she'd worn her braids loose and adorned with those gold beads. She and Isabella's sleeveless dresses were similar, but where Maman's was the deep green of Versillia, Isabella's was black, as always. She and Isabella had been taking a stroll, chatting merrily. When they came upon us, Cera had shot up and kneeled, saluted. And I hadn't. At first, she eyed me with fear, irritation. Those that didn't give respect to the highest ranking priestesses of Rhaea would surely be reprimanded. And Cera, still considered an outsider of sorts, was terrified of such reprimand.

But at six years old, I didn't know this about her, didn't understand that she had, in our long conversation, seen me as an ally in this place. I remembered having fun with her, glad to interact with someone that was so nice and unreserved around me, and jumped up to introduce my mother to my new friend.

I didn't kneel to either of the females, but gave a quick salute to Isabella before hugging my mother's thigh. She mussed the springing curls on my head and listened to me tell her of all the plants I had learned about that day. Then, I turned to Cera, who still knelt on the ground. As I introduced my new friend, I felt my stomach drop. At the time, I didn't have the words for what I saw on her face. Something I now recognized as betrayal shown in her almond-shaped eyes.

After that, she was not my friend. When no one was looking, she would shove me in the corridors. And after I realized that she wasn't playing, I learned to shove back. One day, we had been caught in one of these encounters. But years of her teasing and our quips back and forth, combined with the intensity of adolescent emotions and the burning of our gums as our fangs were coming in, we descended into an all-out brawl. We scratched and cursed and slapped at each other in front of everyone. In the middle of the dining hall. I couldn't recall what she had said to make me lunge for her. Or if I had started it, which at that point, was quite possible.

Maman had been called and broke up the fight between us herself. Still clutching a clump of Cera's hair in my fist, I fumed silently as my mother chastised us. Cera barely kept a lid on her face, trying to stay a mask of reverent respect while the High Priestess lectured her for fighting in the middle of supper. I had never told my mother about my and Cera's terrible relationship, but she wasn't stupid. She stated that she was disappointed that we had let it get this far. I saw Cera's shoulder's slump.

"If you are going to act like little serpents, taking strikes at each other at every turn, perhaps it's best to give you an outlet for the venom you're so eager to spit." I had stared up at her, not trying to hide my confusion. Her deep, brown eyes flecked with gold held a mischievousness that made my stomach curl. It was the same look she had when she gave me that summer project in the gardens, a punishment for stealing a pretty pen from Isabella's office.

My mother took the both of us out to the floral gardens, commanding for no one to follow us, and I could feel Cera seething next to me. At thirteen, I knew logically that she had so much more to lose if she fell into disfavor with my mother. She had just been accepted into the priestesshood at that point, and I knew that she still felt her position was precarious. And at most, I would get parental punishment still laced with maternal warmth. Which was why I couldn't understand why she kept messing with me.

We came upon the training rings that night, the waxing crescent moon rising in the sky amongst the sprinkling of starlight.

Cera and I followed my mother up onto the glowing platform, and she unsheathed the two daggers at her waist. She was always armed, as were all priestesses who had completed their trials. Maman extended both hands and offered the blades to us, hilt first. She didn't explain, but her command was evident enough. I grasped the leather-wrapped handle and felt its heaviness.

This doesn't feel like a punishment, I had thought to myself. I'd observed the sparring on this ring and the one inside the Temple. Ever since I had watched for the first time two priestesses advance on each other with long wooden staffs, I had begged my mother to teach me. One night, I stood entranced while she and Isabella on this very ring went at each other with swords black as night. I had held the image of these two females clashing under the moonlight in my mind since.

My excitement was mirrored in the glimmer in Cera's hazel eyes. She had been wishing to be taught, too.

Maman stepped back to the edge of the ring and called into the night, "Fight, little serpents."

Cera and I circled each other. We made no contact for a long while as we took stock, assessed. We knew each other as girls, then as young adults. But the years had settled us, built us into newer versions of ourselves. I remembered that she slightly favored her left side, and I was sure she remembered that I slightly favored my right. But it had been more than a century since we last stood on this platform.

With each revolution around the ring, we inched closer to each other. We kept our bodies fluid, loose, taunting. She was the one to strike first, and I twisted around her easily. As I landed, I struck her. Yes, we still favored those sides, just the slightest bit.

Suddenly, she came at me in a clash of steel. I countered her swipes with my own, and that beautiful sound of daggers hitting daggers rang out. She was relentless, showing off her centuries of training.

And I met her. I laughed as she came closer, trying to tire me, but each strike and counter I gave only made me hunger for more. We weren't gaining any ground on each other, and I saw a vein tense at her temple. If I had to guess, there were few priestesses that met Cera as I was able to.

"Come now, Death Wielder! Let's see what you can do!" She spat as she struck with her left then right then left again. I blocked, evaded, then felt the sting of her blade on my skin. A knick, but her nostril flared as she smelled blood. Her grin was wild, triumphant, and she came at me harder.

Cera crouched and swiped a leg to catch my ankle, and I jumped. Before I could land, she was up and striking again.

I breathed deeply as I let her come at me in a flurry. "Don't tell me that you haven't mastered *any* of those supposed powers, Mamba! What a waste!" She laughed as we parried.

Her hooked blade caught mine, and suddenly, it was flying out of my hand. She paused for just a moment as she realized she'd halfway disarmed me. I didn't have time to think, and I landed a kick to her front, just as I had done Elián all those weeks ago. I grinned as I heard the breath knock out of her.

My old rival and I carried on, circling and goading. Even down to one blade, I was more calculating, more daring with my strikes. But Cera's defensive work was impressive.

We were irritatingly evenly matched, at one point me knocking her blade from her hand with a triumphant bark. She grit her teeth, reduced to one blade like I was, but as she came at me, preparing her dagger for a strike to my side, I flung my own to the ground to free both hands.

Before she could properly react to what I was doing, I grabbed straight for her armed wrist and pulled her to me. The Rhaean priestess way of fighting was affective, deadly, but there was a primness to it. Most priestesses never fought an actual opponent, where one would bring out anything, everything to win.

I twisted Cera's wrist enough for her to cry out in pain and drop her dagger. At the same time, I pulled her front close into my back as I pivoted around and then flipped her over my shoulder. Her body fell onto the stone ring in a delicious crack, but she was quickly making to rise again.

That wouldn't do.

I dove to the ground with her, drawing her head into my curling bicep and curling my legs around her waist. She flailed in my hold, but her bellowing just made me laugh harder. This way of fighting was all due to what I'd picked up in the seedy, lively tavern rings.

But Cera wasn't giving up, still scratching and writhing to figure out an escape from my hold, so for good measure, I reverted to the priestess way. I drew up all my speed as I quickly released her. But before she could recover, stand, I swiped her curved dagger from the floor beside us and flipped to straddle her hips and force her back down.

A drop of blood beaded on Cera's sun-kissed skin as I held the blade to her throat. Both our chests heaved, adrenaline pumping, and we both bared our fangs to each other. She sneered, and I grinned. She might have been the High Priestess's protégé, but she could still be knocked down.

I held her there, let our audience see that an outsider had defeated her due to her own arrogance. She was a good fighter, but Cera had never had her livelihood depend on the end of a blade. She had never had her *life* depend on the end of a blade. And for that, she had underestimated me. Perhaps not adolescent Meline, daughter of the High Priestess. But the person I was now had learned many lessons that Cera hadn't.

I kissed the air at her and stood, letting her blade clatter to the stone floor while I bent to pick up my own. Not sparing her a glance, I called over my shoulder, "Always fun with you, Cobra. We will be going now. Tell Isabella that I expect to see her tomorrow." The sun was setting, and if Isabella hadn't sent for me now, I knew that she wouldn't today.

Elián extended a handful of green fabric toward me as I stalked down to the gravel pathway. I shrugged into my wrinkled top and led us around the Temple. The high of a match won carried me through the jungle gardens. As girls, Cera and I were evenly matched. She won as many sparring matches as I did. Even when she became a priestess, we were often partnered together. We became some of the best, but it also kept us from throwing fists outside of the rings.

The jungle gardens opened back up to the City of Rhaestras, now bustling with nightlife. The sky was darkening in a mix of orange and fuchsia as we pulled our shoes back on.

"Death Wielder?" Elián's voice was quieter than a whisper, but there was no denying that I had heard him. His eyes held mine for a moment until I broke the contact.

We both straightened and headed back the way we had come earlier today. The smell of fried food carried me toward the market that would be crowded at this hour, and I could feel Elián press closer to me as we were surrounded by more and more people.

The carts and shops that had been closed had now pulled back their shutters and opened up their doors once again. I wasn't ready to go back to our room yet, where my thoughts and Elián's silence would be their own sort of weapons. The chatter of the crowd, the gleeful screaming of children, filled the forefront and background of my mind.

We came upon a large cart with bookshelves built in on all sides. The seller was busy discussing a new release with another customer, but that was just as well. I started leafing through some of the novels in the fiction section.

It wasn't Lee's bookstore back in Nethras, but there were some titles I hadn't heard of on the cart. I remembered how Lee would lean over the front counter at the shop while we'd go back and forth about which of our favorite authors created better plots. Whether he would finally take one of my recommendations even though I always took his. I smiled through the tightness in my chest and nestled a book I thought he might have enjoyed in my arm.

I picked out four more novels, all romance, and paid the delightful older human man who owned the cart.

"A big romance reader, are you?"

I clutched the small paper bag of my purchases to my chest and smiled at the man, "Oh, yes. I venture out sometimes, but I always return to these. You have some that I haven't heard of before, so I am excited."

His light brown eyes were warm, the skin around them weathered and wrinkled in the way of a comfortable leather chair, "I know what you mean. My husband has gotten me to read a few of the ones you selected, and they are quite entertaining. I'm proud to say I'm a converted romance reader." Another customer waved him over to haggle about a box set, and I made my way into the crowd.

The sun fully set, and the moon rose as we walked past each cart and booth in the market. Some were merchants selling clothing, an entire row was dedicated to fresh fruits and vegetables, and another row for meats and seafood. Weaving throughout the main attractions, smaller setups sold perfumes, foreign fabrics and trinkets, and dotted amongst the shops were entertainers of all sorts. A trio with a lute, drums, and a singer played the trademark Rhaestran music that held a light soulfulness I hadn't heard replicated anywhere else.

I hummed along to the classic song they were playing, one about a jilted lover who resigned themselves to finding love again, while I stood in line for a food cart that smelled particularly delicious.

The stout female taking orders took my request for two fish sandwiches with fried potatoes and spiced mango. The food came out hot and greasy and perfect, and I wished Mathieu was here with us. I balanced the food in my arms and led Elián out of the market.

The sound of it never quite left us as we went toward the edge of the city. The whooping of a crowd surrounding a magic act hit my ears at the same time of the soft crashing of waves.

Just near the eastern edge of this part of the city, a lagoon was nestled beyond a stone ledge. The coral and rock formations that separated it from the ocean were too treacherous for ships to maneuver, the beach too rough and rocky for people to really enjoy. Because of this, the area remained fairly untouched, and turtles, crabs, and other creatures walked freely and openly on the sand.

A paved walkway ran around the drop-off to the lagoon, just separated by a chest-high ledge to deter people from jumping down to disturb the wildlife. I settled us at a spot away from the others who had come out to enjoy the view. Guards posted intermittently along the walkway stood silently, watching the waves for intruders and the ledge for people looking to jump.

A few sometimes did, but they were mostly children looking for a thrill or people that were inebriated and wanting to touch a turtle or something. I spread our food on the ledge and couldn't hide the smile creeping across my lips as I remembered the teasing grin Mathieu and I gave each other when our feet hit the jagged beach just before I felt the firm arm of a guard hauling me up to take me back to the city.

The real beauty of the lagoon, besides the untouchedness of it all, was the bright blue glowing waves. While I always loved reading tales, from as early as I could remember, my brother was always searching for knowledge, whether that be science or history.

I'd read of magical princesses, and Mat had researched and learned about the history of our people, of the realm. One particularly lively conversation centered upon us arguing whether the villain in the book I was reading at the time was more cunning than the infamous King of Lylithans whose crimes actually drove the first Lylithan Council to rise some two-hundred years prior. We'd eventually brought our parents into the debate, and they both jokingly agreed, much to Mathieu's dismay, that the corrupt King was no match for the villain in my tale.

One summer, Mathieu had found during his endless studying the scientific reasoning that made the waves glow and tried to explain it to me, but I had decided to still think of it as more the magic of Rhaestras. At night, when the sky and sea both darkened to the same shade, it looked as if the stars themselves were lapping up on the sand.

I unwrapped the parchment paper that held my sandwich and took a bite. Dribbles of creamy, tangy sauce ran down the corner of my mouth, and I wiped it away with the back of my hand. I grabbed some potatoes from the folded paper cone and stuffed them into my mouth. They were hot and spicy and almost burned my mouth in the best way.

"What is that?" Elián was holding his own sandwich and pointed to the banana leaf held closed with twine.

"Mm!" I used one hand to untie the knot, and the leaf unfurled to reveal a pile of sticky red and orange. "It's mango with spices sprinkled on top."

Elián eyed the fruit for a moment before plucking a slice and eating it whole. He looked out onto the bright waves, nodding to himself.

We ate to the sound of the water and the music of the street performers. The grease and sugar sat heavy in my belly, and I cursed myself for not grabbing beers before we had walked out here.

"Death Wielder?" Elián asked again. I clenched my jaw. Cera had to take that shot, didn't she? And he had to pick up on it. Apparently, he wasn't going to let it go.

I waved the question off, "Cera's a jealous bitch who was just frustrated to face someone that's better than her."

He crunched on a piece of potato. "What she said upset you."

"I wasn't upset."

He gave me a knowing glance, "You were upset enough to lose concentration when she said it. It seems like she knew you would react to those words. Mamba."

I groaned and leaned on the ledge. "Don't call me that." He shrugged and continued to eat while looking onto the lagoon. The enjoyment I had been experiencing from the market and our food was slowly dissipating. Elián's questioning and teasing flung the events of today back into my mind, and I wasn't ready.

Our day at the Temple was a total wash, other than my Shadow now having more ammunition to shoot me with and my own bitter nostalgia muddying my emotions. I groused into my hands, "Cera is almost as irritating as you. I wouldn't take anything she says seriously."

Elián balled up the spent parchment of both our sandwiches and set them aside. Through the movement, I heard that quick, amused exhale he liked to give.

"And what the fuck is so funny?"

"You. Her."

"Well, if she's so funny, why don't you go back to the goddess-damned Temple and seek her out. I saw you ogling her. She noticed it too and was fucking eating it up."

He pursed his lips, "Ogling?"

"Yes, ogling. I know what you look like when you're angry since that's how you look at me most of the time. You didn't look at her like that. So, ogling."

He furrowed his brow and turned to lean his back against the ledge. His arms crossed at his chest, "She acts like you."

My whole body froze, "*What*?"

"She acts like you," he said slightly louder.

"I fucking heard you. I don't understand *why* you said that."

He shrugged his large shoulders, "Before she mentioned that you were raised together, I could already tell. You and Cera are very alike."

I gave a sarcastic, resounding cackle and pushed off of the stone ledge. "Fuck you, Elián."

18

18

The next morning, I woke to the sound of thunder. After the market, Elián and I had walked back to the lodging house in silence, and I quickly retreated to my room. I wasn't sure if he slept, if he slept ever, really. Even a bath in the extravagant tub last night couldn't rid my mind of the exhaustion and anxieties that I was feeling. I'd laid awake for what felt like many hours, replaying what Cera had spat at me. What Elián had asked me.

I would be seeing Isabella today, come hell or high water. And if Cera tried to stop me, she would get a poisoned blade to her side.

Would Isabella have the same question as Cera? Would Isabella be disappointed in my failure? Maybe she had given up expecting this of me long ago. Elián didn't ask much about me besides passing judgment on my life choices, so his inquiring twice about what Cera had said did not bode well. By the purse of his lips at my non-answer, I knew that he wouldn't be letting this one go.

I dressed in another breezy outfit, this time with a sleeveless top that matched the rust color of my trousers. I braided my hair back in two plaits and walked out to the front room, mind still abuzz.

Elián sat on the settee by the window, facing the door. He was reading from a thin magazine that he held in his lap, his bare feet propped up on the cushions in the most relaxed position I had ever seen him. Perhaps some good food and the ease of the island were having an effect on him, too. At least one of us wasn't coming out of their skin with nerves.

He didn't take his eyes away from the page as I neared. The

curtains had been pulled back at some point, presumably by him this morning, and wild rain pattered against the glass. I lowered onto the floor in front of his feet and sat cross-legged.

The palm trees outside swayed with the wind, and the clouds churned. The rainy season would begin soon, if this storm was any indication. But my guess was that the rain would clear within the next hour or so, and the clouds would be broken by the sunshine once again.

I propped an arm on the settee cushion by Elián's leg, but he didn't move. His body radiated so much heat, I felt my own skin flushing. A flick of my wrist, and I could have laid my hand on his knee. Part of me wanted to, just to see what he would do. But there was an invisible barrier around him. Not a real one, but something about him made my body resist getting any closer.

"What is that?" The way he held the magazine prevented me from seeing the content of the pages, but the cover read, *Joran, Knight of Honor.*

His eyes flicked up to meet mine and back down to his page, "It's rude to interrupt people when they're reading."

I coughed, mouth agape. His eyes kept scanning, and then he turned the page. I pressed up to my knees and scooted closer to his lap. He didn't flinch as I pressed my hands into the edge of the settee and leaned over.

I peered down on the magazine—no, book—that Elián was reading. It was one of those picture books that were all illustrations and captions. There was a small section of these at the bookstore in Nethras, but I hadn't seen many people read them besides children. I had once watched Marco run around the yard with one of such books clutched in his hand. Judging from the violence and blood on the current page, this one wasn't much suited for little ones. The blocks of pictures showed a battle and many casualties as characters fought with swords on horseback.

"Did you bring this picture book with you?" I asked as I read along with him.

We reached the end of the page at the same time, and he turned it to the next, "No, I bought it yesterday." When had he done that? I must have been so engrossed with my own browsing that I hadn't seen him doing the same. "And I wouldn't call it a picture book."

"What else would you call it?"

He shrugged but didn't answer. Now the main character was escaping on his horse into the woods. He clutched his side from an injury he had sustained in the battle, and the illustration emphasized the weakened state he was in. The shading around that particular block was dark around the edges, implying that his consciousness was waning.

"Did you enjoy the market?" I whispered mindlessly as he turned to the next page. I could see why Marco and Elián were entertained by these little magazines. The illustrator for this particular story was quite good. I didn't much like stories of war, but I found myself wanting to keep reading.

"Yes and no. I liked that beach better."

The corners of my lips turned up, and the hero on the page, Joran, was able to make camp in the woods and begin to bind his injuries. He joked along to his horse that gave knowing 'hmphs' along with him. "I agree. I honestly never thought I'd see those glowing waves again. If coming back to this miserable island was worth anything, it was eating that food while watching that water."

Elián turned the page again, and on this one, Joran and his steed heard the snap of a twig just as they had been about to sleep. The little man on the page rose to a crouch and grasped for his sword. He cursed when he couldn't find it in the dark. "You don't seem miserable here."

Elián's words didn't sink in as my eyes took in the drawing of Joran finally finding his sword and whirling around to face a darkness that had rippling edges. Elián turned the page, and my brow furrowed in frustration to find it nearly blank. The words 'To be continued...' were written above the floating image of Joran's eyes looking scared and confused.

Elián snapped the book shut with a compression of his hand and set it flat on his legs. How could readers of these tiny books contain themselves when reaching a page like that? "Did you buy the next one?"

"Yes."

I realized that I was just staring at the cover of the book as it sat in his lap. Clearing my throat, I reclined back on my elbow, pressing the sharp corner of it into the cushion. Dangerously close to his thigh. I flicked a plait behind my shoulder, "Well what are you waiting for? I want to see what happens."

He tilted his head to the side, just slightly, and I suddenly felt exposed. So naked, that I glanced worriedly at my body to make sure that I hadn't somehow forgotten to get dressed before leaving my room this morning.

"What will you have us do today?" The only part of his body that moved was his lips. He was a disconcerting figure to face like this. He didn't seem to be breathing, just assessing me with that stare, and I couldn't quite put my finger on what color his eyes reminded me of today.

I picked up the thin book from his lap, careful not to touch him, and settled back on my haunches. My fingers flipped through the pages, eyes scanning but not focusing on any of the images. "Go back to the Temple. Meet with Isabella. Hopefully get her approval."

"And if she doesn't want to see you today?"

My head snapped up. His voice was neutral, flat, but he had given my fear the words to grow and form into reality. Now the possibility of such wasn't just an anxious thought, but one my Shadow had obviously felt was a real outcome to consider. What would I do if she refused to see me? Defying or angering Cera was as natural as breathing. It called to my younger self in a splendid way. But to do the same to Isabella? My younger self did not recoil from the thought of disobeying the last High Priestess any more than a daughter does her mother. But to do that to the *current* High Priestess? I swallowed the knot in my throat.

"She will."

Elián straightened his head and shifted in his seat. I saw a flash of script on his left palm, bare without his usual leather gloves, before his fingers curled over it. He stretched his arms toward the ceiling and brought them behind his head. "What does the tattoo on your hand mean?"

"What tattoo?" He closed his eyes and leaned into the arm of the settee. His shoulders arced over the edge, stretching his back.

I huffed and stood. A few moments of tense peace, and he couldn't help but be an asshole again. My bare feet stepped over the thick purple and green rug, stopping at the large window. Just as I had suspected, the storm was letting up. I could see bright blue trying to peek through the clouds as they gave off the last of the raindrops they had to give. We would be able to walk to the Temple without getting soaked in the next few minutes.

I took a deep breath, steeled my spine. Yes, Isabella would see me today.

~

Isabella would not see me today. The walk to the Temple from the lodging house had been wholly unpleasant. The storm had every surface wet, and the blazing sun that had finally broken from the clouds caused the air to mix with heat and steam. We had gotten a later start to the morning because of the rain, and the temperature of the mid-morning made us pay for it. Sweat prickled my brow, my back, and the humidity wouldn't let it evaporate. It just reinforced it.

Even Elián, who seemed unbothered by the heat yesterday, was frowning a little deeper as we made the trek. He still insisted on wearing his heavy weapons and full-length, black ensemble.

The coolness of the front entrance of the Temple was an ominous reprieve, but one I accepted for the oasis that it was. As we had done yesterday, I walked into the altar room, knelt for the Goddess, and lit a candle for Maman. After standing back a moment, I leaned in to light another three. The first available one was beside Maman's, and I dedicated it to Papa. Further down the dais, I found two more and dedicated them to Shoko and Lee. No breeze came today, but the ritual made me feel a bit calmer all the same.

Elián and I sat in the pews for a while and waited. The gardens were outside in that unpleasantness, and the rest of the Temple was unavailable to us without a priestess to give us access. We did not talk to each other, but I was growing restless. I shifted in my seat, counted all the candles once, twice, thirty times. People entered and left, and I traced my gaze over the mirrors and tapestries that hung on the walls.

Rhaea stood watching over it all, hands raised. Someone had tossed gold coins at Her bare feet at some point between yesterday and today. *Which was fucking stupid*, I thought. Rhaea cared nothing for money or riches. Though, I was sure the priestesses would pocket it for Temple use.

The groan of the door and shift in the air signaled someone entering the room, and quick footsteps made their way down the aisle. The periwinkle priestess, Jesyn, stopped before me and gave a deep bow, bringing her steepled hands to her brow. "Meline, Mamba of Versillia. I have a message from our High Priestess and her protégé."

I weighed the sound of the new title in my mind, lips turning down and brows rising as I realized that I didn't hate it. "And what is this message? They've both kept us waiting for quite awhile, and I know they were aware as soon as we'd arrived."

Jesyn straightened but kept her head bowed as she spoke, "Your Highness, the High Priestess has sent word that she has matters to attend to away from the Temple and the city. Cera is giving a healing lesson at the moment but will be here shortly." Not until the message was complete did Jesyn raise her head. Her auburn hair was loose today and spilled down to her lower back.

I sucked my teeth and bit back the rage that roared in my chest. Despite the insult, I would not stoop so low as to lash out at the female for just relaying what she had been told. "Thank you for the message." She gave another salute and quickly left the altar room.

My knee bounced up and down, jostling my clenched fists. I shouldn't have been surprised—Isabella had been playing these games with Mathieu and Uncle as well. Going back and forth with him, only to request my speaking with her after months of correspondence. But she couldn't keep me here forever. She couldn't keep making me come here to only ignore me. Worse, give me a fucking escort in the form of that viper. I already had one shadow. I would *not* be saddled with two.

I scrubbed my hand over my face, accidentally scratching my cheek with my fingernail. How had I been reduced to this by the simple mission to return here and talk? Mathieu and Uncle had been doing this shit for months, and I was already at my wits end from a few days. Once this was all over, I was going to go back to Nethras. I would rest in my bed, in my home, and not do a single thing I didn't want to for the next decade. At least.

"Looks like you were right," I muttered, knee still jumping.

Elián didn't respond, which only made me more irritated. Isabella wouldn't talk to me, Elián wouldn't talk to me, and Cera wouldn't *stop* talking to me. Why had I not brought Tana? "You ignoring me, too?"

He didn't say anything, as usual, and I laughed darkly. Was I fucking invisible?

The groan of the door sounded again, bringing the scent of rosemary and lemon, and Cera's figure appeared in front of us. She always liked using her Lylithan speed when it wasn't even necessary, but I was too angry to make a petty comment about it. Knowing her, she was doing it to annoy me, anyway.

"Sorry to keep you waiting, old friend. What would you like to do today?" She didn't bother greeting me with respect, calling me her friend with the sour sweetness that seemed to just drip from her pores. My fingers twitched at the thought of crushing her throat. She probably saw the thought cross my face, because she smiled wider.

"I'd like to fucking kill you, but your worthless Goddess probably wouldn't like that." I heard a low gasp from somewhere behind us.

"*Our* Goddess would surely be displeased, but I'm a bit excited to see you try."

"Just go back to your lessons or whatever the hell you were doing. We'll be going back to the city." I rose, and Elián followed. I wondered how quickly I could unsheathe my blade and bury it in his side. Not to kill him, but maybe hit his intestines and let the hot, thick blood shower my hand. Lylithans couldn't find nourishment from each other, but I imagined his blood would taste like the cinnamon of his scent and be rich and deep.

My mouth had begun to water when Cera's words made the image quickly fade, "I know that you are frustrated, Meline. But Isabella has her reasons." My eyes focused on her face, and found it stark in its honesty. There was no taunting in the hazel anymore, and her lips were neutral, no hint of that goading smirk.

I clasped my hands behind my back and squeezed my wrist so tight that I felt the veins immediately dilate. "And what would those reasons be?"

Cera wet her lips, "I do not know. Believe me, I do not enjoy watching you like a child. But we both have our orders."

"I do not have orders."

She quirked a brow, "Don't you? Mathieu has sent you here to do what he couldn't. Isabella is not a liar. She said she would speak with you. But she will wait until she is ready to do so. I have served her since your mother's murder, and I have learned to be patient. I suggest you do the same if you want what you came for."

Murder was too gentle of a word for what the Vyrkos did to my mother, but I would let that one slide. Cera was many things, but she was nothing but loyal to Rhaea and her fellow priestesses. She hated me but had revered my mother. Her voice softened almost imperceptibly when she spoke of her.

"I am here because I volunteered to do this for my people. *Our* people, if you haven't forgotten that you are as much Lylithan as you are a priestess of Rhaea."

She shook her head solemnly, "I may have chosen to devote my life to Rhaea, Mamba, but I was born Lylithan. As was Isabella. She will speak with you. Eventually." She turned on her heel and stalked toward the door. And fuck me, but I followed her, Elián in tow.

19

We spent the day roaming the Temple halls, stopping frequently so that Cera could go about answering the questions of her sisters. Her tone was composed as she relayed knowledge and advice about the most mundane issues. What herbs were best to use in a poultice for burns, what weapons she would suggest for a new priestess beginning her training. What males thought about beginning relations with a priestess of Rhaea.

The young human priestess that had asked this particular question had all the gall of youth and a laughably short lifespan. Cera had remained unbothered as she shrugged and imparted that most males, in her experience, did not have any qualms with such details. The priestess didn't even try to hide her hungry glance at my Shadow as she hurried away and joined a group of others.

Elián had no reaction to it all whatsoever.

Cera showed us the library, large and with the dusty smell of old books. But she didn't let us settle into the comfortable seats that ran between the stacks and kept us moving. I knew where we were headed before we came upon a set of wooden double doors.

She pulled them open, and I was hit with the scent of sweat and steel. The indoor training rings weren't as beautiful as the one in the floral gardens, but the sight of them still made the breath catch in my throat. The black stone floor held two large, golden circles that were on opposite ends of the room. Along the far walls behind the circles lay all sorts of weapons, training and otherwise, that were grouped by type. The other wall that faced the door was made entirely of mirrors that extended to the ceiling. Several priestesses sat in their training clothes, stretching and talking happily. But when the three of us entered the room, all eyes turned, and the couple that had been about to go at each other with wooden swords stopped mid-strike.

They all dropped or rose to their knees, murmuring greetings to us, to Cera, and gave the salute of Rhaea. Cera and I returned the salutation, while Elián kept his hands at his sides.

Most of them were disheveled from their training but ran to us with palpable excitement. One of them shouted, "Are you going to fight again? Some of us missed you in the gardens yesterday!" She still clutched the wooden sword in her hand, eyes wide.

Cera chuckled and turned to me, "You had fun yesterday, I could tell. I thought you might enjoy seeing this place again."

I hated that she wasn't wrong. Despite my best efforts, I could picture myself so clearly as one of those that crowded around us. Their gazes kept moving between Cera and me and Elián. Not one of them looked nervous about having him in one of the spaces that was off-limits to outsiders.

"But," Cera clapped her hands in front of her, and my stomach tensed for what was coming, "I was wondering if our guest wouldn't mind showing us a few things?" I almost opened my mouth to respond, but I caught her eyes looking past me. To Elián. "We have never had a Shadow come here, as you may have suspected." A few priestesses chuckled. "And we would be honored if you would demonstrate whatever you are willing to show us, Master Elián."

Oh, she was in for it. I smirked at the impending burning coldness that Cera was about to receive for putting Elián on the spot. For effectively demanding that he dance for them like a circus attraction.

His lips pursed, looking to me, then her, then our audience who was all but drooling. They were eager warriors at various stages of expertise, all hungry to learn. They were also eating up the attention of the mysterious male that had been visiting their precious home.

No one dared to breathe as Elián assessed all of us. Then finally, his eyes landed back on Cera. He shrugged. The motherfucker shrugged.

He took a step toward one of the rings, and the priestesses quickly parted. As he sauntered to the golden circle, he reached to the swords on his back and unsheathed them with a metallic shudder. Someone gasped as if it were the most impressive thing they had seen in their life.

When he reached the center, Elián stood, short swords lowered, and looked at me. He moved his head from side to side and rolled his shoulders. His brows rose, waiting.

"I think he means to spar with you, Mamba," Cera whispered. Elián stood completely still. The priestesses were split in staring at Elián and staring at me.

"Fine," I said beneath my breath. I did as Elián had, unsheathing my blades as I walked to the ring. The Mamba and the Shadow. I could almost hear the gossip that would ring through the halls later tonight.

I settled just a few feet from Elián. He looked down his nose at me, and I must have been fucking hallucinating because I saw the ghost of a smile cross his lips.

When he had come at me on that hill on Dyna Island, he hadn't used weapons. And it had been a fight in the loosest of terms. We'd shared blows, but while his had been near catastrophic, mine had been like the beating of a moth's wings.

Elián gave no warning when he brought his right sword up to strike. He had been standing still and then there was a blade coming down to slash at my shoulders.

Instinct took over, and I twisted, evading the blow. I whirled my blades toward him in an attempt to slash his torso. I wasn't sure what effect the poison would have on him, but it would be fun to find out.

Even though I knew that he was holding back, probably using me as light exercise, I met him with all the seriousness as if we were fighting for our lives. Elián was here to protect me, and I knew that none of his blows would do real damage.

But a stinging slice across my back as I tried to avoid those deadly swords shocked and filled me with glee.

His face remained flatly focused, eyes constantly moving, as we sparred. He wasn't even breathing hard, but I wasn't embarrassed at my own panting. If he was willing to spill my blood, it meant that maybe I was holding my own more than I thought. Or maybe he was just toying with me.

A quick combination I aimed at his chest to no avail caused him to move back to avoid my slashing. I backed away to give even more distance.

I pointed my blade at him, "Next one to land a blow wins." He didn't acknowledge my command, but I knew that he'd heard me.

Elián sheathed his swords. Just like that, he stowed them on his back once again, and for a second, I thought he had given up. Confusion was certainly written on my face, but when he began to stalk forward, fiery intention on his, I realized what he was doing.

Before he could reach me, I sheathed my daggers. I wouldn't give him the satisfaction of beating me while still giving me the advantage of being the one armed. My fists raised to my brow, readying. His hands remained at his sides, but his knees were loose, ready.

I shot out two jabs in quick succession, and Elián blocked them easily. My hook toward his chin, dodged.

Before his fist could make contact with my side, I pivoted around and behind him, calling on all my speed. My feet shifted and slid on the floor, remaining as fluid and efficient as possible. But of course, he knew this way, and he turned with the same almost dancer-like grace.

Elián truly looked enraged now, his face no longer flat with bored determination. I gave him a wink and imagined myself a mist again, just like I'd been taught.

Though his movements seemed to come with an ease akin to breathing, and mine more conscious and less practiced, we began a dance of jabs and kicks that were just as silent as our steps. But they were no less powerful, and I knew that I would bruise from a few of his strikes that skirted my less-than-expert evasions.

Once again, I spun on the ball of my foot to move behind his back, and as he turned to face me again, I brought up my heel, quick as lightning. But instead of connecting with his cheekbone, my heel was caught in his gloved palm.

I grunted as I struggled to break out of his hold, and before I could maneuver away, I was pressed against him. He used his own speed to unsheathe my blade from my waist, and he held my back to his front with one arm, and the tip of my blade to my neck with the other. The razor edge of my own dagger pressed against my throat but didn't break my skin.

The hard muscles of his body pressed into me, and the unnatural heat of him warmed my bones. The arm he used to hold me still was just as impenetrable as when he'd disarmed me the first time. But instead of feeling terrified or angry as I had then, I felt... comfortable. Giddy. My breathing slowed, and I almost relaxed into his arms.

I felt his warm breath on my ear, and his deep voice curled down my spine. "You fight well, my queen. But I fight better." The blade pressed a fraction more into my flesh, threatening to break the skin, "Whichever traitorous Shadow taught you should have done a better job." His words echoed those that he'd spoken during our first encounter. My stomach fluttered, and I felt the most treacherous swell of arousal below my navel. A beat of panic shot through me, knowing that he would be able to smell it.

Though I had come away from our first fight with shame and rage, I was certain that I wasn't ashamed to be defeated this time. He would've been a horrible Shadow if I had won, especially using his own way of fighting against him.

My increasingly racing thoughts were halted when our audience's presence made itself known. The room erupted in ridiculous applause, and Elián lowered his arms, returning my blade to my hip. He put space between us, but stepped up to stand beside me. I commanded my body to cool down—where this new reaction to Elián had come from, I wasn't sure. I looked up and caught him tucking strands of his hair behind his ears, gazing forward.

"Thank you very much, Master Elián, that was quite a match!" Cera called as we walked back to the group of priestesses. The young trainees watched us with wide eyes and barely contained questions on their lips. "And Mamba, I must give credit where it is due. You take defeat well."

"Better than you. Care to show your trainees again how quickly you can be bested?" My smile was saccharine, and she mirrored it. Elián crossed his arms, and I was reminded of what he had said last night. Then, the notion had sounded so ludicrous, but standing here, with Cera and I eerily mimicking each other's posture... dammit.

A priestess piped up and snared my attention. She bowed before speaking, "Mamba of Versillia, would you be so kind as to watch us and impart any guidance you have?" The others nodded enthusiastically, as if they had all agreed before putting this one up to give the request.

A genuine warmth crept over my face when I looked at her, at all of them. Cera and Isabella were intent on making me miserable, but everyone else in Rhaestras had been nothing but kind and welcoming. And the priestesses were especially so, albeit a bit squirrelly. This group was young, none of them appeared to have entered adulthood yet. The energy around them reminded me so much of the children I volunteered with back in Nethras, and my heart ached a bit. Little Marco would have loved the Temple. Somehow, I knew that he wouldn't have felt insecure at all being one of very few males if he were here.

I agreed to the priestess's request, and they fought amongst themselves about who would be first to show off for Master Elián, Cera, and myself.

I spent the rest of the afternoon watching them, laughing with them, and giving critique. Some were fighting their weapons instead of using them as an extension of their arms, some spent more time anticipating their next move instead of keeping an eye on their opponent, and one or two thoroughly impressed me. Even Elián responded when asked about what weapon he had mastered first (the broadsword).

There were no windows in the training room, but I could sense the waning of the day, as did the trainees. Once everyone had fought for us once or twice, they began to resume the stretching they had been doing when we arrived. Cera and I stretched with them while I answered questions about my travels and the world outside of Rhaestras.

When priestesses had served Rhaea for five years and completed their primary lessons, they were permitted to move about the world and to other temples at their whim. These trainees were close to that point, and told me of their plans for where they'd visit first. A few were eager to hear about Nethras, never having been to a city bigger than Rhaestras. Their eyes were wide as I described the sheer size of it.

After a while, we finished our stretching, and Cera asked, "Would you both wish to eat with us? The dining hall should be fairly quiet this early in the evening." The priestesses had become more relaxed around us, and a few audibly begged for us to join them.

I glanced at Elián to search his face for any objection, and when I saw none, I agreed for the both of us.

So, we ate supper with Cera and the other priestesses. We waited in line with them, and we filled our plates from an assortment that was laid out on the far wall of the dining hall. Bread, fruit, roasted meats, and cheeses lined the buffet. I piled mine with as much as I could manage, and the three of us sat at a table near the back. Jesyn joined us, sitting on Cera's right side. I sat across from her, and Elián sat to my right. After he tasted a bite of everything on my plate and deemed it safe to eat, I began to inhale the food.

The three of us talked between our chewing as Elián silently ate his own meal. Jesyn was directly under Cera and had also been an orphan given to the Temple. Her skills in healing magic weren't yet that of her superior, but she was working diligently to improve. I spoke of my cousin and her knowledge in such things, and Jesyn began talking much more animatedly as I relayed the spells I had seen Tana conduct.

"She was really able to attach a severed limb? Just like that?"

I nodded and took a sip of wine from my glass, "Yes, it was very impressive. Especially since humans heal so slowly. She used to visit the Temple quite often with my mother and I, which sparked her interest in the healing arts. If you are ever in Versillia or Nethras, I would be happy to introduce you. She is much better at explaining these things than I am. I don't have any proficiency in healing, apart from what my body does naturally, that is." I speared a piece of sticky cake and brought it to my mouth. It tasted of guava and vanilla, and I hummed as I took another bite.

"Yes, but you have other gifts, too. Don't you, Mamba?" Cera looked innocently at me over her emptying plate, and my shoulders bristled. Maman had drilled in me to keep that part of me hidden from most of the world for my own safety, and though I did not fear what Cera or the other priestesses would do, I did *not* want to discuss it with her.

Ice chilled my stomach, and I felt fingers caress against my senses. The Temple called to it, and Cera's words were too effective at letting it gain slack against my restraints.

It tickled behind my eyes, my throat. Not unlike Elián's voice before, the darkness ran down my spine, and I shivered. With Elián, the sensation brought comfort and slight arousal, but this darkness felt so wrong in its rightness. I was barely able to keep my muscles from vibrating at the feeling. It was begging for the relief of me setting it free.

My retort was weak, but all I could muster was, "I don't know what you're talking about."

Cera glowered, "Enough of the denials. They," she waved her fork to gesture around the room, "may not realize, but I was there. I know what you are, as much as you try to deny it. As much as you try to deny Her."

My fingers were twitching as the darkness begged to be let out, just a little bit. I seethed through my teeth, "*She* has nothing to do with this."

"*She* has everything to do with this. You disrespect Her by denying what She gave you, Meline. I'm surprised it hasn't swallowed you whole."

Darkness began to unfurl at the edge of my vision. This fucking place made it harder to keep it in check, and I wouldn't be able to withstand Cera's interrogation much longer. I pounded a fist on the table and shot a finger at her. She flinched, but I pressed on, "You don't know what the fuck you're talking about."

Even with my finger still aimed at her chest, she shot back, "Of course, I do, Death—"

I shot up from my seat and all but tumbled over the bench. A quenching chill was settling over my skin, and my muscles hummed blissfully. I stalked out of the dining hall, barely aware of the silence that had settled over the cavernous room and the wide looks of concern tinged with fear.

The halls flashed around me while I shook out my arms. The humming was only growing, no matter how many deep breaths I tried to take. I wouldn't let it out, *I couldn't*.

My bare feet hit the gravel, but I couldn't even smell the sweet aroma of the floral gardens. All that filled my nose was the cool muskiness of the abyss.

A leather touch gripped my arm and pulled me to a stop. I lurched against the hold, but was jerked back again. In a corner of my mind, I knew that it was Elián, knew that he had followed me out here.

The darkness swirled curiously around his touch. I felt it swell under my skin, wanting to escape and wrap around the warm leather of his hand and seep into his flesh.

I gritted my teeth, my voice a low growl, "Get *off* of me, Elián." He responded by whirling me around and grabbing hold of both my arms.

A rising sun. That's what his eyes reminded me of today. The sky above was nearly black, but Elián's eyes were two suns in the night. They moved quickly as he searched my face, his jaw clenched and sharp as a knife. He didn't speak, and he didn't let me go.

Earlier, I had found a kind of comfort in his touch, but now, I was afraid.

The darkness inside of me begged in curiosity. Elián's fire only made it grow stronger and my restraints weaker. My vision was darkening and clearing at the same time, my other senses sharpening to the point of pain. It noticed too much, everything. Whatever made Elián's eyes the way they were, made his very being burn, was calling to those dark tendrils that wove through every fiber of my soul.

My voice was even more animalistic, and I bared my fangs to him, "You need to back the *fuck* away, Elián."

He kissed his teeth, "Or what?" His own fangs shone under the moonlight. I rarely saw them since he was so taciturn, but they looked deadly. "What will you do?"

I shrieked into the air between us, cackling wildly, "I don't know!"

No panic, no fear, flashed across his face, but I knew that my eyes had gone black. Though my irises were dark to begin with, the whole of my eyes had surely gone as black as my pupils because I saw the darkness manifest outside of my body. It began to twine around my shoulders like black smoke, just above where Elián still held me before him. The smell of jasmine warred with Elián's burning cinnamon and oak, and I wanted to give into it so badly. To let it consume me and do what it wanted.

He shook me and hissed, but I was so tired. So tired of reining this darkness in. The headaches, the fear, the running. Cera was right. It would eventually swallow me whole, so why not just let it?

Suddenly, my neck was burning. One of my arms was free, and I clawed at Elián's now bare hand at my throat. He didn't cut off any of my air, but somehow, his palm was singeing my skin. The dark smoke around me pulled back, but was no less curious.

The rich awareness of his blood flooded my nostrils and overpowered the jasmine. I felt it under my nails, and I stopped my swiping. My fingers flew to my mouth, and I tasted Elián on my tongue. His blood was somehow deeper, woodsier than I had imagined, and my eyes rolled back. A rumbling moan left my throat at the taste.

The abyss shrunk back into my skin, and the heat at my throat and the blood in my mouth pushed to the forefront of my mind. My toes curled, and I felt the smooth gravel underneath me. My breathing slowed, and I was able to take a deep gulp of air through my nose.

My body was shaken again, and my gaze settled on Elián in front of me. He still showed no fear. His head was tilted, and his eyes narrowed. The humid night air somehow felt cold against my bare throat when he'd removed his hand.

He brought both back to his sides, and I swayed for a moment before catching myself. I took another deep breath, and the trembling ceased.

I winced as Elián said, soft as the rustling of leaves, "Death Wielder."

20

There was a soft knock at the door. I was naked under the sheets of the large bed, and I clutched my pillow beside my face. My hair was still braided, and as I sat up, I ran my hand over the fuzzy plaits. Flashes of last night played in my mind, and I shuddered. The dark tendrils stirred within me at the memory but remained behind my walls. I recalled pieces of the journey home, refusing Elián's insistence to just let him carry me as I stumbled through the streets. I remembered tumbling into my room and stripping before crawling under the covers and letting a similar kind of darkness take over as I passed out.

Soft sunlight trickled into my room through the curtained window, and I heard the front door to our rooms open. Kiava's voice was brief and cheerful as she relayed that a note had been left for me at the front. He didn't respond, but I heard the rustling of paper before the sound of the door shutting.

As I pushed myself out of bed to stand, I expected to feel exhausted, perhaps sore. But I only felt energized and slightly agitated. I showered quickly, almost scrubbing welts into my skin.

I dressed and donned the first thing I pulled from one of my bags. The emerald dress was light and flowed to my ankles with a plunging neckline held together by weaving ties at the front.

Elián was lounging on the settee again, but it seemed closer to the window this morning. Had he moved it? A ray of sunshine landed on his face and upper body as he reclined. He really enjoyed sunning himself like a house cat.

"What did Kiava want?" He flicked his wrist and extended a piece of paper in my direction without shifting his posture. I stopped behind him and pulled the note from his fingers. It was the same hand he had held my throat with last night, but there was no evidence of my scratching on the smooth skin. I saw the edge of the script in his palm before he moved it to rest at the back of his head.

I unfolded the note and read the brief message. My hands began to shake in rage, and heat flooded my cheeks. I wanted to scream. Isabella's handwriting was blocky and severe, and I shredded the paper, letting the pieces fall like snow onto the floor.

"I'm going downstairs to the courtyard." I swiped one of the books I had bought at the market from the table beside the door before leaving the room.

Luckily, there was no one sitting by the swimming pool. The air was a bit cooler after the storming yesterday, and the sun was halfway obscured by the clouds. I sat by the pool, under the shade of a mature palm, and all but tore my new book at the spine when I opened it. I glared at the first page, and forced myself to concentrate on the words. Not on what had happened yesterday now that the darkness was dormant once again. Not on what Isabella had said in her note. And not on Elián settling beside me with his own book.

I had picked up the novel that reminded me of Lee. It was an adventurous story, the main characters starting on a sort of quest for some stolen artifact. Just as I began settling into the first chapter, someone came running outside and jumped in the pool. Water droplets splashed on my bare toes, and I spat, "Do you mind?"

The adolescent male looked me up and down, lingering on my chest and the low cut of my dress before scoffing and starting laps around the edge of the water. I slammed the book shut and began to stand.

Elián cleared his throat next to me, and my head whipped around to him, "Do you have something to say?" He didn't, of course. "Then I suggest you leave me the fuck alone." I sat back on the lounge chair and picked the book up again. The child in the water continued to swim lazily, and I raised my book so that it obscured him from my view.

I read outside, finishing a quarter of the novel and a joint I had brought outside with me, before my stomach began to growl.

Looking up at the sun, I knew that food may be harder to come by at this hour. Most restaurants would be closed until later, and I didn't much feel like venturing out onto the streets anyway. Reading hadn't done much to quell my irritability, and I was one curt word before ripping someone's head off.

Kiava was writing something in a ledger when I approached. She looked up with a pleasant smile, and it only fell a fraction when she caught the surely unpleasant look on my face. She gave the salute of Rhaea and asked, "What can I do for you?"

I didn't return it and didn't bother keeping my tone light, "Can I have some food sent up to my room, please?"

"Yes, of course. Would you like to see a menu of what we have prepared today?"

I was already turning toward the stairs, "No, whatever is fine."

She called after me, "We will have someone send it up to you as soon as possible."

I unlocked the door and threw my novel down on the sofa while Elián slipped past me to check the space. If there was an intruder, I couldn't quite bring myself to care. Perhaps bloodshed would give this anger somewhere to go.

My knuckles rubbed my tear ducts, and the squelching of my eyeballs filled my ears. My knee bobbed up and down as I leaned back into the cushions. This trip to Rhaestras had been a mistake. Agreeing to help Mathieu had been a mistake. I wouldn't be able to do it, and I was going to have to come back to Versillia with my tail between my legs. And Mathieu would look at me with that warm, pitying smile to try to hide his disappointment.

Another set of knocking rang, and Elián opened the door and accepted a tray of food from Verot. He slipped the male a few coins before closing the door.

The food Kiava had sent turned my stomach. The spiced mango, grilled fish, and rice would have normally made my mouth water, but my stomach felt like it had a rock in it. The thought of tearing into the meal made me want to vomit.

"You eat it," I lurched to my feet and began to pace the room. Elián obviously didn't need to be told twice, because he quickly sat with the tray in his lap and began with the spiced mango that seemed to be his new favorite.

I made three revolutions around the room before he asked, "What is wrong with you?" The platters were nearly empty now, and he was still eating. The fish was picked clean, and all that was left was the head, tail, and bones.

"What the hell do you think is wrong? She's still refusing to see me. *Tomorrow* she says. Always tomorrow!" I needed to hit something, but I had better sense than to wreck the room. Keeping myself moving would have to do.

"Cera said that she would meet with you eventually," he said over a mouth full of mango.

"Oh, are you still listening to Cera, hm? You're a fucking idiot if you think she's speaking the truth." Elián raised a thick, black eyebrow and swallowed his food. Before he could speak, though I doubted that he would, I spat, "I don't even want you here, so don't you dare try to placate me, you shifty motherfucker." I stopped with my back to the door and stood over him and his lunch. He was so nonchalant about the whole thing as if the fate of our people didn't depend on this. On this mission. It figured, though. The Shadows hadn't cared much before.

I was about to continue my pacing when Elián put the tray on the low table between us and stood. My fingers curled and dug half-moons into my palm, and I refused to back down. His irises were swimming amber and rufous and gold, and Elián moved around the table with murder in his eyes. Waves of black hair fell in his face as he stalked towards me.

My parents used to chastise me during my adolescent years that I had to be mindful of the way I treated others when I was in these moods. Then, in the throws of my body changing and my fangs coming in, I had been liable to snap at unsuspecting bystanders at the slightest shift in the air.

Now, my Shadow had just been one of those bystanders as the weight of being back in my mother's homeland pressed down on me. I'd felt like I could slaughter anyone who crossed my path when we received Isabella's letter postponing our meeting for another day.

The backs of my thighs bumped into the table that sat in the entryway of our rooms. Nowhere else for me to go, I held my ground as Elián stood over me in that way he had by the stream. His shoulders curled down and forwards so that his mouth hung by my ear. My Shadow didn't touch me, but he might as well have for how his presence made my body stir.

He growled, barely above a whisper, "Count yourself lucky that I am unable to harm you. You would have had my swords buried in your gut ten times over if I had my way." His accent slipped again, the words starting to flex in a rhythm that hit my ears in an irritatingly pleasant way.

Elián pulled back and met my eyes. The stupid, mesmerizing fire was enough to inflate my anger even more, and I glared with all of the fury I felt in my soul, "Why don't you just fucking do it, then? I've been fantasizing all day about spilling your blood again." And instead of trying to squeeze out of the corner he'd backed me into, I stepped forward.

My chest pressed into his as I crossed into *his* personal space. This was the second time our bodies had touched like this, and from what I could tell, his form was all the hard muscles it appeared to be.

His large hands smothered the tops of my arms as he shoved me away from him. But once cold air moved in between us, they lingered, holding on as my back arched slightly over the table. With his bare touch on my bare skin, I felt the heat simmering within him, just as I had last night.

Darkness and boldness swirled like smoke in my lungs, and my pulse hastened. I knew that he could hear it, could feel it as he held my arms. But I couldn't break our stare, and rather than releasing myself from his hold, my hands grasped for the waist of his trousers. I hooked my fingers between the crisp fabric and his waist, and it was no accident for my fingernails to claw into him. Confusion and fire flashed over his face in quick succession.

The hand that held my left arm disappeared, and for a blink, I braced myself for him to hit me, to reject this.

But I instead felt his strong grasp at the back of my head.

He grabbed a fistful of the damp hair that tumbled freely down my spine, and my eyes rolled back at the heart-lurching swell that coursed within me. Elián's hold wasn't painful, but close enough to my scalp that I was unable to move without pulling out many strands of hair. My Shadow's blade-sharp jaw flexed, and he tilted my head back to bare my jugular to him.

It was a position of vulnerability that I had never been in. With anyone. But I went gladly, eager and ready for something, anything. For him to touch me or fight me—I could have gone either way. If I could have reached my daggers, the need could have certainly turned into me stabbing him as I'd fantasized.

He searched my face, stare tracing for a pause that extended longer than I could say. The scent of cinnamon and burning oak was rolling off of him and enveloping me, and I felt ready to burst out of my skin. Those waved strands of his hair that he'd tucked behind his ears fell and tickled my nose.

Then, in an instant, his head flew to my exposed throat. I couldn't see him in his shifted position, just the rest of the room beyond. But I could feel his warm breath on my skin, the hardening length of him pressing into my stomach, and I groaned toward the ceiling.

Though my body squirmed with need, I couldn't remove my fingers from the waist of his black trousers, for one wrong move and he could tear my throat out. I squeezed my thighs together to try and calm the throbbing between them, but instead, a sizzling pulse shot up my body and made me tremble.

"Get on the table," he demanded at my neck.

I immediately rose on my toes, and Elián's grip moved with me as I settled onto the tabletop. My legs opened, begging, and I tried to pull his hips toward me. The absence of them against mine was like a cold slap, and I ached to have him between my thighs.

But he wouldn't move, and instead, he removed the hand on my arm and placed it beneath my skirt. I felt the warm back of his hand on my inner thigh then heard the sound of ripping fabric. My undergarment hit the stone floor in a soft shudder, and I moaned again, wanting this so badly that I couldn't—

His fingers. I felt his fingers, and my hands flew to the edge of the table, nails digging into the painted wood.

He let out a rumble as he discovered the slickness that had been pooling in my lap and all but trailing down my legs, and he did not tease, did not coax.

Elián pushed a finger into me, and the ragged moan I gave in response echoed throughout the room. But I dared not move, and the very restriction was bringing the pleasure even higher. He moved slowly at first, in and out, drawing out another series of sounds from me that could have been described as nothing less than guttural.

And then, by the grace of the Mother, Elián added another finger and thrust them into me, faster and faster, and my eyes rolled back again, spine bowing over the table. All the while, he breathed at my throat, never letting me forget that he could end my life at any moment. His fingers curled to hit that spot inside of me, and my own splintered the edge of the table.

The roaring climax I was reaching was closing in as he added his thumb to circle at the epicenter of my throbbing.

"Oh, Goddess," A part of me hated that I called out to Her, but I was also too far away to truly care.

Just as I felt the slightest touch of a fang at my throat and my desire to lean back and let him drink from me, the grip at my head disappeared. The fingers inside of me disappeared too, forcing a whimper of protest to escape my chest. My upper body swayed a bit at the absence of his force holding me arched and anchored, and my hands clutched onto the edge of the table for balance.

I yelped at searing touch meeting my calves and moving up to firmly grip my thighs. One of the touches was slick, and remembering that I could now move my neck, I looked down. My tongue swiped at my lips as I watched Elián kneel between my legs and, almost angrily, push up my skirt.

But he didn't look up at me, didn't say anything, and before I could form another thought, he threw my full thighs over his shoulders.

His palms settled on my hips, and I moaned deeply, loudly, when I felt his tongue give a long, slow swipe over my slit. I grabbed his hair in my fist, and I could have sworn that he leaned into my grasp.

The rumble of his growl vibrated against my legs while he pushed his tongue into me, nose tickling while I felt him taste me, devour me. And while I couldn't see his eyes, I watched the top of his head bob as he gave me this.

My thighs shook as Elián pulled pleasure from every part of my depths with each curl of his tongue. He didn't move his hands from my hips again, letting his mouth do all of the work.

The erotic sounds of him feasting upon me rang out from between my legs, and my hips rocked against his face, wanting more, needing it all. My fingers clung to him even tighter, and his hair was like silk.

Quick as an asp, Elián's tongue moved to that throbbing and swirled in the most masterfully agonizing pattern. I wasn't sure how he knew this was what would push me over the edge, but the release that had been hovering over me with each plunge of his tongue now crashed into me with a force that rivaled the roughest Rhaestran waves. I shouted out to Rhaea again as the climax of my pleasure washed and slowly settled over me.

My hands were still curled tightly in Elián's hair and on the broken edge of the table, and with the absolute molten state of my body, I was unsure whether I would be able to keep upright at all if I let go.

Not until the tremors of the aftershocks settled did Elián move. He'd still been underneath my skirts, panting yet unmoving.

He shot up, letting my legs fall from his shoulders, and removed his hands from my hips. I was about to reach for him, perhaps pull his lips to mine so that I could taste the mixture of us on his tongue.

But he turned too quickly for me to see much else besides a flash of his face, mouth glistening with the evidence of what he had done. I watched his retreating back, stunned, as he moved to his room and slammed the door.

21

"We'll take two, please." I smiled up at our server and returned the small paper menu to him. The male was quite pale for a Rhaestran, but his accent suggested that he was from here. It reminded me of my mother's.

The restaurant wasn't yet full, but the setting sun was drawing people out of their homes for something to eat. Just as it had done to us.

Ice clinked in my glass as I raised it to my lips. Elián had already checked it, of course, though he hadn't said a word as he did. Our table was in the far corner of the restaurant patio, and it offered a pleasant view of the street. Elián's eyes were focused on the people walking past, on the couple that sat on the patio a few tables down.

After closing himself inside his room for a few hours, he had later emerged, showered and changed. He'd simply said, "I need to feed," and we left the room.

After inquiring at the front desk, Kiava suggested we go here where they had a menu that catered particularly to Lylithans. Elián and I were silent on the walk, and I had requested we eat outside to escape the echoing chatter of the main dining area.

Our server came back and deposited two glasses of blood and a plate of fried squid between us. His eyes lingered on Elián, who had mercifully left his swords in the room and opted for some assortment of concealed weapons. I squeezed lemon over the pile before Elián plucked a piece from the top. He sniffed and ate it quickly.

Twin Blades

Elián tested both of the new glasses, but kept his gripped in his hand. Once he was done, he settled back in his seat, angled to face the street. I picked a piece of the squid, and the batter shattered between my teeth as I chewed.

"Did you not like the taste?" I saw the moment my words registered. His nostrils flared, and he shifted in his seat, resting an ankle over his knee. He took another sip and said nothing. "Elián."

He sucked his front teeth, threw back half of his glass, and finally responded. "What."

"You didn't answer my question."

"And I won't."

I popped another piece of squid into my mouth and talked through my chewing, "We are going to talk about this."

"We will not."

I swirled the blood in my glass and watched it climb the sides before settling back down. They had chosen to enhance it with chilies that mingled with the natural sweetness of the human it came from to create the sweet-spicy flavor that Rhaestrans adored. Though I didn't necessarily need it, I drank the blood all the same. "We most certainly will. Even if I have to command you, though I would rather not."

He finished his glass and rattled the table as he set it down. Elián turned his amber stare to me, "Why must you insist on torturing me with this?"

"Oh, for the love of the Mother, you are so fucking dramatic. I, for one, had a lovely time."

Elián scrubbed a hand over his face and tucked damp strands of his hair behind his ears. He'd changed into a clean set of his casual Shadow attire that matched his hair, and the neckline revealed the glint of a thin, golden chain around his neck. He'd opted to go without his leather gloves tonight, and I couldn't help but remember how his bare fingers felt between my legs.

He rested his hands on the arm of his chair and leaned back. His voice was pitched low, so that no one but me would hear him. "If you want to talk, then let's talk about you, too. Death Wielder."

I bit my bottom lip but otherwise kept my face cool. "Fine. You get one question, and I answer. Then I ask, and you answer. See? I can even be amenable and let you go first." I took a long gulp from my

199

glass.

He narrowed his eyes and asked, "Rhaea is not just the Goddess of Life and New Beginnings, is she?"

"No." I swallowed and worried my upper lip with my teeth. "Why didn't you say anything?"

He clenched his jaw and looked down for a few moments. "I had nothing to say." He waited, but I had set the rules of the game and was going to wait for his next question to speak again. "And you've never mastered this gift?"

A grim smile shot across my face and then was wiped clean, "Not really." I paused for a moment and then continued with my next question, "Is it against the rules you all follow? The Shadows, I mean."

His eyes flickered to the street beside us and back to me, "No, it is not. What is it? The death wielding."

I shrugged, "A little bit of this, a little bit of that. Then why run away afterwards?"

He pointed a finger at me, and I felt my navel stir again, "That wasn't an answer." I couldn't help but grin. Oh, yes, he had opened the floodgates, now.

"Oh, all right! Um, it's what that loathsome title implies. Death, in many forms. Now, *why* did you run away?"

Elián scoffed, "I didn't run away."

"Yes, you did. Is it because you regret it? Or did you like it *too* much?"

He ran his hands past his brow and wrung his hair out before letting his arms fall back on the chair, "What do you want me to say, Your Highness?"

I picked up my glass, "Oh, I don't know. That you couldn't even bear to brush your teeth after you bathed because you wanted the lingering taste of me on your tongue? That would be a start."

Elián's nostrils flared again, his mouth pressed in a thin line. His eyes flashed in the low light of the day, and—I caught the barest, blissful scent of his arousal while a carriage moved swiftly past the restaurant. It was like his normal scent, but with an additional sweet heat, not unlike the blood we drank.

He had no response to my words, but when he had emerged from his bedroom some hours after making me come, he had on a fresh set of clothes and the scent of eucalyptus soap surrounding him. But his breath still smelled like my cunt and spiced mango.

"So, are you quitting our little game, then? Or do you have a response?"

He glared at me while our server came over with a carafe and topped off our glasses. The server didn't even bother looking to me, and he left, lips turned down in disappointment, when Elián made no effort to return his pining.

"I think that server wants you. Since you didn't finish, perhaps he can help you out. Or maybe you did that already in the shower."

Elián looked like he wanted to choke me across the table. "You are a menace."

I barked a laugh and continued, "Elián, if I wasn't sure you'd snap my neck, I would offer to do it for you." He rolled his eyes, but I also caught the quick glance he gave in the direction our server had left. That gave me another bout of the giggles. I wasn't lying in the slightest, but it was also very clear that Elián was regretting what he had done, despite how much his scent belied his words. Possessiveness wasn't something I was too keen on, but smelling myself on Elián with each word he spoke, each shift of his body, kept my own heat swelling.

We ate the rest of our meal in silence and people-watched for some time afterward while the sky fully darkened. Our server continued to try and get Elián's attention, and when he not-so-accidentally brushed the back of Elián's hand with his own, I watched my Shadow hover those assessing eyes up and down the server's body. He sent another round of fluttering at my navel when he pulled his gaze away and back to me, ultimately rejecting the offer.

After supper, we made our way back toward the heart of the city. We passed again through the market, and I tried my best to ignore the glances from passersby toward me and my frowning companion. Though we were more appropriately dressed, we were clearly not Rhaestran, and even some priestesses, who had shed their Temple garb for casual clothing, gave us both salutes of Rhaea when they saw us.

I ended up buying some dried herbs native to the island that Tana might find use for, and I tucked the carefully wrapped sprigs in my deep pockets. Elián followed me as I walked us again toward the outskirts of the city, and the crashing of waves grew louder and louder with every step.

On this end of the city, instead of a fluorescent lagoon, there was a sprawling beach that spanned about three miles. The stars hung brightly overhead, and after removing my sandals, I walked us over the warm, white sand. We came upon a cluster of large boulders underneath a palm tree, and I sat without a word, facing the waves.

The sea air stirred my hair, and I felt the salt cling to my skin. My breaths came in easily and flowed out unencumbered. Crabs scuttled around freely with the lack of people, and I watched as one dove into the earth by my bare foot. Though I had committed to staying away from this land for so many years, the rush and pull of the water was, admittedly, a lullaby I still sang to myself on the worst of nights.

"Why are you so afraid of it?" Elián's voice didn't battle with the shushing of the waves, but seemed to move with them.

Like the Temple, I felt a peace here. Unlike the Temple, however, the peace I felt was far less terrifying. Perhaps that's why I found myself being completely honest with him, sharing what I hadn't before given words to. "It's... unpredictable. And finding that you have been given the gift of Death before you have even been alive for very long—I suppose I've never learned to not fear it." Not to mention the fact that the last Death Wielders had been hunted. The twin Godyxes Aeras and Thryx, along with the God Mortos also gifted some individuals with enhanced abilities or strengths, but never powerful enough to incite unease from the rest of the realm. Rhaea was the most powerful, and the Death Wielders had been feared by many.

Another pull of waves onto the shore, and when they pulled back, Elián whispered, "But you've killed before."

I winced, "It's not—it's not just about the killing." I dragged in a breath, "When I had reached five years or so, my mother, Isabella, and I were attacked while on our way to Rhaestras. They were petty, human thieves, and I hadn't yet understood that my mother could hold her own perfectly well. One of them lunged at Maman with a knife," the darkness shuddered in me at the memory, "the last I remember, I had closed my eyes, screamed.

"They had been a band of five or so... and I killed them all." I rubbed my hand at my chest and swallowed. "It was a matter of seconds, surely, but the Death slashed all of their throats. And—and I didn't come to until I was crouched over the one that had been about to attack my mother. Isabella said I was lapping up the blood like a dehydrated puppy." A sharp chuckle escaped my lips. "When this happens, it's like I'm not really here. It takes over completely, and I don't quite know what I'm doing."

That first time it happened, I had been thrust back into awareness not by the sweet taste of the blood, but by a nearby whimpering. Upon searching the area, Maman and Isabella found a young child that the bandits had been traveling with, and she was even younger than me. She'd seen the whole incident, and the one that I had been drinking from was her mother.

I watched in horror, with her mother's blood running down my chin, while the girl wailed into Isabella's arms. Though my mother comforted me and told me that I had done nothing wrong, tears ran down my face the entirety of the journey.

We ended up taking the girl to Rhaestras with us, but I couldn't build the courage to speak with her. I stayed tucked into my mother's side the whole time, and cringed away from the little girl, as if I should have been the one afraid of her. She was eventually adopted by a Rhaestran family after a short time living at the Temple and had now joined the echoes of the many spirits that called to me when I was too tired to keep from listening.

My voice wavered as I wove the memory for Elián, but he listened silently, intently. When I finished, I felt the ocean breeze carry the rest of my words out toward the horizon.

After a long, long pause, Elián said, "Would it not be better for you to learn to work with this gift? So that you have more control over it?"

"Easy for you to say." There was no malice in my words, just—exhaustion.

Another long pause from him, and then, "You didn't kill me." The first time we met, the darkness had asked to come out, defend me. I still didn't quite know why I'd held it back.

I shrugged, "It's unpredictable, remember?" But it didn't feel like a random response to Elián. His snort conveyed that he thought as much, too. "And—it's not—it's not all killing." I turned to him for the first time since we had come to this beach, and he was looking at me, too. His brow was raised, waiting for me to elaborate, and I huffed, clenching my eyelids closed, "It's like... I can feel it. Death. And if I let it out, that's *all* I feel." My mind went back to that afternoon chanting on the cobblestones.

Elián's eyes were on mine, searching for something. He chewed at his bottom lip, and his irises were glowing embers as they moved. I counted twelve, shallow breaths, before he spoke, just barely over the rustling of the palm fronds above us, "I left because... I had to."

It took me a moment to realize what he was talking about, and now I was the one searching his face. "Why?"

He turned back toward the water and tucked errant strands of his hair back behind his ears. The urge to run my hands through the silkiness made my fingers twitch, but I held back and waited for his answer. Eight breaths, then ten, and then—

Elián was spun around, crouched, and behind me. Or rather, he had put me behind him while he searched the darkened path that led back to the city. I looked at his shoulders, moving just slightly with his slow breaths, then to where he was facing. There was nothing that I could see or hear, but something had caught his attention enough to brace for an attack. I felt the spider-walking sensation down my back, but could detect nothing but the two of us, the beach, and the city in the distance.

"We should go," he said after slowly straightening. The tone of his voice allowed no argument, and I found myself nodding and standing without complaint. We went much more quickly back to and through the city that was still merry and bustling.

Elián tucked my arm in his as he wove us in and out of the crowded market and streets. And though he kept his face and posture at ease, I could feel his large bicep tensed underneath my palm.

We didn't speak until we were back at our rooms, and this time, he didn't let me enter further than crossing the threshold until he had done a full sweep of every inch. Once he was finished, I flopped down in the nearest armchair. I let my senses widen, search around us, but again, all I could detect were the usual noises of the inn and the other guests, the lapping of the pools downstairs. And the air between Elián and I had tightened again.

His jaw was in that hard set, and his eyes weren't the soft orbs they had been on the beach. He retreated back into his room for a moment, and when he returned, they were like hard, glinting gems. The twin swords were again strapped to his back, and his hands were held behind him in what I now labeled as his Shadow Pose.

"What was it?"

"I don't know." On the beach, we had sat close enough to touch, but now, he stood several feet away from me. Neither of us made a move to continue our conversation from earlier, either. Though the questions were at the back of my tongue, I knew that they would hit the air all wrong and completely undo whatever progress we had made toward not loathing one another.

So, I let my gaze slide away from him, to the floor, and then back to my lap. The urge to take back my earlier confessions and reel them into my heart was fierce. Just as I opened my mouth to—what? Demand he forget it all? Bark some biting words to combat the foolish vulnerability I showed tonight?

Before I could, Elián walked toward me, then around and to the corner he had perched himself on our first night. But on the way, he tossed something onto my lap.

I fumbled with the thin, flopping pages, but I realized that it was three of those magazine-like books. I flipped through the pages, and they looked to be the next three installments of the *Joran* story. The one on top of the pile Elián had given me started right where the last one had left off, with the image of Joran's frightened face taking up the entire first page.

I looked over to my Shadow, but his eyes were staring forward at the door. I sighed and stood, clutching the books to my chest. The floor in here felt cold under my bare feet compared to the warm sand of the beach.

Elián didn't say anything before I fully retreated to my room, and I didn't call back to him either.

22

Once again, we climbed the black and gold steps of Rhaea's Temple. Elián had again taken to walking behind me, and I didn't have the strength or energy to argue with him about it. We hadn't spoken a single word to each other that morning, the routine of dressing and walking to the Temple easy enough to follow. I had dressed in another set of trousers and a top, this time matching the deep blue of the surrounding sea. My Shadow, of course, was in his usual black and had once again donned his leather gloves.

We headed for the door to the cella, and upon pulling back the heavy stone, I stopped in my tracks. There was no one else in the altar room besides a female, kneeling at the feet of the statue of Rhaea. Her head was bent, hands at her brow, and I heard the soft chanting of her prayer to the Goddess. It was in the same rhythm of my chanting in Versillia, and I felt my skin ripple with the flow of her words.

Then the lilting prayer stopped, and the three of us stood in a stilted silence. I held my breath, hand still clutched on the handle of the large door, while I watched the female rise. She was dressed in a deep orange set with wide, flowing trousers and a cropped, full-sleeved top. When she turned to face us, a pathetic little cry bubbled out of my mouth before I could stop it, and I was all but tripping over my feet.

I slammed into hard, warm arms that didn't hesitate to circle around and pull me close. In that moment, I was a girl again, and though she was even shorter than me, I curled into Isabella's chest.

She petted my hair in that comforting, familiar way of hers, and I felt a rumbling purr in my chest.

"It is nice to see you again, little serpent." The lulling rasp of her voice drew out another rumble from my chest, and she chuckled.

I didn't notice another had entered the room until the sound of a quick clearing of a throat snapped me to attention. I stiffened then jerked back from Isabella's embrace when I realized who it was.

Cera circled to stand behind Isabella, not unlike how Elián was standing behind me, I realized, and the four of us stood for a tense moment, observing and settling with one another. The warmth in my chest cooled at Cera's intrusion and all it brought. Seeing Isabella after all this time made me forget for a pleasant few moments about the reason I was here and her efforts to avoid me for the three days before. But now, facing the two of them, I couldn't help letting those thoughts seep back into the forefront of my mind. Isabella's kohl-lined eyes tracked this, but she did not step away.

She raised her hand, with its three tattooed fingers, and lightly traced along my cheekbone. And, for a moment, there was nothing I wanted to do more but to lean into that touch, but Cera's face behind her was hard, murderous, and I didn't move. No, things were different now.

Through tightened teeth, I said, quietly, "You have kept me waiting."

She just smirked at my accusation, not denying it in the slightest. Her cascading dark tresses were swept back from her face with a golden band that matched color of her skin. The light, citrusy perfume of her hair contrasted so deeply with the pulsing, mint-scented power radiating off of her. "And now I am here." Her gaze then flicked to Elián behind me and held him for an arrested breath. When I turned my head just enough to see him, he was completely taut and still, save for his head that was tilted just slightly to the side.

"We have much to discuss, Isabella," I said after turning back to face her.

She continued to look with knowing eyes at Elián behind me, "Yes, I suppose we do." When she finally turned her honey eyes back to me, she said, "We will talk in my office."

Isabella didn't wait for a response, and she walked around Elián and me, back up the aisle toward the exit. Cera moved closely behind her, with Elián and me following. They led us down the winding hallways back to the priestess's wings. And then further, Isabella led us to an area that Cera hadn't shown on our multiple tours of the Temple. But my legs remembered the route to the wing of the High Priestess.

I fought my hesitation and the memories when we reached our destination. It was no longer my mother's, but Isabella's office. And the one across the hall didn't smell of the now-High Priestess like it used to all those years ago, but of Cera.

I swallowed my rising discomfort as we entered the large room. The beautiful, sprawling tapestries were still here, and while the other ones of the Temple also depicted the stories of Rhaea, the ones in here showed her in a different light. The one to my left was as black as the walls and woven with the image of a figure, also just as black but with white, shining thread for her rippling hair. Her eyes of pure gold were cast downwards to the babe in her arms who looked back with the same eyes. But this babe's skin was a deep, warm brown, and her soft, curling hair was the color of her mother's skin.

The birth of Rhaea had been painted and drawn numerous times, but this iteration was by far my favorite. And looking at it now, with the shimmering light coming through the stained-glass window, the betraying vibration of my muscles declared that the darkness in me enjoyed it, too.

Isabella sat underneath the large, circular window cast in angular patterns of purple, gold, and green, and the rest of us stiffly settled around her. It was the same furniture as it had always been, and I found myself sitting in the chair that had always felt like mine. Elián stayed standing behind me, as did Cera with Isabella, and we were again in a tense silence.

The High Priestess was the one to break it first. She pulled her legs to sit cross-legged in her seat and her lips curled up, "I hear you have quite the illustrious career, girl."

My eyes widened and then narrowed sharply. "You've been watching me?" The tone of my voice was much less composed than I had planned for this meeting, but when I looked at Cera, she looked just as incredulous. At least, until she caught herself and smoothed her face into an uncaring mask again.

Isabella flicked her hand, "Of course, I have. It's been good to hear that your training hasn't gone completely to waste. Even if you still deny the gifts Rhaea has given you." But her voice was tinged with palpable affection, perhaps even jesting.

I cleared my throat. "Be that as it may, I am here to talk to you about our requests for you to join the new Lylithan Council."

The warmth of her smile chilled, and I felt my skittering anxiety build. "You are."

"Yes. And I'm sure my brother's letters conveyed the importance of this."

Isabella pursed her lips and swept a look down and up my body, "What is your role in this Council, then, girl?"

"I—um—I'm here as you requested. To discuss this."

"Yes, I can see that. But I asked you what your role is in this group your brother and uncle are building." Her thin brows rose, and I battled with my urge to curl into myself.

No, I was not a child anymore. I lifted my chin, perhaps a bit too defiantly, "I am helping in any way I can. You requested me here and have denied me this meeting for three days. I do expect some answer as to why."

"And I don't have one other than that I was otherwise occupied," She flicked a hand again, but this time in the direction to my right. Cera followed the silent command and began pouring mugs of tea from a steaming kettle. She thrust two of them at Elián, who took a sip of one before handing it to me. Isabella eyed the exchange with the same amusement that Cera had on our first day here.

She took the stone mug Cera offered her and took a sip. "You never were one for patience, girl. I don't know why I halfway expected you to have grown into it after all these years."

"Isabella, are you going to join the Council or not? What are you looking for me to say to you that Mathieu hasn't already explained?"

She jutted her chin at me, "Tell me. Have you returned to Versillia to take your place as the queen the people already say that you are?"

"W—wha—"

Isabella flicked her wrist in the air once again, "Do not gape like a fish, girl. Tales of the Warrior Queen, Protector of Innocents of Versillia have reached even our little island. So, I ask. Have you returned to your homeland to take the throne?"

"No! And—and—I'm not next in line, anyway." Though I meant to keep my voice steady, my panic was rising, and stronger than that was my confusion. Why would I *ever* want that?

She flicked her wrist again, waving away my assertions, "That means nothing. You are a daughter and priestess of Rhaea. She does not give such gifts to those meant to just *help*." Where the fuck was this coming from? If I didn't want to be a priestess of Rhaea, a fact I had made very clear since as early as I could remember, then why the *fuck* would I want to be the actual Queen of Versillia?

But my thoughts were racing too much to do more than grasp on the one thing that felt the most solid, "I am *not* a priestess." It sounded stupid and lame as it left my mouth. Surely Isabella knew this. By the way that Cera was looking at her then at me, she was just as confused. Though I had walked and learned and trained with the priestesses, I had never taken their courses or completed their rights.

Isabella's brows shot to her hairline, "Are you not? It would be foolish of you to deny even further what you are." Before I could retort, she looked behind me, "And you, Master Elián. What is your role in all of this?"

I expected him to remain his usual silent self—so much so that his deep voice startled me. I barely suppressed the shiver that coursed through my body. "I am here to escort her highness as she meets with you and another potential member of the Council."

"And surely, you know that she does not need such an escort."

"My experience thus far would beg to differ, High Priestess." Cera's face cracked into a snicker before settling again, and the shivering sensation within me cracked and dissolved in an instant.

Isabella swept her gaze over Elián again and pursed her lips. "And what are the Shadows' role in this?"

"We, too, are here to help in whatever way we can to ensure the prosperity of our people." His words were so calm, they were almost flat. But I felt a fervent undercurrent to them that I had never heard from him before.

"Hm. And are you on this Council, Meline?"

Her eyes held mine, and I struggled to not look away. Was I? Mathieu, Uncle, and I hadn't really discussed me joining the Council officially. What was the criteria for such a thing? And was what I was already doing what a full member did anyway? I had attended all the meetings since my return to Versillia, I had written correspondences and offered my insight, and here I was on a goddess-damned negotiation tour. "Yes."

If she was surprised, Isabella made no indication. She simply nodded and continued to drink her tea. The three of us waited and watched the High Priestess who made no effort to rush her words. Her golden skin was smooth and hard as porcelain, and she swept a finger covered in curling black tattoos across her brow. "Tell me what you have done with yourself since we last spoke."

This time, I groaned outright at her avoidance, "Isabella, I am here to talk about *you*. Specifically *you* joining the Council. Besides. I thought you were watching me, anyway."

"Tell me, girl." I knew this tone to her voice, lined with a razor edge. So, I drew a breath and remembered my mission. Mathieu had sent me here to win Isabella's approval. I would do this.

After my exhale, I launched into when I had last left Rhaestras. Isabella's pale eyes pinioned me where I sat and pulled out my words so that they flowed steadily. I spoke of fleeing Versillia after the series of Vyrkos attacks. Mathieu and I had both left upon our parents' murders with a smoldering kingdom behind us. I spent the next few decades traveling all over before settling into a routine of taking contracts and building a reputation in the tavern rings. Eventually, I bought an apartment in Nethras, and after an extended visit by Tana, she moved to the city as well. My voice was softer, though, as I detailed the attack Tana and I survived on my birthday and my subsequent return to Versillia just a few weeks ago.

"So, that brings me here. I have seen first hand, many times over, the dangers that our people face. I have lost my parents and two of my best friends, among so many others I once knew. The previous Council, though flawed, did some good work for our people. *We* are now trying to do so as well, and hoping to do even better."

"Hm." Isabella finished her drink and set the handleless mug on the short table between us.

"Who would've thought a direct descendant of Rhaea's power would lower herself to fighting for gambled coin from drunkards," Cera took the opening of Isabella's silence to sneer at me.

My lips curled to bare my fangs, and I leaned toward her in my seat, "You can go fuck yourself, you groveling waste of space. I am *finished* giving you any more of my attention."

Cera began to lunge at me, but Isabella shot out an arm that made her freeze. She glanced at her High Priestess, and I watched her jaw clench in bitter obedience. She settled back to where she had been standing and stared daggers at me.

"Though out of turn, she has a good point, girl. You have had ample time to hone the blessings that Rhaea has given you, but I can see, even now, that you recoil from it in fear." Her voice chilled, "you are the first in a thousand years, and you let yourself crumple instead of rise. Your mother—"

"*Don't.*" I shot my finger at her, and though Cera hissed, baring her own fangs, Isabella did not flinch in the slightest. She hadn't spoken of Maman this entire time, but now she was going to invoke her best friend and predecessor to chastise me? That, I would not let slide.

"Even now, *girl*, I can see it sputtering within you. You have turned away from all the work your mother and I did to help you perfect your gift so that it is *you* in control. And yet, you come here, almost weaker in this than when you were a scrabbling *child*."

I shot to my feet, "*Enough,*" I pointed at her again, "I agreed to come at your request, but I will *not* be further insulted by you or your pathetic protégé. Will you agree to join the Lylithan Council or not—*that* is all I want to hear from you next."

She smirked. And waited.

My chest heaved under my rage that, instead of rising, crested and began to fall. "Surely you know, girl, that you must learn to work *with* your powers before they overtake you," she glanced behind me then met my eyes again. "You have given me much to think about, Mamba. I will see you tomorrow."

I barely let her finish before I spun and left the room.

~

I kept walking, kept going, and, soon, I felt the sand between my toes again. This time, the sun was high in the sky, and the heat was suffocating. I hadn't even bothered putting on my shoes when we left the Temple, and I dropped them in the sand as I headed straight for the water. My fingers found my belt and unbuckled it, letting it and my daggers fall. The sleeveless band of my top was shed next, and then my matching navy trousers, until I was fully bared under the sun. I soon felt the cool lapping of the water and kept on so that I could dive under the clear blue. My limbs fought against the tide, then went with it, as I pushed myself further and further into the ocean. Not until I felt the settling of my anger did I stop swimming or come up for air.

My head broke the surface of the water and turned back toward the beach. I had swum at least two miles, but I could still see Elián sitting amongst my discarded clothing and, further away, the lounging forms of a few that had decided to also brave the midday heat.

"Always tomorrow," I muttered to myself.

I swam much more slowly back to the beach, and when I emerged, I at least felt the comforting warmth of my body having been given some sort of exercise. All this stress, and I had skipped my morning conditioning since the day before I left Versillia.

Elián's eyes stayed on mine as I walked naked toward him. I sat on my trousers, already much warmed by the sun, and drew my knees to my chest.

Though my meeting with Isabella hadn't gone as poorly as the worst of the scenarios I had considered, the clenching in my stomach and throbbing of my head signified that it hadn't been close to the good, either. But, of course she was disappointed in me.

I searched the rise and fall of the waves, the sweeping seagulls overhead, and I knew that she was right. My winters in Rhaestras hadn't just been filled with learning about plants or learning how to yield a sword. They had also included sitting with Isabella and my mother as they searched the histories and texts of Rhaea for tales of the Death Wielders. There was limited mention of them, with many theorizing priestesses claiming that Rhaea had ceased doling out such powers after the last of the Death Wielders had been killed off. Rhaea being the Goddess of Death had become somewhat of a secret after this, to prevent more priestesses being killed out of fear that they, too, could contort and deliver Death with just a thought.

Under Maman and Isabella's guidance, I *had* been able to let it in without being overcome with the whispers of the spirits around me.

At night, this had been the worst, but one winter, I had finally been able to sleep the night without hearing a single spirit. And another winter, I had laughed triumphantly as I curled the inky smoke around my fingers before sucking it back into my pores. My mother and Isabella had smiled over the library table at me and requested for me to try it again, which I did successfully.

But after the school, I *couldn't* risk pulling it out at will. That night it had started to inch toward Elián was the first time I'd seen the manifestation of my curse with my own eyes since that horrific day that changed everything. Ending a life with my blades was always justified, often necessary, but ending lives with *that*? Feeling the loss of lives around me with that? A shudder of delectation raced down my spine.

"What did you think of the other installments of the story?" Elián's voice was almost drowned out by the tide.

I rested my cheek on my knee and looked at him. "I enjoyed them. Did you buy the next one?"

He shook his head, continuing to look out at the water, "No. But I can." His skin already looked a half-shade darker here, under the scorching sun. But no sweat beaded at his brow, and he let his hair flap wildly with the sea breeze. The thin chain at his neck shined.

"I would like that." Elián didn't acknowledge my words, just continued to watch the waves, and I turned back to watch them, too.

Eventually I stood and waded out into the water again, but I only went so far as to need to tread water to keep my head above the surface. I floated on my back for a while and let my hair spread out around my head. The sun beat down, and the water crashed around me, over me. But I stayed, letting it push me out toward the horizon and then back toward the island, over and over again.

We were set to meet Roalld in Nethras in six short days, and if Isabella refused to give me an answer by the time our ship set sail in two, what then? Even though she had done this to Mathieu, played games and exerted her own wicked sense of control, the stabbing of her words was so personal. To her, I was a failure, not just disgracing the memory of her deceased friend, but her patron Goddess Herself.

But Isabella would never understand. Cera and Elián would never understand. He didn't have the weight of the Goddess on his back, and the powers bestowed on Cera, Isabella, and my mother were *life*, healing. And while death was its own kind of balm, there was no one to guide me. So what else was I supposed to make of what the fucking Goddess had given me?

The sun began its descent, and I cycled my arms backwards and let my legs paddle lazily. The sand felt even hotter when I made my way back to Elián, who hadn't moved in the time I spent in the ocean. He sunned himself, eyes closed, as I shook off most of the water that still clung to my skin and wrung out my hair. I quickly pulled on my trousers and slipped my damp head through the halter neck of my top. Elián stood and swatted the sand off of his own trousers while I buckled my blades back onto my waist.

"Tomorrow."

23

After returning to our rooms to bathe and change, Elián and I again returned to the streets of Rhaestras. The dress I wore was the color of ripe cranberries, and my Shadow had changed into a clean set of the same clothes he had been wearing this morning. He grumbled when I requested for him to leave the swords in the room and brandish a less-conspicuous assortment of weapons instead, but he eventually complied when I argued that they just brought me *more* attention.

Mentally, I was exhausted from my failure of a meeting with Isabella, but staying in the inn with my silent companion and my roaring thoughts was much worse than venturing outside.

"We're going to go out and try to have some fun, so *please* don't glower and just act like an actual person," I said to Elián as we hit the iridescent pavement. He huffed quietly but extended his elbow to me. And after a second of hesitation, I tucked my arm into his, and we actually began to stroll.

As we went, I pointed to buildings and businesses, indicating which ones were unchanged from my childhood and which ones were different. "And that used to be a bakery that was my mother's favorite." It was now a tavern of some sort, and patrons holding mugs of ale and glasses of wine chatted happily within. Though Elián continued with me in silence, his eyes followed where I pointed each time.

We came upon one of the two pharmacies within the city, and I pulled us inside. It was small and lined with rows of neat wooden shelving packed with medicines and toiletries of all sorts. A fat, orange and white cat was curled up on the counter at the back, and when we approached, it twitched its long tail in interest.

It didn't take long for a small, eager female to emerge from a back room. She blinked her large, blue eyes at the two of us, and her features and scent reminded me of Kiava from the inn.

"Can I help you?" She asked cheerfully. If I had to guess, she had just recently reached adulthood.

The light of childhood was still lingering behind her eyes, and I couldn't help but respond just as cheerfully, "I need to send three letters, please."

"Of course!" She ducked under the counter, and then produced some stationary and indicated a basket that held various writing utensils. "Just let me know when you're ready to send them out!"

She picked up the cat and walked toward the many aisles behind us. Elián leaned beside me against the counter, and I set out on the first of my letters. I informed Mathieu and Uncle of my meeting with Isabella tomorrow. Instead of telling them that the first had gone so poorly, I kept my update vague and framed tomorrow as a continuation of our conversations. I sealed that envelope and wrote its destination on the front. The second letter, I wrote to Tana, expressing my regret for not having brought her, the absolute gall of Cera even after all of these years, and my promise to bring her on my next journey.

The last, I wrote for Nethras. The previous one I sent had described the beauty of Versillia, including my brother's stables and all the various tasks my cousin's coven sisters had put me through. In this one, though, I wrote of Rhaestras, and I tried to paint the best image I could of the city and beaches. The fluorescent lagoon and Temple were difficult to describe, and I included rough sketches of them both to hopefully fill in the gaps that my words couldn't. After three pages, I finally signed off on the letter and sealed and addressed it.

Just as I was gathering them and tidying the counter, the female and cat came back to the desk.

"Ready?" I nodded. She first grasped my letter to Mathieu and my uncle and quickly read over the destination. Nodding to herself, she passed a steady hand over the front. Then, in a practiced, effortless motion, she held the letter between her dark brown hands and released them with a toss of her wrists. There was a fleeting flash of light and my letter was gone. She did the same with my letters to Tana and to Little Marco. "Is there anything else I can do for you?"

She scratched the head of the cat as I reached in my pocket and produced three copper coins and placed them on the counter. "No, that will be all. Thank you!" She nodded warmly and palmed my postage fee.

When Elián and I made our way back outside, the last light from the sun was gone completely, and my stomach was rumbling. But I wanted to keep moving.

We walked into the market, making an intentional path to the food carts that were parked closer to the center. I scanned my eyes over them, inhaling the smell of roasting and frying.

I tugged on our intertwined arms and looked up at him, "Are you in the mood for anything in particular?"

He was looking over the carts as I had, and I couldn't help but admire the hard angle of his jaw and the pleasant curve of his lip that was the supple medium between thin and full. Perhaps if things were different, if we were different people and he wasn't such an asshole...

The thought of Elián's scowl at being called that word seemed comical now, and I didn't realize that I was grinning at him until I saw that his eyes were now on me. They swept up to my hair that was now piled on the top of my head in a mass of frizzy coils, and then they moved down to my face. His thick, black brows tightened just a fraction, "What?"

"I was just thinking about how you reacted when I called you an asshole the day after we met."

I actually giggled this time when he just exhaled and rolled his eyes, "I am fine with whatever. You pick."

Though there were a few seating areas interspersed throughout the market, particularly near the food carts, I chose a vendor that grilled their meat on wooden skewers. I ordered four that alternated large pieces of steak with onion and peppers. They had more of the spiced mango, and I ordered some of that as well. After paying, Elián and I continued to walk, this time chewing on our supper.

We left the market and its crowd and found ourselves walking toward the lagoon. It wasn't clear who had initiated the route, but neither of us refused, and just as we both finished our meat and vegetables, we arrived at the stone ledge.

The waves here were much quieter than the beach on the other side of the city, and we both looked out on the glowing water with mutual admiration. A large turtle moved slowly directly beneath us, and a couple a little ways down pointed at the creature with quiet glee.

"Have you met Isabella before?" I wasn't quite sure where the question had come from. I had been trying so hard not to think of the High Priestess or our miserable morning, but something about the way she had been looking at Elián kept tugging at me.

"No."

I turned to him, and instead of keeping his gaze on the lagoon, he turned to me, too. "She looked at you multiple times like she knew of you. Why?"

He pursed his lips for a moment, actually considering my words instead of denying them outright. He blinked for a bit longer than necessary, and I felt my insides clench. But whatever he had begun to say came out different, flat. "I'm not sure." I opened my mouth to call him on his hesitation and demand what he was thinking, but he added, "I have never met her before."

And this rang true. I wasn't sure how I knew, but when his words hit my ears, an awareness in the back of my mind was assured. I passed my tongue over my front teeth, "How do you think that went? The meeting with her, I mean."

He considered this, too. His eyes went to my hair again then back to mine, "It could have gone better."

The soft laugh I gave was bitter, hopeless. "Obviously."

Elián tilted his head to the side, "And do you? Want to take your throne?"

This time, I threw my head back and barked to the sky. "Why the hell would I want that? And it's not *mine*."

He shrugged the claim off just as Isabella had. "There is nothing that says that you can't. And your High Priestess spoke truth—you are already known to your people as well as to others as a queen. The idea is not as impossible as you are making it out to be."

"El, it *is* ridiculous. I haven't even been there for Versillia through all of this. It's been Mathieu and my uncle this whole time working for our people. If anything, one of them should sit on the throne. And if we're going by birth order, it should go to my brother, anyway."

Elián had a curious look in his sunset eyes, but after a moment, he shrugged, "And yet, neither of them are king. And like you have said before, you are helping now. If you do not want the throne, that is one thing. But Isabella was right in pointing out that it is available to you."

I crossed my arms over my chest, "Well, I *don't* want it. Would *you* trade your freedom to be shackled to a seat and crown full of nothing but responsibilities and politics?"

He answered immediately, "No. I wouldn't."

My shoulders rose, then fell. I picked up the paper cone I had balanced on the stone ledge and held it out to him. He plucked a sticky piece of spiced mango and popped it into his mouth. Again he blinked a beat longer than necessary, but instead of hesitation, it was satisfaction, maybe even delight.

I ate one, too, and then we both took turns eating the fruit until there was nothing but a gloopy mess of orange and red in the empty cup. He took it from my hands and put our discarded skewers into it. "So, what do you do for fun? When you aren't working, I mean." A soft wind swept past us, but it just carried the smell of salt and seaweed.

He leaned an elbow on the ledge and glanced to the lagoon then back to me, "A little of this, a little of that." I gave an insolent scoff and pressed forward, mimicking his posture and waited. It didn't take as long as I expected for him to relent. "I read. I enjoy being outdoors."

I nodded, though these were all things I knew about my Shadow. But he had at least answered the question. "I enjoy those things, too. And do you only read those picture books, then?"

"No. I read other things as well." He turned to look again at the water, trying to effectively end the conversation, though his body was still slightly angled toward me.

And in that moment, I felt a boldness, a desire to shock him from trying to ignore me again. "And who do you spend your free time with, then? Family? Friends? Lovers?"

While I did get my wish in Elián turning back to me, he looked angry again. I didn't expect him to answer, though. "Some."

An admission and also none at all. I pressed, "Master Noruh?"

His forehead wrinkled, and it looked like I had indeed shocked him out of whatever irritation my question had sent him into. "She is my sister Shadow."

I curled my hand in a gesture for him to continue, "Yes, I realize that. But are you friends or lovers? Both? I would be very shocked to hear you are blood related." But he just kept looking at me with that expression. His lips were tightened into a flat line, and he said nothing. I had scented them on each other back in Versillia, and I didn't know why his caginess was bothering me so much.

Though he'd once had his fingers and tongue buried inside of me, I was not deluded into thinking I had any claim over Elián. Perhaps it was due to this being one of the few things about him that I knew for certain. Perhaps it was because he still had refused to acknowledge what had happened between us. And while it hadn't quite changed our dynamic completely, there was a palpable shift.

While he was obviously content to ignore it, I held no such sentiments. Frankly, fucking my Shadow would provide some relief from the tension between us and be a welcome distraction from the mess of everything else.

Each time I bathed since that afternoon, I had pleasured myself at the thought of him between my thighs. I imagined twining my legs around his waist while we glared at each other, moved with each other. When I plunged my own fingers into myself in the steamy bliss of the shower, I thought instead of him pressing me into the tile, fisting my hair and taking me from behind.

He'd said it wasn't against whatever rules or protocols that The Shadows followed, but there was something that was holding him back. Did he still hate me so much that we couldn't take pleasure with one another? He was surely attracted to me, at least physically.

I traced my gaze over his form, and though I hadn't seen much of him, what I had felt so far left me wanting more. When he had touched me, tasted me, he hadn't let me see his face, even though he held me within an inch of my life. In that second, looking over the lagoon, I wanted nothing more than to see what Elián looked like with his head thrown back in ecstasy, what sounds he would make with my fist wrapped around him.

Elián's face whipped around, and his nostrils were flaring.

And that had been on purpose, hadn't it? He could do his best to ignore my words, but the aroma of arousal that my musings had been conjuring would be much harder to disregard. Though I wouldn't call myself the most forward person, I had long ago decided that I had no desire to mince words when it came to sex.

I took a step closer to Elián and closed the space between us, to the point that if either of us decided to take a deep breath, our chests would meet again. He looked down his nose at me, nostrils still flaring, so I pushed onto my toes.

He was still leaning on the ledge, and now I was able to brush my nose against his and feel his breath on my face. Elián still didn't pulled away.

I took another leap and pressed my palms onto his chest, felt his heart pounding beneath his skin. Just before I moved my lips to his, I couldn't help but smirk in triumph.

Everything stopped, and I couldn't even hear the sound of the waves anymore. All that I sensed, I felt, was Elián's soft lips meeting mine and the sound of his heart beating.

I brought my hands to his freshly shaved jaw and tilted my head, deepening my kiss. And again, to my surprise, he met me, tilting his head in the opposite direction and opening his mouth at the gentle prodding of my tongue.

I wrapped my arms around his neck and felt his arms do the same to my waist. The skirt of my dress was short, just brushing the middle of my thighs, and with Elián's hold, I felt it ride up even further. Our bodies pressed together, and it was as though a statue, a sculpture, had come to life and pulled me in. My fingers tangled in the silky waves of his hair, and when my fingernails brushed lightly on his scalp, I felt, rather than heard, the soft rumbling from his chest.

Suddenly, the backs of my thighs were kissing the warm stone of the ledge, and I nipped at Elián's lip. He bit mine back, and our kiss turned into something more frantic, more intense. His hands reached up to my hair, and his leather touch was gentle and firm. He didn't make the misguided attempt to try to bury his fingers in it. Instead, he caressed my curls with one hand, and with the other, he pawed my lower back, pulling me closer.

The desire to kiss him had been swift and devious, but this was—something else. My body was thrumming with lust and a need that, if I had been able to think clearly, should have scared me.

As his tongue curled around one of my fangs, teasing it and drawing out a soft moan from my throat, I had the hot, fleeting thought that I would let him consume me in every way. And the darkness was stirring with the same need as that night it broke past my shields—it longed to unfurl and welcome the heat of my Shadow, to twine with it and maybe just let him truly set me aflame.

Elián moved to my neck, kissing, biting, licking, and I felt the rest of my coherent thoughts slipping away. My toes curled as his grip moved to my hip, with only the leather of his glove separating our skin. I opened my legs even wider and felt him hard between them.

Would he fuck me in front of the twinkling water of the Goddess?

I moved my touch down his chest. He shivered and tipped my head forward again, crashing his lips into mine.

My palm traced further down Elián's front to find the straining of his erection against the waistband of his black trousers. My body somehow felt hotter, even more desperate, and I needed to feel it, taste it, take it.

He groaned into my mouth when I brushed my fingers over the tip. The headiness of this moment, this connection, notched up even higher, and I didn't think at all as I flattened my palm and applied pressure on his deliciously hard shaft. It twitched under my touch, and Elián's lips left mine.

His neck arched back, and I watched with nothing but hunger as I caught his flushed skin and swollen lips and black lashes fluttering on his cheeks. I gripped him further and moved my hand back and forth, wanting to see him come apart, to give him what he had already given to me.

He flinched. The lightning crackling between us stilled, and it was like he turned back to stone. His hands left my skin, my hair, and gripped the ledge at either side of my hips. He bared his fangs, and the lips that had just danced with mine were curled in anger, revulsion.

"Don't. Do that."

I realized that my hand was still frozen on him. He was still hard, pulsing against me, but the burning need in my stomach to yield to him turned acidic and sickening. My hands flew to my chest, and I trapped my fingers within each other. My knuckles cracked at the strain, but my body was still throbbing, fighting with the ebbing desire to touch him still.

But the way he had looked at me—I cut my head to the side and clenched my eyes shut. I fought like hell to breathe deeply, but the waning scent of his arousal twined with mine was mocking in its temptation. I sucked in air through my slightly parted lips. Four shallow breaths, five, six, and I finally felt the warmth of his presence step back.

I hopped down from the ledge, and I felt the slap of cobblestone underneath my feet. Without looking, I reached behind me to grab the cup and skewers from a lifetime ago. Earlier today, Isabella's words felt like a cold blade scraping my heart. But I now knew that that had been nothing, nothing, compared to the way Elián's words and expression turned my insides to ash.

Kissing my Shadow had been such a stupid fucking idea. Considering opening up for him, wanting to give him everything, whatever he asked, had been misguided and, evidently, the opposite of what he wanted. I kept my eyes on my feet as I stomped back toward the city. The taste of him was still on my lips, and no matter how many times I swiped the back of my hand on them, it lingered. It was inside my mouth, my throat.

He, of course, silently trailed after me, but I didn't allow myself to look back as I threw our garbage into a receptacle on a street corner. I didn't allow myself to think of anything other than getting back to my room and being as alone as I could.

When we finally climbed the stairs of the lodging house, and I unlocked the door, almost snapping the key with how forcefully I turned it, Elián's arm shot out to block me when I started toward my door. I jerked back from his touch, and it took the entire time of his search of the space for me to collect myself, straighten my spine. He took his position in the corner, and neither of us said a word to each other.

The slam of my bedroom door rattled its frame. But here, in the darkness of my room, I was finally alone. On the walk back, the pressure in my chest had built more and more, and my shields were failing. Upon the safety of being alone, behind a closed door, I threw my head back and let it out.

All was silent, but my power spilled out of me. It came out of my fingers and my chest, and the inky black was like vines rooted deep within my skin. The tendrils grew and clung to my body, wrapping me in cool reassurance, and I was too exhausted to resist.

I welcomed their embrace, and with each second beyond my walls, the darkness solidified. Maman and Isabella had attempted to train me before, and at that time, I'd grown to feel a tenuous neutrality with my abilities. What happened between us afterwards had shattered that common ground until... until now.

Because now, it wasn't a lashing out that dealt destruction or an assaulting carrier of the voices of troubled souls. The ebony veins swept across my skin with a new tenderness that felt infinite. It was rest, it was solace, and I collapsed onto the bed while the darkness wrapped me in a blanket of the abyss that was always waiting within. Though I had denied it, leashed it, my curse begged to take care of me.

And I allowed it, sighing into its hold that wasn't asking for anything other than for me to let it exist and be alive.

It brushed my ear, like Maman's soothing touch from my childhood, and a new calmness pressed on my heart. I curled into myself on the covers and let Death lull me to sleep.

~

I held my own gaze as I braided my hair. A joint, half smoked, balanced between my lips, and my fingers were careful and unrelenting as they fastened my hair as tight as possible to my scalp. When I had woken up, my power had sunk back into my body, but its presence was more awake and closer to my conscious awareness than ever before.

The two plaits I made sealed themselves as my coils locked into place, and I threw them behind my shoulders. The wrapping paper crackled, dissolved, and ashed into the porcelain sink basin at my inhale.

I was going to meet with Isabella, and she would meet our terms. None of her insults would cut me again. She could throw out her words, and Cera could spit her venom, but I had a new armor, a new cocoon.

My palm flew up and cracked against my cheek, the pain welcome, needed. I finished my joint and my dressing and didn't waste time.

The smoke and steam rushed out with me, and I didn't say anything to Elián as I walked out the door. If I gave myself enough time to think about last night, to think about where I was going, the guilt and shame might creep back up again. And right then, I needed this wall of purpose.

The jungle gardens came nearer and nearer, and I threw off my sandals, not bothering to carry them with me. The guards could keep watch of them or let them be stolen—I couldn't care less. What mattered was this meeting and my mission and eventually returning home.

A hair-thin crack formed at the thought—*where is home, now?* But I commanded the darkness within me to patch over the worry and flatten it into submission. The anxious mumbling quieted to a faint whisper.

And I had been just distracted enough by trying to wield my power within my own mind that I hadn't seen Cera coming until she was before me, blocking my path. I snarled at her, fingers curling into claws. Of *course* she would try to stop me now. But at that moment, I was prepared to kill her before she could try.

The haze of my wrath froze and cleared all at once when I saw her face. Her copper skin was pale, her eyes red. But despite her troubling appearance, her voice was steady and commanding. "Come with me," she said.

But she wouldn't quite meet my gaze. She spun on her heel and began to walk further toward the Temple. I felt my burning intention from earlier turn to ice. "What's wrong?" Cera kept moving, and I now saw her steps were rigid, jerky. She didn't answer me and kept walking while I stayed where I was. "What. Happened." Cera stopped in her tracks, and under the canopy of Rhaea's jungle garden, she slowly turned to me.

And I saw it all in her eyes. The hazel was dark and glassy, and my stomach dropped. I rushed forward and caught her before she collapsed, sobbing. My hands clasped around her, and I felt her shudder, felt her tears soaking my top.

Cera wailed into my shoulder, and I pet her hair. I took it in. "She's gone."

24

I didn't bother counting the breaths. I didn't look to Elián, though I could feel him behind me.

Cera continued to cry into my arms, and I held her tight. No tears fell from me, but I couldn't keep the dry heaves from my chest from joining Cera's. She didn't need to say anything else. I swallowed her grief and outrage and sorrow.

Isabella was dead.

I knew it like I knew the moment my parents had been killed. I knew it like the moment I knew that Shoko and Lee had been killed. Even more, after accepting what my curse confirmed, I could feel that her soul was gone from this realm, too. It was like a chord that tied me to her since the moment our paths had crossed was cut cleanly with the sharpest of shears. It was an absence I knew in my bones when I thought of her.

Cera shifted, her cries grown more subdued after those heartbreaking moments in my arms. When she straightened, I didn't flinch when her brow pressed to mine. It was clammy, and some of my warmth transferred to her. Under the skin of my forehead, my power tingled, and I could actually taste her grief on my tongue. It was a cold burning that surged with every breath she took, pulling back when she calmed a moment, but rearing forward the next.

We took a deep breath together, sucking in the same air, letting it fall out of our noses. One of her tears splashed onto my forearm and trailed down my skin. I started another breath and she followed. When it was complete, she pulled back, but we still clung to each others' forearms.

I hadn't been here when her first High Priestess died, but I could imagine that she had cried like this. And something about that image, of Cera breaking down about my mother in the way she did now, warmed my heart toward her. I could also imagine that the one holding her at that time had been Isabella. Now she was gone, too.

We released each other at the same time, and my eyes swept up and down Cera's form. I knew that she wouldn't speak it now, but I was looking at the new High Priestess of Rhaea.

She turned and led us to the Temple without another word. Elián and I followed, and when the jungle garden finally parted, we came upon absolute silence.

The Temple had always teemed with the chattering of Rhaea's most faithful followers, but now, there was no one in sight. The sprawling, onyx structure seemed even more ominous now. For one of our kind to die, you had to be killed or be very, very old. Just like she didn't have to tell me that Isabella was dead, Cera did not need to tell me that it had been murder.

We walked up the steps, and I felt the crowded, frantic energy coming from the cella. It made sense that most of the priestesses would retreat to Rhaea's altar room to pray to the Goddess and light a candle for their High Priestess that had gone to join Her. The path Cera carved, however, bypassed the cella completely, and we soon found ourselves in the High Priestess's wing. The smell of violence and blood had started itching my nostrils as soon as we started to climb the steps of the Temple, and as we drew closer, it assaulted my senses and made my powers stir.

Cera stopped us at the mouth of the corridor. Isabella had been murdered in her office, then.

I felt a vine of my power flow out of my fingertip, and I let it continue to test the air. Pulling it back into myself felt too large of a feat at the moment, and letting it split and curl around my hand and up my arm felt... good.

I allowed myself a deep breath, and the darkness didn't ask for more, satisfied with how much freedom I was giving it. It continued to slither and pulse around my left hand, but it didn't grow and didn't try to explore anything else.

My feet moved forward, and I crept up to Isabella's door. Her death had been violent, and the smell of her blood was almost overpowering. Though she had been harsh, sometimes incredibly cold, Isabella was *the* master healer. Her powers and blood had brought many back from the brink of death. I pushed the door open and made myself look. The taste of it was acrid, too rich, and for a moment, I felt unable to move.

Isabella was a proficient fighter, having been trained in the way Cera and I and all the priestesses had. She put up a fight. The tapestry of Rhaea's birth was torn at the bottom and on a pile on the floor, the chair behind her desk was tipped backwards, and there was a shattered mug on the floor beside it.

I could see the movement of the struggle, almost like shadows replaying the scene. Isabella had been sitting at her desk, working on something, when someone attempted to attack her unawares. One of our first lessons was to always, always be armed, and Isabella had reacted quickly and taken her own dagger to her attacker. There were quick, angular splatter lines of blood that weren't hers on one of the walls, and droplets of it on the rug. They smelled like sweet, powdery roses.

The fight brought them across the room, where the tapestry had been pulled from where it had hung for hundreds of years. Eventually, whoever it was that wanted Isabella dead got their wish and overpowered her. The large puddle of her blood closer to where I stood told of her trying to draw attention to anyone that could help her. Another lesson we learned training at the Temple was knowing when you were outmatched. Isabella was no fool, and she had almost made it, most certainly to make the intrusion known to Cera or anyone else close enough to intervene. I took a deliberate sniff of the air, and her blood at my feet held two distinct notes. Some felt thicker, heavier, and some were lighter. A throat torn and a heart ripped, then. That was how Isabella had been killed.

I crouched and hovered my left hand over the evidence of Isabella's fatal injury. Lylithans were hard to kill, but even we could not regrow a heart.

My curse was tentative as it unfurled toward the mess on the floor but grew surer as I gave it permission to grow. The vines turned to an inky smoke, and I watched in a mixture of wariness and awe.

It spread over the area, reading it, smelling it, and through its connection, I felt Isabella and her attacker. With my own sense of smell, I already knew of her outrage and the attacker's vicious intentionality. But with Rhaea's death wielding, I felt them as if they were within me. Isabella had not been afraid—she had been furious. Though there was no way for me to know her thoughts in her last moments, I felt her... disappointment.

The smoke turned back into those black vines, and they retreated to my skin, curling around my hand like an intricate piece of living jewelry. I twisted my hand and watched as the vines continued to move and shift, as if relishing the feeling of the outside of my skin. My heart calmed as it became clear that it was, again, here to help me, work with me, instead of incinerating all of those around me. I pushed myself back to stand and felt Cera and Elián's presence at my back.

I glanced over my shoulder, "Were you the one to find her?" Cera nodded solemnly. Stray pieces of her black hair curled around her brow in a messy halo. "And where did you put her?"

She whispered, "In one of the medical rooms. We gathered all of the—the evidence from her body that we could before cleaning and wrapping her. Meline..." She held back a sob, and when she collected herself, she whispered, "Did she—did she suffer?"

Not in the way you are asking, I wanted to say. But how could I explain to Cera, that the only mother she had left spent her last moment, her last second in this realm, being disappointed in herself. So, I said simply, "No. The death itself was quick."

Cera's relief was palpable, and I was glad I was able to give that to her.

She looked down at my hand, where the mark of my curse was still reveling in the outside. I fought my reflex to snatch it back, to hide the evidence of it from the world and myself. But last night had changed something between us. At least for now.

Elián's voice broke whatever trance my power put Cera in, "Can you see who did this?" She swallowed and looked back at me, and her eyes echoed my Shadow's question.

I shook my head, "No. It's not—it's not a clear picture. It was a Vyrkos."

"Well, we knew that already," but her remark was weak and lacked its usual taunting edge.

"I can feel the intention of whoever did this. Like their sole purpose was to kill her specifically. But there were no feelings beyond that," my words were slow but deliberate as I worked through the conclusions as I spoke. "I think whoever did this was sent here by someone else. The killer themselves didn't feel like they had a connection to Isabella other than her being their target."

Cera took an uneasy scan of the office, and I wondered if, when she inevitably took her oaths, she would claim this space as her own. Or was it too tainted, now? The blood could be cleaned, the furniture and tapestries repaired or replaced. But the smell of violent death would permeate for a long, long while.

She turned away, her face taking on a green undertone that I couldn't blame her for, and walked across the hall. She pushed her door open as I closed the one to Isabella's, but that did little to dull the smell of death.

The three of us entered Cera's office. It was about half the size of Isabella's but it was no less extravagant. More tapestries of Rhaea hung on the walls, but they all showed the Goddess in Her maturity. Some were like the depictions of Her in the temple my brother had constructed for our mother—images of Her healing and embracing. In these, She was every bit of the Goddess of Life and New Beginnings. But there was a large one hung behind Cera's black desk that showed the Goddess of Death.

There were no other figures woven around Rhaea. The piece of art displayed the Mother's first born, standing tall and wrapped in cascading lavender fabric. Her hands were outstretched like Her statue in the cella, and from Her three blackened fingers on each hand, extended dark tendrils that curled and turned to a cloud at Her feet.

I stumbled into one of the seats in front of Cera's desk but couldn't take my eyes off of the tapestry. I had seen artwork of Rhaea using this facet of Her power before, but never this particular one. And it had never felt so personal, so familiar. I looked down to my own darkness still weaving itself around my skin, forever shifting.

"What did you do with her blade?"

Cera sat down in her seat behind the desk and looked down at her lap. She took a moment to respond, and through tight teeth, she said, "It was gone when we found her."

So whoever did this took it, then. And I didn't need to speculate as to why, "To ensure their payment, surely."

She furrowed her brow, "How do you know that? Could they not have taken it as a trophy of some sort? To gloat that they had killed a high priestess. The most powerful one in the realm, at that?"

I shrugged, "As I said before, the killer had no feelings toward Isabella other than cold intention." I detected the faint rustle of fabric as Elián shifted behind me. We both knew. "I know it because I've felt this way, myself. When you are hired to dispatch someone, if you are any good anyway, there is no desire apart from getting the job done and getting payment."

Her eyes widened, and she appraised me with this new knowledge. Obviously, Isabella hadn't shared with Cera the information she had collected on me over the years, and my old opponent hadn't known about this part of my career. "And you, Master Elián? In your line of work, is this accurate?"

I didn't allow myself to turn toward his voice, but it was flat and certain, "Yes. Her Highness speaks true."

Her Highness. I tsked and cut Cera a sideways glance, "Can't take my word for it, Cobra?"

A shade of her usual slithering smirk swept her lips, "I have to consider all the possibilities, Mamba."

I felt myself mirror her, and just as I was about to respond, someone knocked and stepped into the office. Jesyn's scent of coconut and sunshine followed her as she walked in and stopped beside Cera. She bowed to her, saluting, before hastily doing the same to me. When she stood, though, I saw the dark blue shadows beneath her large eyes. "The rest of the guards have arrived, and all the priestesses have been notified of the bar on traveling beyond the Temple grounds, Your Graciousness."

"Thank you, Jesyn. Has anything else been found?" The priestess stood stiff, cutting her eyes to me and Elián then back to Cera. But Cera waved away her hesitation.

Jesyn pressed, "Are—" she took a deep breath.

"Out with it."

"There is some evidence of the southern entrance being breeched. The intruder's scent is strong there. But we are still investigating how they were able to enter. Only priestesses are able to access that door." Her eyes were nothing but accusatory as they focused on me. I raised my elbow to rest on the arm of my seat and settled my chin on my fingers. The priestess sucked in a gasp when she finally noticed the shifting on my skin. It tickled my jaw, but I held the priestess's eyes with mine. She dared to think that I had something to do with this.

Cera sighed loudly, "They had nothing to do with this. And if you used your nose at all, Jesyn, their scents are not entwined with the High Priestess's murder."

"But they pointed out that someone had been hired to do this. Could they have not outsourced such a thing? You said you were going to consider all possibilities." She had been listening from outside, then. Probably creeping just on the edge of the hallway the whole time.

I rolled my eyes, "Though I wanted to strangle her for insulting me yesterday, I had no reason to kill Isabella. The reason I am here was to get her on the Lylithan Council. And in case your grief is clouding all your sense of reason, priestess, I would need Isabella alive to accomplish this." Because what the fuck would the Council do now that she was gone?

Jesyn glared at me, but Cera chuckled, "She has a point. Besides," Cera picked underneath her fingernails, "they were both at the lodging house all night during the time of the intrusion. The letters Mamba sent out last night were to her family and to some child in Nethras. They did not communicate with anyone else after leaving the Temple, and, I strongly doubt that the Queen Protector of Innocents hired a Vyrkos assassin to murder the last maternal figure we had in this realm. It is possible, certainly, but there is more evidence to the contrary."

My and Jesyn's mouths hung open. Cera had taken a note out of her predecessor's book, but I didn't feel offended at the fact she had us followed. I would have done the same thing. "How long?"

She flipped her long, unraveling braid behind her back, "Since you disembarked on the island."

My grin was sudden but genuine. Another move I would have made as well. The longstanding rivalry between us shifted again. My mind called back to the presence Elián felt on the beach the previous evening.

I'd also caught her naming Isabella as a maternal figure for the both of us, and the label felt accurate. Isabella had been more than my mother's protégé and best friend. The shame I felt at her chastising yesterday only cut so deeply because of the pedestal I had placed her on before I could consciously do such a thing. When I thought of power, of regality, the first that came to my mind was Maman. And after that, Isabella. And now both were dead.

The four of us continued to theorize about Isabella's murder. Of course, in her position of power, there were many that would feel threatened by her. But the order of ascension to High Priestess of Rhaea was locked tightly within the Temple ranks. There were no outsiders that could possibly have claim to the title, and though she wasn't my favorite person, Cera loved Isabella tremendously. In my —assessment of the murder scene, I knew that Isabella hadn't known her attacker. If she wanted to kill her superior, Cera would have done the deed herself.

So, for what reason would someone want Isabella dead? If it wasn't to clear the way for them to take her position, it was for some other motive that none of us could quite pinpoint. Though Cera was the closest with her, Isabella had kept many of her dealings and comings and goings close to her chest. There were too many variables and too many unknowns.

Eventually, I went back to Isabella's office and carefully walked about the room. My power shifted into that smoke and hovered around my hand. I passed it over her desk, but only felt her surprise and reaction to the intruder. My feet carried me toward the window, and the smell of the unknown assailant stopped there. They must have escaped that way, then.

When I returned to the hallway, I faced Cera, Jesyn, and Elián. The two priestesses looked exhausted, and he looked... blank. I cleared my throat and detailed what I was able to glean from my more thorough look at Isabella's office. There weren't any new details, really, and the females' shoulders sagged at the same time.

"Is there anything else I can do?" I tried to keep the hopelessness from my voice, but it was inevitable. Even letting out my power provided no real help. No real reassurance. Because holding the power of Death only went so far—I couldn't bring anyone back, and though some of the ancient reports from priestesses past spoke of some Death Wielder's abilities to speak to souls that clung to the realm, all parts of Isabella were gone. She had accepted her fate and went to her Goddess as soon as she took her last, shallow breath. We were no closer to finding out who had done this. Perhaps we would never know.

"No. But... I thank you, Meline." Cera jutted her chin at my left hand, and I managed a shaky response. I truly didn't know what I was doing, and Isabella's judgement rang through my mind. If I hadn't been running from my powers all these years, maybe I would be better at this.

"When is the ceremony?"

Cera shifted uncomfortably on her feet, "Tonight." I had never seen the funeral rites of a High Priestess, but the story of my mother's own rise to the helm was clear in my mind. After the prayers and burning of the preceding leader were complete, the next would take the oath.

I nodded. This time tomorrow, I would be boarding a ship to Nethras. And this time tomorrow, Cera would be the High Priestess of Rhaea.

25

My pen hovered over the stationary. For the past ten minutes, I had been struggling with starting my letter to Versillia. How could I tell them that not only had my task in Rhaestras concluded incomplete, but the High Priestess had been murdered while I was here?

The pharmacy's cat eyed me lazily and its tail tapped the back of my hand while I debated. There was no avoiding it, but they would also want answers that I couldn't give. I left the priestesses to mourn and prepare without having to move around Elián and me. We were outsiders in their space, and even though Cera had been nothing but warily appreciative of my help, I knew that she had much more to do than talk with me.

I worried at my lower lip as I finally began to write to Mathieu and Uncle Hendrik. I started by reassuring them of my own safety and then informed them of Isabella's fate the night after our discussion. The fact that it was a Vyrkos assassin couldn't have been a coincidence—right? And would they still allow me to continue to Nethras if they knew that? If I informed them that the office in which I had talked with Isabella became the site of her untimely death not a few hours later?

For those reasons, I left out the race of the attacker and stated that the priestesses and Rhaestran guards were still investigating. At the end, before signing off, I added that I had every intention of continuing my mission of speaking with Lylithan leaders. With Isabella gone, the importance of getting Roalld on board wasn't just significant because he represented my home city, but because we were running out of options.

The same female who had sent my letters last night nodded as I told her the message needed to be marked as urgent. I paid extra for the postage and bid her a good afternoon.

Elián followed me to a café across the street, and I claimed a seat inside to escape our rooms and the heat of the day. I had stuffed Lee's book, as I began to think of it, in my pocket when we returned briefly to the lodging house after returning from the Temple. There was a cluster of low, wooden seats, and I claimed one nearest the large, open window. Though the sun was baking the streets, the wind from outside was cool.

The both of us sipped chilled papaya juice, and I tried to keep my mind on the things that I knew, that I could control.

My book sat opened in my lap, but my eyes were unseeing on the page. Isabella was with the Godyxes and the Mother, now. And Cera, the thorn in my side since I was six years old, was to be High Priestess. A week ago, I may have been affronted by that fact, but now, after seeing the respected priestess she had grown into, I found that I also...respected her. It was clear that she cared about her sisters above all but the Goddess she served. And was that not what a high priestess was supposed to be? Had it not been what my mother and Isabella had been?

I knew, also, that coming here to Rhaestras had tilted my perspective of what Rhaea had given me. As a child, I sat through lessons with my mother and Isabella about Death Wielders, but at the time, it was just more schooling. Since that day on the road where I had killed the group of bandits, there was a block in my heart against my—gifts. There were moments during Maman and Isabella's teachings that showed me glimpses of what it could do if I maintained my control, but I still left it to just those times, where I was sure they could still reel me back in. Shield me from it.

But could they truly have?

Since then, the only times I had felt my power anywhere besides underneath my own skin had been in the most extreme of ways. In Versillia, I laid waste to a battalion of Vyrkos within a matter of minutes. In Nethras, I slaughtered a group of them in seconds.

I bent and stretched the fingers of my left hand. The vines had seeped back into my skin when we left the Temple grounds, but I could almost still feel them dancing around my knuckles, my wrist. And now their absence felt troubling and hollow. For all of my life, I had beaten my power into submission and only let it crest to its full height in times that demanded all, everything.

But last night, when I released it, there was nothing but tender caring. It pressed onto me to calm my shaking and rubbed my ear like my mother. And in Isabella's office I felt a facet of it that I had never felt before. With the little bit of slack I gave, the darkness opened my senses to what Death and destruction left in its wake. My powers were terrifying and vast and still mostly unknown, but they had also proved to be helpful.

The last thing I knew, was that I would be setting my sights on a new goal. Roalld of Nethras was a fairly young Lylithan, and he had risen to power within our community by his business acumen and rumored rigidity. I had only caught glimpses of him out and about, but he agreed in his and Uncle Hendrik's correspondences to meet with me about the Council.

I knew our city, and I had been attacked in our city. Those two facts would hopefully add an undeniable weight to my request for him to join. He wasn't as jaded as some of our older counterparts, and perhaps that would be on my side as well. The task at hand made the reality of going home, albeit for a brief period of time, a bit duller. But at least I could sleep a few nights in my own bed.

The rustling of a page turning drew my attention to my right. Elián sat easily beside me, flipping through the books he had let me read two nights prior. He was on the second one, and I could see the image of Joran's horse glaring as he tried to persuade the steed to let another knight, Viktor, travel with them. By the end of the next issue, I knew, the horse would grow fond of the newcomer.

Elián and I had not tried to talk about last night, and what would be the point? His rejection was all too clear. He was here to work for me and protect me—that was it. Whatever physical attraction we had for one another was best kept ignored. Even if the feel of his lips on mine was still haunting me.

I swallowed thickly when I remembered how he had snarled when I put my hand on him. That was as clear as his words had been. *Don't. Do that.*

I focused back on the novel in my lap and was eventually able to get into the story. It was entertaining enough, but the lack of character development in the name of furthering the plot was disappointing. The day turned into night as I finished it. The heroes successfully retrieved the artifact they needed and returned to their homeland, only to have one of them be kidnapped at the end. I flipped over to the back of the book, and saw then that it was the first in a trilogy.

Elián and I returned to our rooms to pack for our journey the next day, and we ordered our supper to be delivered to our rooms. We ate in our separate areas, and I started one of the romance novels that I had purchased while I sprawled in the bathtub for the last time.

Packing my clothes up again was quicker work than then first time, and after fastening the last bag, I sat on the floor of my room, fibers of the purple and green rug tickling my legs. Tonight, perhaps at that very moment, Isabella's body would be wrapped in linen and brought to the floral garden. Cera would be the one to light the flame and lead the prayers for as long as the body took to burn. And when the body was no more, Cera would take her oath and be judged by the Goddess Rhaea. A High Priestess hadn't been denied as far as I knew—the vetting process up to that point was rigid enough to prevent such things.

I looked down at my hands resting in my lap. My brown skin was darker here in Rhaestras, and the salt and humidity had somehow rubbed it to be even smoother, clearer. My fingernails were long and curved into points, and they reminded me of Maman's. Though somewhat impractical for her line of work, and mine as well, the sharp yet elegant tips had always made her look regal and vicious.

I called on the darkness, and my heart skipped at how easily it seemed to unfurl from the crooks between my fingers. This time, it left from both of my hands, and it was mesmerizing. Like dropping ink into water. As the tendrils grew, they floated and fanned around me like the mist of a cool, early morning.

My power felt calm, content to linger in the air and await my command. And while I sat amongst it, there was no fear.

This ability Rhaea gave me, a fraction of the power that she Herself commanded, smelled like me but also with the jasmine scent of Death. It spread through my body, and instead of my senses sharpening to a painful needlepoint, they honed to a fascinating, yet comfortable clarity.

In the bathing room beside me, I could taste the cascading plant above the bathtub and it's shedding leaves. The intentional death of those limbs was like a cool autumn day, where dying was to make room for new life.

I could feel far in the distance, a soul who had not yet accepted their death. They smelled sweet but stale, like an overripe fruit, and their sadness made me chest clench.

And I could feel Elián in the room beside me.

I inhaled deeply through my nose, and the floating whirls of my darkness angled toward the door separating us. Without the clarity my power provided, my Shadow smelled of warmth, earthily sweet, and with a hint of musk and bitterness that made my mouth water. But as I sat, opening up myself to my power and letting us become one, I felt his own power within him. Within me was darkness, cool and welcoming and consuming, and within him was a raging inferno.

It was the smell of smoke and char from a forest fire, the blazing heat of the sun whilst lying naked on the beach, the taste of peppers so deliciously painful that made one reach for another and another. And then it shifted again, and I felt the soft warming of a hearth fire on a winter night, tasted the first sip of a new cup of tea that warmed weary bones at the end of a long day.

The scent and taste and awareness of him like this made me restless, and my skin felt too close to my body. The few times his flesh had touched mine, I felt a fraction of what I was opened up to now.

My darkness stayed aloft around me, still twirling and twitching and resting, even as I parted my legs, resting the soles of my feet on the itchy carpet. My power wasn't physically connected to my hands anymore, but I sensed an invisible tether that would allow me to yank it back at any moment. And I felt the darkness's willingness to be pulled in whenever I deemed it time.

I let it stay around me, filling me with an Elián that I had only caught a glimpse of, one he had no desire to let me see or feel.

I tried my best to remain silent at the first touch of my fingertip to the wetness between my legs. My back bowed as I added another finger to circle quickly, round and round, and I imagined it was my Shadow's tongue.

My breathing stuttered, my head fell back, and there was no denying the sound of it. I was probably dripping onto the rug, and when I moved two fingers where I was aching the most, a husky moan slipped past my lips. But I couldn't stop, because each breath brought more of him into me, and I could almost taste him in the deepest part of my throat. I imagined his hot skin where his essence enveloped me, and my hips moved rhythmically back and forth.

Just in the other room, when he had done to me what I was now doing to myself, Elián had snatched my hair and threatened my life as he worked to make me come. The memory of his breath on my throat was intoxicating, and my fingers moved frantically in and out and swirling.

I bit my lip, drawing blood, at the thought of those fangs of his grazing my throat. And what would it be like to have him bite down and drink from me? Not to feed, but for no reason other than to truly consume, to pull me into him to be as close as possible.

My climax made me stop breathing all together.

My legs trembled fiercely, and my toes cramped as every fiber of my body was drawn taut. The release was a complete rush of my senses, and the hair on my limbs stood on end. It was as if someone had taken a long brush against the inside of my skin.

When I opened my eyes, the darkness was still swimming in the air, but it had dulled the clarity it provided. I willed my breathing to calm from the quick pants I had been taking, and yes, the scent of Elián wasn't nearly as intense anymore. I could no longer feel that melancholic soul down the street.

I came further down back into myself, and in a test of my gift, I asked it to come back and settle upon my skin. The mist retreated from the air, converging around me in darker, more condensed clouds, and then further it went, collecting into those vines. They packed and shortened to fit like earlier today, making home on the backs of my hands, in my palms, and trailing up my wrists. From a distance, it would perhaps look like a matching set of intricate tattoos, but the markings lived, moved.

They were flush against my skin and followed the curves of my veins, the ridges of my bones, and the dips of the lines in my palm.

Matching, spiraling black climbed my first three fingers, and I thought of Maman's and Isabella's High Priestess markings. They were given upon ascension to match the Goddess Herself and represent Life, Death, and New Beginnings.

I was so engrossed in the similarities between this part of myself and the signal of the Goddess that the knocking on our door made me jump.

My scenting had dulled back to normal, and it felt like a cloth had been draped over my face. Through it, though, I felt her—lemon and rosemary. Cera. What was she doing here?

Elián opened the door to the hall at the same time I entered the front room. He stood back and let Cera enter, alone.

She was dressed in black, flowing trousers with delicate golden embroidery at the hems. The swirling pattern was so much like the form of my own power, it made me twitch. Across her chest lay a black band to cover her breasts, and her hair was at a loose knot behind her neck.

"What is it?" My voice came out worried, surprised. She was supposed to be at Isabella's funeral ceremony and taking her vows.

"Come with me," she jerked her head back toward the door, and her words were a cruel call to this morning. Had it truly been this morning when I had found out that Isabella was no longer in this realm?

I looked at her, confused, "Come where?" I crossed my arms around my waist, pulling my closed robe closer to myself.

She frowned, "To the Temple."

My face dropped like hers, "For what? Did something else happen?" The anxiety was creeping in again, and I felt the power stirring at my fingers.

Cera's hazel gaze flew to my middle, and I watched as she trailed the movement of the veins of Rhaea's gift. The left corner of her lip lifted, and for the second time today, I saw a glimpse of the Cera I knew underneath the sorrow. "No. It's time for the ceremony."

"But—I—I am not a priestess. That is for you all."

Cera tilted her head, eyes still on my hands, "It is for *us*. Isabella was just as much a mother to you as she was to me. You deserve to light her flame with me."

"Cera you don't—"

She held up a hand and swiped it across the air, "I will hear no arguments. And Isabella was right. You may not have spoken the priestess vows, but you are still one of us. Whether you like it or not." And in that moment, she truly was the Cobra and the peer that lashed out at me as much as I had at her and the little girl that laughed with me on that summer day amongst the flowers. She shrugged, "So, bring your guard dog and come. Don't bother dressing, we will provide you with clothes." So she wanted me to traipse thought the streets in my robe.

But it was so much like her to demand this of me, to present it in that challenging way. With Isabella gone and the weight of our people's survival pressing on my shoulders, I found myself clinging to this familiarity.

I knew what she was doing, and I found myself taking the figurative hand she was extending. Elián was watching me from behind Cera's shoulder, but I couldn't decipher his expression. There was no way he knew that I had felt what stirred beneath the stone of his facade, and I wondered how he kept it from surfacing. But he had surely smelled and heard me touching myself beyond the thin wall between us. I turned away from him, unwilling to search his face for more damning evidence of his hatred toward me.

My attention turned back to Cera, and our eyes met. I nodded silently, firmly, to her and followed to the Temple.

26

The full moon was a beacon overhead, almost too bright as it shone down on us as we stood before Isabella's funeral pyre.

This area of the gardens was full of white narcissus flowers the same color of the moon and stars above, and they swayed softly around us. No one spoke, but we were faced toward the figure wrapped in black and gold and lilac on a stone altar. I stood at the back of the crowd with Elián and watched as the priestesses around me closed their eyes and angled their faces and palms toward the sky. Cera stood at the front, nearest Isabella's body, and I caught sight of Jesyn among the high-ranking priestesses just behind her.

Long moments passed in the silent prayer to the Goddess, and though I had no words to give, I mirrored those around me. I kept my eyes open, searching the depth of the night sky, and the darkness within hummed and pulsed. It wasn't a harbinger for destruction as I had thought of it before, but a lullaby, a song.

Instead of unfurling around me in the physical world, I felt my power seep into my mind, showing me what it saw, what it heard. The mourning of those around me tasted deep and floral and bitter, but also pure. Though they all loved Isabella and revered her as High Priestess, they perhaps were those most familiar with the nature of death. Their tears were for themselves, now set to live in a world without her. And they cried in joy for Isabella, now free from all the burdens of this realm and resting with the Mother and the Goddess Rhaea Herself.

Crunching gravel neared and broke my trance. I lowered my chin and found Cera walking toward me. She didn't speak, but she offered her hand. And her face, for the first time I had ever seen, was soft, serene. There was no trace of contempt or competition or judgement.

When I hesitated, her expression changed as she looked me up and down, and I let out a relieved huff. My hand joined hers, and she squeezed it once, twice.

She pulled me forward, and we walked hand-in-hand toward Isabella's pyre. Though my breathing remained calm, I felt naked and almost panicky. The senior priestesses who had wrapped Isabella and prepared the altar dressed me when I arrived with Cera at the Temple. Now, we walked together, dressed in black and violet. Where her band top and airy trousers were embellished with gold swirls, mine were plain, like that of all the others behind me. Save for Elián, who was permitted to remain in his usual ensemble. I felt him remain where we had been standing, and his absence was a strange, cold void.

Cera and I stopped before the black stone platform and the shrouded form of Isabella's body. She had always been slight in stature, but laid out like this she looked so... small. Despite being all too familiar with dying, I had been to few funerals, and those I had attended had mostly been here. I was grateful for the Rhaestran custom of wrapping and burning the dead. Once a life was ended, the physical body took on a strange, disturbing appearance. I didn't think I would have been able to handle seeing Isabella like that.

Her body held whispers of her scent, orange and thyme, but it was growing staler with each passing moment. I brought my hand over the wrapped form and passed slowly over it. Along the way, the veins danced faster, concentrating on my palm, but they didn't move beyond my skin.

At her heart, a dry cry, a gasp, left my chest, and I couldn't help but smile. I could feel echoes of her affection toward me, her love. Even with her biting words the day before, I felt the depth of her tenderness for me, and it was something I had only caught shadows of throughout our time together. And when I brought Cera's image into my mind, hand still circling in that area, I felt the same. Fierce love and protection and pride.

I turned to look at Cera, who had deep tracks of tears flowing down her cheeks. I wasn't sure how to communicate the complexity of what I was able to see—maybe if I—

I snatched her hand, and she went willingly as I placed it over mine. We both watched in awe as the veins wrapped around the back of her hand, tying us both together. Letting her see what I saw. I watched as a bright, bright grin broke across her face, and a torrent of tears flowed. She clenched her eyes shut and nodded over and over while I anchored her to my power and let her see just how much Isabella loved her. I could see the deep respect they held for one another, the stubbornness but also the admiration between them both.

After long moments of Cera knowing, finally, how her mother and mentor truly felt about her, we slowly dropped our hands to our sides. She was never coming back, but that would be okay.

Jesyn stepped forward with a lit black candle. She knelt and extended it toward Cera, who silently accepted. As Jesyn stepped back, Cera turned toward me and held the candle between us. I stared at her, wide-eyed, but she just nudged it toward me until I complied. We both grasped the slender black wax underneath the flame.

We took a joined, deep inhale, and as we exhaled, we brought the candle to the pyre.

The linen wrap caught quickly. Cera and I stepped back to allow the rest of the priestesses to watch with us as all traces of our High Priestess left the realm.

While I watched the smoke curl toward the moon, shame circled in my heart. I hadn't watched my mother's body burn after she'd died that night in Versillia. Nor my father's. After their noble deaths, I just ran, unable to face this reality, this truth. As Isabella's corporeal form turned to ash, I sent up a prayer to Rhaea, apologizing to my parents, Isabella included, for my cowardice.

As if in answer, a soft wind carrying ocean waves, cedar, and thyme ran past me, over me. I rubbed the heel of my palm at my chest, over my heart.

It didn't take long for the body to burn completely—the priestesses not only cleaned their dead but also mixed the perfumed oils they rubbed over the deceased's skin with a sort of accelerant before wrapping. And I was reminded of the Goddess's presence, though She didn't walk our realm anymore. An unnatural breeze swept only the altar, and Isabella's ashes were swept upward. It didn't look that different from the smoke of my power, and we all watched the last remnants of the former High Priestess disappear into the black and white of the stars and sky.

Cera moved to stand before the empty altar and turned to us all.

And now it was her turn to kneel. Her hair was loose now, and hung like a curtain, a veil, over her back and shoulders. Though her tears hadn't yet dried, she no longer looked sorrowful. She was determined. Regal.

She brought her fingers to her brow in the six-fingered salute of the Goddess and bowed deeply to us all. There were no objections, no sound at all, and I followed the rest of the priestesses as we remained standing and returned the salute.

And we waited.

For a long moment, nothing happened. The only sounds were the rustling of the garden flowers and the jungle beyond and our breathing. I opened my eyes, and though she still looked just as determined and dignified, I saw the mask begin to crack on Cera's face. A faint line appeared between her eyebrows, and I felt panic for her. Would the Goddess reject her? Even though we had all accepted her unspoken vow?

Without thought or any direction from me, my power lifted from my skin. Like earlier tonight, it turned into a sort of mist that swept into the air, inching and circling around Cera, who didn't dare open her eyes. Though I still felt the connection to my darkness, it had a mind of its own as it twined around her legs.

Just then, a wild wind coursed through the jungle gardens, rushing toward us. It barreled into our gathering, and I watched in awe. The wind smelled of jasmine and mint, and my hand flew to my eyes to cover them from the harsh current.

Not until I felt the air settle did I tentatively lower my arm, open my eyes. It seemed that the others had done the same, and now we stared.

And stared.

Cera was still kneeling on the ground, but her hands were now at her sides, forearms bent and palms to the sky. Her head was thrown back, and her eyes were wide toward the moon.

I held my breath but saw my power collect and retreat back to my skin. And I saw the six fingers Cera had held at her brow just moments ago. They were tattooed with delicate tendrils. The markings of Rhaea had appeared on her hands and extended about halfway down the copper skin. The blunt fingernails had turned black too, and when she lowered her head and opened her eyes, they were newly flecked with gold that reflected in the light of the moon.

She stood and blinked slowly, and I saw the mixture of surprise and relief on her face. Her new eyes shifted to meet mine, and I brought my hands to rest on my heart for her, my oldest friend. I raised them to my brow, and now it was my turn to kneel.

The others followed me, and we held for an infinite moment, silently recognizing Cera, our new High Priestess.

~

Elián and I rode silently back up the dirt road toward the port. Bhrila and Noxe were just as unsteady on the soft dirt as they had been when we arrived, but we trudged forward easily enough. The sun was just rising, so the air hadn't yet turned to its full heat. Though still humid, there was a coolness that allowed for me to wear my traveling leathers without feeling like I was suffocating. The brim of my hat fluttered with the salty morning air, and I felt that I was almost a new person than I had been nearly a week ago.

We reached the port with no obstacles, and handed our horses' reins over the crew of our ship to Nethras. While we were unbuckling our packs from their saddles, a voice called my name.

I turned to find Cera and Jesyn with three members of the Rhaestran guard behind them. Cera had shed her embroidered ensemble for a simple matching set in a forest green, now free to dress in colors other than black.

At first glance, she looked as she always had with her braid in the pattern of a fish's tail, and the curved daggers sheathed at her waist. Her sandals were the same worn, brown leather. But as we stood before each other, taking in the changes we had experienced in the last few days, I smiled. The markings on her hands swallowed as much light as her eyes now reflected.

"Not going to say goodbye, Mamba?" She raised an incredulous brow.

I chuckled and crossed my arms, "I figured you'd be busy, Your Graciousness."

She snorted, "I think two days ago, you called me a waste of space. Don't bother with pleasantries now. It doesn't suit you. Or me."

"Well," I nodded toward her entourage, "one of them may try to slit my throat if I call you that again now."

She shrugged, "Why have one of them do it when I'm perfectly capable of doing that myself?"

I narrowed my eyes, "You wouldn't come close, Cobra."

But instead of hitting me back with another retort, I gasped as she pulled me into an embrace. My arms rose stiffly but softened as they wrapped around her back. She grasped the nape of my neck, and I hers, and even her scent was changed. Though the jasmine of the Goddess was woven through her, she smelled strongly now of lemon and rosemary and mint.

The two of us, completely orphaned but still standing.

"Thank you," she whispered in my ear.

We pulled back to bring our brows together, and I knew she saw my confusion. But she didn't comment on it, didn't explain what she was thanking me for.

When we stepped away and disentangled our hold on each other, I dropped to one knee and saluted. Like my mother and Isabella, I knew that Cera would be a fine High Priestess. I had already seen that she was a good teacher, and despite our bickering, I always recognized that she was a fierce fighter and leader. Her healing powers had always been strong, and now with the ultimate blessing of Rhaea, she was the most powerful in the world.

Cera snickered but wasn't looking at me, "You don't kneel before your High Priestess, Master Elián?"

My hands dropped to rest on my thigh, and I twisted to look behind me. My Shadow was still standing, though his fist was closed over his chest. He frowned at Cera's words and let his fist fall, "The Shadows only kneel before the Mother and the Godyxes themselves."

But—I looked up at Elián, brow furrowed, and he looked back, blank.

I stood and turned back to Cera who just smirked between the two of us then to the ship behind us. I hadn't registered the crowd that had begun to stare, and many were kneeling for their new High Priestess. The news of Isabella's death had been whispered throughout the city almost immediately after we left the Temple the night before. "Oh, and I will be joining your council, Mamba," she waved a hand toward Jesyn, now clad in the black of her new position, who stood to her right. "Just send the details to Jesyn, and we'll coordinate my traveling schedule for whenever you all meet."

I gaped at her. I hadn't even thought—*expected*—for her to be thinking about the reason I had come to Rhaestras. Isabella's death and Cera's ascent to High Priestess eclipsed the negotiations I had come here for.

She picked underneath one of her black nails, "You don't have to thank me. Just make sure to be at those meetings, too. Your brother always irritated me even more than you did, and I will not deal with him and the other stuffy people he's no doubt rounded up."

My confusion still clung to me—since when did Cera and Mathieu have issues? But I quickly swallowed it away, halfway afraid that Cera would change her mind. I nodded and extended my hand.

She accepted it, and this time, I was the one to pull her in. We clapped each other on the back, once, twice, and separated. She offered no other words, and Jesyn beside her gave a quick bow before they all turned and began walking back toward the city.

After depositing our packs in our double cabin, Elián and I stood on the deck of the ship as it finally pulled away from Rhaestras. The sky was lightening to a pleasant blue now, and I removed my hat and held it at my side. Two days, and I would be back in Nethras, and I felt a new, complex lightness.

Death still clung around me. My parents, Shoko and Lee, and now Isabella, were all gone.

But with this resignation, was a new confidence, purpose. I hadn't failed in Rhaestras after all. And I knew that Nethras, in truth, would be easier to handle than this. I didn't think too hard about Cal and his syrupy games, but on the prospect of being back in my home. Not the one that had been mine by birth, but the one I had made for myself. I left those weeks ago because I couldn't bear walking among the memories of my dead friends.

Rhaea's gift pulsed faintly under my skin, as if reassuring, and I now felt ready to go back there. To write a new chapter for my life in Nethras. One in which I would inevitably, in my own way, secure our people a more prosperous future. So that children like Marco could live long, long lives.

The unknown identity of Isabella's killer tugged at my hope, and no matter how I tried to push it away, it remained at the back of my mind. I knew that Cera would still work toward finding who had done this, and I trusted that she wouldn't rest until she did. And when my Council task was over, if she still worked toward this, I vowed to myself that I would join her.

I turned to Elián and took him in. More uncertainty crept up. "Are you ready for what is next, my queen?"

I blinked at him, "Are you ready for two more days at sea?"

His lips turned down in the deepest frown I'd seen from him yet. He looked out accusingly at the water, "Yes."

And though the past few days had made me think it now impossible, I laughed cheerfully at my Shadow.

PART THREE
FIRE AND ABYSS

27

"Home at last," I sighed as I pushed open the door to my apartment. The invisible barrier, not unlike that in the tavern rings, responded to me immediately and let me cross the threshold. It was a piece of magic that Tana had installed for me, to respond to only myself and those with my invitation, and when I walked through it, there was always a hit of lavender.

I dropped my packs on the wood floor of my apartment and flipped on the floor lamp beside the door. I didn't know what I had expected, but the living space flowed into the dining area and kitchen as it always had. A bound sketchbook signed by my favorite clothing designer sat on the low, white stone table where it had always been since Lee had gifted it to me five years prior. One of Shoko's jackets hung on the back of one of my dining chairs.

I took a deep breath and reminded myself that though their deaths had been unjust and violent, they had accepted death just as immediately as Isabella had. They were resting with the Mother, now, and when I inevitably passed on, I would see them. Or maybe it was all a load of horse shit, and we all died for nothing and turned into nothing. Either way.

"Your Highness," Elián hissed.

I whirled around, and saw him, packs still hanging from his shoulders, standing just outside of my door. Ah, I had forgotten that he wouldn't be able to enter. I crossed my arms and cocked my hip. "Are you going to be nice to me?"

He looked like he was most certainly not, "I am always nice," he seethed. He had been an absolute terror on the journey here, and it had taken all of my strength to keep my spirits up. How was it that I was the one with Death swimming under my skin, and yet, *he* was the dreary one?

"That might have been the funniest joke I've ever heard, Shadow. You've been acting a complete ass, and I would like to know that you're going to treat me and my home with respect before you enter."

Those thick black brows rose, nearly meeting his hairline, "I could easily go back to the Shadow Well and leave you here to fend for yourself. I am not your servant."

Shadow Well. Is that what their home was called? I filed that away under the very limited information I knew about Elián and The Shadows, "I don't want you to go, but I also am trying to retain a bit of peace. So, I ask again—can you agree to be nice?"

He huffed, and the exhale made some of the hair at his brow flutter, "I will—be nice. Whatever that means."

The grin I flashed him showed all my fangs, and his mouth flattened in response, "Master Elián, please come in. Welcome to my very peaceful home." I waved him forward, and he stepped silently through.

He didn't look uncertainly around the doorframe as most new visitors did. As soon as he crossed the threshold, he slammed the door shut, dropped his packs, and began to flit around the apartment. I stood, arms crossed, and waited. I could already smell and hear that there was no one else inside, and I was sure that he could, too. But, it would seem that despite his dislike of me, he was still taking his job seriously.

Elián stopped in the dining area, finished with his search. He brought a gloved hand to the gray jacket slung on the back of one of the chairs. He lifted it to his nose and looked at me, brow raised.

"My friend's," I croaked.

His eyes scanned the large room around us, "Your friend lives here?" Shoko's scent still clung to the walls, even though I could tell it had faded substantially. To him, though, it was surely prominent. I marched forward and snatched the fabric out of his hand. The fleeting scent of Shoko's rose and hyacinth and hash made my stomach plummet, the memories of the last time she wore it already fading. Elián continued to look at me, and now the brow raised turned from curiosity into judgement, "That wasn't nice."

I chewed the inside of my lip and closed my eyes, making a concerted effort to count my breathing. One, two, three. "She's dead. That's why I came back to Versillia in the first place."

That brow dropped, and I saw understanding cross over his face. He didn't say another word, and neither did I. Our journey had been long and uncomfortable, and I felt the tiredness in my bones. Perhaps it was my brewing exhaustion that made it seem like Elián's eyes in that moment softened to a deeper orange color. They reminded me of roasted yams, and—yes, I was also very hungry.

I cleared my throat and turned back toward the living space section of my home. "So, I only have the one bed. You can take the sofa. I think it's long enough for you, and it's more comfortable than it looks." I went to my packs by the door and began gathering their straps in my hands. "You've already seen my bathing room, and you're obviously welcome to use anything in there. We'll have to go out to get something to eat. Is there anything else you might need?"

He remained standing beside the table, arms clasped behind him, and he looked at me now with his head tilted in that way that meant he was considering something. I waited until he shook it quickly. "Well, I'm going to shower and change if that's all right? Then you can do the same, and I'll unpack while you do?" He nodded.

I closed myself in my bedroom, and my shoulders relaxed. The packs slid down my arms and landed with a thud on the floor. Many weeks away, and my room felt stuffy and smelled so much like me. The long, white curtains were closed, and I crossed the room to pull them open. The sun would be setting soon, and the light outside had taken on a color not unlike that of my Shadow's eyes. The last time I had been staring out of this very window, Mat had come to check on me and ask me to come back to Versillia. The Meline that I had been felt a short lifetime ago.

The dark shifting on my hands was testament enough to that. On the ship and ride back to Nethras, I had willed my power back into my skin, and after growing more and more comfortable with it in Rhaestras, I realized how much of a strain it was to keep hidden. The sheer effort of it gave me a headache the entire sail, and I had exhausted all of the hash I packed in that little golden box.

I looked down at my hand now, and the veins underneath my skin looked greenish on my brown skin. Without thought, I exhaled, giving permission. I watched as the veins on my hands seemed to turn black, but no, it wasn't my actual veins. The power seemed to enjoy running along the form of my knuckles and bones and skin, and today, they mimicked the branching of my veins. When I turned my hand over, it ran along the creases in my palms. It twined around the ridges in my knuckles like a collection of onyx rings.

My headache fizzled and disappeared.

I turned away from the window and fell into my returning home routine. The shower I took was perfunctory, and I combed my freshly washed hair into a tight knot at the back of my head. I dressed in a pair of undershorts that I preferred for lounging and pulled on a worn tunic that had been washed so many times, the cotton was incredibly smooth and soft.

Though I was tired, I sped through my unpacking. One of the things I had realized about myself once my contracting career progressed—if I didn't unpack the night I returned, my bags would remain packed and untouched on my floor for days on end.

When I emerged from my room, I found Elián sitting at the table, though his bags were arranged in a neat row behind the sofa. "You can put your things in my closet and dresser if you'd like. I have enough room, I think," I jutted a thumb toward my bedroom.

He stood and began walking toward me. He had taken his boots off, too, and they rested at the door next to mine, "No need. I'm going to bathe." I watched as he bent to pick up one of the bags, straightened, and retreated into my bathing room.

For a moment, I debated on looking through his things. From what I had seen throughout these few weeks, one of the bags was full of neatly wrapped weapons, though the swords he wore on his back more often than not were never packed away. The bag he took with him most likely contained his clothing, which I had no doubt was just as neatly and efficiently packed. He had two more that I was less certain about, but another moment passed and I thought better of it. He might make good on his previous promises to stab me if I went through with the urge.

Instead, I went to the kitchen and palmed my well-used kettle. In a pattern dug deep into the floorboards of my apartment, I filled the kettle with water from the sink, lit the right-front burner, and set the water to boil.

I pulled down a jar of my favorite chamomile tea blend from the Nethran market and filled two spherical tea steepers. I placed them into two large ceramic mugs and set them beside the stove. My fingernails drummed on the counter.

On the wall hung a framed drawing of my friends and I that we had sat for during one of the summer festivals that popped up in Nethras throughout the hot months. Lee's arms were slung over Shoko and Tana's shoulders, and my cousin's arm was wrapped around my lower back. My head rested on her shoulder, and the street artist had captured my subdued closed-mouth grin, Tana's warm smile showing all of her teeth and fangs, Lee's head thrown back in a guffaw, and Shoko's tongue sticking out playfully between her teeth.

Half of those in the drawing were gone, and I rubbed at the healing crack in my chest. The tight fabric of my tunic swelled against my deep breaths, and I willed away the despair.

The kettle's whistle rang loudly over the silence of my apartment, and I shook myself.

As I poured the hot water into the mugs, I felt my Shadow enter in a cloud of steam from the bathing room. "Do you like honey in yours?" I called without turning while I drizzled some in mine.

There was a palpable pause before her answered, closer to my back than I anticipated, "Sure."

I waved the honey wand over the other mug before tossing it in the sink and latching the jar of honey closed. The mugs were already hot to the touch, and I grabbed them both. The smell of eucalyptus and fire enveloped me, and I took another bracing breath before turning around.

Elián's hair was brushed back, and I could see the tracks left by stiff bristles. He hadn't shaved, and the shadow of his burgeoning beard was even darker than it had been this morning. I pushed the mug toward him, and he took it with his left hand. The tattooed one. The writing was neat and slightly flourished, and the characters looked vaguely familiar, though I couldn't decipher them. It appeared to be one word—maybe it was a Shadow marking?

He brought the mug to his lips and took a sip. His other hand stuck casually in his pocket, and my eyes followed the movement. My brow crinkled, "*What* are you wearing?"

Elián looked down at himself, "Clothes?"

He was dressed in black per usual, but the full sleeved tunic was almost as tight as mine, and it clung to the hard panes of his chest and shoulders. His trousers were loose and tightened at the waist by a drawstring and dark, charcoal *gray*. Was—was he wearing pajamas?

I asked as much, and he looked back at me, just as confused, "Yes?"

A passing, traitorous thought inquired whether he was wearing undergarments underneath those trousers, and I risked a glance downwards before clenching my eyes shut. No. It appeared that he wasn't. I walked around him with my tea in hand, giving a wide berth, and sat on the sofa.

If he noticed the heat rushing to my cheeks, he made no mention, nor did he comment as he leaned his back against the counter before the drawing I had been staring at earlier.

We sat in silence for a long while, drinking our tea, and I wondered how my home looked to him. It was fairly neat, due to my cleaning before leaving for Versillia. There was an eclectic mix of prints and drawings from Nethras and lands far away on the walls, and there was a large bookshelf that spanned one of the living space's walls. Trinkets from my travels sat amongst the books, acting like a log of where I had been and enjoyed.

"So, was I right?"

My gaze flicked back to Elián, still standing in the kitchen leaned up against the counter, "Right about...?"

"Is it easier now that you have practiced controlling your gift?" He nodded to my hands that held my mug, where my power was visible on my skin.

I rolled my eyes and took a sip of my cooling tea. I thought a moment to open my mouth and cut him with a snide remark, but I decided instead to flex my power. The ship here from Rhaestras was more crowded than the one we had taken from Versillia, and Elián's scowling the entire way left me feeling unenthused to let the tendrils wriggle about.

But now that I was home, and he was pressing me, it seemed as good a time as any.

It wasn't a matter of explicitly telling my power to unfurl, but an unspoken intention that acted immediately. The little bit that I had tasted in Rhaestras told me that I hadn't been necessarily fighting some foreign curse thrusted upon me. I hadn't been infected by Rhaea in some cruel decision—it was part of me like my skin, like my blood. And, unfortunately for me, Elián, Isabella, and Cera had been right. Strangling it had been hurting me. Not only that, but the days that I had acknowledged it within myself, let alone let it out to play, had left me feeling more in control than any other time I could remember.

So, when I flicked my wrist toward my Shadow, the shiver up my arm wasn't from fear but relief.

This time, the vines lengthened and curled toward Elián and looked just like those that sometimes grew along the facades of homes in Versillia. It branched, not needing a solid surface to rest. My chest thrummed with the use of it, and a smile curled at my lips. *If he is so intent on being right, let me show him what I've learned.*

He hadn't seen what I had released in the privacy of my own rooms, just at the ceremony and Isabella's office. A large part of me wanted to scare him, even though within the black wasn't the part of me that would kill. But he wouldn't know that.

Elián remained where he was, hands still on his mug and in his pocket, and eyed the tendrils creeping toward him. They felt like they had no end, the well within my chest infinite, drawing from the Goddess Herself.

When they reached him and a branch began to curl around his arm, I gave a silent shudder. He didn't move, looking upon it with utter, infuriating calm, while I felt like I had just taken my lips and dragged them around his forearm. I felt my face flush with the warmth of him, even through the fabric of his tunic.

It was addicting, and my darkness wanted more.

More branched off and twined around his torso, caressing his chest and shoulders. I could feel his heart, silent but betraying that this was affecting him, too. But he remained silent, not looking at me but eyes tracing the part of me that was wrapped around him. If I wasn't mistaken, his lids had lowered a bit, but I was also distracted by what the touch of my power was doing to me. I had felt him in all of these places, but this was a new facet that my physical contact couldn't quite encompass.

And then, some of the black met the bare skin of his neck, and a full-body shiver almost made me spill my tea. Elián's eyes closed, and I ached while I watched his head fell back. It was how he had done when I'd grabbed his cock as we kissed before the light of the fluorescent lagoon, and I was just as transfixed.

I could taste his flesh on my tongue, and when I looked down and saw the tenting of his loose cotton trousers, my mouth watered.

His whole body was entwined with me now, like tiny snakes that wanted to cover and feel every part of him. One crept over his ear, feeling like I had dragged the flat of my tongue around the upper curve of it and into his wet hair. The scent and taste of him was somehow stronger here, and I had to stifle a moan because I knew that it would break this trance. He wasn't afraid of me or the Death all over his body. Judging from the soft flesh of his neck that was open toward me and welcoming the vine that circled it, to him, it was—good.

To me, the darkness was a comforting abyss, and I wondered what it felt like for him in this moment. The dark pink of his tongue peeked out and wet his lip, and I had to clench my thighs together. But there was no hiding the scent of my or his arousal. It was filling every inch of the large room.

And I wanted so badly to go to him. At that moment, I would fucking crawl. I could make out the outline of the head of his cock from here, and I could imagine how it would fit in my palm, how it would feel encircled by my fingers. What he would look like standing over me while I took it in my mouth.

Don't. Do that.

My jaw clenched hard as I remembered Elián's words the last time I had touched him. I scrubbed my hand over my face, and I didn't need to will the power to retreat. It just did.

The expansive nothingness that the darkness brought was probably like some kind of spell. I knew first hand how good it felt to give into it, and he hadn't explicitly given me permission to do this, had he? Even with him leaning into the pleasure it was invoking, he hadn't spoken his consent, and that fact made my mouth immediately dry, my stomach curl.

I wouldn't do that to someone—I couldn't, and the fact that I had been made me feel so ashamed. As if it felt the same way, the vines retreated all the way under my skin, to where the only evidence of what I'd done was the thick arousal in the air and the trembles racking both of our bodies.

I slammed the mug I had miraculously held onto this whole time onto the low table beside me and leapt over the back of the couch. I mumbled a pitiful, "Sorry," as I went to my room and closed the door behind me. With the space between us, I drew in a shaking breath.

Fuck, what had I done? The pulsing between my legs was torturous, but I just went to the chaise before my window and sat on my hands.

My thoughts kept racing between focusing on the activity outside and imagining how Elián would feel deep in my throat. And then the shame would wash over me in another surge. I hadn't felt this worked up since I was an adolescent, and I groaned in frustration. So far the side effects of testing my new power had been nothing but positive and helpful. But if it made me want to jump on my Shadow, who I was sure hated me more days than not, and demand he rut me into the ground, I would need to keep a better hold on it.

I remained there, in front of the window, all night. I didn't trust myself to walk back to where he was. The wall between us was one of the few barriers that gave me a modicum of control, and I didn't dare lie down or get into the shower. My hands prickled underneath my thighs, but I couldn't let them go, because they'd just end up between my legs. And he would know.

But I couldn't help hoping, imagining, that he would knock on the door and demand I come back. Ask me to come back and *do that* again.

He didn't of course, and I tried my best to focus my ears on the cacophony outside and not on searching the silence in the next room.

28

I stood at my door, tapping my foot. Elián was in my bathing room dressing, and I was having a hard time calming my nerves. The hash I had smoked hadn't helped, and keeping my powers under my skin and locked in the vault in my soul was giving me a splitting headache.

My palm ran over my loose hair and the assortment of clips that held it away from my face. I straightened my deep blue, embroidered vest and matching trousers. It was one of the outfits that Mat had commissioned for me, and I was surprised how much I liked it. My blades were sheathed in my heeled boots, and I switched to shifting between my feet.

The meeting with Roalld was to be at one of his restaurants in the city center, and it somehow felt more intimate than sitting in his office. There would no doubt be the eyes of my neighbors but also his entourage on me. Most likely intentionally placed about the space so that they could monitor our conversation.

If I could handle doing this with Isabella and Cera, then someone at least one-hundred years my junior would be nothing, I tried to reassure myself. But the way my heart was beating, it was like I was anticipating he'd hold a blade to my throat and another to my back. However, even those types of situations I had been able to maneuver and gain the upper hand. So why were my nerves making my lungs and heart work overtime?

Elián finally emerged, and I barely gave myself time to look at him before I flung open the door and began to march toward the stairwell. He dressed in a simple black jacket and trousers and no weapons to be seen. But even my quick glance had told me many things.

I rubbed my hand at my chest as we walked out into the cool air. The sun was just an orange sliver on the horizon, and I weaved us through the paved Nethran streets. I pushed away the images of Elián with his tailored clothing and tousled hair and focused on the task at hand.

Roalld had been welcoming enough in the letters I had read over before leaving Versillia, but my negotiations with Isabella had gone in a completely different direction than I had anticipated.

And she'd been fucking murdered.

So I wasn't putting any hope behind the congenial tone in his correspondences.

The restaurant was only a fifteen-minute walk from my apartment at a leisurely pace, and with my jitteriness, we made it there in close to seven despite the busy streets. It was tucked into the ground floor of one of the tall brick buildings characteristic of Nethras, and as I went for the wooden door, Elián reached around me and pulled on the iron handle.

Roalld had been made aware of my guest, and Elián and I had agreed that he would continue to assume the demeanor of my companion when we were out in public. I reminded myself that it was to keep me safe while not drawing attention. Just like the weapons I knew he had hidden on his person. He stood beside the open door, and I stepped through with a nod in thanks.

"Name, please?" One of the restaurant staff asked without looking up from their post near the door. Judging by their scent, they were Lylithan like Elián and I, and they were dressed in a crisp beige ensemble. This restaurant was usually too stuffy for my or my friends' tastes, so this was only my second time here. The marble floor beneath our feet was shining it was so clean.

"Meline Richerre," I included my family name in the custom of Nethras. It felt strange to speak the name aloud, as I didn't use it often, but the city was influenced by a myriad of customs, and the human one of using both names was one that many had adopted.

The restaurant host, thankfully, did not seem flustered by reading my name from the log book of reservations and turned to show us to our table. As I started forward, I was startled by a soft press to my lower back. I looked up, almost panicked, to see my Shadow looking forward, but his brow was raised, as if waiting for me to protest his touch. But I felt grounded, and my nerves calmed a bit. He was doing this to play his role, just as he had let me hold his arm through the island market a few days ago.

We had talked briefly on the journey to Nethras about the importance of him looking as little of a Shadow escort as possible. At least outside of meeting rooms.

In Rhaestras, I was already well known as a high priestess's daughter, so having a guard wasn't strange. But here, that would draw even more curious looks. And what would happen to my reputation if other tavern ring fighters saw me with my own personal babysitter? I'd never live it down.

Elián had grunted his assent to this plan, this farce, so that I may still be able to keep my good name in the life I held outside of being an heir to Versillia.

We followed the host into the large dining area with its low lighting and cozy tables, and I had to remind myself that his touch at my back was nothing more than him following through on my request. Even if his warm, bare palm had no right to feel that good.

We came upon a table tucked in the back corner, where one could remain obscured by the other booths and tables but with a nice view of the entire space. Roalld Grevane was a slighter male, but his back was rod-straight in his seat.

He smiled softly at our approach and stood. As we neared, he extended a hand toward me, and I met it with my own. The skin of his palm was dry but smooth, and his cool blue eyes held mine a moment. He grasped my hand pleasantly and squeezed his other atop it before releasing both. Roalld nodded quickly but respectfully to Elián, and the three of us slid into the booth.

A server came by and deposited a crystal carafe of blood between us without a word. Roalld extended a hand for us to be the first to drink, and I waited for Elián as he poured a glass. His fingers were deft and graceful, and I made a point to look out the window behind Roalld instead of Elián's lips. And though Roalld was almost as good as Elián at masking, when Elián took a sip, the telltale sign of hunger showed through so quickly that I almost missed it.

I felt a mixture of irritation and relief when Elián handed me the glass he had deemed safe. It made me think of how the priestesses or that café server had fawned over my Shadow, and it also made Roalld seem less intimidating. I passed my gaze over him, and though he was all clean lines and reeked of money, he was just another person. He was no Isabella, that was for sure. I could do this.

Roalld poured his own glass and took a drink of his own. His pale brown jacket matched his short, neat hair and had shining golden buttons down the front. "Meline Richerre, it is a pleasure to officially meet. I hope that your journey back to Nethras went well?"

I nodded and smiled politely, "Yes, thank you. It is good to be home."

"And your companion?" This time, Roalld's mask stayed in place when he looked pleasantly to my right, where Elián sat at the end of the booth bench.

"Elián. Thank you for allowing me to meet with you as well." I almost choked on my beverage—I had never heard my Shadow be that polite to anyone, not even Mathieu or Uncle. For a moment, I feared that he was flirting, but his face remained pleasant stone. He leaned back a bit in his seat and angled his shoulders slightly toward me.

Roalld offered another nod to Elián in return and turned back to me, "So, let us get to it, then. The last Lylithan Council was before my time, and though I've been made aware of the rationale of starting such a thing again, I'd like to hear from you why I should become a member." He sat back and waved a hand for me to make my argument.

I cleared my throat and straightened my spine. This was what I had been preparing for, my points arranged in a thorough list in my brain. "Well, I am sure you're aware that our people are few, and with recent attacks, the need to organize is all the more imperative. I survived a brutal attack during The Killings, and I have lost parents and friends to those that wish us harm for one reason or another," I took a breath and placed a hand over my racing heart. "I know that you have many commitments and responsibilities, but we would be honored to have your presence and expertise on the Lylithan Council."

Roalld nodded, glass in hand, "Yes, and it appears that there has been another targeted attack here," he pursed his lips, "and you were correct that I am a busy male."

"We have requested local leaders of areas with larger Lylithan populations to bring the voices of their people to this Council, and as a citizen of Nethras, I know that I would greatly appreciate having my voice and my neighbors' in these conversations."

He nodded again, but his expression gave nothing in either direction, "That is understandable. But are you not already doing this? I am trying to decide if joining this is worth my time and efforts, and if there is already a Nethran at the table, why need me?"

I worried at my bottom lip. He had a point. The moment stretched as my mind raced for an adequate response that would still convey my competence but also the absolute need for him to accept. Flattery, then. I inhaled and leaned forward, "It is true that I have a seat at the Council table, but I did not grow up here, as I know you did. In truth, we do not have any members that have the business acumen to keep our ambitions and plans realistic and in check. You would bring a unique voice that would not only benefit the Lylithan citizens of Nethras, but provide us the foundation to make this a lasting and strong vehicle for change."

Roalld nodded again, perhaps deeper than before, and my shoulders relaxed a fraction. What I said was the truth—none of us could boast building an empire from the ground up, and we needed a shrewd voice to keep us grounded. If his reputation proved accurate, and judging by the way he conducted himself, I was inclined to believe it, Roalld was just that person.

I relaxed further as Roalld's questions turned logistical in nature, and as we discussed over a simple yet elegant dinner of roasted fish and vegetables, he ceased asking *why* he should join but how.

Elián remained a steady presence throughout our conversation, offering backing to my statements when Roalld inquired his opinion. At the end of the meal when we stood to leave, Roalld extended his hand. But this time, instead of taking mine like he did in greeting, we shook, and I couldn't contain my grin and thanks for his agreement.

And this time, when we stepped outside onto the street, I felt like a boulder had been lifted off of my shoulders. Elián extended his arm to me, and I took it without hesitation. Roalld had proved to be an agreeable person, albeit a bit curt, and I now had my second approval. If I didn't think it would make Elián frown, I would start skipping down the streets.

"Thank you for your help back there," I said as we walked toward the pharmacy I frequented.

I felt Elián shrug his shoulders as we both remained looking forward. His statements didn't seem to particularly sway Roalld to my side, but they definitely bolstered my arguments. Whatever animosity there was between us, I was reminded, again, that Elián was taking this seriously.

We entered a much larger pharmacy than the one in Rhaestras, and as we walked to the counter arm-in-arm, I had the thought that perhaps I had judged the Shadows wrongly. When The Killings occurred, they were nowhere to be found, as far as I knew. And though they wouldn't have been able to prevent all the deaths that occurred, a large group of expertly trained Lylithan fighters would have saved many.

But they had joined this cause for a reason, and he was one of three that seemed committed enough to help us. That counted for something.

The older male who was often working when I popped in went to a back room at my inquiry about any letters I had received since I'd been away. He walked slowly back to the front carrying just one.

I broke the Versillian seal and read the longer message Mathieu had sent while Elián and I had been sailing from Rhaestras. He expressed sadness at the news of Isabella's death and updated me on his and Uncle's progress.

Their negotiations had yielded mixed results, and we were still looking to encompass more areas of Lylithan interest that would fully round out the Council.

Fortunately, Mathieu wrote, *King Cal of Krisla has finally written back, and he expressed interest and excitement in speaking. He's agreed to a meeting with you in three day's time.* He included details of the lodging already reserved for me in Krisla, courtesy of Cal, and I felt a clench in my stomach despite my good mood. That would mean we'd have to leave tomorrow.

Fortunately for the Council, unfortunately for me, I thought. At the counter, I hastily wrote a letter to Mat and Uncle about securing Roalld as an official member of the Council, how the negotiations had gone, and that they could include him here on out on all Council correspondences. I also included the news that Cera had agreed as the new High Priestess and to include her as well.

Once my letter was sent, I took Elián's solid arm again as we left. I ran another hand over my vest and straightened my shoulders. Cera and Roalld, and now Cal. There would be another day to worry about meeting with him again. Tonight, I resolved, I would revel in my success.

"So, what would you like to do? It's early." I looked up at Elián as we weaved around the others that walked in the mild early evening weather.

He shrugged again, "It is up to you. You know this city better than I do." For some reason, this admission excited me. I started to steer us in the direction of my second favorite tavern.

My Shadow and I both stopped at the same moment, and someone behind us cursed before almost colliding with our backs. Neither of us moved as I filled my nose and lungs frantically with the scents around us. Memories of blood and a torn tapestry flashed through my mind.

Whoever killed Isabella was here in Nethras.

29

Elián leaned against the brick wall of the alley while I stood facing the street. He tucked his hair behind his ears before crossing his arms at his chest.

"Why don't you just cut your hair or tie it to keep it out of your face?" I snapped. His brow raised in silent challenge, but before he could speak, I muttered, "Sorry," under my breath. I had requested he be nice, and now I was the one finding it difficult to do the same.

"Are you sure you can trust this person?" I nodded and glanced toward the door leading into the building on my left. He'd be here at any moment and would hopefully be able to provide some answers.

After scenting the assassin on the streets, Elián and I had trailed the scent before it was muddled and lost amongst the sea of others that were out and about on this busy night. Right before we lost it, though, we were led to a tougher area of the city than where we had met with Roalld. Though the streets were still fairly clean, vacant and boarded-up establishments started popping up. And then I had an idea.

Elián and I stood waiting, listening to the ruckus of the tavern we stood beside until its back door opened.

A grinning, bare-chested male with black skin held onto the door handle, and his sharp, gold teeth were unnaturally bright in the dark alleyway.

I walked to him and extended my hand. Grimm grabbed it and brought me in for a warm one-armed embrace. When we pulled back, he looked me up and down and did the same to my Shadow.

We *were* dressed rather formally compared to his simple gray trousers and boots. Though his smile didn't falter, I felt Grimm's gaze turn from congenial to assessing, "And what have you gotten into now?"

My hands rested on my hips, and I lifted my chin. "Nothing I can't handle. But I do need your help."

He chuckled, and his voice was a soft rumble in the dark space, "Well then, lass, let's hear it." He looked again behind me to Elián, "Must say, I am surprised to see you with one of them, though."

I didn't hesitate, just shrugged, "He's a good fuck, what can I say?" Grimm snorted, but my response seemed to satisfy whatever questions he had brewing in his mind. Hopefully Elián would forgive me later. "So, can we go somewhere? It stinks back here." I waved a hand at the full garbage barrels around us.

Grimm grunted and turned back down the dark corridor, clearly meaning for us to follow. We weaved around crates and boxes stacked against the walls before coming upon an almost empty room. The wooden chair I sat in groaned as I leaned forward. Grimm had led us to one of the back rooms where I knew first-hand few legal activities occurred. I'd met with employers in many a place such as this, and I was fairly certain I had been in this particular one once before.

My elbow rested on the wobbly wooden table between Grimm and I. I pressed my thumbnail into the flesh of my fourth finger until I felt my skin break. A drop of deep red blood beaded on my skin, and I pushed the finger toward Grimm.

No longer grinning, he touched his rough finger to my bleeding one. Now stamped with my blood, my friend brought his first finger to his mouth. I watched his throat bob as he tasted. His lashless eyes closed, and he leaned back in his own seat.

Beneath the black lids, I could see the Mind Walker's eyes shift and search my memories, "It was earlier this evening and four days ago. A Vyrkos scent I don't recognize. Got any ideas?"

I wasn't sure how old Grimm was—I didn't know much about his people or how they aged—but he had been a successful ring fighter for a long time. He was respected and had a hand in all sorts of dealings in the rings and behind the back room doors. And many also sought him out for this very thing.

After a few moments, his eyes flew open, and he whistled, "Lotta blood, lass."

I sighed, "Tell me about it. Know who did it?"

He looked behind me at Elián, but no hint of teasing was in his face as he addressed me. Grimm was good for not riffling through sensory memories that you hadn't asked him to search. Well, unless someone had paid him to. Though it was a risk, I needed answers, and Grimm had never proved untrustworthy before. I'd won him a lot of money over the years—he was the one who'd encouraged me to start in the rings, after all. It was in his best interest, as well as mine, for us to remain friendly.

"Huh, yeah, I know that one. Newer one of the dead ones in town. Seen him before hanging around that tavern they all seem to love. Each time, he's always leaving with or outright fucking someone." Grimm chortled and tilted his head, "Matter of fact, you both might actually be his type. What with your warm blood and pretty fangs," he gave a lazy wave between Elián and I.

I nodded gravely. "You got a name?"

He shook his head, "But he's got gray hair, same length of your new pet's," he jutted his chin behind me, "and those red eyes. 'Bout half a head taller than you."

I committed the description to memory and stood. "I owe you one, Grimm," and he nodded, smirking, but I also knew that he was adding it to my list of debts. And though we were friends, Grimm wasn't one you wanted to owe.

He turned his unsettling stare to Elián, and his face grew teasing, "This one impress you with her fighting, then, Shadow?"

Elián glowered at Grimm, and responded dryly while glancing at me heading toward the door, "Absolutely."

I jutted a thumb to Elián as we left, "Take up my debt from Dyna with him. He's the one that has the rest of your money."

Grimm's only response was more raucous laughter, but the sound was faint in my racing mind, my plan already taking shape.

~

After briefly returning to my apartment, Elián and I again took to the streets, looking very different from how we had earlier that evening.

The leather of my trousers shuddered softly between my thighs as we walked, and I passed an absent hand over one of my daggers sheathed at my thighs.

I glanced quickly over at him while we crossed another street, noticeably less-populated than the last. He was back in another set of his leathers again, and though he was striking in both this and his more formal Shadow attire, he seemed much more comfortable in the fighting clothes.

When I'd quickly run down the plan I'd formed during our walk back to my home, Elián remained disbelievingly silent. I knew that it was a long shot, but I knew what we'd find at the Vyrkos tavern that Grimm had mentioned. And his information on our target blossomed into a plan that I needed his help with.

While I'd slicked back my hair into a long, singular plait and buttoned the leather collar of my backless top, I turned to him and squeezed my eyes shut, "If you help me, I'll tell you as much as I know about the Shadow that taught me your ways."

And he froze.

After five breaths, waiting with my shoulders almost at my ears, Elián grunted his agreement—to help me. I certainly wasn't going to argue, and after he'd swiftly changed his own clothes, he asked clarifying questions about his role in the next few hours. He even nodded along when I provided my thoughts and explained all that this would be requiring of him.

Another half hour, and we'd scoped out the location for the third part of my plan. And that, too, was surprisingly up to his standards. Along with planning, I'd also prepared arguments supporting each step, each rationale, in case he protested.

I kept looking over at him to see signs of his displeasure of what I had suggested. But, it seemed he was trusting me in this, at least to get to the answers as to which Shadow betrayed their secrecy. No protests came, and then our destination was in sight.

The tavern was exceptionally busy at this hour, most of its regular patrons now out in full force under the darkness of the night. *Good*, I thought. There was more chance of us finding him if there were more people here. And sure enough, the scent of our target appeared and grew stronger the closer we walked toward the establishment. Though I was no longer holding onto his arm, I felt Elián stiffen and catch a whiff of our target as well.

His swords were back—there was no sense in trying to hide who he was here. Those that knew of me were likely to know of the Shadows, and if he was as good as I thought he was, they'd know of him, too. Grimm recognizing him for what he was, even when dressed in formalwear and with no introduction, proved that very quickly.

So, tonight, we'd play into it.

There were a few that were drinking and smoking outside, leaning against the brick of the facade and talking. Most were dressed in black or some other dark color, and nearly all had those glowing, red eyes. They shone in the low light in a different way than Elián's amber ones. The blood color was somehow cold, and it signaled the reality of what they all were.

A few turned to watch us as we went inside, but their looks were more curious than anything. One nodded at me in greeting, and I returned the gesture.

The light was just as low in here, considering that all those inside didn't need artificial illumination to see. A group of musicians played harsh music in the back corner, and a long, dark wooden counter stood on one wall. Black leather booths lined the opposite. There were a few tables that sat in between, but the rest of the floor was clear for people to stand.

Many talked casually over drinks, but some were taking advantage of the lack of inhibitions at The Grave. The name of the establishment was fitting, considering most of the people here were technically dead. And though Lylithan's weren't known to be prudes, exactly, the Vyrkos *were* known for their propensity for public displays.

A female with tumbling black hair was looking up with tears in her eyes as a male thrusted into her mouth just beside where the band was launching into another song. Another two males seemed to be seconds from unlacing their trousers, judging from the intensity with which they were rubbing against one another. Many who were by themselves were looking hungrily at those that were engaged in heavy petting or kissing or outright fucking.

I grabbed Elián's hand possessively and pulled us across the floor for all to see. My skin prickled with the feeling of all those watching us, some wary, some hungry, and I made sure to slightly exaggerate the swishing of my hips. When we reached the bar counter, I leaned my elbows on the surface and immediately felt my skin stick to the wood. While I fought the urge to cringe at the remnants of liquor and blood that I would surely have to scrub off later, I felt the press of a warm body behind me.

Elián's hands came to rest beside my elbows, and he leaned against me. The material of his leathers was thicker than mine, but no less smooth. I felt the seam of his close-fitting jacket against my bare back, but no other part of him touched me yet. Though, it was enough for me to need to swallow before the barkeep turned around from filling a mug of ale.

His thick, pale arms were bare, and his brown leather vest was straining against his broad chest and belly. The pale brown of his hair was in a severe knot, but once his crimson eyes met mine, his lips pulled into a genuine grin.

Though his teeth were blunt and straight now, I knew that something very small could trigger his razor-sharp fangs to distend. I grinned back at him, flashing mine that were always present. "Look who's finally fucking graced us with her presence! What'll you have, Em?"

I kept my voice even, despite the feeling of Elián's breath on my neck. He leaned down and traced his nose along the curve down to my shoulder and back up again. "Whatever you've got that's strong. And two."

Jon's grin grew suggestive as he took the two of us in, "See you caught yourself a Shadow. I would say I'm surprised, but then I'd be lying."

I raised a brow, immediately reminding myself of Elián running his face along the curve of my ear, and touched the tip of my tongue to my fang, "And what's that supposed to mean?"

He chuckled as he poured two short glasses of brown liquor, "Means that since I've known you, your sweet little warmth loved a good challenge." And then his grin dropped altogether, "Was really sorry to hear about Shokes, you know. She's missed, but it's nice to see at least one of you again. Not sure why that group did what they did, but I want you to know that we were all heartbroken to hear about it."

I nodded. What else was there to say? Gratefulness for the astute barkeep swelled in my breast when his smile returned, and he pushed the drinks toward me. I started to reach into my pocket to pay him, but he shooed us away with a grunt. I palmed the glasses and pushed back from the counter, straight into my Shadow. Elián's large hand slid to my waist, and his scent wrapped me in its heat. The two of us turned back toward the floor and began to find a spot.

The presence of our target was hard to ignore, but I kept my gaze forward as we crossed the floor again and sat at one of the booths. Elián slid in first, and he lounged, large legs spread and arms leaning against the back of the seat. I slithered in after him, and instead of facing the rest of the room like he was, I rested my knees on either side of his thigh, straddling it.

I thought of Cera sneering at me and the offending stench of garbage, and when Elián's gloved hand gripped my hip, I added the thought of cold, cold showers. We raised our drinks to each other and clinked glass before taking a sip. Another request I made of him. He couldn't investigate my food and drinks while we did this, but since we'd watched Jon pour them, there was very low chance of the alcohol being poisoned. Had to admit, though. I kind of missed the ritual, having gotten used to it over the weeks.

Elián's hand traveled up to my bare back, and I felt the pressure of his gloved palm and bare fingers against my already sensitive skin. I set my half-finished drink down on the table behind me and brought my hands to his chest. His heartbeat was steady, calm, and I marveled at how unaffected he was. Though my power was tucked into a tidy corner of my mind, I felt the both of us tremble at Elián's hold.

He was still looking at me, and I caught his persimmon gaze making a pointed cut to his left and back. I felt more eyes on my back, hopefully the pair that we were interested in, and leaned into his ear. My hips ground against his thigh, and I tried my best to conjure the memory of when I had once been ordered by my parents to shovel horse shit and clean out the stables with my brother.

Elián's scent was sweet torture, but I somehow managed to keep my voice as professional as possible and completely at odds with what my body was doing. "Turn me around."

He obliged and surprised me with the blatant use of his strength.

He spun and settled me between his thighs. Now I could see the obvious glances our way. We were two warm-blooded Lylithans in a pit of Vyrkos. Predators and prey at the same time.

I'd forgotten how it felt to be here, in a sea of those that hated me or coveted me or envied me. I saw a few familiar faces from my days of visiting as Shoko's pet and then her friend, but it didn't matter. Though I'd had many fun nights here in the past, there was a specific end goal to my presence tonight, and it wasn't getting fucked for all to see. Probably.

With more and more glances our way, Elián and I continued to play the part of wanton patrons.

Which one is he, which one is he?

Elián wrapped his arm around my middle and pulled me against him until my back was flush with his front. I felt the hard bulge of him as well, and the need to fan myself was ratcheting higher and higher. At least I could be assured he wasn't completely unaffected by our little act. How my Shadow could be fully outfitted in leather and not show a bead of sweat was beyond me, because against him like I was, I felt blood flood my cheeks.

And though the Vyrkos watching us could derive about as much nutrition from our blood as we could from one of our own kind, they were drawn to the life within Elián and I all the same. Time after time, Shoko fussed and fawned over that very thing—where my insides were living and beating, hers were like crystal shards.

Elián bodily grabbed my thigh and threw it over his so that, though completely clothed, my open legs under the table were as much of a suggestion as any. I leaned my head back to rest on his shoulder. He picked up his glass again, but instead of putting it to his own lips, he brought it to mine.

"Drink," he said, rough and low with command. *Damn, he's good at this*, I thought. It wasn't a competition, but I suddenly felt the need to not be outdone.

I reached up to grip the back of his head and let him pour the alcohol into my mouth. His breathing was still steady, and I couldn't have that. Not with the right person still not making themselves known. We were drawing a sizable audience, egging on the others that were also in similar positions, and I'd be lying if I said I didn't want more. This was a play both of us had agreed to... it also made it that much easier that I relished the feeling of his touch. Shit, I was so pent up, it was a wonder I hadn't jumped him at this point.

He set his glass down again, all the while letting me hold him as if we were the only two in the room. Elián gave a quick pass of his thumb over my lips before settling back to hold at my throat. My breathing hitched, and I had to consciously steady it.

His face was nearly touching mine like this, and though I still felt a vice tighten against my lungs at the thought of kissing him again, I flicked my tongue and caught the soft flesh of his upper lip.

The look he gave me, all heated and seductive, left me about to melt, and I had to chant to myself *it's fake, it's fake, it's fake*. He pulled back to fully nuzzle my ear, and I couldn't hide my shiver against his hardness.

Quietly but just loud enough for the sensitive ears of the rest of the room to hear clearly, Elián rumbled, "Careful, wicked girl." His hand that held my jaw tightly turned my head, angling me slightly further to the left than straight forward, and I caught sight of slicked, gray hair. "Your beauty has everyone wishing they were me right now," he brought his other palm to my inner thigh, dangerously close to where I was growing wetter by the second, "I wonder what they'd do if I let them see how pretty you are when I make you come."

I wriggled against Elián at the precise moment I locked eyes with the one we were seeking. My Shadow's cock twitched behind me, and my moan was as much from lust as it was from victory.

"So—what? Your plan is to seduce him?"

"Are you opposed to getting close with a Vyrkos?" It wouldn't have been *out of the realm of possibility considering many Lylithan's feelings on the matter.*

Elián's mouth twisted a bit, but he shook his head, "No. I've met many Vyrkos. I have... little issue with them." He cleared his throat and continued lacing his boots, "So, your plan?"

I shrugged, "I'm prepared to pivot, but seduction feels the quickest route considering what Grimm said. But if you don't feel comfortable with it, say the word, and I can figure something else out."

He searched my face. I knew that I was asking a lot of him... and with what had happened in the past, I was expecting his refusal more than anything. But to my surprise, my Shadow snorted, calculating glint in his eyes, *"All right, Your Highness. We'll try your plan."*

The Vyrkos male that had killed Isabella was here. In this tavern. His nostrils were flaring, and his fangs were drawn while he watched me writhe against Elián. Though my words were to my Shadow, I spoke them at my target, "And what if I want them to see? Maybe let one or two join you in fucking me." I thought we had every pair of eyes on us now, and spurred on by that fact, I moved my hand atop Elián's at my thigh and cupped myself with his hand.

Elián growled in my ear, "All the shit you talk about Shadows, they'd be watching me wreck that filthy mouth of yours before I—"

A female with dull brown hair was suddenly in my line of vision, blocking me from the heated stare of my mark. She slammed her hands down at our table and peeled her lips back from her fangs. "Why don't you get rid of that pathetic little breeder, and I'll show you a good time, Shadow?"

I knew this one—what was her name? Valyrie? Again, it didn't matter. She was one of Shoko's old flings that had barely hidden her jealousy when my best friend had taken up with me. I think Shoko and I had once fucked in this very booth, actually. Either way, Valyrie or whatever-her-name-was was hindering my avenging Isabella. And though *she* didn't know that, she thought she could seduce Elián away from me.

The air of our audience was shifting, adding burgeoning bloodlust to the mix. Something about the turning process made Vyrkos more animalistic than they had been as humans. Though anyone was capable of being territorial, they wouldn't respect anything other than me confronting her challenge with the same energy.

My hands ripped Elián off of me, and I shot to my feet. I leaned against the table and hissed, baring my fangs and showing my fury, "Back the fuck off. He's *mine*." Never mind that she was admonishing me for being Lylithan when Elián and I were the same race.

His hot palm smacked my ass, and I couldn't focus on the meaning behind it. Was it purely for the act, or was he reminding me to not get too wrapped up in this one who didn't matter? Whichever, I let myself arch and yelp at his touch, which just enraged the challenging female even more.

I laughed in her face, and Elián spanked me again, paying her no mind. "Best go find someone who actually wants you for a change," I spat.

Her eyes widened, and I could see her anger flare at my blow. Had she really thought Elián would just push me aside and—what? Mount her in the middle of the room? I laughed again, and she snarled back at me. She was taking this moment to prove herself to her people, and on a normal night, I might let her walk away without fully bruising her fragile ego. But the way the target of all of this was eyeing Elián and me with even more hunger, it was too good an opportunity to pass up.

The muscles on the female's shoulders tensed in a telltale sign of her next move, and I let my instincts take over. I launched myself over the table and brought her to the ground. She screamed, and a half circle of onlookers began to form around us as I straddled her.

My fist collided with her cheek, and I grunted in satisfaction at the crunch that rang out. She was a shit fighter, but I let her flip me just to see what she'd do. The left side of her face looked wrong with her fractured cheekbone, and it was no issue to block her pathetic swipes at my own.

I popped my hips up to make her lose balance, and she tumbled over me. The powdery sweetness of her accosted my nose, but I continued to let my training guide me. I wrapped my arms around her back and flipped her so fast, she stared confused at the ceiling. My elbow struck her jaw, and her eyes rolled back in her head. There were a series of cheers and chuckles at the quick defeat, and I stood, probably looking every bit of the wicked girl that Elián had called me.

Those hot hands of his palmed my hips and ground my ass against his rock-hard cock. I spat on the unconscious female and was met with more approving looks. It was barbaric, but I'd earned more of their respect tonight. And Valyrie wouldn't be messing with me anymore after this quick defeat.

Elián's teeth nipped at my earlobe, and his hair tickled my neck. "*Fuck*, you make me so hard." That wasn't a lie, at least. Again, Elián had angled us toward the reason we were here, and he didn't need to say his invitation aloud. I knew that we were both holding the Vyrkos assassin's attention and that there would be no mistaking it. His voice dropped lower, "I'm going to make you scream."

I bit my bottom lip and moaned while he continued to grind me against him. One of his hands disappeared, and I watched as he tossed back the rest of my drink. With a pointed glance toward the silver-haired male, we turned and left. Well, Elián pulled me outside, and to them, it looked like he was taking me away to fuck me elsewhere.

To me, though, I knew he was starting the second part of my plan for me. I had enough sense not to protest, but his hand on my ass as we left was clenched tight in irritation.

The alley behind this tavern was even filthier than the one we had met Grimm in. But this was part of the plan, and I breathed past the absolute stench of rancid blood, piss, old cum, and overflowing garbage buckets. Luckily for us, there was no one back here, and the telltale sound of steps a few paces back made my heart quicken in anticipation.

Elián hoisted me in the air and pushed me against the brick facade of the building. His hands dug into my thighs, and I arched my neck to him. Our mark was fully sauntering to us now, and Elián inhaled at my throat. He angled his head toward the newcomer, and I let out another moan at the press of his hips against mine.

A new, horrible voice curled my insides, "She's a fiery one, isn't she?" I could *smell* Isabella's blood on his breath. It was faint, but it was there, and my body vibrated with anger.

But as I struggled to keep up the act, Elián rolled right along, "You have no idea. The mouth on her is something else."

"Oh, I don't doubt that," he was leaning against the wall next to me, now. He was dressed in black like us, though his leather was more like Elián's. Whether he was looking for a contract when he came to The Grave, a quick fuck, or both, I didn't know. Again, it didn't matter. He had killed Isabella, and I was intent on finding out why.

My Shadow kept on nuzzling my neck, and I turned to face the male. He was looking between Elián and I as if he couldn't decide which of us he wanted more. Though I wanted to scream and rip his throat out like he'd done her, I licked my lips, which made him palm his crotch.

"What do you say, wicked girl?" Elián swiped his tongue along my neck, and my eyes rolled back like the female I had just knocked out. "Care to show him how you swallow a good, big cock?" The male groaned and had already started adjusting his trousers as he watched me look at his crotch and nod. "Do a good job, and I might reward you with mine," Elián punctuated his order with another nip at my ear and then released me.

My boots smacked the paved alley, and Elián stepped back to let me move and stand before the one who had snuck into Rhaea's Temple and murdered the last mother I had in this realm. The Death within me was fighting to come out in reaction to my rage, but I managed to keep the mask of a different kind of heat on my face.

I wasn't without Elián's warmth for long. While I went to my knees, I fought the urge to gag as the assassin's arousal flooded my senses. But then Elián's hand rested on the top of my head in what would look, outwardly, like a possessive and encouraging touch. Something about the way he held me, though, I knew that he was grounding me.

"That's right, vicious girl. Take what you're owed." Elián's voice was gravelly with lust, but I knew the words for what they were.

The pale, silver-haired Vyrkos was looking at me hungrily, fangs drawn and tongue slithering over his lips. I fought the gag in my throat by thinking of my Shadow behind me while I tugged at the laces of the assassin's trousers. My plan had dictated that I fully distract until he was too in the throws to put up a fight, cause a ruckus. Though I was in good standing with the Vyrkos of Nethras, I knew it would be foolish to assume they'd see my attack as warranted and not come to their brother's aid. But the thought of pulling his cock from his trousers already made me want to vomit.

I glanced up from his untied crotch to see his head thrown back in anticipation. My fingers reached in toward the Vyrkos's cool skin as I looked back at my Shadow, as if asking for a lover's approval.

Elián raised a brow, silently stepped away, and I leapt to my feet. My jab was a calculated strike at the assassin's nose, and the breaking of his bones and thud of his scalp against the wall made my darkness shiver. I watched with cold eyes as he slumped to the ground, and Elián and I got to moving on part three.

30

The rat squirmed in my hand, and for a moment, I thought I was going to retch. The air in the abandoned building was stale, the windows all boarded up. The only light was from the slivers of moonlight through the slats.

Elián checked the silver chains for the third time, and they were locked tightly. He held the key made of the same metal, and placed it in his pocket. The sexual tension between us went cold the second the Vyrkos assassin had hit the ground, and he stood close, yet much further away from me.

His heated words and possessive touches were still in my mind, and I shook my head to try to dispel the fog they created. The black veins were back on my hands again, and they offered me a bit more clarity. Enough to focus on the task at hand.

I ripped the squealing rodent's head off and made sure to direct the spray of its blood on the ground and not on me. If his arms weren't bound behind him, the assassin would have been able to reach out and touch my body. But he was still unconscious, black blood clotted on his face, and slumped in the chair we had propped him up in.

The scent of the dead rat's blood stirred him awake. It was unnerving how his nose gave a quick sniff just before his eyes snapped open.

He lunged forward for the source of the blood, unseeing as he snapped his mouth with fangs already lowered.

"Good, you're awake." I flung the rat parts away from me and wiped my hands on my trousers, already coated with dust and blood from Elián's and my tasks getting ready for our interrogation. Or torture, depending on which way this one would swing.

It took a few moments for his mind to catch up, and I waited, letting the silence settle in the air and hopefully unsettle him.

His eyes whipped back and forth between me and Elián, who had one of his swords in hand. The assassin's lip curled back, revealing more of his fangs, "You fucking *bitch*."

I crossed my arms and rolled my eyes. "Oh, calm yourself. I could have just killed you outright."

He spat on my boots, "What do you want?"

I unsheathed one of the daggers at my thighs and twirled it with a flick of my wrist. "Nothing too complex, really. You were sent to kill the High Priestess of Rhaea a few days ago, and I want to know why. And by whom." I shrugged.

His sneer dropped, and he looked at me blankly for a moment. But then he threw back his head and cackled in a grating pitch.

Once he had gotten it out of his system, he said, "I don't know what you're talking about."

My patience was nonexistent, and I had been ramped up to the edge all night with no real release. I slashed my blade across his cheek, and he screamed at the poison stinging his flesh. It was just enough to break the skin, but it would sting like all hell.

His screech turned to more unsettling laughter, and I felt the vines stir faster on my skin. He hadn't noticed those yet, apparently. Which made me even angrier—how had he been able to take Isabella unawares and dispatch her? It had to have been be stupid luck. "I've heard of you, you know? Batting your eyelashes to hustle money and steal all the good contracts. You're a fucking worthless cunt!"

And here we went. I was well aware how some of my more disgruntled colleagues saw me, but I had long ago made peace with the fact that they were just insecure. I felt no shame at using my body to fight as well as entice when it brought me closer to my goals. He was just upset that I had used it on him and how well it had worked. And I didn't hear him saying the same thing to Elián, who had used his body to seduce just as much as I had. If anything, he was the one to offer me up to the small male.

"You're going to have to be much more original than that. I get quite cruel when I'm bored, and you're starting to bore me. Talk."

When he just glared, I struck again on the other cheek, but he remained silent this time.

I stepped back to keep myself from plunging my blade in his heart, and Elián, to my surprise, replaced me. He crouched, and though I couldn't see his eyes from where I stood, I imagined that they were more distressing than the Vyrkos's could ever be. "You're going to answer all the questions my queen asks of you, or the least of your worries are going to be scratches from a blade."

The male didn't say anything, but he also didn't try to insult Elián the way he did me. Typical. Though they were immortal once turned, the Vyrkos still seemed to hold on to their human sexist bullshit more often than not.

Elián pressed to stand and then punched the male in the stomach. He doubled over as much as he could with his restraints and spat out black blood onto the floor.

My Shadow switched places with me, and we spent the next few hours trying to get answers. Whoever had paid the assassin had chosen well. After his initial outrage at being taken unawares, he committed to silence, even though his end was certain. When he did open his mouth, he cursed us both, but his insults were all directed at me.

When his ear hit the floor, "You worthless slut," as I licked his sickly sweet blood from my dagger.

After Elián thoroughly shattered his already broken nose and dislodged a few of his teeth, "Fuck you."

I plunged my blade into his side for the third time, "I'm not telling you shit, so why don't you just fucking end it? Or do you need his backup to do it? Is that how you handle all your work, bitch?"

I'd rolled my eyes again on that one and twisted my dagger in slow circles, "You really are boring me."

When I stepped away, though, Elián's eyes were flames much brighter than the Vyrkos' red ones, and his fist connected with ribs this time. I heard them snap, and my mouth watered. He wasn't using his sword, just holding it with one hand and letting the other do all the work. "You won't be leaving here alive, so you might as well just tell us what you know, and she'll end you swiftly."

The Vyrkos assassin, whose name we still didn't know, looked between the two of us. One of his eyes was already swollen shut, and the other one was heavily bruised. The wounds of my blades had done as much damage to him as Elián's blows, but he still wasn't budging. I had to give it to him, at least. His employer had picked a loyal assassin. Or whoever had hired him was scary enough to keep the male quiet until the bitter end.

He managed to wheeze through his broken bones, "Then why don't you just step aside and let your little slut do it, then? Or is she that much of a coward? I'm not telling either of you shit. I hope her mouth is really as good as you said it is, because her attempts to get me to talk are pathetic." He rolled that good eye to land on me, "Thought you'd be more impressive than this," he spat more blood on my boots, "what a waste."

His words didn't phase me in the slightest, but my scoff choked in my throat before it could sound into the dusty room. I watched as the assassin's head lifted off of his shoulders after a sharp, silver blur. Elián had the gray hair in his hand, and I watched the severed head, still gaping, burst into flames.

31

I was frozen. I had been prepared to keep torturing the bastard all night, even keep him up past daybreak when he'd be exhausted and delirious. It was why we had selected this particular spot for the last part of my plan.

But instead, I was watching my Shadow become a whirl of jerky, black movement. It was almost too fast for me to track, but I watched, incredulous and in awe of him throwing the flaming head onto the stone ground and turning to the body still sitting in the chair. The restraints gave a metallic snap as he ripped it from the silver chains.

He lifted the corpse from the chair as if it weighed nothing, and it, too, began to smoke and then catch. From his hands that I belatedly noticed were now bare, his gloves seemingly burned off.

He flung the body on top of its head that was now black and still burning, and the rest of Isabella's murderer began to be consumed by giant, licking flames.

My Shadow hadn't stopped moving until that moment, and he stood, watching the body burn. I was fixed on his back, expanding and constricting quickly with his panting. His hands that were apparently capable of starting literal flames curled and flexed.

There was no smell of magic, of aether being wielded. Which meant—that fire had come from *him*.

Six breaths coursed through my lungs. Six breaths where the only sounds in the abandoned building were our heartbeats and the crackling of the body being consumed by Elián's fire.

He slowly turned to me, and I gasped.

The first time I met my Shadow, I could see his rage. Over the course of our time together, I had seen his eyes change color and intensity each day, sometimes each hour. While he was able to don that Shadow mask, his eyes often gave him away.

Now, they weren't just shifting shades of auburn or gold, but hauntingly beautiful flames swimming within his irises. The blazing of that stare was nothing I had ever seen before, and my heart picked up an even faster beat. My darkness crept up my arms in curiosity and anticipation.

But his sculpted brow was crumpled while he looked at me, and his jaw was flexing harder than I had ever seen it. His shoulders were drawn, and though his breathing had slowed, he looked to almost be preparing himself for some sort of onslaught.

Perhaps he was right to assume that would happen, though I would not be running from him in terror or rebuking him for this power he was able to wield. Our playing earlier tonight had already left my body fidgety, and crackling bolts of desire just ran through my veins even stronger.

I rushed forward without thinking, and when I clutched the front of his jacket, he flinched but didn't pull away. With the fire, there was another emotion swimming in his eyes. Something sad, something regretful.

I grasped the back of his neck and pulled his head down to mine, where I was close enough to feel his breath on my lips. When he didn't make to pull away, I closed the distance and planted my mouth onto his.

My lips did not bother with softness while I took in whatever emotions he was feeling. I opened myself up to take whatever burdened him, all but begged for it. The fear I had for kissing him again was washed away—I just wanted to taste and comfort him.

Elián hesitated for a moment but then responded in kind, letting his lips part when I nipped at his bottom one. Our tongues tangled in a way that was no act, no playing. There was no one here to seduce aside from each other, and I again felt that need to open myself for anything and everything he would give me.

Elián brought his hands to my back, dropping the sword with a clatter. I moaned at the near-searing sensation on my bare skin and pressed my hips to his. He pressed back, and I felt the evidence that his desire was overruling his senses in the same way mine was. Before, when he'd held to me, I had to dangle along the line of restraining myself but also convincing an audience of my desire. But now, I let my mind go and the need within take over.

When I moved backwards, he followed, keeping our mouths glued in a mess of lips and fangs and tongue. I turned and shoved him down, and thrill ran up my spine at how easily he obeyed.

Before he could even land on the chair just occupied by the body burning next to us, I was on him. Elián gripped my hips as I straddled and moved them against his. The aching spot between my thighs rubbed against the hardened length of him, and I didn't even attempt to suppress the moan that escaped my body. My fingers tangled in the soft waves of his hair as I broke away from his mouth, kissing down his jaw and neck. When a rumble in his chest rippled into mine, I moaned again, all the while rocking against him.

Elián shuddered and cursed, "Merro". It was a word I didn't recognize, his accent around it deeper, stronger, but I couldn't think about it now, couldn't ask about it now.

When he started to pull me away from him, I whimpered in protest. Only for his mouth to shoot to my chest. One of his hands moved from my hip to the back of my neck, steadying me as he leaned me backward.

He found one breast and attacked it with his tongue. The thin leather of my top was still skin-tight enough for me to feel every painstaking swipe, and release came so close, I could easily claim it. Elián tickled and teased my nipple and the golden bar through it, and my eyes rolled back in my head, hands still in his hair, as I held him to me.

Then he moved to my other breast, and as he did, the hand gripping my hip to bruising was gone. I wriggled, demanding it back. But he still had me pinned with his other hand at my neck.

Elián's thumb started working between my legs in slow circles. All thought, all sense left me, and when I squirmed, writhed again, he found the spot that I needed and moved it faster. He was going to make me come through my clothes, and at that moment, it felt like the most erotic thing I had ever experienced.

I was gripping his hair so tightly that I knew I was pulling too hard. But my toes and fingers were curling beyond my control, and the pressure was building too quickly to do anything other than let it take me. My hips ground against his thumb erratically, and for the first time that night, I regretted my outfit choice because I wanted the flesh of his thumb against my skin.

As I was wriggling on his lap, mind plotting how to get out of my clothes but unable to keep a thought for more than half a second, he bit down on my nipple just enough to draw pain. And, with his scalding palm at my neck and his thumb moving in just that way I needed, the pressure coiling and curling from my core exploded.

"*Fuck,*" came from my throat in a raspy hiss. But he kept licking me, this time languidly with the flat of his tongue, and his thumb didn't give me a moment, either. And just as the stars cleared from my vision, the pleasure ratcheted up again. I knew I'd pulled out some of his hair by now, but he kept on all the same while I came again. This time, though, I was beyond words and just grunted like an animal.

He stopped his licking and kissed his way up my chest to my neck and brought both hands to my back, rubbing his hot palms on my bare skin. I was still trembling from the thunderous releases he'd given me, and I knew that soon, I would want more.

Elián leaned back in the chair, bringing me with him, and I loosened my grip on his hair. My hands found his chest, and his breathing was deep as he inhaled at my neck, letting his fangs graze over my skin. *I could stay like this all night,* I realized.

I lost count of the breaths we sat like that, but Elián still being hard underneath me nudged at my mind, my body. This was the second time he'd given pleasure to me without taking it for himself, fleeing before I could reciprocate.

I gripped his face and instead of meeting his lips with mine, I flicked out my tongue to tease his top lip, once, twice. His cock jerked underneath me, sending another pang of pleasure shooting up from my lap. But I was determined now.

"Elián," I started to move my legs, attempting to slide off of him. The fire on his face had settled to something calmer, and his hands flew to my hips, trying to keep me in place.

But I couldn't have that. "Elián," I looked him in the eyes and almost lost my breath, "I want you to fuck my mouth now." His eyes were still simmering, but the colors moving in his stare weren't flaring like they were before. They were a soft crackling hearth instead of a roaring forest fire.

And I could see the protest there, too, felt it in the way his grip wasn't letting me go. He began to shake his head, but I cut him off, "I do not allow just anyone this privilege, so take that into consideration before you say no."

His eyes flared for a second, as if about to challenge me. But another moment passed, and he softened, huffed, and nodded. It was all I needed.

This time when I made to slide down from his lap, he let me. When I had knelt before the now-dead Vyrkos assassin, I'd felt utterly disgusted. But kneeling before my Shadow now, I felt nothing but a desire so staggering, that my fingers were shaking. My mouth was watering, and I so badly wanted the primal taste of him on my tongue.

When I brought my palms to his knees, he allowed me to nudge them open, and I had to focus to unfasten him. His gaze was so intense, I felt it even with my face toward the laces and buttons of his leather trousers. I barely got the damn things untied before he sprang free.

My teeth bit down on my bottom lip as I took in the beautiful length of him. He was long and thick and smelled like the rawest version of his cinnamon and oak. How had I lasted this long without tasting him?

My palms rubbed his thighs as I briefly contemplated on how to start. I wanted to watch my Shadow become utterly undone, to make that stone facade crack and split until the real Elián was revealed to me. I'd seen glimpses of his true self within our arguing or more companionable moments, but I knew there was so much of him that I didn't know. And I wanted it all. I wanted him to burn me alive.

Once I decided how I would proceed, I looked up at him, slowly. And my gaze beneath my darkened, kohl-lined lashes had the effect I'd hoped it would. His mouth was parted, just a bit, and his tongue snuck out to swipe at his bottom lip.

He moved a hand gingerly to my temple, letting it trail over the curve of my ear, along my jaw. It was so sweet and caring, and perhaps at another time, I would want that treatment from him. But this was not the night for it. When Elián had agreed to my seduction plot, I told him to do and say whatever to me that he needed to. And the fact that his touch had been strong, his words commanding, I had a sneaking suspicion that this was how he'd want to take me.

I shook my head, and he raised a brow.

The huskiness in my voice pleasantly surprised me, "When you and I first met, you shattered my wrists," he flinched, but I pressed on, "do not try to be gentle with me now." And then I moved in.

I palmed the velvety smooth base of him and hovered my lips over his tip. Puckering, I let a trail of saliva slide out of my mouth. I moved my fist up, twisting slightly, then back down, letting it become slick and ready for me, and his cock somehow grew harder. He shuddered and then I swallowed him down.

I wasn't lying when I told Elián that I didn't offer this to just anyone, but I didn't let my fear of being out of practice deter me. The taste of him in my mouth was better than I'd imagined, than my power was able to theorize, and I fought the gag reflex reacting to him hitting the back of my throat.

My darkness was still out, concentrated on my hands, and he bucked deliciously at my touch. I sucked and constricted my throat, making the most obscene of sounds but not caring in the slightest.

Elián's hands were then gripping my scalp, and I groaned around his invading length. He managed to get his fingers clasped in my hair around the thick, singular braid, and he used it to pull my head back so that just the tip of him was in my mouth. I swirled my tongue around it, licking up the moisture that beaded there, and moaned again at the slightly salty taste of him. With another word in that foreign language, he pushed me down again to meet his thrusting hips.

I gripped Elián's thighs while he indeed fucked my mouth.

My nails dug into the leather, just to return the little taste of pain he gave me earlier. He hissed as he thrusted, "Fucking—take it so good," and the fabric of my top and skin-tight trousers was too much. The fluttering in my chest and the tears springing from my eyes while he thrusted into and out of my throat were too much. I brought a hand to that aching above my slit, but I immediately wished it was his.

"*Meline,*" His voice was breathy now. His cock was pulsing on my tongue and in my throat, and his thrusts were becoming jerky. He was close, and I sucked harder.

With being already primed from earlier, the sweet exertion of letting him fuck my face, the rubbing of my own fingers, and the sound of my name on his lips again, I came for the third time. My scream was muffled by him in my mouth, and the vibration of it was *his* undoing. His hips shot forward, and his hands held me down in a steel grip as he came with a roar that racked the entire building.

His hot seed shot down my throat, and I hummed as I took each spurt of it until Elián settled back into the chair. His hands fell from my scalp down to dangle at his sides, and he panted as if he'd been running for days.

I pulled back slowly, letting the flat of my tongue drag as I released him. I swallowed and licked my lips, proud of myself for not wasting a single drop. Rich and wild, the taste of him was everything I'd imagined it would be.

When I brought my gaze back up to him, the tense anger and sadness that was in his shoulders was gone. His eyes were halfway closed, and his fangs rested softly on his bottom lip.

So this is what it looked like to see him completely wrecked. I had expected to feel utterly triumphant, and though I did, I also felt... warmth, longing.

I ran my hands softly up his legs. Pressing down on the tops of his thighs, I brought myself to a crouch before him. I leaned over and planted quick kisses to each of his fangs.

"Come on. We should probably get out of here." If the screams of our captive hadn't alerted anyone of our presence here, the roaring of our orgasms surely would. I stifled a giggle, seeing clearly the moment my words snapped Elián out of the afterglow of his release. But I couldn't keep the satisfied grin from creeping up my lips as I watched him shoot up from the chair and clear his throat. He tucked himself back into his trousers and redid the laces and button. His eyes flitted to me then to the sword on the floor, and he grabbed it, sheathing it with the other one at his back. I had never seen him flustered before.

He moved around the now smoking heap of ash and toward the door. Elián stopped and turned back to me, clearing his throat again. My grin settled into a smirk as I followed him back out into the alley and then onto the street.

We didn't talk on the trek back to my apartment. I just followed his lead without protest as he meandered down side streets and more alleys in a nonsensical weaving to deter anyone tracking us. But I thought he was buying himself time to brood. I could almost *hear* the wheels of his brain turning, trying to make sense of what we just did. Of what he did. Yes, I had kissed him because I couldn't bear to see the look in his eyes. His rage left me wanting him in a way I had never wanted someone in my life, and that had fueled some of what I had done. But the sadness and shame that was on his face... I couldn't stand it.

While I was not regretting anything that transpired tonight, nor was I angry with him for killing the one chance we had at getting answers for Isabella's murder, I knew that he was. I moved through the city streets at his side, keeping my eyes forward, but I could feel him descending into that place again.

We snuck in the back door of my apartment building, the one that practically none of my neighbors used, and made our way up the steps. Elián took one of my spare keys from his pocket and unlocked the door for us. He proceeded to search the place while I closed the door and flipped on my lamp in the routine we'd completed many times now. He walked slowly back to the living room this time, though, and the tension between us was thick and crackling and made me shift between my feet. His eyes were back to their normal state, and they looked the color of liquor in the dim light.

Elián opened his mouth, decided against whatever he was about to say, and closed it. So I rushed out, "I don't regret anything that happened tonight." His jaw clenched, and worry churned in my gut. By the set of his face, I found myself steeling for rejection or indignation or—

A frantic pounding at the door startled me, and before I could whirl around, Elián had me behind him. He flung the door open, pulling in the stranger and slamming them against the wall.

32

What the hell? I would need to ask Tana to reinforce the barrier sooner rather than later, because my Shadow seemed to have pulled that person through the threshold with ease.

Elián had a sword to the intruder's throat when my mind caught up. It took the person in Elián's grasp longer to register what had happened. Not until Elián bared his fangs at them, growling, did they begin to thrash under his grip. But it was no use. One wrong move, and Elián would either cut their head off or tear out their throat.

I shook my head to clear the arousal that crept up my spine as I watched Elián handle the intruder. And then I recognized the trembling person under Elián's grasp. Tears streamed down the chin of the cloaked person, but I didn't need to see their whole face to smell who it was. I rushed to Elián, and clawed at his arm, trying to pull him away.

Elián's face whipped to mine, and he let out a snarl, all the while still keeping his grip and the sword held still. He hissed at me, and I hissed right back, "Fall back, Elián!" His eyes narrowed, and he turned, ignoring me. "Elián, that is an *order*. Let them go." I saw my command as his charge push through the haze of his instinct to protect, and he slowly lowered his weapon. Steps scuttling up the stairwell hit both of our ears at the same time, and we stiffened. But the person bounding up the stairs didn't hear us, nor did they see the scene through my open door until they were on the threshold.

I gritted through my teeth as I saw the fear in the newcomer's eyes, "*Elián*, let them go. They're a *friend*," and now I directed my words to the person in his grasp, "Whitley, I'm sorry."

Elián slowly eased his grip on their throat, and when he released Whitley, they slid to the floor, clutching at their chest. I turned to little Marco as he stared at us with tears in his eyes. He must have followed Whitley here, and he couldn't stop staring at the sword clenched in Elián's fist.

"Please, Marco, come in and shut the door." The little one's lip trembled, but he obeyed. He crouched down to Whitley and moved his hands helplessly over his shivering caregiver. Bile rose in my throat when I saw the fear in Marco's face turn to anger. Whitley was Francie's mate, and they worked at the children's home with her, taking care of Marco and the other orphaned children that lived there and—fuck, fuck, *fuck*.

We all remained silent, and no one moved. Whitley was still taking in deep breaths, doing their best to recover, but I saw the gray tint their brown skin had taken. Marco was glaring between Elián and me, and bless him, he crouched in front of Whitley as if to protect them from another attack. And Elián stared down his nose at them both.

After a moment, I realized that he was waiting for my command. *Would he cut down this child if I asked him to?* I shuddered and pushed away the thought.

I said softly to try to de-escalate the situation further, "Elián. You can stand down. This is Whitley and Marco, and they are friends of mine. Whitley works at the children's home where Marco lives, and where I've helped out for a few years. Please." Soundlessly, he backed away until he stood next to me, and I released the breath that I had been holding.

I lowered to a crouch, "I'm sorry, Marco. My friend here is just trying to keep me safe like you're keeping Whitley safe. And Whitley, I'm sorry that Elián frightened you both. I hope you aren't hurt."

They took a few deep breaths. And after clearing their throat, Whitley lowered their hood and rasped, "I'm fine. It's fine. I just— I've never had a sword to my throat before." They let out a half-hearted chuckle, running a hand over their short, white curls, and Marco relaxed.

I brought a hand to Elián's calf, and he flinched at my touch before backing away, giving the three of us on the floor some room. We'd have our conversation later, then.

Marco and I let Whitley come down from the inevitable adrenaline rush they had experienced. And Elián stood at my back, ready to intervene should any sign that the situation was changing arise. I spoke to Marco in soothing tones, thanking him for looking out for Whitley and asking if he was hungry or thirsty. Sure enough, his weary eyes turned bright at the prospect of something to eat.

"Whitley," they were starting to look better, the grayness almost completely gone, "are you able to stand? We can go sit at the table while I get Marco something to eat. And I'll make us some tea."

Whitley nodded quickly and carefully stood to their feet. They didn't wobble, and I breathed a sigh. The three of us made our way slowly to the kitchen, and as we rounded a stock-still Elián on the way there, Marco wrapped his small hand in mine. He eyed Elián with a mix of trepidation and awe.

Whitley and Marco took seats at the table, now dressed with a bouquet of blush begonias I'd bought upon my and Elián's arrival to the city. I put the kettle on the stove and took down four mugs from the cabinet, all the while monitoring the tension slowly dissipating from the room. The dread I felt from scaring Whitley and Marco, though, sat like a stone in my gut.

I crouched before Marco and asked him what he would like to eat, "I don't have much, but I think I have enough to make you a sandwich. It won't be as good as Francie's, but I'll try." I smiled at him and flicked one of the strawberry ringlets on his brow. The stone seemed to double in size when I saw tears well in the young boy's eyes and spill over.

My knees thudded as they hit the wood floor, and I took both of his hands in mine, "What's going on?" But he didn't answer with anything other than tears tracking down his dusty cheeks.

I looked over his shoulder to Whitley sitting beside him, and though their shoulders were square, I saw the worry. My whole body stilled, Marco's hands in mine, as I steeled myself for the news to come. With the commotion of Elián almost painting my threshold in blood and bodies, I hadn't quite thought through why these two would be here. And how they knew where I lived. I stared unseeingly at the bouquet and tried to parse through my racing thoughts.

The stone in my gut grew again, pushing now on my lungs and heart. I tried to breathe deep, but it got in the way. My heart beat frantically against the dread, no matter how much I willed it to calm.

A squeeze in my palm brought me back, and I managed to ask, "What's happened?" Because the only way Whitley would know where I lived was if Francie told them. And per my instructions, Francie was only to come to my home should there be a threat or danger that they couldn't take care of themselves. A last resort, I urged her. But she wasn't with them.

Whitley opened their mouth, but a high-pitched whistling came out instead. We both flinched, and I realized that it was the tea kettle. I began to rise, but the boy resisted me trying to break our grasp. My thumbs rubbed soft circles on the backs of his hands, but he held on still.

He jutted his dimpled, tear-streaked chin behind me, "Why doesn't *he* get it?" Looking over my shoulder, I saw that Elián had crept up closer behind me. Just three feet or so separated us, and he was staring down at me. I quickly searched his face for something, anything, but he was locked down. I'm not sure why I expected something different.

But he was not my servant, and the whistling was becoming unbearable. So I gave a swift kiss to Marco's brow and released our grasp.

The smell of chamomile immediately relaxed me, and luckily, I still had enough honey from my last trip to the market to add to each of our mugs. I placed the one with an extra dollop before Marco, and another before his caregiver. My own warming in my palm, I extended a mug to Elián. He quirked that damn brow, and I almost splashed the tea in his face. See how that fire protected him from a good scalding.

He must've read the intention on my face because he took the proffered mug in his right hand and drank while sheathing his sword in one swift movement. I took the seat opposite Marco, and Elián stood at my side. I wished that he would sit down but had no energy to start that argument. Thankfully, Whitley and Marco's shoulders were no longer drawn, and their breathing had relaxed substantially.

"Tell me," I requested softly over my steaming mug.

Whitley took one sip, then another, and shuddered. They then reached slowly into their trouser's pocket, failing to take discreet glances at Elián. But he made no move to leave my side. In fact, the fool was looking mighty relaxed with a hand resting in the crook of his crossed arm, sipping his tea.

"The children, Lydia, and I went to the river this afternoon, and Francie hung back to start prepping dinner," they let loose a ragged sigh and fiddled with the folded paper they'd retrieved, "and when we returned, there appeared to have been a struggle in the kitchen. Things were thrown all over, and on the counter, there was this note. That's all that was left, and Fran was gone." They reached over the table and offered me the paper. When I unfolded it myself, there was a single sentence that left me cold.

I wanted to vomit but managed to keep my face steady. When I sat forward, leaning my elbows on the table, my bare back peeled off of my chair. And I remembered what I must look like to them, black fighting clothes and blades sheathed at my thighs.

Elián's voice startled all of us, "Do you have any idea why someone would take her?" I was grateful for his smooth rumble, and the stone in my gut, at least, had stopped growing. Part of me wanted to reach beside me for his hand, but I was unsure of how he'd react enough to keep my hands around the note.

Whitley shook their head and stared into their mug. They were usually all quiet smiles, but their mouth was pressed in a hard line. Tremors intermittently racked their shoulders, and I wondered if Marco weren't here, would they let show the true weight of their worry? The young boy, at least, now seemed to have stopped crying. And he looked over Elián in that unabashedly curious way that children do.

"Fran seemed to think that you would be able to help in case something went really, really wrong. And I think," they cleared their throat, "I think this would count as such. We already talked to the city guards, but they seemed just as perplexed as we did. I've spent most of the night trying to figure this out myself and with Lydia. But we need help." Whitley's ash gray eyes pleaded mine, and if my well hadn't gone dry, I think I would've sprung a few of my own tears.

I turned my head to my left, speaking to Elián now, "I think we should go and see what we can find. We might be able to pick up on something." A few beats passed, and he didn't respond. I looked up to him, but he was looking back and forth between Marco and Whitley. When he was done assessing and came to whatever conclusion, he glanced back at me and nodded.

Whitley sighed again and ran their hand over their head. Tea gone too cold for my taste, I stood and prepared the sandwich that I promised Marco. While I did, Whitley asked him how he managed to follow them through the city without them noticing. The boy detailed how he was able to remain at least a block behind Whitley while still keeping them in sight, making sure to walk close to others so that he didn't stand out. Part of me wanted to gently let them know that while the boy was clever, Whitley most likely lacked the training to be effectively aware of their surroundings. But when I turned around with the cheddar and apple sandwich on a small plate, I caught sight of Elián's slightly pursed lips. An expression that I had learned through these weeks to signal faint amusement.

Marco took the sandwich and began inhaling, muttering a couple thank you's as he gobbled it down. A few bites from finishing, he pointed a finger over Elián's shoulder and asked through a mouthful of food, "Would you show me how to use one of those?" They boy hadn't been doing a very good job at hiding his fleeting emotions in regard to my Shadow, and I couldn't help but smirk at his landing on being impressed and intrigued.

It was the night for Elián to constantly surprise me, it seemed, because his voice took on a softer tone with Little Marco, "And what do you know of swords, boyo?"

Marco straightened in his seat while he chewed and swallowed the last of his sandwich. He crossed his arms at his narrow chest, "I know a lot! And Lady Em has been teaching me!" Marco looked at me, "I did my exercises and drills every day like you said!"

I grinned, "I knew that you would. Truthfully, you did better than me, because I've forgotten mine more days than not. I think you're on the road to be a great warrior, Little Marco."

Marco turned back to my Shadow, "See? Lady Em is the best fighter! And she's taught me all sorts of things about swords and daggers."

Elián pursed his lips again, and I wondered how often he interacted with children. When did Shadows start training? If I had asked myself two days ago if I thought Elián would be kind and patient to a child, I would have laughed away the notion. But I watched, utterly amused, as Marco and Elián went back and forth about what I had taught the boy and whether he was worthy of a lesson from Elián.

The corners of his lips were tilting up in the barest hint of a smile, and I could hardly believe it. "We have to go see about this Francie, but I will show you my swords before we part. If you can be helpful, I may even let you hold them."

Marco shot up from his seat and headed for the door, "Let's go, let's go! We need to save Francie!"

The three of us adults followed behind Marco, but as I locked up and we trailed after him toward the children's home, I felt that hopeless feeling creep up again. Though I had two political victories, the past few weeks had yielded a dead Isabella, a missing Francie, and a relationship with my Shadow that was becoming more convoluted with each passing day. I was far less confident than Little Marco that finding his caretaker would be a simple feat.

33

The scene in the kitchen of the children's home wasn't as bad as Isabella's office, but it was just as ominous and just as Whitley described. The kitchen was in disarray, while the rest of the house was in the type of orderly chaos that was characteristic of the small children's home. They'd been here specifically for Francie, then.

Whitley had asked Lydia to keep watch of the children upstairs, all of which were asleep anyway, while the three of us and Little Marco combed over the scene. The boy had been told to go up to bed, but he refused over and over, and I could tell that Whitley was far too weary to keep arguing with him.

I turned to the two of them, "Both of you need to swear to me that you will not speak of what I'm about to do." I had kept my powers within my body since Elián and I left the site of our interrogation, but they were far more useful when I gave them freer rein. And though I could tell that no death occurred here, perhaps they would be able to show me *something*. The urge to use them had been tickling more and more at the inside of my mind, and upon entering the kitchen, the request was more of an incessant itch.

Whitley looked confused and even more exhausted but nodded. Marco puffed his chest and didn't look tired in the slightest. He spoke quietly but seriously, "I swear it, Lady Em."

Though I hadn't been a good student when Maman and Isabella were teaching me about the history of Rhaea's Death Wielders, one thing that I always recalled was how they'd been eradicated.

I nodded to the both of them, and though I sure as shit didn't need his permission, I glanced at Elián. He stood close enough to be able to touch my back, and at that moment, I wanted nothing more than his steadying hand. The way he had caressed my face while I knelt before him held a delicate care that I hadn't felt in so long. Perhaps not since Shoko. Hers and my romantic relationship ended for a myriad of reasons, but that care from her had been plentiful, and I hadn't realized I'd taken it for granted until it was gone.

But Elián didn't touch me. He'd caressed me and pleasured me and held me tonight, but something had changed by the time we got back to my home. He'd put his wall back up again, and I didn't know how to move beyond it.

Also, he could create fire. We would most definitely have to talk about that later.

My Shadow gave me a slow nod, though, and that breadcrumb of encouragement relaxed my shoulders more than it had any right to. So, I walked to the corner of the kitchen and stood in front of the back door. The entirety of the room was before me, as were the three people staring and waiting for me to do something. I closed my eyes and inhaled, though I didn't really need the preparation. Whitley and Marco weren't Rhaestran priestesses, they weren't my brother or Tana or Elián, so sharing this with them made me feel incredibly vulnerable.

I exhaled, and let open the iron gates of my mind. When I opened my eyes, the black smoke was curling out of the dips between my fingers. Two breaths, and the smoke had flooded the room. It circled around Whitley, Marco, and Elián, leaving a ring of clear air so as to not touch them. I focused on what the darkness was able to find and not on the stunned expression on both Whitley and Marco's faces.

Again, I could see like a murky memory the scene of the struggle that had ensued. I could see Francie chopping something, and the air around her vibrated with her absent humming. She was taken unawares, just as Isabella had been, when a stranger burst through the door that I was now standing in front of. I couldn't quite hear what she had said to the intruder, but it felt like she was demanding to know who they were, baring her fangs and telling them to leave. She wasn't a trained fighter like Isabella, but she had wielded that kitchen knife as if it were one of my daggers.

The intruder wasn't Lylithan, but the scent was somehow tangy and musky at the same time. And as I watched the scene play out, I watched them meet Francie's Lylithan speed with an equal quickness. They were eventually able to knock her out with a blow to her head that made me flinch. Though the intruder wasn't much taller than her, they threw her over their shoulder with ease just before fishing a piece of paper from their pocket. They left it on the counter and walked out of the door with Francie.

The vision cleared from my mind, and I blinked a few times to refocus on the present. A warm hand touched my back, and it wasn't until that moment that I realized I had been swaying. I swallowed and brought my hand to my chest, rubbing at my breastbone. I shook my head once, twice, to try to further clear my head. My hands were now swirling with the living tattoo, but the coming down process was hitting me hard.

It had been a tremendously long day, the elegant but small supper with Roalld was long gone, and hours of politicking, seducing, torturing, whatever Elián and I had done, and now this were taxing my body greatly.

"Do you have tea here? And we need a chair." A gruff voice behind me asked.

Whitley had gone pale again but nodded quickly. I tried to drag in a deep breath again, but it was much shallower than I needed.

Next thing I knew, that warm hand had pushed me into a chair that Little Marco had swiftly brought over from the dining room. Elián crouched before me and swept his eyes over my face, my upper body. "How do you feel?"

I blinked a few times and resumed rubbing at my chest, "What?"

He brought that large hand again to touch me, and this time he held it to my forehead in the way you would a sick child. Part of me was incredibly embarrassed—I had used my powers in much larger displays than this, and what I saw in the vision of Francie's kidnapping was nowhere near as bad as Isabella's murder. What was wrong with me?

"Rest here." He'd used that commanding voice with me again, and though I *was* exhausted and in need of rest, I felt a stirring at my navel and in my chest.

He pulled away, and his imposing form was replaced by Little Marco's much slighter one. Sitting was continuing to make me feel better, and I registered the look of worry on the boy's face. However, I was relieved to see that he wasn't looking at me with the thinly veiled apprehension that Whitley was. "Are you okay, Lady?"

Marco reached out his small hand and held the one that I had in my lap. He squeezed it once, and I stammered, "Y—yes. I'm just tired, is all. It's been a very long day."

Little Marco nodded gravely, and his mouth worked as he was deciding what to say next. "Your eyes went all black, Lady Em. Did that hurt?"

Before I could answer, Elián's hand was thrust into my line of vision, and he carried with it a steaming mug of tea. I reached for it and took a sip to wet my dry mouth. It burned my tongue a bit, but I couldn't care less. It wasn't chamomile, but it was warm and sweetened with just the right amount of honey.

"No, it didn't hurt. I'm sorry if I scared you both," I said quietly.

Marco shook his head fervently, "I'm not scared! Can you teach me how to do that? Or—what even was that?"

I smiled down at the boy. He was so eager to learn anything and everything. I shouldn't have been surprised that he would see that darkness and be nothing but curious. "I'm afraid not, Little Marco. I was born with the ability to do that. And even I don't know everything about it yet."

Whitley cleared their throat from where they were leaned against the wall opposite where I sat, "Did... were you able to find something?" Though they were still tentative, the fear in their tone and gray eyes was gone.

I took another gulp of tea, guzzling down half of it, and licked my lips, "I don't know what the city guard was able to discern, but I saw someone take Francie. They were just as fast and strong as she is." I glanced around the kitchen that was still a mess, "The disarray is because she fought them like hell."

Whitley closed their eyes and nodded vigorously. A lone tear escaped the corner of their eye, and Marco left me to go hug his caregiver. "It's okay, Whitley. We'll find her!" Marco hugged Whitley's waist, and they hugged him back.

Elián reached his hand out toward me, and I stared at it, confused. He bobbed it up and down once, and I placed the mug in his palm, not sure if that's what he was asking for. His fingers closed over the bottom of the blue cup, and I watched Whitley and Marco continue to embrace and comfort each other. Elián pushed the tea back toward me after a second or two, and when I took it back from him, I found the mug just as hot as it had been when he'd first given it to me.

My head snapped up to look at him, but he was already pulled back with arms crossed over his chest. *Oh, yes, we will definitely be talking about this.*

While I finished the rest of my tea, I described what I had seen with all the details I could relay. They all nodded along seriously, but I found myself being even more frustrated than when I had arrived. I didn't really have any new information for them, and it was Isabella's murder all over again. Yes, I knew who had killed the former High Priestess, but the reasons as to why were still a mystery. And now another person I cared for was gone, too.

I groaned and rubbed at my temples. Life had been much simpler a few months ago. There was little uncertainty fighting in the tavern rings, and most of my contracts had been straight forward deals that I didn't think twice about after they'd been fulfilled.

Shakily, I stood after downing the last of my drink, and Elián crept closer like he was preparing for me to faint like a weak maiden. Just to prove him wrong, I walked to the sink and rinsed out the mug, washed it with a bar of soap and brush that rested near the faucet, and set it on the drying rack.

Little Marco's timid voice made me turn around, "Um… Sir Elián? Would you show me your swords now? Did I help enough?" He was clutching his hands behind his back and had crossed half the room toward Elián.

My Shadow uncrossed his arms and nodded. I watched with another strange sensation in my chest and saw him unsheathe his short swords in a quiet shudder of metal on leather. Marco crept forward, eyes wide with awe.

Elián held his weapons, handles toward Marco. "Now, based on what you said Meline told you, you know that these are not to be treated as toys. They are some of my most prized weapons, and you will handle them with care. Do you understand?" Though his words were firm, Marco was not deterred. He nodded solemnly and reached a hand toward one of the leather-wrapped hilts. "And I don't need to tell you that they are heavier than they appear. Best just hold one at a time." Marco nodded again and closed a hand around one of the swords.

Elián didn't let go of the sword until Marco had brought his other hand to grip the hilt as well. I watched his arms drop a bit as he got used to the weight, but he recovered quickly. Marco's grin showed a handful of missing babe teeth and the absence of fangs that wouldn't appear until his adolescence.

Little Marco gave an experimental movement and lowered the hilt in front of his center. The blade tilted upwards, and he held it just as I had taught him. A fierce swell of pride filled my body when he turned to grin at me, still holding the short sword steady. In his child's grip, the sword looked as large as a broadsword, and he was handling it with the care that I had preached and Elián demanded.

He turned back to Elián who still stood holding the other sword. "Am I holding this right?"

Elián shrugged, "You would not normally hold it like this, as they are meant to be wielded as a pair, and you would fight with one in each hand. But with only one, that is the correct stance." He nodded toward Marco's feet that he had grounded, shoulder-width apart and with knees slightly bent.

Marco nodded, "Could—could I try holding the other one, too? I've been doing all the exercises Lady Em taught me, and I'm getting stronger every day." He looked at Elián with all the seriousness of a fighter in training. *Yes, he would very much enjoy life at Rhaea's Temple,* I thought.

Elián tilted his head and looked at Marco for a long moment. I was halfway worried he would refuse the boy, but he eventually gave a quick nod. Marco slowly transferred the sword he held to one hand, and once he was able to handle it steadily, he reached for the other.

Elián slowly transferred the hilt to him, and I watched Marco's determined face light up when he was able to handle the weight of both. Now, he stepped one of his little feet back to further ground his stance, and he pointed both blades slightly forward, toward my Shadow.

Elián was circling Marco and began making comments, directing him how to adjust his stance. "How's this, Sir?"

Between instructions, Elián interjected, "I am no 'Sir'."

When Elián had made a full revolution and had no further comments for Marco, the boy asked, "Then how am I to address you?" His little rust-colored brow scrunched in confusion, but he kept standing the way Elián had told him to.

"I belong to the Shadows, and we are no knights. You may just call me Elián, but if you want my title, Master Elián will do."

"What's a Shadow?"

Whitley cleared their throat, but I was the only one that looked over at them. The dark circles under their eyes were even more apparent, and behind their head, through the small window to the outside, I caught sight of the lightening sky. The sunrise had snuck up on us, and with the kidnapping of their mate and the other children that would surely be waking soon, I was further reminded of how worn out Whitley must be. Just looking at them made me feel tired. "Perhaps it's time we try to get a bit of sleep, Marco. And I'm sure Meline and Master Elián would like to rest, as well. We've taken up quite a bit of their time."

The boy pouted his lip a bit but nodded. Very carefully, he tilted the swords until he held them hilts up, and pushed them toward Elián. He bowed his head, "Thank you for showing me, Master Elián."

My Shadow retrieved them tenderly and stowed the weapons once again on his back. He surprised me again, though, by crouching before Marco so that they could better look each other in the eye. Though he was still a head taller than Little Marco like this, his tone was as serious as he would speak with anyone else. "You are welcome. And the Shadows are a group of fighters like me. Your Lady Em was right to teach and train you, and I expect you to stay consistent with this." When Marco nodded vigorously, trying his best to mimic Elián's stern expression, Elián brought his fist to his chest.

Eyes wide, Marco straightened his spine and mimicked the gesture. They nodded to each other, and Elián stood. "Do you need anything else?" He directed his question at Whitley, and I had to shake my head to remember why we'd even come here. Francie was still missing, and I hadn't been able to help figure out why or where she had been taken. And I had already run out of time to help any more. Elián and I would have to leave in a few hours for Krisla, and I was coming to terms with the fact that this was further like Rhaestras. I was leaving without answers and relying on others to figure out where I had failed. I took a weak swallow.

Whitley shook their head and ran a hand over their short hair, "Aside from having my mate back, no. I appreciate your willingness to help. The guards are still investigating, and if anything else comes up, I will send word." They drew a breath and released it, "I just don't understand what they think we would have stolen."

"Return what you've taken, and she'll be returned," the note had read in cramped common-tongue. None of us were closer to identifying what that meant, and I doubted the guards were, either.

I pushed off of the counter and walked to Elián. On the way, I mussed Marco's curls, and we both headed for the side door. "We will be leaving the city later today, but I won't stop trying to find her. I swear it."

Whitley gave a grateful turn of their lips and gave Little Marco a quick pat on his back toward the hall. I'm sure they had to remind the boy to go to bed most nights, but he didn't protest at the clear urging to go sleep. "Goodbye, Lady Em and Master Elián. See you soon!" And then he dashed down the hall.

With a wave to Whitley, Elián and I took our leave into the brightening dawn.

~

My Shadow and I sat at the outdoor counter of my neighborhood café. There was no food at my apartment after feeding Marco, and the growling of my stomach had become quite distracting. Though we'd gotten a curious glance from the staff that had opened the café for the day, no one commented on our attire or apparent weapons.

My chocolate filled pastry was flaky and buttery and delicious, and I bobbed my head as I chewed. Elián had ordered one also but had finished his in two quick bites. Roalld's elegant supper hadn't been quite enough food for him, either.

"We'll have to bathe, pack, and then head to the livery yard." Luckily the stipend Mathieu had sent me with was more than enough to cover the rental fees for boarding Bhrila and Noxe.

Elián nodded and took a sip of his bitter drink. Though I was prepared to order tea for us both, my Shadow had cut in and requested black coffee with his breakfast. I'd tried the beverage numerous times throughout my life, but I couldn't get past the taste.

We took time to finish our meal, and as I gathered our empty plates and mugs, I spoke quietly, "Thank you for your help last night. All of it—everything." I wanted so badly to talk to him about what had happened between us at The Grave and afterward, ask him about his fire powers, but it didn't feel like the right time.

And in confirmation, his jaw flexed as he stood. He tilted his head to the left then right, and I heard a muffled cracking. Elián didn't speak of his end of the deal in helping me with the Vyrkos assassin, and for many reasons, I didn't bring it up. He rounded the counter and faced the street before us, "Come on."

I sighed. He wouldn't be able to avoid it forever. Not only did I have the taste of him now, but I had seen that I wasn't the only one harboring a gift from the Godyxes. Though the events of the previous few hours had softened me greatly toward Elián, there was so much that he wasn't telling me. And I was intent to ask him about all of it.

34

The three-day journey to Krisla felt twice as long with my tired bones. Again, I had to travel with my powers hidden, and we'd had to leave so quickly that I didn't have time to buy more hash before we left Nethras.

On the third day of our travels, we'd been riding all morning on the main road in tense silence. We'd only spoken to one another about the tasks at hand, and even when we rested in a roadside inn on the first night, our words were perfunctory and logistical. With the warming sun peeking through the trees and heating the air, I tested the waters. "So, how are you feeling?"

"About what?" At least he wasn't disregarding my question. Elián was annoyingly prone to ignoring any inquiry that he didn't want to address. I kept going back and forth between being irritated with and longing for him. Now that I had regained my strength, he was content to leave me a wide berth.

I shrugged, trying to appear as nonchalant as possible, "Everything that happened in Nethras, I suppose?"

He held onto Noxe's reins with ease, but the stony mask he wore on his face didn't hide the discomfort he was feeling at my question. I'd purposefully left it open so that he could address any of the events he wanted to. I was certain if I'd outright asked him to let me suck him off again, he might breathe flames. *Could he even do that?*

He sighed, "I feel fine."

More annoyance surged in my head, and the exertion it caused made my restraints on my powers wane. Some of the black veins crept out onto my hands, and I couldn't bear to pull them back. Thankfully, no one else was on this stretch of the beaten path, so I let the release of it relax me. My headache lessened. "I am not trying to make you feel uncomfortable. But I would like someone to process everything with."

"I'm not uncomfortable."

"Are you certain about that?"

"Yes."

"Then would you let me suck your cock again?" Silence. Just like I thought. "Or will you tell me how you are able to make fire out of nothing? What about that?"

"Your Highness." His voice was reprimanding, and it was making me even angrier. Just when I thought we were making strides, he would pull back again. It was exhausting, and I was holding onto the last dregs of my patience.

I let go of Bhrila's reins to stretch my arms out wide, "Elián this is fucking ridiculous. Through our time together, you have seen me at my worst and helped me *torture* someone. You tasted me, and I tasted you. Forgive me if I would like to discuss *something* of substance. Perhaps reflect on all the fucked up things we've seen and encountered!"

My voice had grown higher in pitch at the end to where I was almost shrieking, but I couldn't bring myself to care. His withholding was turning me into a version of myself that I didn't like, but I couldn't seem to stop reaching for him, seeking him out. I was beginning to hate the hold he had on me.

"What do you want from me?"

Now I was screeching, "What do I want? I don't know El, just—just fucking *something*! In one breath, you care for me, and in another, you run away from me! If you haven't been paying attention, I've lost many who are dear to me, and you have seen two of these occurrences first-hand. If we're stuck together for the time being, I'd like a little bit of fucking support, you asshole!"

My chest was heaving, and I belatedly realized that my yelling was distressing the horses. I reached down and brought a hand to Bhrila's mane to soothe her. I muttered apologies while I tried to get a handle on my breathing.

The sound of Elián kissing his teeth made me flinch and look over at him on my right. He was glaring at the road before us, but I knew that it was my words that he disliked. I had regained a bit of my composure to let him turn over what I said. One thing I had learned about him in these weeks was that if he did deign to answer a question, he would do it when he was ready, never before.

And surely enough, he said barely above a whisper, "You are not the only one who was orphaned by The Killings, Your Highness." I flinched and didn't even dare to breathe. And due to my patience that took tremendous effort, he added, "I told you that working with your powers would give you better control," Elián turned to me and set those radiant eyes that mimicked the sun to my dark ones. "The advice I gave was from experience."

I waited for him to say more, but he set his attention back on the road, and we fell into silence once again. I wanted to kick myself for being placated by his breadcrumbs again, but the solemn way he spoke made me believe that the little bits he shared were actually very large, indeed. I'd asked him once about his family, and he hadn't really spoken of anyone, had he? And now with what he said, I knew why.

Were his own powers why he never seemed frightened by mine? Ours were vastly different, but he never looked upon my Death with terror or even caginess. It was as if it were just another part of me like the hair on my head or the color of my skin. Something to make note of and move on.

When the morning turned to afternoon, we entered Krisla.

As soon as we crossed the threshold of the large iron gates, I felt my stomach knot, and the sensation only grew worse the further we went.

It seemed that each stop we made, Elián and I were making our way to cities that were larger and more crowded than the last. Krisla was northwest of Nethras, and though it was technically a seat of monarchical power as opposed to the sovereign Nethras, Cal had long ago opted to manage his kingdom like a charismatic businessman. And while he still touted himself as King of Krisla, I knew that Cal was no Roalld, and he was no Mathieu or Uncle. While he was all smiles, Cal was a cruel bastard.

The brick towers of Krisla were even taller than in Nethras, and the place was annoyingly crowded. I had never longed for the easy island city of Rhaestras more than when I lived here. The wealthy were easy to spot, dressed in their dark, expensive fabrics that glimmered under the glowing lights that lit the overcast day. Those that were less fortunate tried their best to avoid the pompous, judgmental glances of their neighbors.

Per Mathieu's instructions in his letter, Cal made a personal reservation for me at an inn called The Moonbeam. After asking a stranger in ragged clothing for directions, Elián and I soon came upon what appeared to be one of the tallest buildings in the city. A uniformed human man rushed out of the entrance upon our arrival along with an adolescent Lylithan female dressed in the same neat gray tunic and trousers. They welcomed Elián and I, and the female took our bags while the man took our horses.

When we entered The Moonbeam, the interior was dressed in black furniture and black walls, and the floor was a pristine gray marble. The dark colors were accented with silver everywhere, and it all felt very cold. Expensive, but slightly unwelcoming. My guess was that Cal owned this place, and the decor choices further confirmed. The female led us to a set of double doors that parted and slid into the depths of the black walls at our approach.

She entered the space that resembled a large closet first, and Elián and I stepped in after her. The wallpaper in the small compartment resembled twinkling stars in the night sky, and I rolled my eyes at this design choice as well.

The magic of these lifting contraptions wasn't unfamiliar to me, but it was something that was rare in other cities. Few were so crowded to where they had to build upwards instead of outwards.

But The Moonbeam had such a thing, and once the three of us were inside, the doors slid closed. A hovering, glowing light bobbed above us, and the female said clearly, "Penthouse suite." I sighed.

It took eight breaths for us to reach the top, and I watched the inside of the walls as we were lifted to the top floor of The Moonbeam. Though I had snuck out of Krisla in the dead of night the last time I was here, it seemed that Cal was still wanting to impress me. No doubt, he was up to something nefarious.

The doors of the lift slid open to reveal a short walkway lined with an exquisite silver and blue rug that led to an ornate, black wooden door. The female who had remained silent, even in her refusal to let us carry our own things, fed a key into the lock above doorknob that looked like a crescent moon.

When we stepped inside, more magic lights, suspended toward the ceiling like multiple moons in the sky, softly illuminated the space. Leave it to Cal to not think simple electricity was enough to light this large inn.

The suite was even bigger than our room in Rhaestras had been, and it was fitted in the same black, silver, and blue. The sleek leather sofa was big enough to fit seven or more, and one wall seemed to be made entirely of glass. There was a small kitchen area fit with a cooling chest, sink, cupboards, and stove and was just beside a door that certainly led to the bedroom. Another door on the other side of the kitchen was open, and I could see that it led to a large bathing room done completely in black tile.

It was a large gesture of Cal's wealth, but at least I knew that I would be comfortable here.

Elián got to checking every nook of our home for the next two days, and I tipped the female before she spun and left.

~

I spent the next few hours resting, washing my body, and unpacking my scant outfit for the evening. The silk had gotten a bit wrinkled from being folded away, and I hung it in the bathing room to hopefully straighten out amongst the steam from our showers. Elián's ensemble, however, somehow looked crisp as he unpacked and draped it on the back of the sofa.

The room came with one bed, like my apartment, and my Shadow had taken to the sofa like he had the brief evening we'd spent at my house. Whether he actually slept that night after I had caressed him with my darkness, I wasn't exactly sure.

My gut continued to churn as my meeting with Cal loomed closer, and I rehearsed my speech over and over. While Isabella had been stubborn and Roalld quiet and calculated, Cal was much more unpredictable. His moods changed swifter than the tides, and I had to be prepared for anything. I didn't know how I'd stayed with him and in this city for as long as I had.

I pulled a chair from the small but just as elegant dining area and set it before the stove. This, at least, didn't require any magic. I used a match from a book in the adjacent drawers to light the black appliance and set the size of my flame.

The heavy iron comb I'd brought from my apartment invoked a barrage of memories, most of which were hazy and filled with a cold hedonism I hadn't let myself think of in a long, long time.

I propped the tool on the stove, directly above the flame, and sighed heavily. I was doing this for our people. I would do this.

Once it was thoroughly heated, I grasped the insulated handle of my old straightening comb and brought it to the first parted section of my hair. A bit of smoke rose as I passed the comb through my kinky curls, but I didn't let my detestation for the ritual stop me.

"What are you doing?" Elián appeared beside me, nose wrinkled. He eyed my grooming with baffled judgement, and he held his hands crossed at his chest.

I barely looked up at him. "I'm straightening my hair."

The curl of his lips was apparent in his tone. "Why would you ever do that?"

I furrowed my brow as I let the now-straight section I had been working on fall. Now without a hint of texture, it reached all the way to my lap and brushed my thigh. I started to work on the next section, "I used to do it all the time when I lived here."

"Why?" He pressed.

More smoke rose in the wake of the straightening comb, and once the section was as limp as the first, I rested the comb back down on the stove. I looked up at him now, and he appeared almost horrified as he eyed the straightened bits of my hair and the curly sections still held back and awaiting their turn.

"Because Cal liked my hair this way." And I was going to use every tool at my disposal to win him over. Elián looked even more affronted, and I sighed, "I know the smoke can get annoying, but hopefully I'll be finished soon. Now, unless you're offering to heat the comb yourself, I need to get this done before I get dressed."

He grunted and spun on his heel back toward the sofa, leaving me to finish straightening my hair. The task itself was a tedious one, and I had forgotten how long it took to get through all of my thick hair. I had to maneuver slowly and carefully so that I didn't fucking burn myself or singe my strands, but I eventually made it through every section.

When I turned off the stove and stood, my scalp felt wrong. The air was too close, and I kept touching the silk that was so uncharacteristic of myself. I was uncomfortable, and that insecurity didn't lessen with each glance I made toward Elián. He was reading another one of his picture books, but I had the feeling that he wasn't scowling because he was unhappy with the story. But it was no matter—I was doing this.

I retrieved my outfit for the night and closed myself in the bedroom. The bed was ginormous and set against the wall below more glowing lights.

The room boasted another expensive and exquisite black rug, and I realized that the white comforter, sheets, and pillows were to make the bed like the bright moon in a sea of black. I huffed a low snicker and planted myself at the large vanity beside the bed. My hair looked as dark as Elián's in this state, and my dusky skin was dull. Or perhaps that was just a reflection of how I was feeling being back in this city.

I opened the small bag of my cosmetics and set to work on my face. Shoko's voice trailed my mind, and I swallowed thickly. *All you need is a bit of color and some darkening around your eyes. Good as new, honey.*

My chest heaved another sigh, and my palms wiped at my face. *What a fucking disaster.* I allowed myself twelve breaths. Twelve breaths to let myself shake with dehydrated weeping. All I wanted was to have her here to play with my hair, to use her ability to make me look pretty in a way to cheer me up. What would she say about all of this?

"From what you've told me, Cal's a piece of shit, but you know how to deal with his kind. Knock him the fuck out with your words and your clothes and your hair and your face, make him do what you need, and laugh all the way home. You can do this, honey."

"That's what she would say," I muttered to myself.

At the end of the twelfth breath, I struck myself on the side of my face, and the stinging pain was enough to snap me to attention. I could fucking do this.

The kohl I'd used a few nights ago was put to good use as I emphasized the corners of my eyes. I darkened my lashes even further with a tiny brush dipped in a small pot of black pigment before swiping a rosy color from a similar pot over my cheeks.

My fingertip rubbed the same color over my lips, and I watched as I turned into a version of myself that I had long ago hidden in shame. It wasn't the color on my eyes and face per se—though I didn't wear cosmetics daily, I enjoyed using them for nights out and when the mood struck me. No, it was the combination of them with my limp hair that threatened to hurtle me back to that female.

The veins on my hands crept out and began to crawl up my wrists and arms. The cool pressing of them on my skin felt nice, and I exhaled. When I looked over myself, I knew that Cal would see what I wanted him to. The broken temptress that fucked and raged alongside him for nearly a decade.

I could do this.

The silk of my skirt and top had indeed loosened and let go of its wrinkles, and I dressed quickly. It was one of my outfits that I hadn't worn in a long time, but it fit just as well as the last time. I didn't pull on any undergarments, furthering the illusion I was trying to set, and pulled the skirt on until it rested high on my waist. The swirling blues and pinks of it reminded me of the early hours of a spring morning, and the top matched with the same pattern. It was more just a band of fabric that covered my breasts, and I carefully lifted the circle of its strap over my head to rest against the back of my neck. My straightened hair was just as smooth as my clothes, and it fell just past my navel. I left the bedroom, carrying my pink sandals in one hand and my daggers in another.

Elián was standing facing the front door, and he, too, had changed. He was wearing the tailored jacket and trousers he had worn when I'd chosen him for this journey. His hair was slightly damp, and his dual swords were gone in exchange for the large one he wore at his side. He was striking, but the acknowledgement of this fact only left me feeling more wilted.

My voice made him turn around. "Would you mind holding my blades? If you are able to?" The way he was looking at me made me feel incredibly scrutinized, but I kept my spine straight. His irises flared, and he didn't hide his search of my body and face.

Quite frankly, his surveying was threatening to chip at the nerve I had been working up. I cleared my throat and tried again, "Elián?

Can you just put them in your boots or something?" I gestured to my outfit, "I have nowhere to put them without ruining the appearance I'm going for, and I don't want to leave them completely." I gave a weak laugh and felt fucking stupid.

That seemed to snap him out of it, though, and he tucked a lock of his hair behind his ear. He nodded, crossed the room to me, and grabbed my daggers. I watched as he swiftly buckled my sheaths at his legs, and I swallowed at the glimpse of a golden, muscled calf dusted with dark hair.

When he straightened, the air stirred and brought a current of his scent wafting toward me. Comfort and heat and ruin. But I couldn't focus on that. I went to the sofa and sat, and I nearly slid right off of the leather with the slipperiness of my skirt. After steadying myself, I bent to fasten my feet into the strappy sandals. They were wholly impractical, but they completed the image that I was trying to paint for my meeting with Cal. If there was anything the King of Krisla loved more, it was the illusion of ownership. Wearing an outfit that he'd had made for me, and the implications of my still having it even after I'd left him decades ago, would hopefully soften him to my negotiation.

While my fingers worked at the stringy straps, Elián rumbled, "Your Highness…"

Still bent over, I raised my head to look up at him through the hair that was falling in my face. I huffed and shook my head, trying to clear it from my vision. "Hm?"

He opened his mouth and closed it, and I saw the muscle of his jaw flex against his newly shaven skin. I sighed and went back to addressing my shoes.

"I am… sorry."

I sat up, shoes now on, and pushed myself off the sofa. My lips turned down, "Sorry for what?"

Though his face was still stoney, his eyes had changed to a rich orange color, "I am sorry for… not… being more supportive. Or helpful."

I tilted my head, and my hair shifted about my shoulders and back. My mind was too focused on my meeting with Cal to fully deduce what he was trying to say to me, so on the way to the door, I waved off his apology. "No need to be sorry. You're here to protect me, and you've never failed me in this. Comforting me is not your job. Don't worry about it."

~

The servant walked us through the large foyer of Cal's home. His name was Marcus, I remembered, and after recovering from my shock that he still served his king, I tried to give him a warm smile. When he returned it, the welcoming expression never reached his red eyes, and the wash of shame was swift and fierce as it swept through me.

I had gotten too used to Elián playing as my companion during our time in Nethras and half our time in Rhaestras. He trailed behind me, for now in Cal's home, there was no point in pretending that he wasn't my guard. I rolled my shoulders back while we walked behind Marcus through the hall toward the formal meeting room. Cal had many homes, and though his city was incredibly crowded, this one boasted nothing other than unnecessary extravagance at the city center. Whenever he was in town, he stayed here, and when I had lived with him, this gaudy house was my home, too.

It wasn't cozy like my family's Versillian estate, nor was it simple but rife with memories and treasured items like my apartment. Cal's sentimentality extended to *who* he owned, not what. The furnishings were dark and expensive, just as the inn he'd set me up in, but I could tell that the pieces had been chosen only due to the image they projected. Priceless black and silver carpets, and enormous paintings of himself, his ancestors, and beautified versions of his kingdom eclipsed the black walls.

On our way to meet him, Marcus, dressed in a simple and clean black suit, trailed us past a painting that left my feet stuttering.

The bastard.

I stared angrily at my naked back. The two males beside me now stood in silence while my eyes swept the damning artwork. My skin looked pale, and maybe it was the darkening of the Rhaestran sun that was still apparent on my flesh now, but that version of myself looked sick. Cal was thrown back lazily on an ornate settee, his legs wide and hand possessively gripping my waist. His silver crown was tipped with giant sapphires and was no doubt the real center of the painting. It was the cruel pair to the diamond and sapphire collar around my neck.

The way the still version of me was twisted and caressing his sharp jaw, the curve of my right breast and peek of a brown nipple highlighted, told all of what I had been to him. My lashes were cast dark and heavy, and a sultry smile curved my blood-red lips. I could almost feel the soft velvet of that seat under my hand that had propped me up when we sat for this addition to his art collection.

His mistress. His pet.

When Shoko had first called me the term, I'd recoiled, but her sweet words and touches, even after hearing all that I had done, helped me reclaim the word. But *this*—it threatened to undo all of that.

Elián's voice brought me out of turning back into *her*, "Your Highness." Two simple words, but he imbued them with velvet concern, and underneath that, a simmering rage that I knew all too well.

I flicked my eyes to him, now beside me, and he looked downwards then back up. *Shit*, I thought when I saw what he'd subtly pointed out to me. The veins on my hands were darkening with my power trying to rise to the surface. If there was anyone, *anyone*, who I needed to shield Rhaea's gift from, it was Cal.

With a breath, I commanded my Death to remain hidden and quickly reinforced the iron wall in my mind, building it higher and thicker than before. How was I going to be able to meet with him *and* keep my barriers in tact? They seemed to crack or fall completely without my leave when I was emotional or overwhelmed, and this meeting, judging by this unpleasant surprise, was going to be just as upsetting as I'd anticipated.

Writing a letter to Cal was one thing. Seeing him and feeling the barbed caress of his words was another. And being confronted with yet another version of myself that I had long buried might be the thing to break me down.

Marcus cleared his throat, "Are you ready to see His Majesty?"

"You can do this, honey," I thought of Shoko's voice again. She'd been the only one I'd told about my years in Krisla. At the time, I was so in love with her, and she was so angry about all that I was holding back. She was prying into my past, and at each resistance of

mine, her eyes, like beautiful garnets, grew sadder and sadder. When she pushed me for *something*, I told her the worst of me. And it wasn't just what I'd done in and my resulting fleeing from Versillia, or abandoning my brother, or not seeing my parents' bodies properly burned once they'd died.

It was also what I had done here.

Part of me wanted to push her away with my story. I told her all of the disgusting details, and when I was finished, migraine threatening to split my head in half, she just looked at me with all the love and understanding in the world and held me. Even after our romantic relationship ended, she never looked at me differently, never struck me down.

I nodded to the male that had been witness to that version of myself in the painting—he might have even been in the room when Cal and I sat for its artist—and gave him a wider smile than I had upon entering Cal's home. "Yes, thank you, Marcus." Though he didn't move, I caught the surprise that chipped his flatly pleasant demeanor. No telling what he saw in the years since I'd been here. I added, "And, I know that it is no consolation, but I am very, very sorry for all that I did to cause you pain."

Again, his brows tilted up a fraction, but he didn't otherwise acknowledge my apology. That was fine. I just needed to say it.

He turned on his heel toward the receiving room, and Elián and I followed. Another thing I hadn't truly considered in my ruminating about this meeting was Elián knowing about this part of my past.

Perhaps he'll finally just kill me.

I shook my head quickly at the thought, and my palm itched to slap myself again. *Focus.*

Another two Vyrkos servants stood on either side of carved double doors. The motif on the dark wood showed the rolling of hills, soft clouds, and a full moon above it all. If it didn't fill me with such foreboding, I would have thought the artistry quite impressive and beautiful.

The two servants hardly even glanced our way, but upon our approach, they opened each door in one synchronized movement. Though Cal's cologne permeated every inch of the home, an onslaught of his scent hit me as soon as the doors slightly parted. It was vetiver and tobacco and felt like silk and blood. The allure of it was powerful, and that had been what drew me into him in the first place, hadn't it?

After leaving Versillia, I wandered the realm in my own tumbling self-destruction, and my random travels led me to a city I hadn't been to but twice before and many years prior. Krisla had swiftly struck down the growing uprisings that Lylithans now referred to as The Killings, and I found the city had no shortage of liquor and drugs and blood, and more importantly, those that didn't know me. It was a cruel act of fate that that one night, while reveling in wine and the blood of a beautiful human who'd let me bury myself in his neck, I caught the attention of the King of Krisla who was now staring at me like a priceless jewel returned.

35

Cal was already standing, halfway across the large room, and I turned my steps into the slinking prowl fit for the King's pet.

Marcus walked me right up to him, and I willed with everything in me for my heartbeat to slow. I could show no weakness, lest he pounce and fight to drag me back. There was a reason I'd left in the wee hours between night and day when he'd been sleeping heavily after a night of debauchery.

The King of Krisla was an arresting male, and in his crisp, royal blue jacket and trousers, he exemplified royalty, indeed. The silver buttons of his jacket were polished to the point of shining like diamonds, and though no crown decorated his blonde hair, I knew that it would match his ensemble perfectly.

He was almost as tall as my Shadow, and when I was finally before him, his grin was coquettish and held knowledge and unspoken intentions.

You can do this, honey, rang through my mind again, and instead of baring my fangs at him, I grinned back. I would not let myself become the female in the painting, at least not on the inside. But on the outside, dressed like the morning to Cal's night, I could act like her.

"My darling," he drawled and reached for my hand. I met him, and he brought it languidly to his mouth. Perfect lips, perfect face, perfect hair—that was Cal. He was a warm-blooded Lylithan, but his smooth lips sent a chill through me.

"Cal," I forced my voice lower to match the sensuality in his tone.

And though my powers were locked tightly in my mind, I felt like I could taste Elián's growing anger behind me. *Focus.*

"You've returned to me. Have you found your room at The Moonbeam to your liking?"

I inhaled, watched Cal's clear perusal of my breasts, and exhaled, "It is lovely, and I expected nothing less from you." But he didn't immediately reply. His pale blue eyes were slowly tracing every curve of my body, and I remained still to let him.

It was how I'd always dressed here. Elegantly, scantily, and to his preferences. He wanted others to envy his owning of me, and at the time, I'd felt prized. Not in the way of a partner, I later realized, but in the way of one's most obedient dog or an expensive piece of jewelry. Protected and valued, yes, but never an equal and always expendable when it came down to it.

He actually licked his lips when his gaze swept the scandalously high slit of the skirt, and I knew that he could see the lack of undergarments. The delicate silk left little to the imagination, and if it slipped too far in one direction, my sex would be exposed to the air. In the past, it'd provided the teasing image he'd wanted and easy access for when he felt like slipping his fingers or cock into me. And at the time, I'd delighted in it.

"You look just as delicious as the last time I saw you, darling," he finally said, eyes still on my exposed thigh. "My mouth was practically watering when I received your letter," he still had my hand, and he raised it to his mouth again. He kissed my knuckles, but this time, his tongue joined his lips. For a beat, I was revolted. His touch brought memories of mercilessly feeding from a Vyrkos while Cal's blonde head was buried between my legs.

I knew that was what he was trying to do—conjure memories of our lecherous past. I'd dressed and primped myself for him, and flattery was the sure-fire way to get Cal's attention. So, I shoved away the memories of our time together and instead thought of a head with rippling black hair in my lap. I thought of searing hot palms holding my full thighs instead of Cal's icy ones, and the satisfied flaring of Cal's nostrils let me know that he could smell my fabricated desire.

"You know, I was very disappointed when you left, my pet." His azure stare pinned me where I stood, and a beat of panic threatened to blow apart my disguise. The timbre of his voice wasn't just a playful reprimand, and I had heard it many times before.

Marcus cut in and asked, "Is there anything else you need from me, Your Majesty?" And the way Cal's stare grew colder and hotter at the same time, I knew that Marcus would pay for his interruption.

But the break from Cal's attention brought me back, "Actually, Cal, I would love a glass of wine. Surely Marcus remembers what I enjoy."

The wrath on his face softened as he turned his eyes back to me, "Of course, darling. While we wait, please sit and indulge me with what you have been doing for yourself since you left me."

I suppressed a flinch at his words and let him pull me to the more casual lounging area at the back of the room. The long, wooden table at the center was for strangers, and the sofas and armchairs were for guests.

All those years ago, I would have sat on the ground between Cal's legs, resting like a tiger in wait and purring at his touch. Something to dangle and entice. And, in our game, when one of his guests would become too familiar and leer, or even sometimes touch me, Cal would slacken my gilded leash and let me rip them to shreds.

This time, though, I wasn't heir to a destroyed kingdom, but liaison to the new Lylithan Council. And I was no one's pet.

Elián took his post behind my back, and I clung to his presence more than was sensible. He was a withholding asshole, but he was one of few anchors I had to the person I was now. Cal lounged across from me, appraising in silence, and I leaned back to show my ease. Though I wasn't tall, my shapely leg appeared longer with the tip of the pink heeled sandal on my foot, and I milked every moment as I crossed it over the other.

Cal didn't even look at my face as he said, "Please update me with all my pet has gotten up to."

Even though I'd carefully crafted myself like his, the fact that Cal still saw me as his property curled my insides. The urge to eviscerate him pulsed within my ears. "Oh, I have been quite busy, but I'm afraid I'm here for a political matter, as you already know."

His laugh was like the rustling of satin sheets, "And what do you know of politics, my darling? If I'm remembering correctly, you were always more than content to just sit and fist my cock during such meetings."

My smile shrank, reducing to a slight tilt of my lips, and I let a tinge of my anger combine with my words. I couldn't help it. "Things change, Cal. And I come to you as a representative of the Lylithan Council with an offer for you."

Marcus returned then with a tray containing two empty glasses and a bottle of red wine. I couldn't care less of the vintage, the request had been more to keep Cal from draining Marcus within an inch from second death in that tense moment, but I accepted the glass he poured for me all the same.

Before I met it with my own lips, I passed the wine behind me without taking my eyes off of Cal. The brush of Elián's fingers stole my breath, touching mine for a second too long to be accidental. And that small touch helped ground me even more.

"Afraid that I'll poison you, pet?"

Elián lowered the glass back to me, passing his inspection, and I gave a dark laugh as I took my first sip. I made no comment on the wine, though it was good. "Of course."

That seemed to fan Cal's ire even more. He hummed contemplatively into his own glass, and when he pulled it away, setting it on the wooden table beside his seat, his lips were tinted a red that looked unnatural against his pale skin. "What I can't seem to figure out, darling, is why I would want to throw my support behind a regulatory body that could hinder my own way of life here. What would my people do should *their* way of life be hindered?" He meant the Lylithans that dwelled within Krisla's walls that were given freer rein than other citizens. The Krislan guard had an unfortunate habit of being unable to solve crimes when a Lylithan was involved.

I didn't hesitate—his selfish response was one I had foreseen, "No regulations or laws have been set yet, Cal. Join us, and you have a hand in crafting a future for all of us. It will be a more... democratic process than you may be accustomed to, yes. But all current members are well aware of the costs of sowing seeds of resentment. Our goal is to reach flexible understandings that will benefit us all."

He ran a hand down the front of his jacket and picked an invisible piece of lint from the fabric, "And what, pray tell, is in it for me?"

"Besides being able to lay the groundwork for hundreds of years to come?" Cal was nothing if not self-absorbed.

But he shrugged, leaning back on the settee and spreading his arms wide. In that moment, he looked exactly like the Cal in the painting, save for the crown. And I knew that it was no accident. He turned his palms to the ceiling, "I am thriving here, pet. Why would I want to jeopardize that and have some pseudo-government breathing down my neck? Just because you now turn your pretty nose up at our ways here in Krisla, does not mean that the thousands of other Lylithans will decide to do the same."

A pulse of black Death flared in my mind, and I hid my wince by tossing my hair over my shoulder and giving a haughty laugh, "Oh, come now, Cal. You rage and taunt and kill."

The King of Krisla guffawed at my indignation, and it took everything in me to not shatter my glass and splatter wine on my silken ensemble. He shook his head and tsked loudly in the room that was feeling too close, too tight, "Such judgmental words for a female who used to fuck and rage and taunt and *kill* as much as her king."

I put my glass down on the table between us in a beat of self preservation and picked my fingernails. My thoughts raced with the ways I would like to kill Cal. Perhaps string him up on the wall behind him and let all his subjects line up to take turns striking him in whatever way they saw fit. Or I could have Elián help me subdue, strip, and lead him through the streets with a spiked collar around his neck like the dog he truly was. I would laugh at every curse and glob of spit from his people that remained poor and oppressed under his rule. Because even in his prejudice, there were many Lylithans that were struggling along with those of other races.

The crown jewels of Krisla would be broken and parceled amongst the hardest hit of his people, and then I would throw him at their feet before laughing back to Nethras.

Or maybe I could just leap across the table between us and rip his heart from his chest.

It would be fitting, as I had seen him do that very thing to too many. The look in someone's eyes when they watch you snatch their heart, the confusion then disbelief then pain before going slack was a sequence I would never forget.

The voice that slipped from my mouth was of someone else, and

Cal's feline grin froze on his face. "You are not my king. And I bow to no male."

We stared at each other for more, thick moments, and I let Cal's accusations wash over me. In all reality, his words were no worse than what I already thought of myself.

Cal was the first one to break our connection, just as I knew he would be. While my Shadow was skilled in becoming stone save for the flaring colors of his eyes, Cal had no such ability. He was porcelain, ice, but his face betrayed every sick and murderous thought he was thinking. Beneath the charm and smooth voice, the foul glimmer in his eyes, the violent curl of his mouth, and the velvet of his threats could never fool me. Even when I had sat on his lap, I knew what he was. I had just been too broken to care.

I was different, now, though. Cal looked beyond my shoulder and finally spoke, "And you, Shadow. Do you bow before this false queen and her honeyed words?"

I didn't dare turn around to look at Elián, but judging from the heat radiating off of him, he didn't take kindly to Cal's posturing. His voice was clear, but just as I knew Cal, I knew Elián. His tone held the razor edge he'd used just before breaking my arms. How long ago my screaming curses at him seemed now. "The Shadows belong to no kingdom, nor any ruler. We are showing the Lylithan Council our support toward their cause, and I have been hired to escort her highness in her official duties."

"Hm." Cal's gaze slid back to my legs, and I waited for him to speak.

The sudden flash of amusement in his face sank my chest. For a moment, I worried if he could smell Elián on my skin or vice versa. It had been three days since those heated moments in the condemned building in Nethras. Though, logically, I knew that Elián and I were far superior fighters than Cal—I wasn't even sure he *knew* how to use a weapon for anything other than taunting—we would probably not be able to overthrow his guards should he be able to call to them. And though I only belonged to myself, if this monster of my former lover were to even suspect that I was pet to another, we would certainly see the height of his wrath.

But what he said next brought a different creeping sensation up my back, "To join the Council, I have two stipulations."

I didn't breathe, "Please, do tell."

"I want them," he pointed to Elián behind me, "and I want a permanent seat."

If I'd had any wine in my mouth, I would have spit it in his face. Instead, I gave a choked, incredulous laugh, "Has all your raping and pillaging truly rotted your brain?" I knew that this was not the way to go about this, but the gall of him was astounding. To have a fair and just council would mean that none of us could remain seated on it forever. We were immortal, and new voices would need to be heard. And wanting to have the Shadows in his back pocket— was he truly insane?

Cal didn't visibly anger at my words. He did, however, rise from his seat and retrieve a piece of paper from Marcus's outstretched hand. He tossed the letter onto my lap before taking his seat once more, and I refrained from touching it. I could read it from where it sat, damning us all.

I recognized Uncle Hendrik's script, and in it, he assured Cal that a permanent seat could be arranged. The letter held no Versillian seal, and that fact made me grit my teeth. He was having side conversations without Mathieu and *bowing* to Cal? I schooled my features as much as I could, "Any offer my uncle has given you is an error on his part. Such an appointment would necessitate full Council approval," if it were even possible.

He waved away my words, "Oh, I am content to wait while you and your uncle do what you must. Because if I do not have a hand in these *regulations* you all seek to enforce, I will certainly make my opinions known." He didn't have to voice the rest. His threat was apparent enough. Krisla held the highest number of Lylithans and had been virtually untouched by The Killings. And though this was due to the Vyrkos that lived here already being beaten far into submission, the fact remained the same. If the King of Krisla spoke against the Lylithan Council, our efforts wouldn't even get off of the ground. Cal could kill it before it truly came to fruition.

"You would be so selfish in spite of all the good we could do? To increase our population rates, offer our people protection and *stability* that they haven't known in centuries?" I was losing my calm now, but I couldn't help it.

He sensed this and gestured to the air around him, "I see no problem here. The Lylithans in Krisla are thriving and populous. We need no Council to help us."

"They are populous because you give them free rein at the expense of all the others that live here." I spat.

Cal huffed, "We just respect the food chain, darling," flicking away the notion that anyone he could feed from would be considered his equal.

I grasped at another straw, "You will never have the Shadows. *We* don't even have them."

"I do not believe you, pet. You have one behind you now who is content to guard you with his life. And if what I'm told is true, so do your brother and uncle. You claim that you've hired them as escorts, but your Shadow's words show commitment enough. I'm sure as a *permanent member* of the Lylithan Council, I should be given even broader access."

For a moment, I almost did rise from my seat. It would be so easy to let the let my power run free and watch the onyx smoke trail down his throat and nose and suffocate the life from him. But Cal raised his glass to his lips again, and the red of the wine reminded me of the curls on Marco's head. Lylithan children like him deserved to be born and raised and grow and live, and killing Cal would no doubt kill the Council just as swiftly. It wasn't the Vyrkos who had bucked against us that split the last council wide open. The trust of the people and lack thereof were far more dangerous.

So, I wiped the anger from my face, and replaced it again with a slinking grin, "You have given me much to consider, Cal. I shall bring your terms to the other members, and we will discuss."

He matched my tone, "Yes, I'm sure that you will." And then he stood, signaling the end of this meeting. "I must say, darling, I was disappointed to see that you hadn't brought your knives with you."

Elián's gloved palm reached down beside me, and I let him pull me to a stand without a backwards glance. If Cal thought anything of the gesture, he surprisingly revealed nothing. I absently smoothed my skirt, "Oh, I did not trust myself to have them at the ready. You would be dead by now if I had."

His grin pulled so far that I saw the lethal points of his fangs, "But we used to have *so* much fun with them." And here was his parting shot. Flashes of the feeling of drunkenly stumbling over bodies while we laughed in this very room. A group of humans and Vyrkos had once requested to meet with the King to discuss the treatment of their respective people in the city of Krisla. Cal and I, the royal mistress, fed them a feast of expensive foods and wines, locked the doors, and drained them all.

While a Vyrkos male screamed under the King's bite to his throat, Cal had thrown his head back and laughed, "*So humorous how turning misleads you to think of yourselves as predator. You are nothing more than* food." And I had laughed along with him, draining the same male with my own bite at his wrist. I remembered how Cal had stood over them, grunting for me to cut him with my dagger while he pumped his fist over himself. We'd sat on these very sofas, high on our own debauchery, fucking all the rest of the night with bodies lying around us, our hands at each other's throats as we came.

The Killings had murdered many of my friends and my parents, and while I would give anything to have them back, I couldn't deny that the Vyrkos were right to be angry with us. My other Council members were naive to the true depravity of some of our brethren, and with my seat, I would confess my own sins in example.

I let a small smile spread over my face, but it was from anything but happiness. "I will atone for my sins, Cal, as will you." Though I held little stock in the Godyxes or the Mother besides the obvious power bestowed upon me, I was under no illusions that my soul wasn't tainted as black as my ability to wield Death.

Elián held my hand as I rounded the sofa, but when we headed behind Marcus out the door, he didn't let it go. My Shadow tucked my hand into the crook of his arm, and I was again grateful for his physical grounding. Our gait fell into step, and I felt somewhat tethered to his power. Enough so, anyway, to call over my shoulder, "Always a pleasure, Cal. Though I did like you better when I was bending you over and fucking you. Perhaps there'll be time for that yet." If the icy silence was indication enough, my words had the desired effect. Though, neither Elián nor myself turned around as we left.

~

The air in Krisla felt dirty, tainted. The city itself was a marvel with its towering structures and elegant citizens with noses in the air. It was a place of innovation with the way that magic was harnessed and woven into the fabric of everyday life. Those same floating lights lined the streets, and hovered outside of shopfronts. To maintain such infrastructure was no doubt costly, but it was another example of the wealth of Krisla.

However, upon deeper inspection, the affluent district where Cal's home sat told everything of who took priority in the city. The point of my Council tour was to travel to lands where Lylithans tended to call home, and Krisla was definitively the largest. Looking around, it was evident as to why. Elián and I found a charming little pharmacy a few blocks from Cal's, and upon entering, there was a Lylithan male behind the counter that greeted us warmly, though there was no hint of recognition in his eyes.

I sent a letter to Mathieu specifically about the outcome of my meeting with Cal, and I all but snapped the pen in half as I recounted the King's demands. I would tell him about Uncle's secret negotiations in person, should Uncle be able to somehow intercept my communication.

As I wrote, a human entered and requested to send a letter as well. The same clerk was much shorter to what I turned around and realized was a young girl. She cast her eyes down and fiddled with the front of her plain dress after briefly meeting mine.

When I finished my letter and sealed it, I gave the clerk the destination and declared that I would pay the girl's postage fee as well. The clerk looked comically confused before shrugging his shoulders and accepting an exchange of coin from Elián. I threaded my arm back through his, and on our way out, the girl nodded and muttered thanks without looking at me.

The two of us stopped at a small restaurant that smelled enticing enough to attract my now-rumbling stomach. I hadn't eaten anything since we'd arrived in the city, and my Shadow tugged us even further toward the door when I tried to protest. While in Rhaestras or Versillia, I'd feared embarrassing reverent recognition. Here in Krisla was much more dangerous. Though the humans and other mortals here were certainly too young to remember me, the immortal citizens, particularly the Vyrkos, surely would.

But I breathed past the anxiety that fluttered in my stomach and sat beside my Shadow in the dimly lit restaurant. Judging from its location and patrons dressed just as formally as we were, the meal was going to cost us a considerable sum. But the warm bread Elián ordered for us made my stomach feel even more empty, and I decided that I would order everything on the menu if I needed to.

We didn't speak while we tore through two baskets of bread and small bowls of soup. Though I definitely had an appetite, my Shadow's seemingly bottomless stomach put me to shame. Our loud chewing and slurping would have been welcome in Rhaestras, but it was drawing sideways glances from more than a few seated nearest us.

After our dishes were cleared to ready for the next course, Elián asked softly, "How are you feeling, Your Highness?"

Now that the dry agony of my empty stomach was quenched somewhat, the reality of my situation had been creeping back in. My Shadow's words made them effectively slap me in the face. Cal hadn't outright refused, but it was clear he had already made up his mind before I'd arrived. Before coming here, I was worried he might try to tempt me to stay. But the point of the meeting was to size me up, taunt me, and fuck me up in the head more than I already was. Cal didn't want me back—I had already insulted him enough by leaving.

"I'm fine, Elián."

He grunted and waited as the server deposited our entrees before us. Elián checked my elegantly plated noodles before digging into his large and bloody steak. "I am here if you are wanting to... process what happened."

I choked around my food and needed a gulp of icy water to clear my throat. "Oh, Goddess please, no." He frowned toward his plate and said nothing else.

We left with full bellies, and I made sure to deposit a large tip into our kind human server's hand before exiting into the crisp air. If I thought my home city was crowded, Krisla was much worse. My Shadow and I pushed past a steady, heavy stream of Krislans of all sorts toward The Moonbeam.

The large inn was a black pillar in the skyline, and we were only two blocks away when a shout left me swiveling my head around. "The Tyrant King's whore has returned!"

Several people turned either to look at me or the source of the voice, now voices, that were chanting 'whore'. The rock in my gut began to grow again, and my power rattled my internal barriers, asking to come out.

But Elián was already pushing me behind him. Around his shoulder, I saw them, a group of about six with blood-red eyes that were heading toward us. Would they attack me with all of these people around? By the way the bystanders were beginning to back away, that outcome seemed more and more likely.

One of the angry group members had pushed past to stand a few feet from us, and I watched, wide-eyed and pathetic as she hissed, "You killed my brother! Do you remember, bitch? Or was he just more fodder for your games?"

Another came to her side and pointed, "They paint you as Protector of Innocents when you are a *murderer*!" He spat towards us, and the wad of saliva landed just on the tip of Elián's boot. My Shadow hissed, baring his fangs, and I tightened my hand around his arm.

Though they hadn't said anything to confirm the suspicion, I knew that this was Cal's doing. Elián and I hadn't done anything to draw attention to ourselves. We were two among many of our kind on the streets. I was dressed how I used to when I was indeed their Tyrant King's whore, but during that time, I rarely walked outside of Cal's homes. He lived extravagantly and met all of my desires—there was rarely a need for it.

It was too much of a coincidence for this to be happening just after my horrid reunion with Cal.

The other four crept closer, and I could tell that Elián was trying to push me in the other direction. Though they had only been hurling insults so far, the impending violence was obvious enough to taste sour on my tongue. I watched the veins on the back of my hand dilate and pulse black with the quickening beating of my heart.

I knew soon that Elián would either fight them or whisk me back to the inn and bar us inside until day when the Vyrkos would be unable to follow. The thought of running or striking them down, though, made the stone grow larger. I'd been running for so long, and look what it had done. I'd fled Versillia only to get caught in Cal's web and let him turn me into the murderous female they were justifiably calling me. When I'd snapped out of it, I didn't face those I'd hurt—I ran again and tried to bury my wrongs. Finding love and acceptance and volunteering at a children's home, for Goddess's sake, didn't change a thing.

Before he could stop me, I sped around Elián and toward the group that had converged in front of us. They flinched before seeming to grow even angrier, but I raised my palms. "There are no words that I can say to truly recompense for what I have done," I swallowed dryly and looked to the female who'd said I killed her brother, "I am truly sorry that I have caused you and your family such pain. I am not here to hurt anyone, and I have not been the King's mistress for nearly one-hundred years. His sins now are his alone, and I do not take the effects of mine on you all lightly."

A few seemed to relax their shoulders, but the two that had been shouting the loudest continued to bare their fangs at me. The female I'd addressed screamed, "Lies! I don't want your *apologies* when you drained him and *laughed* at his cries!"

Her words seemed to snap the others out of the placation my words had provided. I tried to find what else to say and came up with nothing. They inched closer, and I belatedly noticed Elián had drawn his sword and was standing beside me. I remembered that I didn't have my blades, and my fists clenched. *Where were the city guards?*

The female lunged for me, and before I could scream for her to stand back, Elián's sword was a silent blaze as it was suddenly engulfed in flames and cut the Vyrkos down. Her body caught fire and toppled to the ground. The wide-set eyes and round, full mouth on her face quickly became indiscernible as they were consumed, and I was reminded of Shoko's head rolling into a table leg on my birthday.

A mixture of grief and fear and depression threatened to come out of my throat like vomit, and I couldn't hold back my power that was coming out of my palms like angry snakes.

There was a moment of tense silence where no one spoke. There were no sounds, even from the onlookers that gave us a wide berth, and then there was a bellow from the male that had spit on Elián's boot, "*Murderers! Demon!*"

The others were frozen but remained bent and ready to pounce.

My Shadow's form was still tensed, and I knew that if anyone moved, he would burn them all.

But that wasn't what was worrying me. "*El,*" my voice was already trembling. My vision had already taken a sharper tint, and the sound of hearts racing, people panting, and teeth clicking were clanging around in my skull. This turn in my power had happened enough times that I knew what was to come. Soon I wouldn't be able to control myself, my conscious mind locked behind that barrier while Rhaea's power lashed out to snuff out any threats.

He cut his glowing glare to me, and his lips thinned when he no doubt saw my blackening eyes. My head was throbbing, and I knew that my power slithering toward them was as lethal as it looked. It wasn't the curious vines that had explored Francie's kitchen or Elián's body. This was pure Death, and I so badly didn't want it to reach them.

The Vyrkos backing away from us was the last thing I remembered before a sharp pain at my neck, and my consciousness was gone all together.

36

I was burning.

My throat was on fire, and I sputtered, gasping for air and clawing at my neck. Beads of sweat clung to my brow, and I flew to my feet. I hissed and swiped at the air around me, unaware but uncaring. I just needed to get the threat away from me. I need to—

"*Your Highness,*" my bones rattled at the voice, and my muscles relaxed. I shook my head, trying to clear my mind. Where was I?

I remembered accusing red eyes and the wide ones further back. Flames and a head and spit. I blinked a few times and felt soft grass under my toes. Where were my shoes? My palm stung my cheek and threw my head to the side.

That deep voice hissed, but it didn't sound threatening. Strong hands encircled my wrists and held my arms taut at my sides, and I remembered my bones being shattered. I struggled to release their hold, my body jerking and hair flying all about my face, but they wouldn't let me go. I was trapped.

"*Meline.* Listen to me," I thrashed again but to no avail. "You are safe. You are in your suite at The Moonbeam. There is no one here besides you and I." My bucking slowed, but I couldn't—who was—

Now my arms were being restrained by one hand and another gripped my chin. I wanted to throw my head from his grasp, but the warmth reminded me of something. My flailing stalled even more.

"You are safe. I've got you." Twin suns were staring at me, and I followed their light. I sucked in breath after breath until my chest slowed its heaving. The suns had me. They said I was safe.

"That's right. Breathe." I nodded as much as I could and did as the voice said. Black hair fluttered with the force of what he told me to do, and I saw behind it, the room we were in.

A table with chairs and beyond that, a kitchen with my straightening comb still resting by the stove. The Moonbeam, Elián said.

Elián, my Shadow.

I took another quenching inhale and the details came careening back. Cal, a timid girl, a basket of bread, angry eyes, a burning body, and Death. My hands flew up and shoved at Elián's chest. He let me go and took a step back from me.

I slapped myself again, and that seemed to do it. Yes, we were back at our penthouse room at the inn. The soft grass under my feet wasn't grass at all but one of those silk rugs. Elián brought me back to our room after the confrontation on the street had gone horribly, horribly wrong. "I'm fine, I'm fine," I said as I ran a shaky hand through my smooth hair.

He looked... angry at me. He was scowling, and the folds of his brow were deep in his disdain. "Do not lie, Your Highness."

My hands smoothed down my front once, twice, three times. I was still in Cal's silk outfit. Despite everything that had happened, I couldn't help but remark on the fineness of the garment. Isn't that why I'd kept it in the first place? After what had happened, I'd expected for it to be in tatters or stained beyond repair, but no, it was without wrinkle and just as fine as it had been the day the seamstress had finished it.

"I'm not lying to you," I puffed out a gust of air.

Elián closed the space between us and leaned down so that our faces were almost level, "You almost lost control, and I had to knock you out before you laid waste to half of the city. Do. Not. Lie. To. Me."

I scoffed and shoved him away from me once more. His smell was too comforting, and his words were too harsh. Replaying the last few moments that I remembered before waking up here, I knew he was right. The swell of power had been like before, but different. It didn't take over my body and push me to fight—it wanted to be released and raze. The black this time wasn't abyss but an infection of Death, and even now, I could feel it in the corner of my mind.

But fuck him for thinking that I owed him anything. "Thank you for doing your job. I am fine now, Elián."

He growled and clenched his fist at his side, "You said that you wanted me to process about things with you. Now you do not want to talk to me." It wasn't a question, but it was a clear accusation.

My agonized laugh came out more like a sob, "What the fuck do you want me to say?" My hands raised in the air like they had on the road. "I *was* a tyrant king's whore. I *laughed* while Cal killed hundreds—maybe thousands for amusement. I joined in, and I sat like an ornament for *years*, Elián. Those people down there had every right to want to kill me." My chest was heaving, but I was already going, my words spewing out of me like a geyser.

The memories of another great sin, almost rivaling my time as Cal's pet, threatened to crack the last bit of my sense, "Do you know what your Warrior Queen did to earn that title, Shadow? I *did* raze the lot of them to the fucking ground. And I protected children and saved some of the other teachers, like Francie," I swallowed but pressed on, "but do you know what they did when they saw me coming? They decided to kill as many children as they could. We lost even *more* because of me. The children I saved watched their friends' tiny hearts being ripped out of their chests while one of their teachers unleashed Death. Any good deeds I've done since living here won't change that or my sins in Krisla. Cal called me a false queen, and that's what I am! So, there's your fucking truth!"

Elián just crossed his arms, so I continued, voice trembling, "You called me a waste and spoiled and a menace, and now you know how right you were." I rubbed at my temples, cursing that I didn't have anything to smoke to take the edge off. I hadn't spoken about what I'd done in Versillia, the true cost of my *gift*, to anyone. Shoko had been aware that *something* bad had happened. And Francie knew I had some power after witnessing me let it out that night, but she also knew better than to bring it up. She was gone now, though, and it felt like I'd failed her, hurt her, again.

The screams of the children and my friends and Cal's posturing were stuck to my skin like grime.

"Your Highness."

I screamed, "Don't call me that! I am well aware of the contempt you feel towards me, so just forget what I asked of you!"

He growled again and wrung the hair at the crown of his head, "I do not—I don't feel contempt."

"Then what? Pity? Rhaea curse me, Elián if you pity me, you might as well just burn me alive right now. Is that why you let me touch you? You said it yourself those weeks ago that I was lucky that you let me live." I give a dark chuckle, "You don't know how wrong you were."

"Your—I am—I just—" He scrubbed both of his large hands over his face.

I rolled my eyes and crossed my arms, "Don't even bother. You know what? I don't even know why I tried or why I cared. You have your job, and I have mine. Now you see the fucked up female that is *your queen*," my lip curled as I said the blasphemous name, "so you can stop whatever the fuck it is you're trying to do right now. Because after this, I will go on with my life, and you'll go back to being the shifty Shadow you are, and you don't have to—"

My jaw was clutched in a grip so tight, I couldn't even think about moving. Outrage burned my cheeks, and it mixed with the heat radiating from Elián's fingers. Through clenched teeth, he seethed, "For the love of the Mother. Stop. Talking." And, I was so taken aback, I did.

We stared at each other for who knows how long. I wasn't sure what he saw in my eyes, but the colors in his were moving again. Auburn and amber and gold swam, and all the anger I felt was drained away, lost.

Then, his eyes broke and tracked downwards, landing on my parted lips. He didn't give me a second to wonder what he would do next before his mouth was on mine.

His hand on my jaw disappeared and reappeared holding the back of my head. His fingers easily found my scalp as they twined in my hair, and the warmth spread down my neck.

Elián's other hand gripped the small of my back, just at the waistband of my skirt, and I almost forgot how surprisingly tender the feeling of his lips on mine was. With the hard lines and sneers and short words, Elián's smashing kiss was unsurprising. But there was a softness on the edges of it that left me melting into his hold. Cal and the accusing Vyrkos were nowhere in my mind. All there was was Elián's mouth on mine and his strong body before me. My hands gripped the collar of his jacket as he pulled me even further into him.

And then I was facing the wall, my hands flying up to brace against the dark wallpaper of our room. It was smooth and cool underneath my palms, and Elián had one warm hand encircling the base of my throat, the other on my waist with his arm wrapped around my middle.

He inhaled just under my earlobe, and exhaled, "You want to do this?" The softness of his breath left me trembling against his grasp.

My teeth clenched my bottom lip, and I nodded as much as I could with him holding my throat. The hand on my waist moved to my side, trailing down until it hit the high slit of my skirt. He moved slowly, and I couldn't hide the moan while I was forced to wait while he moved under the silk, over the swell of my thigh, and to the slickness between my legs. I felt a soft growl rumble in his chest as it pressed on my shoulders, and desire pulsed in my veins. He circled the spot that'd been screaming for his touch, and my body jolted, rolled my hips against him.

I spread my legs further as his finger worked on that exact area that he must have remembered from the last time. In his arms, covered and pinned by him, my eyes rolled back in my skull.

I threw my head back to rest on his shoulder, and he answered by sinking a finger into me, then another, and then I was grinding between his hand and the rest of his body. All the while, he trailed his nose up and down the curve between my jaw and shoulder. The hardness of his cock pressed against the small of my back, and I needed it—needed more than just his hand or mouth this time. And I made to tell him so, but then he curled the fingers inside me, still circling with his thumb.

"Elián," My mind had gone hazy, and I couldn't think of anything beyond the pleasure he was coaxing out of me with his touch. My legs trembled as it threatened to take me over.

Another growl radiated from him, and he kissed up my neck while he fucked me with his fingers. His breath was warm on the shell of my ear, "Now, let my name be the only word out of that wicked fucking mouth of yours." And I was so stunned by his words that the swell of my orgasm crashed into me, his name on my lips again as I groaned.

My body was tingling and shuddering, and he swept me up in his arms while I came down. A part of me far away remarked that this must have been what he'd done to get me back to this room. He'd rendered me unconscious so that I didn't do something I'd regret then carried me back here so that I could be safe.

Not until I was placed gingerly on the bed did I open my eyes. The city lights coming through the window were brighter than they were in Nethras, but the room was still dark. Elián didn't make to command on any of the magical lights in the elegant bedroom, and he instead knelt at the foot of the bed.

I propped my elbows on the mattress and looked down at him. In our room in Rhaestras, he'd refused to look up at me, keeping his head down. Now, though, he didn't balk from returning my gaze.

He gently pushed my knees open and settled between them, and my feet brushed against the solid edges of his sides. He shot a hand under the skirt, grabbing the waistband from the inside.

"What are you—"

He tsked, "You can't do what I say for longer than five seconds, can you?" And then my skirt was torn from my waist. Cool air kissed my bare skin as he tossed the silk over his shoulder and moved his hand to the band of my top. Like the skirt, he gripped the fabric from the inside, his hand between the top and my chest, and ripped.

My nails gripped the bedspread as I refused to squirm under his stare. Even if said squirms would also be due to the desire that was drawing taut all of my nerves and muscles. My naked skin prickled when I looked at him, still entirely clothed. The wetness pooled even more between my legs, and his nostrils flared.

Elián remained silent, but he tracked down my body until his eyes landed on the source of my arousal. With those hot palms, he moved one of my legs over his shoulder, then the other. His eyes again flicked up to mine for just a second, and then he descended.

My back arched at a dizzying angle, and I screamed over the sounds of him lapping me up. He started with a long swipe up my whole entrance before flickering the tip of his tongue at that exact spot he now knew was my weakness. My mouth dropped open in a silent scream as I watched him devour me. And he watched me back, with those blazing eyes of his, that infernal eyebrow raised.

Still looking up at me, he pushed two fingers in, and I shouted out his name again as my elbows gave out underneath the weight of my writhing. The intense swells of pleasure rippled from where Elián went at me with a fervor that was unmatched, and I knew that my fingernails were shredding the silky sheets beneath me.

My toes curled, and my legs clamped Elián's head between them. His tongue moved in taunting swirls, and he added another finger to the two already thrusting in and out. It didn't take long for the tidal wave to crash into me again, and my back bowed as I screamed his name into the air.

A few soft whimpers escaped my lips, the aftershocks surging and settling between my legs. While they did, and my conscious mind came back to the forefront, Elián released my thighs and stood. That was the second time he had tasted me, and after the day we'd had, it felt like... an apology.

Elián towered over me, looking every bit a shadow in his black-on-black suit. He unbuttoned and shed the embroidered jacket first, letting it fall to the floor in a soft sigh of fabric. Now I could see the thin gold chain he wore, and there was a small medallion hanging from the gold links. Then he grasped the collar of his black tunic and pulled.

My mouth began to water. I realized in this moment that this was the first time I had ever seen Elián's body uncovered. His Shadow uniform had seemed like a second skin, one I had taken to just be part of him. And his muscles were just as cut and rippling as I'd pictured, but it wasn't the unmarred deep suntan that I had expected. Elián's skin was covered in faded scars and black tattoos.

My eyes roamed over illustrations and script on his chiseled stomach, much like the small tattoo in his palm. I caught a flower blooming on his chest just below the gold necklace he wore, a large snake coiled up his left arm and over his shoulder. But there were too many more to focus on, not when my body was still trembling with need.

I sat up, collected my knees underneath me, and scooted closer to get a better look. My own marked hands roamed the hard ridges of him and felt the slightly raised flesh of his ink. I kissed the rose that lay just over his heart, and the skin faintly beat against my lips.

Elián gripped my hair and angled my head back so that I was forced to look at him. And, I wondered how I could ever question his wanting of me. It was front and center on his face in the burning of his eyes, the flaring of his nostrils, and his lips and chin were glistening with me.

He brought his lips down to mine in a kiss that both emptied and filled my lungs. I tasted the salty sweet of me on his tongue, and I curled mine around one of his fangs. Elián's heat was lighting me from within, and I knew that I could grow addicted to this feeling.

The fist he had in my hair tightened even more as our bodies pressed together, and the fabric of his trousers scraped my overly sensitive skin. The bulge of his cock was impossible to ignore, and I reached my hand down to palm and feel it jerk at my touch. He bit my bottom lip as I rubbed the flat of my hand against his shaft.

Elián broke the kiss by tugging me back, and our noses brushed as we breathed in each other's air. "How would you like me to fuck you, my queen?" His voice was low and rough with desire, in a way that sent a shiver down my back even though his hold on me was warm.

"However you want to," I breathed.

He leaned in closer, so that his lips brushed against mine, "And if I am not gentle?"

My tongue flicked out and swiped his top lip, "Then all the better."

He released the hand on my hair and brought both of his to my bare hips. He pushed me back, eyes on my pierced breasts as they heaved with my panting. "Get back on the pillows," he commanded.

Not taking my eyes off of Elián, I scooted back on my knees until the cluster of white pillows leaning against the headboard touched my toes. I reclined back like he told me to, pressing into the feather-softness of the bed. My hands rested on either side of my body, and my legs were slightly bent and spread so that he could see all parts of me.

He made me wait again. Wait while he took in all that I was offering him. Not just my body, but an obedience that I had never given him before, never to this extent.

He unbuttoned his trousers and pulled them down.

If the clothed Master Shadow Elián was an imposing form of deadly strength, Elián naked was a god. The way his eyes blazed even in the darkness was not of this realm, and the scars and tattoos that covered his skin continued down his thighs and told of centuries of experiences and battles won. A few locks of his hair fell about his brow, their own kind of shadow on his sculpted face.

And the way he looked left me close to climax again without him even touching me. He fisted his cock in just the way I had imagined he would while those burning eyes traced every inch of my body. My breasts felt heavy under his gaze, and I longed for his hands on me, his cock in me. But more than that, I wanted him to command me. I wanted to put myself at the mercy of his desires. So, I waited and stirred under his watch.

He rounded the side of the bed, hand still pumping over himself. I tracked each and every movement of his muscles as he climbed onto the bed and knelt between my legs.

"Arms above your head," his command was breathy but firm. I did as he said, and he brought his other hand to my wrists. His grip was unyielding as he held my hands against the cool wood of the headboard.

His other hand stopped moving and held his long, thick shaft steady while his hips moved toward mine. Both our faces tilted down to watch him guide the tip to circle between my legs. "Fuck," I breathed.

Now slick with my arousal, he brought it to the center of my throbbing, and my head fell back. I came again, and this orgasm was a quick shuddering breath that he didn't let me come down from. He just continued to move his tip in torturous circles.

It was too much. I was too sensitive, but he didn't stop. My wrists tried to pull from the headboard, but his hold didn't budge. He slapped his cock against me, and my hips rose from the mattress as I saw stars.

He released my hands and finally gave me a moment to come down. His mouth found my breast, and I held him to me as I tried to catch my breath.

Elián groaned softly as he sucked and circled his tongue around the golden bar hooked through my nipple, and I moaned over his head, finally having the heaviness there attended by his touch. With a trail of his tongue, he moved to the other, biting in a way that sent euphoric shocks through my body.

Elián's hands then found their way under my thighs, and the width of his upper back spread my legs even further as he pressed toward me while he sucked. The backs of my thighs nestled against the crooks of his elbows, and my feet dangled in the air, spreading all of me even wider.

I felt his cock nudge at my swollen heat and gasped. He released my breast with a wet pop and brought his brow to mine. Our eyes were locked, and he pressed his hips, inching into me excruciatingly slowly.

My face crumpled, mouth dropped in a silent moan, and his eyelids drooped in pleasure as he pushed the tip that had been torturing me into my walls. They stretched to accommodate him, not just his tongue or fingers like before, and he gave me a moment to adjust. We breathed together, and he pushed again, this time seating himself halfway inside.

"Elián—" he shoved the rest of himself in, and I couldn't keep my eyes open any longer. The sweet kiss of pain while he stretched me combined with the overwhelming ecstasy of him filling me to the brim. I bared my throat again as my hips pushed against his.

He pulled back, tilted his hips, and rammed into me. Again and again and again.

He built to a steady, harsh pace, and I was reveling in the feeling of our bodies being joined in this way. It was more than I could have ever asked for and everything I'd wanted. There was nothing that had ever felt like this. My darkness was twining further up my arms and down my body, as it, too, relished, *reveled*, in Elián's taking.

"Look at yourself," he gritted while he thrusted. When my eyes remained closed as I took each pulse he gave, he demanded, "*Look*, Meline." My eyelids fluttered open, and I tilted my head down to see myself opened wantonly. I watched as his large body speared into me, and mine somehow swallowed him. "Look at your tight little cunt taking all of me." My teeth bit into my bottom lip at his crass words. He was right, I could feel him in every single crevice inside of me.

After his next thrust, Elián pulled out completely, and I cried in outrage as he left me empty. But he responded by flipping me

348

around. His hands rough with callouses gripped my hips, and I was on my hands and knees. He left me there for a moment, with only the sound of his ragged breathing, and I couldn't help but shake in anticipation. I arched my back to present myself to him, "Please," and I didn't feel a hint of shame for begging.

A crack echoed in the room just before I felt a searing pain on my right ass cheek. I yelped at the sudden strike and the lightning bolt of bliss it sent through me. He did it again, this time on the left, and I moaned when he immediately seated himself to the hilt. He brought one hand to fist my hair at the base of my skull, and then Elián truly fucked me.

His hips pounded, and all I could do was dig my fingers into the sheets and meet him, thrust for thrust. My screams turned to choked grunting, and he groaned as his cock touched that spot inside of me that made my eyes roll back. I felt more and more sizzling slaps of his hand, and my vision nearly blacked out from the intense pleasure.

Before it could completely clear, I was hoisted up, and his chest pressed against my back. He brought a hand to my throat to steady me, the other to between my legs. I was enwrapped, cocooned, and it was as if my blood was on fire.

He circled his fingers and continued to move inside me. I felt his lips and fangs graze my shoulder where he rested his head. His breath smelled of me and the liquor from our supper, and I inhaled, wanting to let it fill me, too. I reached my hands back to rest on his hips and felt the flexing of his muscles as they moved back and forth.

Breath on my ear, he panted, "Give me one more, my queen." That title that I abhorred sounded so sweet and sinful on his lips, and I clutched the back of his neck. He tightened the hand that held my throat, cutting off some of my air, and my nails dug into his flesh. All the while, he moved his fingers and his cock, and I exploded again. The scent of his blood hit my nostrils, and the wave of pleasure deepened.

His hand on my neck eased and moved to palm my breast. The other he brought to my lips, and I took his fingers into my mouth without thought. I sucked my own juices off of them, and he grumbled into my ear. "Tell me where you want me to come."

I released his fingers with a smack, "I want you to fill me up."

"*Fuck*, Meline," he pushed me back onto the bed. My face pressed into the mattress, and my fingers clenched the sheets. With one hand, he tilted my hips into the air.

Elián slammed into me. He was everywhere, and my body greedily accepted each stroke of his while he all but split me in two. His other hand covered mine while the bed muffled my screams, and his rhythm built to an impossible speed.

I came again with his name on my lips and tearless sobs leaving me hoarse. And while my release crested, Elián roared with his own.

His thrusts gradually slowed while he spilled his seed, and I felt the warm liquid fill me and overflow.

It was peace, exoneration, and I felt the unmistakeable prickling of phantom tears. I'd never told someone all of this, everything. He'd seen me as the Tyrant's Mistress, the murderer of children, and wanted me, *saved* me, anyway.

Elián remained pressed into my back, breathing raggedly while my body milked every single drop of him.

Once finished, he slowly pulled out, and we both moaned at the sensation. I felt his seed spill onto the sheets.

"Stay there," he said. As if I could fucking move.

The chill of his absence was soon replaced by the gentle touch of a warm, damp cloth. Elián wiped between my legs, delicately cleaning me. I remained sprawled on the bed as he took care of my body and then left the room again. When he returned, I felt the mattress dip with his weight. He pulled on my back, and I found myself lying on his chest.

Eyes springing open, I tried to sit up to look at him, but stinging on my rear made me hiss and flop back down.

He smoothed a hand over the cheek I had just tried to transfer my weight onto and rubbed in tender patterns. He didn't hold me to him, just let the contact of our chests and his hand connect us.

"Was I too rough with you?" Elián asked after long moments. He transferred to the other cheek and began rubbing that one.

I had honestly begun drifting off, now properly fucked and sleep threatening to take over. "Hmm?"

He caught my jaw with his hand, and I opened my eyes to find him searching my face for something. Some sign that I wasn't all right with what happened. "Was I too rough?"

I gave him a sleepy, sated smile, "Rough, yes. Too rough, no." His face softened. He let my jaw go, and I settled back into his side. "I'm not usually much of a cuddler, you know."

His calming circles paused. "Me neither," he said quietly and resumed. I brought my hand to his chest and gave him my own calming touches. He had a light patch of black hair there that grew amidst the ink.

A sudden whistling from the front room made me flinch, but his hand held me still. He slipped wordlessly out of the bed, and I propped myself up on my hip, careful of the soreness of my backside.

Elián emerged naked out of the darkness with two steaming mugs in one hand and a bundled cloth and a small jar in the other. My jaw dropped before I snapped it shut with a soft click.

He put the mugs down on the side table beside the bed and settled onto the mattress, this time sitting upright. "Turn onto your stomach. You can prop up on your elbows."

I did as he said, and felt a coolness on my ass. I whipped my head around to see that he had fashioned some sort of pack of ice from the cooling chest in the kitchen and had placed it where my skin was still reddened from his spanking.

Elián stretched his legs forward on the bed and handed me a mug of tea. He held his own and drank, brows raised at me.

I knew that I was looking at him as if he had grown another head, but I couldn't help it. Shaking myself, I took a sip of the tea and moaned, not unlike how I had just a few moments ago. "Chamomile?"

He shrugged, "There wasn't any honey, so I added some sugar to yours."

I hummed into my mug as I took another long gulp. Elián seemed to take this as an answer to whatever question he had been asking himself.

He set his back down on the table and retrieved the small jar. Shifting his body to face mine, he removed the lid and released the smell of peppermint. He pressed the cold back to my ass as I sipped, alternating between the two sides as the cloth became more and more damp. The stinging on my skin was now just a faint throbbing. My empty mug was removed from my hands, and I laid down on my chest.

The cool cloth was then replaced by the pads of Elián's warm fingers that were coated with a thick cream of some kind. "What is that?" My voice was muffled with my face pressed into a pillow underneath me.

He slowly worked the cream into my skin and spoke low, "It's a soothing ointment."

"Mmm," I closed my eyes and inhaled deeply. Though he had been rough before, his touch now was nothing but gentle, and the throbbing of my skin lessened. He was silent as he spread the cream over my skin, massaging my muscles as he worked. I felt his fingers move to the tenderness at my hips where he'd held me and begin to spread the cream there, too. "El?"

His fingers stilled for a moment before continuing, "Hm?"

"Where are you from?" He didn't answer, just kept rubbing. I pulled up onto my elbows and craned my neck as much as I could, only to see just the edge of his body as it sat hunched over me. "You never answer any of my questions." He'd demanded I be honest with him, but he still wouldn't do me the same courtesy.

His voice was deep and steady as he continued to massage me as if it calmed him, too. "Yes, I do."

I rolled my eyes, "If I asked you five questions right now, could you agree to answer each one?"

He kept on moving his hands, kneading the muscles in my lower back, "Fine."

His response stunned me. What was I to ask? I hadn't thought he'd actually agreed to it, but now I needed to seize the opportunity. "Where are you from?" I whispered and held my breath, longing for the answer more than I realized.

He didn't hesitate this time, but had I not been listening for it, I would not have heard him answer, barely a whisper, "Zonoras." The vowels sounded round and full on his tongue.

I had never heard of this place. Had he not spoken the name with such held back emotion, I would have accused him of making it up. "I've never heard of it. Where is it?"

"In a desert," was all he said.

I didn't like whatever was creeping into his voice and the fact that I had brought it there. The name of his homeland rolled around in my mouth. It felt strange yet familiar, but I kept quiet. Would I insult him if I asked what the state of his home was now? In the back of my mind, I already knew the answers to both. So I asked a different question, "Do you like being a Shadow?"

This, he answered quickly and louder, "Yes." Another hit of peppermint met my nose, and his fingers brushed aside my hair. He rubbed the cream over my neck, and I groaned as he worked it into my muscles. I hadn't even registered that I was tender there.

A bit dazed, I chose my fourth question, "What does the tattoo in your palm say—why place it there?" Though he had so many tattoos that I wanted to just lay him down and ask about each and every one, I was most curious about this one. It was the only tattoo I knew about before tonight, the only one that was apparent when he was fully clothed.

"That was two questions, Meline." My stomach flipped hearing him speak my name so casually. He had mostly used it in the throws of sex. Saying it now as he tended to my body felt so vastly different, but I couldn't begin to pinpoint exactly how.

"Can you make them count for one?"

"That's another question."

"For the love of the Mother, El! Just answer how you want to, then."

He moved to my upper back, running the heels of his hands along my spine and the curve of my shoulder blades. Though these parts of my body hadn't been roughened by him tonight, they melted under his touch all the same.

"Leandro. He was... my brother." Was. I didn't expect Elián to continue, but he did while he massaged my back, "My mother... she claimed that we had been born hand-in-hand. Whether that was actually true or not—we slept that way as babes. Even as children, then as adults, if we slept beside each other... we would always find the other's hand." Though he spoke as if he had never uttered the words before, I thought I could hear the faintest smile ghost his lips.

Twins.

Twins were almost unheard of for Lylithans, and though I could understand the bond between blood-siblings, I would never understand that connection. They had come into the world together, and now Elián walked the realm alone. My heart ached for him, but

I knew better than to offer sympathetic words. I knew he wouldn't want them.

Lips pressed softly at the base of my neck, and I shivered. He spoke over my skin, "I will give you one more." He pressed another kiss to my back, and my mind drifted to sexual places.

Abruptly, he pulled away, and I felt him rub more cream, this time on my wrists. I realized that he had been referring to my questions. Scrambling out of the arousal that had been creeping into my mind again, I asked the first thing I could think of, "What is your favorite part of my body?"

His laugh was little more than a shuddering of breath, but it was there. For the second time since I had met him, Elián properly laughed. "That is your last question?"

"Yes. Of course it is."

Gentle fingers brushed my hair from my cheek and tucked it behind my ear. I heard him close the jar of ointment and felt him sit back against the pillows beside me. "Your mouth."

I turned to rest my head on my other cheek so that I could look up at him. I narrowed my eyes, "Why—because I once sucked your cock? I would have thought it was my breasts or ass or cunt for all the attention you paid them tonight."

He raised his brow, and I was amazed that he had no wrinkles on his forehead for how often he made the gesture. "You're out of questions, my queen."

I puffed my lips and blew out a gust of air. I wanted more answers, all of his answers, but he had given me more than he'd agreed to. More than, I suspected, he had given to anyone. At least, in a long, long time. Fair was fair, and after multiple releases and the events of the day, exhaustion was taking hold. I closed my eyes and nestled my pillow between my face and arms.

Movement on the mattress alerted me that he was getting up. My brow furrowed, but I kept my eyes closed, "Where are you going?"

His warm breath brushed over my eyelashes as he leaned over me, "To stand watch in the front room and let you sleep. I have been a bad Shadow."

My words were already slurring as sleep was taking over, "Don't you need to sleep, too?"

"I need to do my job more than I need to sleep. And I have a feeling you will be dead to the world for many hours." He was right, though I didn't like it.

The soft press of fabric kissed my backside. Elián smoothed the bedsheet over me, and if I hadn't already been drifting off, I would have asked him to stay regardless. With other lovers, even Shoko, another person clinging onto me for longer than a few minutes left me feeling caged and too warm. If what he said before was true, it seemed he felt the same. But I at least wanted him in the bed beside me.

Just before sleep took me, I sensed his presence leaving my bedroom, but I heard no click of the door closing. The last trailing thought I remembered was my wondering if he would watch me as I slept.

37

My lids softly fluttered open, and I was met with a pleasant, soft, gray light filtering through the room. The white of the sheets almost glowed against my brown skin. My straightened hair pooled beside me and tickled the tiny hairs on my forearm—I had forgotten to put it up before going to bed.

My groggy mind seemed to finally get enough footing to remember what had happened last night. A pleasant soreness between my legs pushed away the fleeting thought that it had all been one of the few dreams I'd had about Elián since we met. But that was easier to accept as fact, that it had happened, than what the utter relaxation in my shoulders asserted. What the silence around the edges of my mind asserted.

A silence that I only noticed because it was so foreign. Elián fucking me until I was sore and voice almost gone from screaming I could wrap my head around. Especially with what had already been building between us. The other two times we had done things, they were like a short reprieve to tide us over, but never completely relieving the tension that had been growing. Hadn't that been partly why I had egged him on? In those moments where I'd screamed at him, it wasn't really Cal or the Krislans I'd wronged that were in the forefront of my mind. I was angry and exhausted yesterday, but I also knew that I had to be the one to push us both over the edge.

What seemed almost like a dream, though, was what had happened after. Elián had accepted me, soothed me, massaged me. Confided in me. In a way that felt so foreign in its rightness and...

domesticity? Were either of us even capable of such a thing? Or was it just the haze of great sex that let us become different people for a few moments?

I stretched my arms and legs, swiping them over the soft sheets. I remembered Elián essentially tucking me in before he left the room last night and felt a bit dizzy at the thought. Sleep was taking me over, but the burning request I had on my lips, for him to stay in the bed with me, was still there. I could taste it on my tongue, along with the lingering taste of him and myself and the both of us.

Straining my ears, I couldn't hear anything from the front room. But that didn't mean a fucking thing, I had learned.

Closing my eyes, taking a deep breath, I let my sense of smell push to the forefront. The bedroom, the sheets, my hair, all smelled of him, but a more solid hit of cinnamon and burning oak wafted from the front room. I hadn't realized the upset that had been creeping up my throat at the prospect of him being gone. *He's supposed to stay here to protect you, you idiot. And why are you worried about him leaving, anyway?*

Gathering myself up, I pushed the sheets away and swung my legs over the side of the bed. My feet met the cool floor, and I stretched my arms over my head. Whatever cream he had smoothed over my skin and massaged me with, along with my body's own propensity for quick healing, left me just a kiss of what I let him do to me.

My past lovers had run the gamut over the centuries, and the gentleness or roughness we had enjoyed together varied wildly. But the fire in Elián's touch and the way my body craved it, swallowed it whole... that was entirely new.

I knew that whatever made his eyes look the way they did, made that fire, was looking to rage. He kept such a hold on it, I didn't think he even thought about it anymore. Maybe he had been doing it for so long, he didn't even know he *was* doing it anymore. But I saw it when my own abyss taunted at him, asked the flames to come play so that I could bask in them.

He would know that I was awake. I sighed at the knowledge that I would probably never master that silence he slipped into so effortlessly. My fingers combed through my hair, which took an annoying amount of time with the rat's nest that had formed in the back. But this being due to Elián's fist holding me taut so that he could take me quelled some of the irritation.

I didn't bother putting on anything and just walked out of the bedroom. My hair swiped across my lower back and partially covered my breasts, and I saw his head and bare shoulders rise above the back of the sofa. He didn't turn to me, which was just as fine. He must have pulled the curtains back a bit at some point because the room was filled with more of that soft light from the cloud-filled skies outside.

I rounded the sofa and saw that he held one of those books he'd bought at the market in Rhaestras. *How different things were back then.*

Was he rereading it? From where I stood, I could make out some of the drawings of *Joran*, and they were ones I didn't recognize. Had he been saving this next one from me?

I stopped in front of Elián, but he didn't lift his head, his eyes still scanning the page he was on. His fingers lazily turned it, and I felt a soft shift of air between the gentle patch of my pubic hair and my navel. And this, of course, made my core flit in that unmistakable way. I knew that the scent of my rising desire would have reached his nose by now, but he made no move.

Impatiently, I snatched the book out of his hands, and he allowed me. I was irritated that he was toying with me by not acknowledging my presence, and even more irritated that he could have easily held onto the book instead of letting me have it.

I held the magazine to me, spread with one hand so that I could look over the drawings and captions. With the other hand, I grabbed the bit of hair that hung over my left shoulder and threw it over my back, exposing my breast.

The page he'd been on showed just three blocks of drawings, the one in the middle being the largest. Joran had just been punched in the face by a fist whose owner was out of frame. In the largest illustration in the middle, Joran's face was blown up to show a confused and pained look, but the spittle and curses written flying out of his mouth made for a comical image instead of a serious one. The last, smaller image on the page was of him lying in a ridiculous heap on the ground, his face one of bewilderment that also signaled that he wasn't that hurt.

A throaty chuckle escaped my throat, and I turned the page. But before I could settle my eyes on the next scene, strong, warm hands palmed my hips and pulled me forward. I dropped the book to my side, onto the sofa cushions.

Elián gripped my waist while I sat straddled over his lap. His clothed lap, much to my disappointment. He had pulled on a pair of those soft cotton trousers he'd worn in my apartment.

I looked up and saw that his hair was all tousled waves. How much of that was from my fingers or his own running through it, I wasn't sure. Though he had surely stayed up all night, his eyes didn't look tired. They were the color of the ripe, rich flesh of a mango. The kind that grew in Rhaestras and that I would eat while air-drying on the sand with drops of saltwater still clinging to my eyelashes.

He searched my face for a moment then let his gaze roam down my jaw, my neck. They settled on my breasts, and I could see the minuscule movements of his eyes as they followed the swell of my breathing. His hands slid between my ass and his thighs and pulled me up so that I was half kneeling over his lap.

I braced my hands on the back of the sofa as he took my left breast into his mouth. His tongue teased the gold of my piercing, and I felt his fingers squeeze tighter. From the way he held me, I knew that my lips were pulled open, and the smell of my desire was already starting to fill the room. But he didn't move his fingers at all to feel the wetness there. He kept them still, holding me up so that I could relax all of my weight into him. He kissed and licked as if he wanted to learn every tiny patch of my skin, working slowly, almost sleepily, as if he had all of eternity to relish in my flesh.

I twined my finger around a lock of his hair that ended in a little loop, almost a curl but not quite. The graze of his fang against my nipple made me moan over his head, but he didn't get any more intense than that. He switched to the other breast, approaching it with the same lazy teasing. I wouldn't have been surprised if I was dripping into his lap.

"Just like other males. Get some tits in your face, and you're gone," my husky laugh was quiet and ended in another moan.

His mouth stopped moving, and he leaned back, though his arms still held me aloft. Those mango eyes met mine, and that infernal brow was quirked. The deep pink of his lips was slick and slightly puffy from his kissing. "Other males?" My stomach did a flip at the apparent possessiveness in his tone. That—that was unexpected.

The hands underneath me shifted, and I sat on his forearm now. His right hand grabbed my chin and brought my face closer to his. My own scent twined with the smell of chamomile and mint on his breath, "I'm going to properly punish you one day for that wicked mouth of yours."

The corner of my mouth tilted upward, "I thought that was your favorite body part of mine? Although it seems you may have changed your answer to my tits."

He didn't smile, but his eyes flared a bit in amusement. My smile grew wider. "It's still your mouth, you menace."

I leaned forward, lips brushing his, "Not hating me so much anymore, are you, Elián?"

He whispered, "Don't say that too fast. It's still early in the day."

"Well," I twirled my finger around another lock of his hair, "I think you owe me more than six answers before you start laying claim to me." I was pushing it, I knew. But I couldn't stop thinking about last night. How Elián had spoken about himself while being gentle with my body.

"Okay."

I was so sleepy and still fuck-drunk that it took a moment for his agreement to register. "Okay, what?"

The hand at my chin was gone, and I heard the shifting of fabric, "Okay, I will answer your questions."

My brows shot up, "No matter how many?"

His lips met mine for a short but warm kiss. He only pulled away enough to have room to speak, "No matter how many," and kissed me again.

I knew what he was doing—the telltale scent of him had released into the air of the room to twine with mine. But perhaps this time, I would be able to have both his flesh and his answers. I squirmed a bit in the seat of his making until his hands palmed my ass once more. He shifted his grip to my hips, letting me decide what I wanted to do, whether I was accepting this or not.

"Were you born with your fire powers?" I allowed my knees to bend even more, until I felt the head of him just brush my skin. Elián sucked in a quiet breath at the sensation, no doubt feeling how wet I was, but he wasn't getting any more of me unless he took me seriously. I was done with his ignoring and half answers. One night of sex and humoring me for a few questions wasn't going to change that.

"Yes."

That wasn't enough, though. I wanted more. I needed it all. "Who taught you how to control it?"

His eyes were halfway closed, but I could see them focused on my lips as I spoke. "My mother." Elián's hands made slow movements on my hips, but he did nothing else. He was content to sit with me or let me swallow him, and I felt power in this.

So much power and so much desire that it felt like my brain wasn't working properly. Now he said he was going to answer all of my questions, and I was finding it incredibly difficult to think of any good ones. The feeling was too heady, and I wanted him in me more and more each second. "C—can you make a flame for me right now?"

I felt cool air on my hip with one of his hands gone, and he brought it to just beside us. In sleepy awe, I watched a lone flame appear in the center of Elián's palm. What he and I were able to do—it wasn't magic. Those like my cousin or the priestesses were able to harness the energy around us and bend it to their will.

But my darkness and Elián's fire came from within us. If all the aether of the realm were to disappear, he would still be able to draw flame, and I would be able to wield Death. The very flame he conjured twitched with our breaths shifting the air, and I realized that it was the same colors as his ever-shifting eyes.

Elián turned his wrist so that his palm was facing downward, and I watched the flame skate around to the back of his hand. He gave a slow fluttering of his fingers, and the small orange and gold fire trailed under and over his knuckles like a shooting star.

Underneath me, Elián's heart was steady, and he didn't stop the languid petting at my hip while the flame danced for me. It looked easier than breathing for him. I was impressed and jealous, and ridiculous, stupid pride coursed through my chest.

My hips sunk further down onto his lap, and I took the head of him into me. The both of us sucked in a synchronized gasp, and he clenched his outstretched hand into a fist. The flame disappeared immediately, but I wasn't disappointed. What he showed me felt like a promise, so I asked my next question, "Why did you run away from me after the first time you tasted me?"

He brought his mouth to my neck, and I felt the warm press of his lips, "Because... I didn't trust myself. To stop."

I sank lower and groaned at him stretching me again. Elián's breathing was a bit quicker now, but he stayed still where he was, "Why were you so angry at Cal's last night? I could *feel* it." Try as I did to ignore his rage to focus on maneuvering around Cal, I couldn't help but pick up on his simmering.

His swallow was loud enough for me to hear above my own heart rate picking up, but he still answered, "Because I could see what playing to that—*vendaco*—was doing to you," he swallowed again, "I wanted to take you and bring you back somewhere safe." I had no idea what a vendaco was, but my mind was able to decipher his meaning.

"...Are you afraid of me?"

Before the question was barely out of my mouth, he growled, "No." My hair shifted and spilled with my frantic nodding at his answer. Though I had seen that he'd never been truly scared of me, I realized in that moment that I needed to hear those words. He'd heard of my crimes and seen another glimpse of what Rhaea's power could make me do. And yet, he said he wasn't afraid.

I let him sink in even more, and now he was halfway inside. My whole body was trembling with the need to fully seat myself, but the fear of this moment passing, me losing my chance, was holding me back.

"Will you," I licked my lips, "will you promise to keep answering my questions later?"

And now he was nodding, too. His nose and lips tickled the curve of my neck, "Yes, my queen. I swear it." *My queen.* When he said those words, they sounded like the furthest thing from the sarcasm he'd had when we first met. The title coming from his lips now felt like warmth and care and absolution.

My head threw back, and I let go of the tension in my legs. With my prolonged arousal, Elián's length had no problem sliding the rest of the way in, and he widened his legs so that I could feel the base of him flush with my skin.

We held there for one breath, two.

I grasped his jaw with both of my hands, and brought his face to mine once more. He didn't hesitate, nor did he flinch when my eyes met his. It was like the flame he'd drawn for me was skating around his pupils now, and I watched it while I raised my hips again.

My thumb brushed his lips, feeling the soft flesh there. And I saw the creeping vines of my darkness twining around my fingers, including the thumb that was on him.

I started to lower again, slowly, until I saw the tip of my Shadow's tongue meet the edge of my fingernail. A whimper left my lips, and I sheathed him entirely once again.

He moaned, and still watching me, took my thumb between his teeth, holding my touch and my power inside his mouth.

While I built up to a blissful rhythm, Elián held my eyes with his mouth still around my thumb. He moved underneath me, meeting my hips with his own in soft thuds, and his touch was the balm I needed to push away the guilt of what happened yesterday. My Shadow, who hated and grumbled and protected now knew about who I had been.

He saw what I was capable of now that my power was let out and a part of me, and he let me see what the Godyxes had given him. And maybe that was why I had picked him over Master Noruh for this journey. For I knew that his flame and my abyss were of the same kind of gift. Even under flinty mask, I'd sensed what was underneath from that moment on the hill. With every insult and every barb, I had been pushing so that he'd push back. I wanted him to consume me with his fire the same way I wanted to consume him with my darkness.

And with him holding me between his lips, I knew that he wanted it, too.

The release that was coming over us inched closer and closer, and I replaced my finger with my mouth, with my tongue. We groaned into each other, and my hair fell around us like a curtain. My chest pressed and slid against his in this fucking that didn't feel like fucking at all. Last night, he'd given me what I needed—to yield the reins on the flimsy sense of control I'd been grasping at, and through delectable pain and ecstasy and vulnerability, Elián grounded me.

But now, as we joined face-to-face in the early morning, it felt... profound.

I started to come first, bringing Elián's head to my neck and clutching his hair. The burst of my orgasm was peeking when Elián's body thrusted roughly just before he gave a sustained, ragged moan at my throat. We trembled against each other while his seed painted my walls, and our breaths remained synchronized as they slowed. We sat for a long while, my fingers still in his hair and his still clutching me to him, and I wanted nothing more than to stay like this forever.

Forever?

That preposterous word was like launching headfirst into the Rhaestran sea. It felt sudden and staggering, and before I could recover my breath to the relaxed cadence it had been, Elián shifted beneath me. He pressed on my waist the same moment he pulled his shoulders and head back to be able to see my face.

Those straight, black brows weren't pulled down in a scowl or raised in challenge. They were drawn in a look of soft concern that made blood rush to my freckled cheeks. "What is wrong?"

And when he was looking at me like that, with his eyes all molten, gooey and ripe mango, I forgot what had startled me in the first place. "Nothing."

"Did I hurt you?"

"Hurt me?" I brushed my fingertips over the straight and curved lines of his face. His nose was longer than mine, and its slope fit his face so perfectly. The bow of his lip was smooth, and I touched mine to his in a delicate kiss, "I am not a soft flower, El."

His hands absently trailed along the outside of my thighs, and his almost-silent chuckle stirred the air between us, "Oh, I am aware." He paused before choosing his next words and didn't quite meet my gaze, "I know that I have... upset you many times. And I am... very sorry for hurting you when we first met. I deeply regret my actions."

The quivering in my chest at his guilt made me shift uncomfortably, and I was reminded that he was still in me. I'd long ago forgiven his attack, but the apology was unexpected and nice to hear.

I threaded my fingers in his hair and combed it back and down his scalp. The strands themselves were thick, and they undulated under my touch like a soft tide, "You're not upsetting me now." He chuckled again, and I didn't even attempt to contain the slight grin pulling across my face.

"Come," he said and lifted us both off from the sofa. I involuntarily clung to him and wrapped my legs around his waist while he carried us to the kitchen area. He grabbed a crisp towel from beside the sink as he leaned me against the counter, the smooth wood cool under my naked skin.

Carefully, Elián pulled his hips back from mine and released the seal of our bodies. I watched his cock pull out and be replaced by the undoubtedly expensive cloth.

When he'd wiped all of his leavings away and tossed the towel aside, he remained close and let me run my hands up and down his chest. My feet dangled toward the floor and bumped softly against the black cabinets. I circled the rose over his heart and whispered, "Why this one?"

He'd been watching my face, but now his head turned down to look where I was pointing. He answered the same as he had for one of my previous questions, "My mother."

Soft patters of rain began to hit the windows, and I asked, barely any louder, "Tell me about her?" To put his mother, the one who gave him life, over the strongest signal of his living aside from his eyes communicated a love that I related to. She was the one who had taught him how to wield his power, and I could tell even now that he missed her tremendously.

I felt him nod, and he began to answer. His voice was low and steady, and all the while, he made slow circles along the thickest part of my hips. "Roza," he said. She was named after the flower he had inked on his body, and she had been born and raised in Zonoras. It was where he had been born and lived before becoming a Shadow. Her skin had been like his, and her hair just as black.

My head flew up at what he said next, and I couldn't believe it. "She was a priestess of which godyx?"

Elián nuzzled my forehead for a moment then answered, "Zoko." The Goddess of Strategy and Combat and Rhaea's younger sister. If I weren't in such a trance from his admissions, I would have laughed.

"And She gave you this power? And your mother had it, too?"

"Yes and yes, though it appears that our Goddesses gifted us in different manners."

My head tilted, "What do you mean?"

Elián cleared his throat and continued, "You specifically were chosen by Rhaea. No one in your line has held such power, yes?" When I nodded, he continued, "My mother's line has always been loyal to the Goddess Zoko. Many generations back, She gifted my mother's line with the flames, and it is passed down through each child."

But—I had never heard of such a thing. For a godyx to gift someone with a facet of their power, that was an anomaly in of itself. The Godyx Thryx was known to parse out small gifts here and there, Their intelligence shared with a select few. The God Mortos chose a few mortal champions each generation to share His strength with, but the Goddesses were much more mysterious, powerful.

For one to gift an entire line... that was a miracle, a tall tale. His eyes shifted colors again as he saw my confusion. "So. Your mother and your brother could do what you can?" He swallowed and nodded. "And... how many in your mother's line are there now?"

The lift of the corners of his lips wasn't a smile but a somber shift in his expression, "One."

I knew that was what he was going to say, but to have it confirmed silenced me. Elián had told me of his brother's death, implied his mother's, and said that he was orphaned by The Killings like I had been. But that solitary word held such an endless loneliness. I wanted to wipe it from the air, but even if I were able to stuff his answer back into his mouth, there would be no changing that Elián was the only one left.

"How?"

I didn't need to elaborate. He tucked a lock of his hair behind his ear before bringing his hand to my waist. "Killed." He breathed a sigh tinged with a side of his anger I realized I hadn't yet been privy to, "First, my mother and the rest of her family when Leandro and I were away at the Shadow Well. We had just been sworn in to the Shadows. Then, my brother and father when they were caught in a city that was being swept by a Vyrkos uprising. They'd been trying to help those being slaughtered but lost their lives in the process. I was finishing up a contract at the time."

The nauseated feeling returned. Another sin to add to my pyre of shame. How many times had I denounced the Shadows for lack of assistance during those horrible years? And Elián hadn't said anything, not a word, when I basically cursed his family's sacrifice. What else didn't I know? I swallowed the knot in my throat, "Elián... I am... so sorry for what I've said to you. I—"

He grabbed my chin, "Nâ." There it was again—a language I couldn't quite place but sounded so familiar. The way he said the word, the vowel was round and further back in his throat. By the set of his jaw, it meant he wanted me to stop what I was saying, and his face showed no ire, just more of that concern.

I worried at my upper lip with my teeth. He didn't want me to apologize, but there was no excuse for what I had surely made him feel. "El, I am..." but I decided to change course, "How are you feeling?"

His head tilted now, looking at me with that appraising way of his, and I imagined the whirling sound of his mind working to figure out what to say.

There was also a part of me that wondered if anyone asked him the question often. Were there other Shadows he was close with? Master Noruh or Master Jones? The handful that I had met ranged in personality and appearance, and I could imagine that they interacted quite often at this Shadow Well. Did they look after him when his mother was killed? Did they mourn with him when his father and brother were?

"I am well."

I nodded around his hold, but he didn't release me. "And, ah, what do you want to do? Today, I mean."

He looked over to the window, where it still showed a light rain outside, "We should leave the city."

The thought of riding our horses through the rain sounded like the last thing I wanted to do. But he was right. It was day, so running into more angry Vyrkos wouldn't be an issue. "Did any guards intervene before you brought me back here?"

"No." I'd figured as much. My suspicion that Cal had been behind the group that'd accosted us last night was solidifying. If he and Uncle were already making their own secret negotiations, he didn't even really need to meet with me. Sicking on me a band of disgruntled people that we'd both wronged was just a gratuitous twist of the knife.

"And my daggers?"

Elián nodded toward the bedroom, "I put them with the rest of your things."

"Who are you and what have you done with Elián? You haven't said one rude thing to me in almost two days." I planted a kiss on the rose for Roza, and felt another rumble of laughter in his chest.

When I pulled back, I saw that he had one brow raised. "Do you want me to?" And then his lips turned down, "What did I say to you yesterday that was rude?"

I huffed, "You insulted my hair!" I pulled on my straightened locks for emphasis.

Though he'd fisted my hair last night to keep me anchored for him, he touched it now with trepidation. "I did not mean to insult." When he let the strands fall limply from his fingers, his lips turned down even more, "It just... doesn't look... right?"

Now I was the one tilting my head and appraising him. It was another tectonic shift in our relationship, and I didn't know what to make of his words or do with the implication of his preference if that were indeed what he was struggling to describe. "Well, um. Perhaps we should get ready to head back to Versillia, then?"

He grunted in agreement and stepped back to let me down. The floor was colder than the cabinets, and I immediately missed Elián's warmth. There wasn't much to repack since we hadn't been in the city for longer than a day, but we both moved more slowly as we settled into this change and the reality that this journey was ending.

After pulling out a set of leathers to wear for the three-day ride to report back in person, I turned to Elián who was cleaning and repacking his weapons. There was a peace to him, tan skin almost illuminated from within, when he passed his own black cloths over the blades and pommels. He had a myriad of daggers and knives, but he saved cleaning his dual short swords for last. He surely sensed my staring, but he didn't call attention to it.

Still naked, I began to riffle through the drawers and cabinets looking for... that. The kettle was still on the stove from Elián using it last night, and one of the cabinets beneath the counter contained a basket of bagged tea blends. After setting some water to boil, I held up each bag to my nose, looking for the one that smelled almost exactly like spearmint but not quite. The fourth bag I tried was the right one, and I plopped it into a mug.

"Would you like some tea?" I called over while I continued to identify and separate out the different blends available to us.

"Sure," he answered.

For him, I chose a bag that smelled of clove, orange, and cinnamon, and just as the kettle began to whistle, I poured our cups. Elián thanked me when I placed it on the table in front of him, and I hummed into my own before taking a sip. Leave it to Cal to own an inn with complimentary contraceptive tea.

"Um, El?" He didn't answer verbally, but he raised his head from the final pass of his cloth over his sword. "Would you like to take a shower?" The stall in the bathing room was as extravagant and simple as the rest of the room, and it would be faster if we took the shower together, rather than taking turns. Maybe.

Possibly.

He reached for his tea, and I waited for him to drain it completely. I wondered if he could ever be burned, considering he held the power of fire within his veins. Judging by the way he gulped the scaldingly hot drink, the answer seemed like 'no'.

Elián sheathed his swords, weapons all cleaned and prepared for our voyage, and stood. He started toward the bathing room, and I marveled at the muscles shifting at his shoulders and upper back as he walked. Another foreign word in that clean, elegant script was scrawled across his upper back.

The sudden urge to draw him was almost overwhelming, but with that came the uncertainty of if I could do him justice. The movement was a prowling that I didn't think I would ever be able to capture, no matter how many times I tried.

The starting of the shower was almost a cracking whip in the silence of the room, and then he was standing in the doorway. "Let us bathe then, Your Highness."

That small voice in my mind whispered again, *What changed?* And I truly didn't know, but the thought of Elián washing me while pressing my body into the smooth tiles of the shower stall was far more enticing. I downed the rest of my tea and followed my Shadow into the bathing room and reveled in his cleansing of me from the inside out.

38

We left Krisla with as little fanfare as when we arrived. There were no angry mobs, no guards blocking our path, and no Cal. The rain carried on until well into the afternoon, but it was light enough that the two of us and the horses didn't mind too much. My hat provided some cover, and Elián was in perhaps the best mood I had ever seen him. We rode close together and under the cover of trees as much as we could, and between stretches of silence, we talked in a stilted rhythm. It wasn't a complete burst of a dam, but more honesty flowed between us. Little to no jabs were thrown, and if there were, they were followed by a snicker on my part or a cheeky frown on his.

When we'd stopped at a clearing for the horses to rest and drink from a small stream, we ate from a cache of dried meat Elián had in one of his packs. Though it was far different from when we'd stopped for a similar rest at the beginning of our journey, there was still an awkward settling between us. He hadn't tried to touch me since The Moonbeam, and I was stubbornly waiting for him to be the one to initiate. I battled with my need to feel his skin and lips on mine again and trying to rebuild my shriveled pride. It left me feeling grumpy, and I tore into the chewy meat while I contemplated until it was time to pick back up again.

That evening, we stopped at a busy inn just off the main road, and I ignored his look of surprise when I asked for a room with one bed. We requested to have our food sent up to us, and after setting our things down, I began to undress my damp and clinging traveling leathers. I draped them over a chair to dry, and when I turned, Elián was still dressed but staring at me.

"What?" I looked behind me then down at my body clad in my undergarments. They were black and unremarkable.

He swiftly turned away to start rearranging his packs and muttered, "I am having a difficult time trying to not be distracted."

"Distracted from what?" I smirked and gave my lower back a little arch that pushed out my breasts and ass, just to see what he'd do.

He glanced over for a second, then shook his head. "From my *job*, Your Highness." Ah, so that was his hesitation. I relaxed a little. The insecure part of me was worried that despite everything, he still truly disliked me. Him being too honorable when it came to his job was much easier on my ego.

I rolled my eyes and began to walk over to him, "Well, we both can protect me very well, and if the both of us are half-paying attention, then I'm still covered, I think."

He retrieved a bundle of folded fabric and placed it on the bed, "I don't believe it works like that."

I shrugged, "Well, if it will help you, I will do my *very* best to keep my feminine wiles to myself and not seduce you."

"There goes that wicked mouth again."

Elián stripped off his own soiled leathers, and set them out on a chair beside mine before changing into those soft pajama trousers. Our supper was soon delivered, and he set up the spread on the bed. It was more stew, as that was a staple of almost every travel stop, but the wine we secured wasn't half-bad. We sat cross-legged on the bed with our bowls set up between us, and I made no secret of my ogling Elián's bare chest and arms.

"Can I ask you something?" He looked up from his bowl that was nearly empty and waited. "How did I ruin your contract when we first met?"

He cast his eyes downwards, and his jaw worked in a guilty rhythm of clenching and releasing. He scraped his spoon to gather the rest of the stew and ate it before putting his bowl down. "When you... stole the circlet from my charge and he discovered it missing, he became so angry that he canceled my contract. That irritating human said that it was part of my job to keep him from getting pickpocketed," Elián snorted and shook his head.

I tilted mine, "But surely you saw what I was doing before I left."

"Oh, I saw. I just didn't care until he nullified my contract."

"So, you found the one who had hired me and decided to enact revenge?" My brows were almost at my hairline.

He lifted his broad shoulders and ran a hand through his hair that was wild from the road, "It wasn't difficult. I was angry, and he was on the island to meet with you."

I couldn't help but laugh. With everything that had happened, I wasn't upset anymore. Never would I have predicted what would transpire between the two of us. Never would I have predicted that I would be sitting across from the one who had disarmed me in such a way and just be thinking about climbing atop his lap.

"Well, I suppose I did get a nice bit of jewelry out of the altercation." After returning to Nethras, I'd thrown the bracelet down in one of my vanity drawers amongst my other jewels and hadn't thought about it since. It was a lovely piece, and perhaps now I could wear it without becoming enraged at the sight.

Elián set his empty bowl to the side and stretched his arms over his head, much to my delight, "I still have your money. I will get it back to you."

I was so entranced by his stretching that it took me a moment to respond, "That only seems fair," but the words didn't have the edge that I'd intended. He was keeping good on his promise to answer my questions, when I... hadn't been doing the same. Perhaps he thought it would cause me distress, but Elián still hadn't pressed me about fulfilling my end of our deal. I cleared my throat, "The Shadow that taught me," my fingers fiddled with the spoon in my hand, "he had dark skin and long, locked hair." Elián's eyes narrowed, but he was otherwise still. I continued, pressing for honesty, now, "We'd—I was just outside of Vharas and had just finished with a contract and had been shopping before heading home."

My voice wavered under Elián's assessment, but I kept on, telling of how I'd heard a scuffle in the alleyway on my walk back to the lodging house where I'd been staying. The seedier area yielded a cheaper room, and I'd reasoned that I was deadlier than anyone else I may have encountered. But my daggers were easily accessible, just in case, while I walked. That's when I heard a struggle, and upon reaching the mouth of the alley, I saw the Shadow being attacked by a group of four. Though I believed Elián would have been able to handle being outnumbered in that way, this Shadow was on the ground, with the armed group descending upon him. I'd leapt into the fight, buying the Shadow time to recover, and we fought, back-to-back, and killed them all.

Blood coated our fronts, my daggers, and his long, curved sword. When we finally faced each other again, I'd prepared to bid a quick farewell, thank him for the fun. But, instead, he looked aggrieved, *embarrassed*. That I had helped him. So, I'd sheathed my weapons and tossed my hair behind my shoulder, *"Seems like you owe me a debt, Shadow."*

I took a bite of my cold supper and winced, "He agreed to show me, as long as I told no one, and he never shared his name. We parted ways when the sun rose." Elián seemed to not even be hearing me now, as he stared into the distance, jaw working on whatever my story, my truth, had provoked. But he didn't seem upset with me, and after seven breaths of me pushing my food around my bowl, he grunted and nodded, acknowledging and accepting my answer to his long-standing question.

I put my half-finished food onto the side table beside my goblet of wine and almost closed the space between us, longing for his touch, for *something*. But it was like he saw the plan forming on my face because he was suddenly standing and then stacking our dirty dishes into a neat pile by the door. Still bare-chested, Elián slung on his short swords and stood in the corner with the best view of the door and window.

His hard features smoothed as if he'd placed a veil that muted his emotion over his face. I grumbled, "Are you seriously not going to sleep? When was the last time you laid your head on a pillow, Elián?"

The veil didn't lift, but he murmured back, "I am not. And your apartment sofa, I believe." He believed. Goddess, that had been days. At least he was still keeping good on answering anything I asked him.

"Honestly, I'm more worried about having a sleep-deprived guard than none at all."

He shrugged woodenly, "I have gone far longer without in far more dangerous situations. You sleep."

"Whilst you do, what? Eavesdrop on our fellow patrons all night?"

His answer was a shrug, saying that that was exactly what he'd probably end up doing.

I settled into the bed and opened one of the romance novels I'd bought in Rhaestras. The pages were crisp, and the spine creaked when I opened to the first page. Immediately, I felt more relaxed with the book in hand, but Elián standing like a too-realistic statue in the corner of the room was tugging at my resolve.

"'There wasn't much I'd put stock to in this world, but one thing I never counted on was seeing those golden eyes staring across from me. I saw them every night in my dreams, but now, here they were in the flesh.'" I pursed my lips after reading the first two lines aloud. I gave a glance to my Shadow and just caught him flicking his eyes away.

That bolstered my confidence, and I continued, filling our room with my narration so that both of us could enjoy the story. Elián had never given me an inkling that he enjoyed romance stories, but he didn't tell me to stop, either. I made my way through one chapter, then another, and when I paused to take a sip of wine to wet my lips, he looked at me expectantly, as if annoyed that I'd stopped. I felt a shameful flush on my cheeks and continued, reading until the early hours of the morning before falling asleep with the book on my chest.

The second day of traveling proceeded similarly to the first. Though the rain had stopped, the fog clung to us for the entire morning, and even when it cleared as we continued northeast, the sun never did peek out from the clouds. Another inn, more stew, and more reading ensued, and I felt the air of the land become more familiar as we started the third day.

We'd stopped at the inn from the beginning of our journey the night before we were to arrive back in Versillia, and Elián's more frequent glances showed that he picked up on the turning of my mood. Since waking up on the sofa in Krisla, the two of us had been sharing a sense of serenity that I knew was coming to an end.

With that came many questions and realities that had been running through my mind on a constant loop when he finally asked me what was wrong. We were packing up our things to make the last few hours' ride to my family's estate, and for a moment, I considered lying and saying everything was fine. But the look of patience and concern on his face left me unable to do so. I drew a deep breath and stated as I gathered my things, "I'm okay, but. When we get back, there will be many things to do. And I..."

"What is it?" Even with my back turned, I could tell that he was tilting his head while he looked at me.

"I," I clenched my eyes shut in embarrassment but forced myself to continue on, "when will you be leaving?"

He remained silent for so long, I turned around to face him. Perhaps he hadn't heard me? But our eyes met, and he was pulling his hair behind his ears. Finally, he said, "My contract is over once I get you home."

"Oh." He cleared his throat and looked at the floor. When he'd started as my escort, I wished over and over that I'd chosen someone else. And I knew that we would most likely part ways once I got back, but I just... Elián coughed again and turned to start piling our packs on his shoulders. Once he gathered them all, he led us out the door to start the last leg of our traveling.

Bhrila and Noxe trotted softly on the road, and faster than I thought possible, we were about two hours from Versillia. Elián and I didn't chat at all as we rode, but the question I'd been turning over in my mind was running out of time. Of course we somewhat ran in the same professional circles, so crossing paths wasn't outside of the realm of possibility.

But I wasn't ready for whatever we had to end just yet. It sounded pathetic and clingy, but I swallowed my fear and blurted, "Elián."

"Yes?" The rumble of his voice was enough to make my back relax a bit.

"When you—when we get back. Do you have another contract lined up?" Because that would make my next question a moot point. Part of me hoped that he did so that I didn't have to ask what I so desperately wanted to know, but I was going to lose my chance if I didn't find out now.

"Not currently. I was unsure if your negotiations would take longer than expected."

Both of our eyes were on the road, and not having to look at him gave me another boost of courage. I bit at my bottom lip for a moment before asking in a rush, "Well, if you don't *have* to go, would you maybe want to... stick around Versillia for a little while?" When he didn't immediately answer, I went on, "Obviously, there's no commitment, but I could use your input on my reports to my family and the Council, and to be frank, I'm starting to enjoy your company, and the estate and city are quite beautiful, and I'd love to show you around, and perhaps it would be nice to just be El and Em and—"

"El and Em?" His interruption left me sputtering, and I hadn't even really been paying attention to what I was saying. I thought I'd gotten used to his silence, but my anxiety was getting the better of me. When I snuck a look over to him, his lips were pursed in a familiar way that gave me a bit of hope.

I snorted, "Okay, that does sound ridiculous. But... you can think about it if you want?"

He tilted his head left and right, and I relaxed further, "I will."

I exhaled half of the breath I had been holding. The tension between us didn't disappear all together, but he hadn't completely dismissed the idea. Though I wanted more than anything to know his answer now, I forced myself to fill the silence with more innocuous conversation. We discussed our favorite moments from the *Joran* series, which I still hadn't caught up to him on. I faked throwing my hat at him when he accidentally revealed a detail I hadn't gotten to yet, and I swear I saw him almost crack a smile.

Soon we crossed the threshold into Versillia, and I waved at the guards that stood at attention on the road. They bowed, and I guided me and my Shadow toward my family's home.

39

Mathieu and Uncle weren't back yet, according to Diana who met us out front, which was just as well. I wasn't ready to divulge everything that'd happened just yet, and I was still unsure of what to do about the information Cal had supplied about Uncle Hendrik's maneuverings.

I couldn't look at Elián while I dismounted and Diana began to unfasten my bags. Now was the moment, but I wouldn't be the one to ask for his answer like an impatient, inexperienced schoolgirl.

So, I stalled by rubbing Bhrila's mane and doling thanks and sweet praises for carrying me to many new lands while being nothing but a good steed. When Hyvan came to lead her to the stables, I gave him detailed instructions of how to treat and take care of her after such a long journey to many strange places. While the young male nodded seriously at each extravagant request I had, Elián dismounted Noxe and unfastened his packs. Diana had already disappeared into the house to take my things to my room, and once all of Elián's were off of Noxe, it was just the two of us after Hyvan pulled our mares to the stable.

"Your Highness?" My pulse skyrocketed, and here it was. He was leaving, I was sure of it. Which was fine, I supposed. Those moments of affection had been nice, but I needed to remember the task at hand. When Mathieu returned, I'd have to discuss with him Uncle's under-the-table dealings with Cal and the possible shit storm that would cause. There could be a misunderstanding I wasn't seeing, but the more I thought about it, the uneasier I got. Was Uncle

Hendrik planning to usurp my brother as rightful heir to Versillia? He was my father's younger brother, so he was older than Mathieu and perhaps more familiar with running a thriving kingdom.

But they had been working together on the Lylithan Council for so long, I knew that such a scheme would be a gutting betrayal for Mathieu. Hendrik was one of two family members we had left. Losing another to nothing but greed would be devastating, but he had to know.

"Your Highness?" Elián asked again, and by the sound of his voice, it wasn't the second time he'd said those words.

I took a deep breath and straightened before turning to face him. Yes, he would leave, and I would face this without him. I felt my lip begin to almost quiver, for Goddess's sake, and I rubbed my hand over my mouth to hide my shame.

"Yes?" It didn't come out completely clear but was close enough.

"I have thought about what you said, and—"

"I hope that I haven't made you feel pressured, because that was the least of my intentions. I just—I don't know what I was thinking. Obviously we haven't... You've got a whole life to get back to, and I *don't* want to come off *spoiled* or like I expect such things from you —" the rest of my words were muffled by a gloved palm over my mouth. It tasted like worn leather, and I knew the skin underneath would taste like fire and cinnamon.

"I was going to ask you where to put my things." His apricot gaze was softly uncertain in a way that melted my insides and worries, and I blinked away the panic that had been fueling my stupid rambling.

My answer was muffled against his hand until he pulled it away with another look that was almost a smile. "Ah, in my rooms. We can go now?"

I expected him to say, 'Are you asking or telling,' but he just took a step back to shoulder his packs and wait. My legs stuttered to action and walked us inside.

He moved behind me, and I tried to keep my footsteps steady and not trip over the racing in my chest. Elián was agreeing to stay awhile. Not as a work obligation but because he wanted to. He wanted to spend time with me.

I never thought I would feel so at home in my childhood rooms again, but I found myself almost as relaxed as I would be in my Nethras apartment. Diana was about to start unpacking my things, but I shooed her away. She made a pointed glance to Elián before she shut my door, but if he noticed, he didn't react.

"You can put your things in here," I waved him to follow me to my bedroom, and he put his packs down in the corner. His leather-clad body seemed impossibly large in the already sizable room, and I drew an audible swallow as I tried to see my bedroom through his eyes. It was clean, thanks to my brother's staff, and there was a homey tidiness with my stacks of books on the nightstand, overflow of shoes lined next to the door, and glass ashtray on the windowsill.

I expected him to want to make quick use of the adjoining bathing room or begin to unpack or reorganize his things, but the wall behind my bed caught his eye, and he walked over to it.

Elián stared for a long while at the drawings and sketches I'd hung there, and I tried to look at them with new eyes, too. Again, the improvement of my skills was evident across the pages, but a few of them were objectively... good? A faint swell of pride coursed through me when he lifted a finger to point at the drawing of Maman, "The Godyx Aeras blessed you as well, it seems."

I ran an awkward hand over the braids running down my scalp, "Ah, well I wouldn't say *that*."

He shrugged, "I would." And turned around to begin unpacking. We worked in an easygoing silence until my bags were completely empty and half of his were.

Despite his agreement to stay with me for a few days, he still made no move to kiss or touch me, and I still wasn't breaking the barrier I'd erected for myself. If he wanted me, he would have to say it with explicit words or action, and he hadn't yet.

"I'm going to shower," I tried, but he just nodded while he spread his change of clothes out on my bed. I hid my disappointment and scrubbed the dust and sweat off my body in the shower. After emerging with a sleeveless, cropped vest, long skirt, and wet hair, we switched places.

He showered alone, and I absently pulled on accessories for our evening in Versillia. A golden chain belt that I'd managed to keep from my mother's collection, and a matching set of earrings Tana gifted me a few years ago. Elián easily agreed to me showing him around the city tonight, but I found myself ridiculously worried about what he would think of everything and why he hadn't tried to touch me again.

My anxious combing of my wet hair left my curls clumped and shiny, and the pins I stuck at my temples to keep it out of my face scraped my scalp.

Elián stepped out of my bathing room then, his hair wet like mine, the ends in those not-quite-curls, and I really wanted to twirl my finger over them again. He was wearing that tight black tunic he'd worn in Nethras, and I surmised that it was the most casual outfit he could muster if he'd only packed Shadow clothing. Did he wear anything else when he was home at the Shadow Well?

His trousers were a nondescript pair in the same black, but the lack of tension in his shoulders and brow made him even more handsome. If he told me to turn around and hike up my skirt for him, he wouldn't be able to even fully get the command past his lips before I'd be bent over the bed.

But he did no such thing and instead dropped his luminous eyes, "Will you have to hide that here?"

That snapped me out of my fantasizing, and I raised my hands. The veins were black with my relaxing in the privacy of my room and the safety I felt around him. I rotated my forearms, watching as they changed to the normal, faintly greenish color against my brown skin. My head immediately felt heavier, but I had no alternative.

I dropped my hands to my sides, and just an hour after we'd arrived, Elián and I walked out of my family's estate toward the city.

Though we didn't touch, we walked the cobblestoned path side-by-side. He'd left his swords in my room, but I knew that he was like me in never going out unarmed. Perhaps if he let me run my hands over his body, I could find where he'd hidden a few knives or a cleverly placed dagger. Mine were tucked into my boots, and the weight of them made me feel steadier, more confident.

I narrated our stroll by pointing out my childhood haunts, and he nodded along when I brought up anecdotes where the other sides of the inside-jokes were mostly long dead. The pastel shops and homes looked rich in the waning sunlight, and the streets of my birthplace had an ever-present floral scent.

Though there were quite a few other Versillians also taking

advantage of the pleasant evening, no one bothered us save for the occasional wide eye or nod in my direction. After weeks in town, the newness of my presence had worn off substantially, to the point where I could almost pretend that I was an anonymous citizen on a stroll with a friend. Was that what Elián was to me, now?

We continued slowly through the city until I asked if he was hungry. He immediately said yes, and I brought us to one of my and Tana's favorites.

The lights were low to create an atmosphere of cozy intimacy, and I pulled Elián into a dusky pink booth. A familiar server asked if I would like my usual red wine, and Elián ordered a short tumbler of liquor. We spent the rest of our meal discussing our favorite novels, mine a romance and his an action tale, though he admitted that he was interested in the one I'd read aloud to him on the road. It was a lengthy book, and we hadn't yet finished it all. Perhaps he'd want to borrow it?

When we left, I hadn't been paying attention, what with my rambling and mind churning out more and more worries about the Council and whatever Elián and I were, and I found myself steering us toward the Versillian temple for Rhaea.

Even after I realized, something carried me forward, and I didn't stop until we were standing before the ivory steps. I looked up at the bastardized place of worship that was a dedication to Maman, and I didn't realize I'd been trembling until Elián's unnaturally warm palm rested above my low-slung skirt.

"I almost forgot that this is what most of them look like," he said.

I nodded, because I had, too. And after spending so much time at the true Temple recently, this one seemed even more offensive, more heartbreaking.

I didn't know what came over me, but I began to climb the steps. It was much smaller than the one in Rhaestras, and the silence seemed even more eerie. The constant chatter of priestesses used to grate against my nerves when I'd been a girl, but now, I missed the pleasant buzzing. Elián's hand didn't drop from my back, and once again, I let him ground me as we crept past the extravagant depictions of my Goddess healing others beneath rays of sunshine.

She smiled sweetly at those that were sick or looking at Her with reverence, and I may have imagined it, but the expression didn't carry to Her eyes. She *did* heal, I had to remind myself. But even that benevolent power wasn't a clean one. Healing the wounded or sick was messy, gory business. I doubted Rhaea did such things without a speck of blood or vomit on Her robes and with a smile on Her face like She was looking upon the most beautiful of sunrises.

We made our way into the pristine cella and stopped before the statue of Her. The one that didn't look like Her at all, and I felt my tie to the Goddess pulse just under my skin.

With no one else in the temple besides the two of us, I let the vines show on my hands as I thought about Cera and Isabella, and that turned into the mystery of Francie's kidnapping that was still unsolved. I had completed my initial goal of securing two members for the Council, and I knew that I should be proud of that. But all that surrounded felt like it was in disarray.

I tilted my head to look up at my Shadow that wasn't my Shadow anymore. He was already looking at me, and the most random of thoughts charged forward when I met his amber eyes, "Can you breathe fire, Elián?" I whispered the question that I so desperately clung to. To pull me out of the spiral of despair rising in my gut. We hadn't discussed our powers at all during the journey, but now I wanted nothing more.

Instead of laughing at me or asking if I was implying that he was like a flying lizard, he cocked his brow in that way he always did, and blew a gust of air through his nose. But it wasn't air, it was— smoke. I stared, bug-eyed while his chest expanded again, and he blew more out of his nose.

I whirled around and shoved Elián on his chest. He yielded a step back as I exclaimed, "What the *fuck*? You could do that this whole time?" But that was a ridiculous question. I eyed him suspiciously and crossed my arms, "Go on, do it, then."

For a moment I thought he was going to refuse, but he mimicked my stance and puckered his lips as if he were about to start whistling. Instead, he blew a puff of flame that extinguished as soon as he closed his mouth. I laughed in wonder and demanded that he show me thrice more. I was sure that I was acting childish, but I didn't care.

More longing, more excitement filled my heart. Alone in my mother's temple, I stretched my palm toward Elián in silent request, and he watched my power curiously while it curled in black tendrils toward him. He raised his hand, and from his skin, a trail of flame flickered and twisted to meet my darkness. If I hadn't spent many hours deciphering his face, I would have been fooled by the steely expression. But his eyes widened minutely when our powers met, and bright white sparks popped where they curled around each other. They continued on toward the other wielder, and soon my arm was encircled by ribbons of crimson and orange flames, while his was by pitch black vines. Though warm, the fire didn't burn as it touched me, and I felt like Elián was truly consuming me.

The same must have been true for him, because he was the one to rush forward and crash his lips onto mine. His tongue was hot and sent my body into shivers, and then I was clutching the bottom of his tunic. Elián's fingers were threaded in my still-damp hair, and I was losing all sense with him finally touching me, taking me.

His hand was still wrapped with my power, and he held my jaw as he kissed in a near frenzy. He bit at my mouth, and I bit back, which seemed to just make him grow even hungrier, more desperate. Whatever bind Elián held himself in to resist this snapped with our powers intertwining, and the taste of him on my physical body and in my mind was enough to make me forget any and every worry I had.

He pulled back, and we both stared at each other, panting and still twined with fire and abyss. He swiped his thumb over my lips, once, twice, and there he was.

No mask, no shield, and though he was still an amalgamation of hard lines, they weren't sharp cuts of a sword, but stability, strength.

His lips parted and he whispered to me before the sensitized Goddess, "Just El and Em?"

I nodded and grinned with every one of my teeth just before he pulled me in again. I finally sunk my fingers in his hair, and I gave him that scratching of my fingernails on his scalp that had made him shiver. Sure enough, I felt his body and fire vibrate around me, and he said something in his language under his breath. Around his lips, I asked, "What's that mean?"

Elián licked and sucked at my neck in a way that felt like he was doing it other places, and then he groaned when I put my hand between us to touch the straining against his waistband, "It means you're a fucking menace." I yelped and moaned into the stale temple air as he ground his hips against me.

I needed him now, to feel his heat inside me, but when I began to unfasten his trousers, he caught both of my hands and pulled them away.

I froze and flinched back to see him. That moment in Rhaestras had been so upsetting, I was sure that I wouldn't be able to handle if he did it again, but when he turned me and gently pressed on my shoulders, I felt a stir of anticipation.

My palms smacked against the white marble of the raised platform of the altar, and I felt strong hands grasping and kneading my thighs and hips. I blinked franticly while Elián touched me over my clothing before Rhaea, and I knew even more of my power was spilling out around us. The tendrils that weren't curled around me or him were spilling into the air like the smoke he'd breathed, and I wouldn't have been able to reel it in if I tried.

Elián lifted and pulled back my skirt, and the pinch of him pulling at my undergarment before I felt even more warm air on my nakedness left me shaking on my feet. All the secret parts of my body were spread in the torch-lit cella of Rhaea's Versillian temple, and when I groaned at the first swipe of Elián's tongue, it was like a prayer.

I stared up at the smiling Goddess, and it felt like She was looking upon me with smug blessing while Elián plunged two fingers into me. My back arched, offering even more to him, begging him to keep this going forever, and while he added another finger and pumped, I felt his teeth close over the fullest curve of my ass as if he wanted to devour me in all ways possible.

That was enough to make my eyes roll back and exclaim to Rhaea as She watched down on Her last Death Wielder being taken on Her altar.

And he wasn't done. The obscene slurping of Elián kneeling behind me didn't stop when I came. He replaced his fingers with his tongue, and his hands palmed my hips. He tilted me even more so that he had full access, and I briefly saw that the entire floor was crawling with my darkness, save for a ring of flame that was more like rays of sunshine around us. But instead of shrinking from the light like any shadow, my Death weaved and danced with the fire

Elián released.

He plunged and plunged his tongue into me at the same time he pulled my hips back onto his face, and it was everything to keep my arms and legs from giving out.

"*Fuck Elián*, I—can't—I don't think I—" I sputtered around the tormenting ecstasy of him and us and this that I had been waiting for.

His smack on my skin wasn't as hard as he'd done that night in Krisla, but it silenced me at once. He gave a punishing swirl of his tongue, and said, rough and low, "You can, and you will, Meline." And then he dove back into me, but this time, he added a gently prodding thumb just above where he was sucking out my very soul.

The sensation of that naughty thumb pushing into me there sent lightning crackling to the tips of my fingers and toes and the ends of my hair that was dangling over my bowed head. My body thrusted back on him for more—I was so close again, it was agony, and then he curled his tongue at the same time his seeking thumb nudged its way just inside. And I was falling.

Elián caught and turned me onto my back while I was still writhing with what he'd done to me. The marble of the altar was like ice on my skin, and that with the heat of Elián in and around my body just drove me higher. My pathetic whimpers were inescapable when it felt like every morsel of my being was alternating between being on fire and frozen over and over.

When I regained some control over my body again, I looked down at where he had been, and was immediately spellbound by his glowing eyes. He was like a panther before me, prowling as he crept up onto the altar where I lay and pulled my skirt off my legs in one swift tug. The golden belt remained, and then he was pulling my vest open, too. I'd regained enough sense to help him with the rest of it and assist him out of his clothes in a frantic set of tugging on both our parts. The gold of my belt matched that in my nipples and around Elián's neck, and I sat up to lick and bite at his shining metal.

His throat vibrated against my tongue, almost in a purr, and I wasted no time scooting all the way forward so that his hard cock prodded my dripping cunt. We both moaned at the sensation, but he pulled away again. This time, it was with his proprietary control of my hair, and I resisted until he commanded, "Ride me. Now."

I brought my hands to Elián's muscled chest decorated with ink as black as my power all around us, and I shoved him down onto the marble. His head landed just before dangling over the edge, and now it was he who was looking up at the Goddess.

My thighs were still shaking slightly from the pleasure I'd already felt tonight and in anticipation for more, and when I climbed atop Elián, I marveled at the sight before me.

The entire room was black and shifting with my power like clouds in the night, and immediately around us was Elián's fire. The darkness wasn't an infection but the cool release of Death. And his fire was the demand of Life. It wrapped around me, caressed my flesh, as if a thousand of his tongues were tasting me. More curling vines crept over his supine form, and they twined in his hair like a dark crown.

I angled myself above the head of Elián's thick, hard cock, and oh Mother take me, he was even bigger from this angle. Not impossible, but I shuddered with the mere piercing of his tip into me. Elián was holding my hips, keeping me steady, but even he was trembling with need and pleasure. My neck arched as I sank down even more, and my moans became a steady sound amongst our breathing and racing hearts.

Flames and darkness were playing all around, and I felt warming brushes of light at my temples and around my face. I glanced down again, and Elián's blazing eyes were looking up at me in lust and awe. "My queen."

I dropped, and our hips met in an anguishing thud. "Oh Goddess, *fuck*. You feel too good," I cried. He did feel bigger like this, and I was fuller than I had been in my life. Though exhausted, my thighs worked us into a harsh pace as I rode Elián, and his hands were gripping my hips so hard I knew I was going to bruise.

His face was contorted in reverent ecstasy, and the swelling of my own bliss was enough to let out another pulse of my power. It swept the cella in dark, curling clouds, and his fire flared higher. My Shadow who accepted all my truths, all my sins, and still looked upon me the way he did, touched me the way he did.

I closed my own hands over his to encourage for more, and he obliged, helping me rise and plummet against him until I was beyond all coherent language. Elián fucked me from below and was spitting a series of moans and grunts and curses that joined mine.

But even with the rise of my release, I needed more, wanted everything.

I leaned down, still rotating and grinding on him, and nuzzled into his throat. His hands moved to hold my neck and back, and his hips were rising so that he could keep thrusting as deep and hard as before. Both of our bodies were covered with a thin sheen of sweat, and we slipped and slid against one another while I opened my mouth and let my fangs nestle just there.

It was a move that many of our kind would see as an offending act of dominance, but a primal need to consume every bit of Elián was in charge of me, now. And instead of flinching away, Elián just kept groaning with the thrusts of his cock and held me tighter to him.

I sank my fangs, and my mouth was flooded with his blood that was hot and rich and spice. "*Merro,*" he roared, and while I drank up all that his pumping heart was giving me, Elián curled us both off of the stone. The taste of him was decadent, and it felt like my very soul was on fire with him inside of me in all ways. Our pace had slowed but hadn't stalled, and now our fucking was languorous with Elián sitting and me still riding.

Then I felt the request of his own fangs at my throat, and I clutched his head to my neck. The pain of his bite was sweet, and my answering release was slow and strong. My nails dug into Elián's back, breaking his skin, but that just spurred him on.

It felt like the two of us would continue on like this. On and on and on in an endless loop of giving to and consuming each other.

Elián moaned into my throat, and I felt his cock within me stiffen even more and let go. The force of his seed filling me drove me into another wave, and all the while, Elián held and licked me.

It was a magical, bittersweet eternity in his arms while we settled into this new world that we created together, and our powers settled back into our bodies. The darkness and flames receded until they were faint ribbons that adorned our arms.

I scratched the back of his head, and the sight of his lips smeared with my blood was something I would never forget. Elián kissed me softly, and the taste of both of us on each other made me believe that we could have this thing. This peace, this connection, this rightness that I'd only truly felt in his arms.

40

40

Elián's right arm held me as I leaned my shoulders into his chest. His left rested on the lip of the tub, and I ran my finger over the script in his palm while the bathwater steamed around us. The glow of the moon and the candles by the sink were all that illuminated the bathing room. Our breathing was joined, and Elián moved his thumb in small circles along my rib cage.

"I can hear you thinking very loudly, my queen," I exhaled and nuzzled my head in the crook of his neck. Elián gave a tender kiss at my brow, and I felt the rumble of his chest as he hummed.

I sighed and flicked the water with my free hand. The stillness, the warmth, with Elián was so nice. "I feel like I could stay in here all night."

"And what are you thinking?"

My circles around his brother's name got faster, "You. Me. Us and Francie and Isabella and what all of this means for the Council moving forward. What all this means for everyone. All the answers we still don't have."

Elián moved his hand that held me to my jaw. The water dripped off of his fingers and trailed down my neck, and he tilted my head so that he could see my face. The gold of his necklace reflected in his eyes that were the same color of a sunset. It was a gift from his mother, he'd said when I asked. The small circular medallion was etched with a single drop of a flame, and she'd given both he and his brother the matching chains for good luck and protection when they reached adolescence.

Elián pressed his lips to mine in a sweet anchoring that relaxed my shoulders. "Later?" He breathed over my mouth.

I smiled and nodded before pressing my lips back to his. "Yeah, later." I settled back into his chest and felt both of his arms close around and embrace me. Our legs tangled together down the length of the tub, and one of his knees peaked above the water.

Sleep was coming over me before a niggling question finally swam to the forefront, where I was able to pluck it and give it voice. "El, are you doing something to keep the bath hot? We've been in here for a long time." I rotated my head slowly on his shoulder, and my breath caught in my throat.

I peeled off of his chest, and bathwater splashed onto the floor with my sudden movement. Elián's brows pulled up and he held my elbows, "What's wrong?"

I gripped his face in my hands and peered at him wildly, excitedly, "Do that again!"

"Do what?" His voice wasn't as panicked, but was tinged with trepidation.

"Smile!" The grimace he gave, a poor excuse for pulling his lips up and showing his teeth, made my own smile drop. "No, no, like you did just a second ago."

He smiled again, this time closed-lipped and softly. The skin of his cheeks pulled back, and on the left side, was one of the most amazing things I had seen in my life.

Elián's lips fell, and the worry in his tone came creeping back, "What is wrong, Meline?"

I pressed my wet finger where the little indent had been when he gave me that soft smile, "I didn't know you had a dimple. It's right here when you smile like that."

He gave a long exhale, and he smirked. The little indent in his cheek appeared again, and the realization that Elián was smiling in this bathtub with me more than he had in our entire time of knowing each other felt like a divulgence of a secret between us.

I leaned back into him again, and ran my touch over his thighs under the warm water. "I'm going to do my best to continue making that dimple appear, don't you worry."

He snorted and nipped his teeth at my earlobe in a move that was both sexy and playful. We'd hastily dressed and left the temple once

I was pretty confident that I could stand without faltering. Once back in my rooms, I suggested that we draw a bath and lay together for a while.

It had surely been an hour or two, now, and it seemed that we both had the energy for more. While my hands were still on his legs, Elián's sneaky fingers skated down my inner thighs. I shamelessly parted them as far as I could in this position, and even in the water, I knew he could tell how ready I was.

"Are you always this wet for me, my queen?" he whispered in my ear, and the tickling of his hair and beating of his chest behind me only deepened his words.

"Well, when you fuck me the way you do, I can't really help it." My voice was already breathy with his circling touch, and my nails dug into his skin.

He chuckled then asked, "That night in Rhaestras, when you touched yourself like this, what were you thinking about?"

Part of me wanted to ask him 'Which time?' or say something like 'I don't know what you're talking about,' but with the mischievous glint to his words, I knew that he was liable to punish me like he said he was going to and maybe stop his ministrations all together.

"You. I was imagining that it was your fingers then your tongue and then your cock," He placed an approving kiss on my cheek then my neck and continued to move the pad of his finger while I rocked against him. The rippling indulgence was intimate in this dark room, but I still needed to get him back. "And after you tasted me the first time, what did you do for those hours locked away in that room?"

He tsked before swiping his tongue on the shell of my ear, "I showered and drained my cock four times to keep myself from losing control."

"And—" a moan broke my train of thought for a few breathless moments "—when did you stop hating me?"

"When I watched you pace the inn on our first night on the road. You sang to yourself while you were unbraiding your hair. Which turned out to be very impractical of you." His judgement was punctuated by the penetration of his fingers once, twice, and a third time while his thumb circled, and I arched, whining through my nose. Elián licked and kissed the tender skin underneath my ear, and he held me while my climax rose and dispersed.

His touch moved from between my legs to trail patterns along my stomach. "And when did you stop hating me, Meline?"

Elián's usage of my name still left my chest flittering, "I didn't realize it then, but when I watched you stand in that clearing, just enjoying the sun on your face. It was the first time you didn't look wrathful."

He chuckled, "I recall that being the first time you called me an asshole," and hugged me tighter. We both relaxed into each other.

Elián kept the water hot like I liked, and both our breathing slowed in impending sleep. We'd fucked and drank from each other, so it was only right that we find safety in this, too.

I was just about to drift off when I felt his body stiffen beneath me. His sleepy grumble sounded above my head, "Your cousin is coming." My forehead crinkled in confusion for a moment, but then I could hear her hurried footsteps and scent the warm patchouli preceding her. Elián began to sit up completely, but I mumbled for him to stay in the tub with me. "You are okay with her seeing us?"

And this made me furrow my brow even more. Did he mean her seeing us naked in the tub? Or seeing us together at all? Either way, I answered that I didn't care if he didn't, and I sighed in relief when he leaned back once more. My eyes remained closed, and I nuzzled back against his collarbone. Elián rested his cheek against the crown of my head, and I was really hoping that Tana would scent the two of us and turn around.

But she kept growing nearer, and she was already talking before she even entered my bedroom, "I can't *believe* you were just waltzing around the city without sending for me. With all—" Tana's steps slowed to a sudden stop in the threshold of my bathing room, but neither Elián nor I stirred.

After absorbing the reality that I wasn't alone in my bathtub, which, she should have smelled him if she had been paying attention at all, Tana pulled over a wooden bench that had been sitting flush against the wall. She plopped down, and her tone changed to one of curiosity and amusement, "Hello. I see you two have gotten along well."

She wouldn't be leaving after all, then. I should have known. I popped one eye open and tried to give the best glare I could, "Yes, and we were—"

"I'm Tana. I don't think we were properly introduced," she looked over my head to where Elián was resting his, and a surprising bite of jealousy gnawed at the back of my throat. I'd told him that I didn't care about her seeing us together—and I didn't—but the thought of her seeing him was unexpectedly unpleasant. I'd just started getting accustomed to seeing Elián in anything other than fighting leathers or his other Shadow clothing, let alone naked. And the fact that Tana was beautiful and cheerful and looked so much like me had me immediately feeling testy.

"Hello, Tana," he said simply and clutched me tighter. Elián's amusement felt like a warm chuckle in the depth of my belly—a residual affect of our blood sharing, no doubt, and I smacked his thigh underneath the water. If I could feel his amusement, he felt my jealousy. *Great.* I had never shared blood in the context we had, and I hadn't been aware of the strong affect it would have.

Tana turned to me again, "So what's this I hear about you getting back hours ago and not letting me know," she flicked her eyes to Elián and back, "I assume this is to blame."

I rolled my eyes, though I realized that without Elián, I *would* have sent her for her as soon as I'd gotten back. But I wasn't going to admit that to her, "Well, we've had a long journey that hasn't been the best."

My generic answer was still too much for my perceptive cousin. She straightened, "What happened? Were you able to get the High Priestess's approval? How was Nethras? And Cal?" She fired off her questions, but I was caught up on the fact that she obviously didn't know what happened to Isabella. I could feel Elián's confusion, too, like an added layer to the slightly tart emotion I was already feeling.

"Ah... have you not heard about what happened?"

"What do you mean?" Her brows tilted up together in the middle.

I peeled my back away from Elián's chest and leaned against the side of the tub. His hands went to my waist under the water, and I reached out for Tana's. Though she wasn't close with Isabella, she'd spent a good amount of time in Rhaestras with Maman and I. She was no stranger to loss, more so now than ever, but I knew she was more sensitive than I was.

She looked even more worried with my voluntary touch, and I took a breath and told her about what happened in Rhaestras. All of it. How Cera had stalled for Isabella for days, and one morning when we arrived at the Temple, we found that she'd been killed. Tana brought her other hand to grasp mine, and her sea-green eyes grew watery.

"I'm so sorry, Leen," she kissed my knuckles, and I gave her a wan smile. I felt Isabella's absence from this realm like a burn to my tongue. Each time I poked at it, the feelings would stir anew, but they were also healing quickly. It was the same with Shoko, Lee, Maman, and Papa. They would always be part of me, but death was inevitable. If anyone knew that, it was me.

But the unjustness of their deaths would most likely haunt me forever. I didn't tell her or Elián that part, though I knew they'd suspect as much.

"So, the new High Priestess?" I smirked, and her face dropped. "Oh, no."

"She and I... well I don't know where we are. But we've reached a new level of understanding, I think."

Tana blew a frustrated breath that stirred a golden lock that wasn't tucked under the pink ribbon she wore in her hair. "I suppose you have to after enduring something like that." We did know from experience, after all. "And no one knows who did it?"

The warm touch on my waist tightened. Guilt, a feeling I knew all too well, wedged in my chest, but the heat of it wasn't mine. I hoped that my affection and forgiveness for him was flowing through this bond that we had, and when I felt his hands loosen, I knew that it was.

I didn't want to draw attention to him, as we hadn't really discussed that night, so I just gave the vaguest truth. "Someone was hired to do it. We tracked him down, questioned him, but he wouldn't budge."

She gave a knowing smirk, "And I'm guessing this assassin is no longer living?"

I grinned, "No. His second death was sweet."

Tana cocked her head to the side, "A Vyrkos, then? Interesting. Do you think they knew about her possibly joining the Council?"

I winced. I had thought about it, but I didn't want to further fuel prejudice between our two races. "It's possible. But he didn't seem to have a personal connection to the issue. It was just a job, though he did seem genuinely afraid of revealing who hired him."

Tana looked contemplative instead of angry, and I let out a silent sigh. I knew that Tana wasn't quick to judge the Vyrkos, especially after Shoko became such a close friend and opened us up to her people, but I'd secretly worried that the attack in Nethras had pushed her closer to the views most other Lylithans held. *That* was an uphill battle that I still wasn't sure I was ready to fight, but I knew that I must. Our oppression of them was inexcusable, and their actions in rebellion, killing so many that we loved, was also inexcusable. But I understood the anger for our injustices. If this Council were going to truly make change, we needed to pull the problem up at the roots.

She was looking off into the distance, "You know, since you've been away, I've really been thinking about your birthday. The attack was so random, and from what you've said, Nethras is a far cry from places like Krisla. Or even here. There's wariness, yes, but Lylithans and Vyrkos live in relative peace there."

I nodded along with her. It *was* strange. "And if it was an attack like those during The Killings, why Shoko?"

"Some of them were people she knew, Leen. She was so angry."

I swallowed, "It's all so strange. Rhaestras has virtually no Vyrkos population that I know of, so I don't know why they would want her dead, either." But the fact that the attackers at the tavern and the assassin were both Vyrkos when there were reports of more uprisings… it didn't *feel* like a coincidence. What were we missing? I told Tana about Francie, though I didn't scent any Vyrkos in the children's home where she'd been taken.

"So three strange attacks, and all on people connected to—"

"Me." My heart rate started to pick up. I'd taken it personally, the murder and kidnapping of those close to me in these recent months. And apparently I'd been right to.

The three of us sat in a somber silence with this truth. Shoko, Lee, and all the others at the tavern died in an attack on *my* birthday. Isabella was my second mother, and she'd been murdered during my first visit back to Rhaestras in over a century. Francie had been kidnapped once I was back in Nethras for less than two days.

It's all my fault.

It was irrational, but I couldn't help feel the statement stamp on my forehead. But could it be correct? Attacks were spreading again, and the Vyrkos in Krisla definitely still knew me. What if this was their revenge? Not to kill me, but those around me?

Elián pulled me back to him, and I let my and Tana's hands fall. My legs curled up to my chest, but not even his grounding touch could dispel the truth. This was because of me. Death was only fair in that it came for us all, but this was *wrong*.

Elián pried my hand from my legs, and brought my open palm to his lips. Tana eyed the movement with more curiosity, but she didn't comment on Elián's intimate comforting or the vines crawling up my arms. She'd seen me lose control a few times, but this was surely the first time she saw my power like this.

He still held my wrist, keeping it warm even above the water, and his soft rumble drew my mind. "Meline says that you are a magic user, yes?"

Tana looked at Elián more seriously, and I saw the moment she focused on his eyes. She didn't answer his question, which was unlike her. But suddenly, her body froze in recognition, and Elián's blood that had fused with mine stirred in... fear? All of his emotions were tinged with a heat that I wasn't used to, but I recognized the bitter taste in my mouth.

My cousin leaned forward then, and her expression changed to one of wonder, "You're one of the Fire Bringers, aren't you?"

Fire Bringer. Why did that sound so familiar?

Elián's arms tightened fractionally around me, and it brought me out of my whirling thoughts. I straightened and raised my chin, ready to defend him. He'd told me he was the last one of his line, the last of these Fire Bringers. The spectacle of him saving me in Krisla could be explained away as magic, but I knew that the depth of Elián's power was far wider than that. For the two of us, there was no bottom to that well.

Whatever Tana saw on both of our faces had her blanching, and she raised both of her hands, "Whoa, I didn't mean to—I just. I thought you had all been killed." And then she winced when she realized what she just said.

I twisted and brought his face down to mine to pepper his lips with supportive kisses. Being connected to him in this way, however long it would last, was giving me access to the inner workings of my former Shadow that I'd never dreamt of. He was flitting so fast between guilt, anger, and sorrow. All of it was hidden so deeply, but his blood in my veins couldn't lie.

My fingers rubbed the stubble emerging on his jaw, and I felt him lean into my touch. His arms pulled me even closer, and neither of us loosened our embrace when Tana cleared her throat and spoke shakily, "I'm sorry. I just got excited to make the connection. I won't —tell anyone."

I opened my eyes in time to see Elián glaring at her over my head. I'd guessed as much that he didn't readily share his fire wielding, just like I didn't share my death wielding. And now here were two people he barely knew knowing his secret.

My lips met his again, and he tore his gaze back to me. "She won't, El."

"Um... you were asking me something? I am a witch, if that's what you were wondering?" She smiled nervously at him, trying to smooth over her blunder. Though he was far from the calm he'd been just a few minutes prior, I felt the sharp flare of his emotions quell a bit.

He assessed Tana for a long while, and the two of us sat patiently while he did, giving him time. "I once met a witch who could gather information from objects. About the owners of such objects. Can you do that?"

My lips pursed in confusion, but Tana nodded in comprehension, "Ah, yes. I've never done it myself, but I am familiar with the particular spell for this. It would let me see the past moments it was used. If it held a significance to the owner, I might be able to get more. Why?" She looked back and forth between us, "Do you have something?"

He looked down at me expectantly, but my lips just turned down in more confusion. What the hell was he getting at? "Perhaps she can help with what you stole from the High Priestess's office, my queen." His brow lifted, and realization dawned on me.

I blew out a gust of air in his face, and he smirked when it rustled his hair. Without thinking, I raised a finger and placed the tip of it in the dip the dimple formed, and I knew he was holding it just for me to feel. "Here I was thinking that I was a pretty good thief."

When I'd gone back to look at Isabella's office one last time before we left, the blush-colored pen was lying on the wooden surface of her desk. I didn't think about why I was drawn to it, but I took it during my final assessment and assumed no one had seen me. Cera, Elián, and Jesyn hadn't said anything, but *of course* he'd noticed.

I didn't have anything of Francie's or from any of the attackers, but I was also unsure of how Isabella's pen would be helpful.

Like she could read my thoughts, Tana tapped a slender finger to her chin, "It could provide some insight. Maybe it could tell us why she refused to meet with you for days. That doesn't feel like just a scheduling mishap to me. This was her first time seeing you in decades, and she acted like it wasn't important? Unlikely."

I turned over Tana's words, and I felt stupid for not seeing it. Elián and my cousin were obviously better at seeing the forest when I was still stuck in the trees. At the time, I thought she'd just seen me as a disappointment, but I now had her love for me confirmed, her pride. A mother like that wouldn't ignore their returning child for no reason. And Cera seemed sincere in that she didn't know why. But she'd told me that Isabella must have her reasons, didn't she?

Maybe we could find out what those reasons were. It was a long shot, but maybe it had something to do with her murder.

"You just need the item I took?"

Tana nodded, "I'll need to gather some ingredients to fully cast the spell, but that shouldn't be too hard." She turned to look out the window beside the tub and then back to us, "Come by the house in the morning with it, and I'll have everything ready."

She stood and walked the bench back to the wall. Before she could leave, though, I called after her, "And then maybe we could get some lunch or something? To catch up properly?" I knew that she was taking my ignoring her today in stride, but I also knew that she'd come here because she was hurt.

She stood in the doorway and looked over her shoulder in an excited smile, "I would love that! I'll see you tomorrow." Tana tapped the doorframe twice and then left.

Once the sound of her footsteps became too distant to hear, I turned to face Elián and straddled his lap. It was becoming one of my favorite sitting positions, and by the way he held me, I knew it was his, too.

"Fire Bringer?" He hadn't used that name for what he was, but the way he reacted to the title told me that it was one he'd been called before.

Thankfully, the tenderness had fully returned to his eyes when he looked at me now, and he didn't hesitate to answer. "What the rest of the world called us. Until they deemed us too dangerous to live."

Again, his words kept scratching at the back of my mind. Why did this all sound so—

"Now, my love, see here," Maman was reading a dusty old text beside me while I was drawing one of the new flowers I'd seen that day. It had speckled petals that were green and purple. All I had was a pen with black ink, but the dots I carefully placed looked enough like what I'd observed.

"Meline. Are you listening to me at all?" My mother's sharp tone made me look up. She usually didn't mind if I drew while she sat and researched, but apparently what she was saying was important.

"Yes, Maman. I know that it is important I remain cautious. We've been having these conversations for years now," I grumbled and got back to my drawing. Truthfully, these conversations made me uncomfortable. Most of the records of those given the Goddess's curse like me were about the destruction they could cause and their resulting slaughter. There used to be a handful every generation, but now I was the first in many, many centuries.

She nudged my shoulder with her own, and I sighed. I looked over at the book she had spread between us, but the illustration showed a female with a black veil covering her hair. Her hands were outstretched like all the depictions of Death Wielders displaying their power, but instead of curling black, what left her palms was fire.

The artist drew a field burning before the female, and her eyes looked strange. It was hard to tell since the author had undoubtedly used just a black pen, but like my orchid drawing, I felt they were still able to capture the horrifying beauty of her eyes. In small, neat script above the illustration was the word, 'High Priestess of Zoko. Fire Bringer'.

I looked at Maman, who'd grown quiet. Her lips that were usually full and either smirking or outright laughing were now flat and almost trembling. Her brown and gold eyes looked so haunted that I placed a hand on her arm. She looked down at my touch, and the golden beads in her braids tinkled with the shift of her head, "There are many who fear those blessed by the Goddesses, my love. I know that these conversations are difficult, but I only wish to prevent you from falling to the same fate as your predecessors and the others who have been hunted," she gestured down to the page of the female with fire hands, and I gulped.

She put her arm around my shoulders, and I let her mint and ocean scent comfort me. But I couldn't stop looking at the female's eyes and the fire she brought.

"You said your mother was a priestess of Zoko?" He nodded. And then I took a wild guess that seemed less and less wild as the memory of studying with Maman became clearer. "Was she... Zoko's High Priestess, El?" I closed my eyes to try and remember how the female had looked on that page. The eyes were like Elián's, but I assumed his people all had eyes like his. But the slope of her nose and angle of her jaw...

"Yes."

I swallowed. It didn't change anything, really. But it somehow shifted things, too. There was no way he could confirm it for me now, but I had no doubt that the female in that book had been his mother.

He ran his hands up and down my sides, "Are you all right?"

I nodded, "I was just thinking...what a cruel twist of fate wrung by the Goddesses' hands." Elián tilted his head, not following my train of thought, and I elaborated, "The last Death Wielder. And the last Fire Bringer. Both children of slain High Priestesses."

Unease was rising up my spine, but Elián gave me more soothing touches. "Perhaps."

I dropped my brow to his. Everything was so complicated, and it was just going to get worse. Cal was going to remain a problem, there was still no word from Whitley about Francie, and our plan tomorrow to look further into Isabella's murder seemed more fruitless each time I thought about it.

But this, I breathed in Elián's scent, this was good. The endearment flowing between our blood bond was enough to keep me from descending into my spiral, and I clung to it by the fingernails of my mind.

"What do you need, my queen?"

Judging by the hard press of him between our stomachs, he already felt what I needed, but he was sweet for asking. I held his face in my hands, and my breasts pushed against his chest. "Fuck me, then sleep with me."

My eyes were closed, but I felt twin dimples form under my palms before the press of Elián's impassioned kiss. I knew that he was smiling for me, and whilst he made good on my first request, we groaned each other's names like a lullaby.

We didn't pull on any clothing after we finally stepped out of the bath. I knew that it had been days since he'd slept, and with the way he'd pushed my body over the edge again and again, I was just as exhausted as Elián must have been. I pulled back the covers on my bed, and they were cold with lack of use when we nestled underneath them.

I'd told him that I wasn't much for cuddling, and he agreed that he wasn't either. But when Elián pulled me into his chest and folded his strong arms around me, I didn't even think about pulling away.

41

"Okay, stay just like that." I directed Elián and took a sip of my minty tea. We were sitting at the table in my rooms, and the plates and platters that'd contained our breakfast were scraped clean and stacked at the edge of the table.

My pen scraped lightly on the paper of my old sketchbook, and Elián kept his head positioned like I asked while he looked out of the window. The world was just waking, and the scene outside was tinted with soft golden light. His eyes seemed brighter like this, and when we'd sat down to eat, I asked him if he'd be all right sitting for me.

I created a soft wave just above his ear, shaded the underside of his cutting chin, and I got lost in my capturing of Elián like this until I was staring down at a simple, yet surprisingly accurate depiction of him. I tried my best to mimic the markings on his chest and the rippling of his arms.

All the while, he'd remained completely still and let me take my time. He was lounging shirtless in his chair and head angled toward the window. When I finally turned my sketchbook around for him to look at the drawing, he picked it up with both hands and studied long enough that I started to shift in my seat.

"You are gifted, my queen," his voice was thick, which would have confused me had I not still been able to sense him in my veins. The connection was fainter now this morning, but I felt a stirring of many emotions that felt gooey and sweet.

"Thank you," I gestured to the drawing, "you can have it, if you'd

403

like?"

But he shook his head and handed the book back to me, "No, you keep it." He jutted his chin toward my bedroom, "And add it to your wall." He gave me another soft smile, and my chest fluttered. I ran my fingernail along the innermost edge of the page and tore it cleanly from the book.

I drained the rest of my tea and stood. My muscles were deliciously spent, but my mind felt clear. I'd slept all night in Elián's arms, and I greeted him by slithering down to settle between his legs. I felt that he was already awake, but he hadn't made to move at all. When I'd gotten my head over his lap, he was already hard, and I swallowed to bid him good morning.

"We should get dressed now, I suppose." He followed me into the bedroom after finishing the last bit of his coffee, and the smell of it on his breath when he bent me over the edge of the bed was enough to make me want to give the beverage another try. After he cleaned between my legs, I hummed as we dressed in otherwise silence.

The wide-legged trousers I pulled on were the same color as my eyes, and the long-sleeved wrap top was pushing the limits of the changing season. But the bright, floral embroidery along the neckline and cuffs drew my eye. I buckled a leather belt around my waist and affixed my daggers in the sheaths.

When I turned around to Elián, I saw him in basically the same outfit as last night. "Do you always wear black?"

He looked down at himself, "No. Just when I'm working." I tried to imagine him in a different color, but all I could picture was the dark gray I'd already seen him in, which was basically black. That traitorous whisper that always spoke my fears sounded in the back of my mind. We hadn't really talked about how long he'd stay here. He was cycling through the clothing he brought, but to call attention to it might burst the bubble we were in.

Instead of bringing up difficult conversations, I piled my hair on top of my head and pulled on my boots. "Ready?" He nodded, and we proceeded out of my rooms.

In another act of boldness, I touched my hand to his while we walked beside each other, and when he didn't pull his away, I took it in mine. My fingers interlocked with his, and I saw him glance down where we were joined and raise a brow. He squeezed his hand tighter, smirking to himself. Another small victory with him that sent my heart fluttering. I really was a blushing schoolgirl, after all.

Some of the staff that we passed looked at the two of us with inquisitiveness, but no one said anything besides greeting. We didn't talk on the half-hour stroll to the city, which was just as well. He didn't drop my grip while we proceeded, and my other hand relaxed loosely in my pocket. Maybe I could ask him to extend his stay? Or that we could visit each other when he eventually took up another contract?

The yellow witch house was the color of the inside of a boiled egg, and clusters of lilacs bordered the white door. As we walked up the short stack of brick steps, the door swung open to reveal my cousin in a white blouse and light green dress that complimented her eyes.

She tried and failed to hide her grin when she looked to Elián's and my hands, but she new better than to mention it aloud. I rolled my eyes at her as we walked into the home that smelled cloyingly of many herbs and oils. Even after helping regularly in the weeks leading up to my travels, I hadn't gotten used to that smell. It was a wonder I could scent Tana at all.

We politely declined her offer of beverages, and she led us out back to a patio that overlooked the wild but sensical backyard. Each plant held its purpose and a specific area of the ground, but to an untrained eye, it might've looked overgrown.

The three of us sat at a small wrought iron table that was already set up with a bundle of herbs, a matchbook, a clay bowl, and a candle. I reached in my pocket and pulled out Isabella's pen. It was slender and ended in a sharp point.

My fingers brushed Tana's as I passed the pen to her, and though warm, she felt cooler to the touch than I had been accustomed to these past few days.

Elián reached an arm over the back of my seat, and we both watched Tana prepare the rest of the spell. She lit the wide, white candle and then the bundle of herbs that she held over the clay bowl. They caught and smoldered, and eventually, burned completely. The burnt remnants and ashes fell into the bowl, and she carefully nestled the pen on top of the still-smoking herbs.

I'd watched my cousin perform spells countless times, and magic-users weren't at all rare. But the stirring of aether around us while

Tana muttered under her breath always made me feel a bit wobbly. She whispered to it, persuading it to mold and grant her access to its depth of knowledge, and when she suddenly quieted, I knew that it was happening.

Her eyes moved quickly back and forth under her closed lids, but the rest of her body stayed rigid. The trees surrounding the house and yard rustled above us.

"I will be refusing your request to join the Lylithan Council," Tana's droning voice made me jump a bit in my seat. I didn't dare say anything while she was still working, but the words made my fists clench. Isabella had refused?

Fifteen more breaths in silence while watching Tana expertly work the magic that was coursing through her. Her golden ringlets shifted with the spring air, and the syrupy scent of aether twined with her lavender.

With a slow rolling of her shoulders, Tana opened her eyes and blinked quickly to readjust to the light around us. I twisted uneasily in my seat, and Elián was already looking at me. His face remained open and unmasked, and I felt the softness of concern coming from him. He leaned over and pressed his lips into my hair, and my shoulders relaxed a fraction.

"You said that she refused the seat on the Council."

Tana cleared her throat and nodded, "Yes, I saw her write the letter. What was she wearing when you met with her?" I described the orange ensemble and golden hair band that Isabella had worn, and my cousin's lips turned down. "It was that same day, then. Judging from the light coming through the window, it was mid-afternoon."

I rubbed my hands over my face and tried to process what she was saying. Isabella hadn't spoken her refusal to me, but she'd written it after our meeting. Was she going to inform me of her decision at our scheduled meeting the next day? Or would she further insult me by keeping me in the dark?

"Did you see anything else?"

Tana sat back in her chair and crossed her arms, "There was another day, perhaps when you all first arrived. She had been holding the pen when Cera came to her, complaining about her orders to keep you occupied." Tana twisted her mouth and quoted in Cera's clipped voice, "I don't see why you're having me do this. If you're going to decline, just tell her and spare us both the torture." In Isabella's deeper voice, "You both were never good at exercising patience, girl. I need time for her to be here, to *see* and be away from her meddlesome brother and uncle. You will help me get it."

I groaned and put my head in my hand, "To see *what*, Isabella?" But there were no answers to that question. She was gone, and she hadn't been letting Cera in on her plans, either.

"Did you see who she was addressing the letter to?" Elián asked.

I assumed that it was to Mat or the Council in general, but Tana answered, "My father."

My body went cold, and Elián's arm stiffened around me. Another letter written specifically to Uncle. I leaned forward, "Did you see what else she'd written?"

"She just stated her refusal. It was only one sentence. Why?" She was starting to look worried, and I didn't want to pull her into my scrambling thoughts. It couldn't be a coincidence that Isabella and Cal had been writing to Hendrik specifically, could it?

Elián was frowning contemplatively, and we shared a silent agreement that, no, it had to be connected. Did Mathieu know about these correspondences? It could be nothing, but...

"What? What does this mean?" Tana asked when I pushed my chair back and stood.

"Is your father back in Versillia?" I needed to speak with Uncle about all of this. If I went to Mat with bogus claims, I would feel like a paranoid fool. And I wanted to see Uncle Hendrik's face when I confronted him. Give him less time to concoct excuses.

Tana scrambled out of her seat and followed us as we walked round the side of the house this time. I didn't want to deal with the smell or the waking witches inside. "Um... he wrote that he was set to arrive this morning. What's going on, Leen?"

"Nothing so far. I just need to speak with him. I'll be back to grab you for lunch!" I called over as I continued toward the city center. It wasn't fair to keep her in the dark, I knew, but Tana loved her father. I wouldn't go spilling my unfounded accusations to her. If it was true, I'd cross that bridge, but right now, I didn't want to cause her any undue pain.

My footsteps were clipped and echoed in the halls of the center of the City of Versillia's operation. There were several meandering about or working at desks, and I tried to school my face so that I didn't stir worry. I forced a smile and short pleasantries at those who greeted Elián and I.

We climbed the stairs to the top floor, and I came upon Uncle's office. The door was open, and he was sitting at his large, oak desk, still in traveling clothes and studying a stack of papers. When I entered, his expression started soft but quickly turned to worry.

"Niece, it's good to see you." He looked behind me where Elián had taken a spot at my back as if he were my Shadow again. Uncle nodded and turned his eyes back to me. "Is there something I can do for you? I was just reading over reports of your progress." He gestured to the paper in his hand that was a copy of one of the letters I'd sent over the past few weeks.

I remained standing and crossed my arms, "I have some questions for you."

He dropped the paper and folded his hands over his desk. "All right..." And I was struck again with how much he looked like Papa. Their eyes were the green of the Richerre line, but his and Papa's were darker than Tana's or Mat's. His wide, strong nose made me think of all the times I'd seen Papa wrinkle his own in laughter.

"What have you promised the King of Krisla, Uncle?" I studied the sweep of emotions over his face, looking for a tell. His lips pursed at my question, and he studied me in confusion.

"I have promised nothing. My correspondences to him were introducing the idea of joining the Council, but I haven't spoken with him since before you wrote your letter for us. Why?"

I narrowed my eyes, "And Isabella? What have you spoken to her about?"

"I haven't spoken at all to the High Priestess, niece. What's the matter?" He looked concerned, now. He called her High Priestess, which was either clever or evidence in his favor.

I chose to bring up Cal again, "During my meeting in Krisla, he stated that he was promised a permanent Council appointment. By *you*." Again, Uncle kept his face a mask of innocent confusion, but something shifted behind his eyes.

He suddenly stood, "I must go," and I felt Elián tensing. Uncle looked over the two of us, jaw clenching and eyes narrowing, but he said nothing else.

"We aren't done, here." I said through tight teeth. The stone in my gut was growing again, but we were in this, now. He was denying my claims, but his refutations didn't feel... complete. He was hiding something, I was now absolutely certain.

But he just repeated that he needed to go, and Elián and I watched silently while he quickly rounded his desk and left the room in a blur. I turned around, mouth twisting, and Elián was still staring narrowly where Uncle had left. Where he'd *fled*.

"We need to go warn Mathieu," I breathed. Uncle Hendrik was certainly going there to plead his case, to beat me in revealing his... whatever it was that he'd done. His undermining my brother, certainly. And his... perhaps his... murdering of Isabella.

And so we charged back toward the outskirts of the city, toward my family's estate. We ran and ran, my heart thundering in my chest. Now that he was cornered, what would Uncle do? What would *Mat* do?

Whatever it was, we would face it together. I wouldn't leave him this time. I'd stand by my brother, and serve with him, and we would make a better way for our people. I leapt up the front steps with Elián behind me, and burst through the door, letting the wood fly back and rebound off of the wall with an echoing crash.

We followed Uncle's scent to the back of the house, to the observatory, and I slowed to a crawl, to silent steps that allowed me to hear what was being said. Shouted.

"What is the meaning of *this*?" A booming voice bellowed, and Elián and I crept closer. He was a silent support, as always, and the brush of his hand on mine grounded me once again.

"The meaning of what?" The cold voice retorted.

"What have you *done*?" I crept forward more, willing my damn heart to calm. But Goddess damn me, as I tentatively looked through the doorway, my eyes were immediately met by Jones, standing with arms crossed and almost vibrating, ready to strike.

Uncle and Mathieu whirled to look at Elián and I in the corridor, and the rage on both of their faces was only further evidence of the violence crackling in the air.

"What did you *do*, Mathieu?" I frowned at my Uncle's bark at my brother. He stood tall as my father, looking down on Mathieu and

Jones.

My brother's mouth twisted, and he swept his gaze over our uncle, his partner in all the good work they had been doing for decades. "Nothing," Mathieu furrowed his brow at Uncle, showing true confusion, and I felt my shoulders relax. I didn't know what was going on, what was happening, but we could sort it out. We would figure it out.

Hendrik blanched at my brother, taking a step back as if he were truly frightened, but no, that wasn't right. Why would he be—

Mathieu spun on his heel to walk back toward the glass wall of the room. The blue of the clear sky and the rich emerald green of the rolling Versillian hills felt like they were surrounding us.

My brother was still in his dusty riding clothes, as was Jones, and he poured two fingers of liquor at the cart beside one of the leather sofas. And when he raised his head from the ritual I'd seen him and my father do many, many times, I hardly recognized him.

His eyes were... blank.

And now they cut to Jones, and he gave a curt, businesslike nod.

I was thrown behind a wall, Elián's back, and I heard a wet crunch, then the shudder of metal on leather. Something hit the carpeted floor.

My hand shoved Elián's arm, and I pushed around him. Jones was still standing where he'd been, looking as if he hadn't moved. Mathieu took another sip of his tumbler, but was now gazing dispassionately at the floor.

Between us, Uncle's head was about three feet away from the rest of his body that had also fallen and was now lying prone on my father's favorite rug.

My chest heaved, and I looked back at Mathieu who was—not Mathieu.

42

"Mat, what—what—" Elián's arm extended in front of me, trying to push me behind him once again.

Mathieu drained the rest of his glass and started to pour another. He shrugged while he removed the stopper on the decanter.

"Mathieu," I pleaded, "What is going *on*."

My brother lifted the shimmering container, "I believe you know what's going on, sister," he poured another two fingers into his glass and placed the stopper back in the decanter.

He palmed his drink and shoved a hand into the pocket of his brown leather trousers. My brother looked down at our felled Uncle, our father's little *brother*, and smirked. The twist of his mouth was one I had never seen on him before. It was detached, it was—amused.

A shivering realization was coming over me. Uncle had heard my accusations and…

I echoed Uncle's last words, "What did you do, Mathieu?" I whispered above the erratic beating of my heart and the blood rushing in my ears. My hands were shaking, and my power was curling up the entire length of my arms, now.

Mathieu eyed it with a purse of his lips that looked like Maman's, "To what are you referring?"

My whole body was trembling now, and the boulder in my stomach rattled my bones, "Did you..."

He took a swig from his glass and raised a brow. But it was nothing like Elián's teasing expressions. It was expectant, cruel. "Did

411

I make a deal with the King of Krisla to ensure his cooperation? Did I pay that disgusting mercenary to dispatch your High Priestess? Yes and yes," he took another sip and smirked again, "Thanks for the tip, by the way." I recalled telling him of my work, the few establishments I frequented that posted contracts up for bid.

I started to sway on my feet, the room beginning to spin. *"Why?"* I screeched, screamed. The only thing keeping my knees from buckling was my clutching to Elián's arm.

Mathieu shrugged again, dusted the front of his jacket, "Because she refused me. Denied our offer."

"But—but—the letter had gone to Uncle and—"

"And she sought to turn him and you against me," Mathieu went to a smattering of papers on a nearby table, and began to read, "'I do not accept your offer. You will not have what you seek. I see you, and so will she.'"

Elián was trying to pull me back even more towards the door. But my eyes were still on my brother, still reeling from his words. My mouth went painfully, painfully dry. "What did Isabella see, Mathieu?"

He tossed the letter down on Uncle's body, where blood was soaking the rug in a near-black pool. "It doesn't matter now that the bitch is finally dead," he kicked his boot at Uncle's head before him, and I felt bile rise in my throat. It rolled just as Shoko's had and—*it couldn't be.*

"Mathieu... did you—did you have something to do with—"

"Your disgusting former lover finally meeting her end?" He supplied. "Is that what you want to know?"

My palm rubbed at my chest. *This wasn't happening, this wasn't happening, this wasn't happening.*

He scoffed and looked at me with sharp disdain, "Oh, *spare me,* sister. Yes, I organized it, as I did the other Vyrkos attacks across the realm. Is that what you're looking to hear? You weren't responding to my invitations, and I needed something to make you want to leave Nethras, just as I needed the push for the others to join the Council. Those heathens are especially simple to rouse." He shook his head in bewilderment and took another drink.

I gagged, felt the vomit kiss the back of my throat. Elián tried to move me another step backwards, but I refused to go. The male before me, he *was* my brother, but he also wasn't Mat. Mat was smart and quiet and *kind*. But this was… "And Cal?"

His cheeks pulled back to show his fangs in delight, "All too eager to support my bid when the time comes. Using Uncle's name in the letter was just to cover our tracks, of course."

"Wh—what *bid*."

He rolled his eyes and proceeded a step toward me. "To lead our people toward a prosperous future, of course," he said innocently, dangling the tumbler from his hand.

It was a sick mockery of what I had been quoting with all my hope and fervent rehearsal. To Isabella, to Roalld, to *Cal*. "But the *Council*."

He stared at me with wide, knowing eyes, and spoke slowly as if I were a child, "Was a means to an end, as it has always been."

"A means to *what* end, Mathieu?"

He took another step closer, and I resisted Elián trying to back us away, ignored the growl rumbling in his chest.

Mathieu's gemstone eyes went even colder, his face twisting into a disdain that… yes, perhaps I had seen whispers of throughout these past few months, maybe throughout our *lives*. The frustration, the tightness of his lips. But—I'd read them as typical of siblings, of quarreling between a little sister and her older brother. Of a brother trying to care for his stubborn, broken sister.

"Do you know what they called me when I came back? When I returned to this kingdom that was still just as damaged as the night we left?" I felt stuck, frozen, but I managed to shake my head, "King of Ruins," he seethed. "Even with everything I've done—"

"But—but you've put Versillia on the road to becoming even greater than what Papa did! And that's what brought me back. To support *you*."

He looked at me as if I disgusted him, and my heart sank further into my chest. "I don't want your fucking support. You being here was always just a means to an end, too, same as my deal with Cal," Mathieu took another step forward, over the growing puddle of Uncle's blood.

"But, Mathieu, you *asked* me here," I knew I sounded whiney, hysterical, and it only seemed to further his distaste for me.

He threw back the rest of his drink, "Better to keep you close just in case."

"In case what?" I flung my hands up.

"In case you tried to take the crown and spoil it all."

I flinched, my eyes widening. A ridiculous, shrill laugh left my lungs, "I never *wanted* the crown, Mathieu! You're the rightful heir, anyway. And I would have *gladly* stood behind you as you took it. What don't you understand about that?"

"It's not a matter of *want*. *I* wasn't blessed by Rhaea and the fucking Mother herself! No matter if you seek the crown or not, there will always be those who see you as the rightful ruler over me. King of Ruins or Queen Protector of Innocents?" He laughed harshly. "But now it doesn't matter. I will be king of us all." And I felt a curl of understanding. Isabella had *asked* me about taking the crown. And so had Elián.

I stumbled forward, past Elián's outstretched arm and closed the space between me and my brother. He had to *see* that I didn't want this. There was no one standing in his way of that.

But my feet squelched in the pool of Uncle's blood. Mathieu had killed Isabella for... seeing that he was keeping me close to ensure that I didn't—challenge him?

But no, no, no, more realization swung into my head. My thoughts started reeling again. Ajeh, Quen, Edan, *Cal*, they were all —"'The Council was a means to an end,'" I quoted him. It was never about starting another Lylithan Council. It was about him, and only him, rising to power?

He huffed, "Took you long enough. You see, Mother always favored and coddled you, Goddess knows why. You were always so fucking oblivious." The heel of my hand rubbed over my breaking heart. What was he *saying*. Maman loved us both.

But then I thought back to his monument to her. I'd conceded that the full scope of Rhaea's power was kept secret from the rest of the world, so he had to build a temple to her, for our mother, like the rest of those in the realm.

But even Papa, who loved Maman with all of his heart had never done such a thing. There was no need for it when Versillians' regard of the Godyxes was mostly secular. Bile rose in my throat again—it was an insult, a *slight*. Against me and Maman.

"Mat... what did you do with Francie?"

His brow wrinkled. He looked confused, surprised, but that must have just been more of his pretending, more of his mask, "Who's Francie?"

I started to argue, to demand he tell me what he did with her, but there was a blur of movement to my left, and I whirled around to see Jones grabbing Elián's arms.

My Elián looked enraged, bucking against Jones's hold, head thrashing as he managed to get one of his arms free. But then his eyes raised to me, and the color drained from his face and from his mango eyes.

And then an exploding, searing pain punched through my back.

43

I lost control.

My grasp on it had never been so futile as it was when it came to her. Meline, my queen. I felt the blade pierce her heart as if it had stabbed mine.

When she confronted him, I saw the violence and resentment behind her brother's masterful mask before he let it fall and revealed all of his hatred toward her. And then he lifted and used her dagger against her.

Jones, the *traitor*, held my arms while Mathieu stabbed my queen.

She never thought her brother would be the one to hurt her, try to kill her. Or else she would've never turned her back on him, but when she saw Jones grab me, I watched her eyes widen just before she was felled by her own blade.

Everything seemed to stop in that moment. Her eyes that were the color of the richest soil that yields the most beautiful flowers locked with mine for a second, then went distant. He just let go of her. He was going to let her fall to the ground like nothing.

I exploded.

The windows of the glass room shattered, and my flames poured out of me. Jones was foolish to try to hold onto my arms, and when the fire coursed out of me in an inferno, I was free.

I gripped *him* by the throat and watched his sea-glass eyes melt down his cheeks while the rest of his face charred and split like roasting meat. I threw him through the broken metal supports of the windowed wall now blown open, and sank down to my knees.

Her brown skin was dulling, and the flames on me grew higher, hotter. Rhaea's dark mark was still on her skin, but it didn't dance across her flesh as it normally did. More panic was rising over me, and I ripped her dagger from her back and let it fall to the floor with a muffled clatter.

My arms wrapped around her as gently as I could manage with the rage still racing through me, and I held her to my chest. Distantly, I realized that I was screaming, and my fire covered us in a cocoon of orange and blue and white.

I wiped a thumb at the trail of her blood trickling out of the corner of her mouth, and that wasn't right. She should have been healing, the bleeding stopping. But it was just getting worse. My hand on her back was becoming drenched, and her heartbeat was waning.

I put my brow to hers and rocked her softly. She should be healing, she would be okay, she was—

"P—poi," I pulled back and saw her looking at me, gaze no longer far away.

"My queen, what is it, why are you not healing?" Drops of water splashed on her cheeks, and her black, beautiful lashes quivered.

"Bla—pois," and she moved her eyes slowly, too slowly, to look down her nose. Her hand flinched and landed at the middle of her chest. The blade hadn't broken all the way through, but I knew that it had hit her heart. I searched her face, dusted with freckles like stars in the clearest night, and another roar left my chest, this one understanding.

Her blades were poisoned.

And it was in her heart. She wouldn't survive this.

Her pulse was already deadening. I could hear it. I could feel it like the draining of my own life, and no, no, *no*.

"Mm... eh..." I shushed her. She wasn't crying. My queen was looking up at me with a bloody smile on her face, and my tears spilled onto her dry, full lips. The flames around us flared higher, and I cursed the Mother, the Godyxes, for letting *my*—

It was a fool's last ditch effort, I knew. But the panic had taken deep root in my chest, and I was nothing more than a grieving, scrambling mess. I didn't even feel the puncture of my fangs on my wrist. When I pressed my bleeding skin to her lips, she started to shake her head, and I shushed her again. This wasn't *right*, this was not going to happen.

After a few drops made their way into her mouth, I saw the flare in her eye when she tasted them. Her tongue did dart out, and though she was too weak to hold my arm to drink, I kept it steady and felt the soft pulling of her lips. My people weren't known for their healing like hers were, but maybe, maybe—

Someone was hovering just outside my wall of flames, but my eyes were on *her*. But the drinking was slowing. I felt my heart quicken as hers slowed even more. It wasn't working, the poison was too much. Her skin was paling, and my arm beneath her was now dripping from her wound. There was nowhere I could get her in time. Moving her might make it worse, and and and—

My love who had Death in her very veins wasn't going to survive this.

She was no longer drinking, her lips moving against my skin. I reluctantly pulled back, and she licked away my useless blood so she could try to speak again.

I leaned my ear to her lips to hear her, tried and failed to keep my trembling from shaking her. "Had—" she coughed up blood, some of mine, some of hers "—had fun. W—wi—you." And I couldn't contain the laugh, the sob. She was such a delightful menace, and she was going too cold, too quiet.

When I looked down at her again, her eyes had grown distant once more, unseeing. The thudding of her heart was almost nonexistent, and I pressed my lips to hers, then to her brow, then to each cheek. Her pink peppercorn and lilac scent flooded me, and I wanted so badly to drown in the taste of ocean breeze coming off her skin.

"Leenie!" A faraway voice called behind the roaring of the flames around us and my own heaving. Without her, there would be nothing. She had brought light into a life that I hadn't even realized had gone so, so dark.

"Master Elián!" There it was again. It wanted to take her away from me, even this moment. It didn't want me to even have these last seconds with her. My snarl, hunched over my dying queen was not a sound I had made before, but I would die before they tried to take her away from me any more than she was already leaving.

Yellow, round like a sunflower, danced behind the dying walls of my fire, but that couldn't be right. I tried to peer between the licks of the flames, but my queen giving a wheeze turned me back to her. It didn't matter. All that mattered was this taunting, beautiful, female that consumed and danced with me in a way I had never known before. Despite my pushing her away, writing her off as a vapid, petty thief. She commanded me. She was endless, and every look from her threatened to steal all the air from my lungs.

Even now, with her staring up at me but not, I felt like I couldn't breathe. I was choking with my cries, and it would be any moment, now, and I—

A shaking hand pushed on my shoulders, and I felt so weak, so hopeless, that I relented before snapping my head up and baring my fangs.

And it was her. Meline, it was her with her own tears in her eyes. But, but that wasn't right, either.

I furiously blinked my tears away, and it wasn't her. It was the golden witch. What was her name? The witch's hands were pushing under mine on my queen's back, where her own brother had used her blade to kill her. The witch's other hand pressed on my queen's chest, over her quiet heart.

"… blood burning up the poison…" and I could smell the telltale sweetness of magic stirring. But I could barely feel her now, it wasn't going to be enough, just like I hadn't been enough.

More of my tears splashed her face, her cousin's hand. I bent to kiss her brow again, couldn't bear to look in her still eyes.

"*Fire Bringer,*" The witch hissed, and I despairingly met her gaze. "*Give her more, now.*" The witch nodded down to my hand that was caressing my queen's brow and resumed murmuring, chanting, with her eyes closed.

What was she—

"*Now, you lovesick idiot,*" the witch hissed again, but it wasn't her words that spurred me to action. It was a gurgling inhale in my arms. And then a louder, clearer, thud.

I stared down at my queen with wide eyes. "*For the love of the Mother, feed her.*" The witch was shouting in my ear, and I tore fresh punctures in my healed wrist. I pressed it to her mouth once again, and the witch and I held my queen beneath the stir of fire and aether that was flowing around us.

The golden witch kept chanting, and I kept feeding, feeling the pull of Meline's drinking grow stronger, more frantic. I looked up to the bare sky above, still blue in the midday, and for the first time in one-hundred and twelve years, I pleaded to my mother's Goddess. *"Lo pava, mé sana Zoko,"* I prayed to Meline's Goddess, *"lo pava, Rhaea,"* and I prayed to the Mother, *"lo pava, Matra, sa yamita vitir, é sahmo."*

Our words coursed louder, filling the space as the golden witch beseeched the aether to work and flow, and I begged for *Them* to save her. To let us succeed.

Distantly, the sound of shouts were ringing, but we just kept praying, kept giving, and then the thudding was louder, steadier, and there were hands gripping at my arm, holding it there.

My queen's eyes were closed. Not in death, thank the Mother, and I kept giving to her. I realized in that moment that I would give her all, absolutely everything, if she needed.

The witch's hands moved to feel at my queen's brow, to brush the hair that stuck with sweat to her face. "You're going to be okay, you're going to be okay," and I joined her cousin in giving praises, encouragement. She was actively lapping from me, and the laugh I gave now was with wonder, shock. Even now, her skin was warming, slowly returning to her usual, gorgeous color.

I felt my own energy begin to wane while she drank, but it didn't matter. She would take what she needed and *live*.

"We have to go," the witch's voice that was normally light was now heavy with emotion that I cared not to decipher or ask about. Meline was too weak, not ready, and though she'd now stopped drinking, her eyes still weren't opening. I brought her closer to my chest, listened for her breathing, her heart. The thudding was strong, now, almost its regular rhythm, and her breaths were slow but steady. The wound on her back, I rubbed my palm over it a few times to be sure, had closed.

"Fire Bringer," the witch hissed again.

"Don't call me that," I bit back and showed my fangs to her once again. It wasn't rational, nor was it fair, a small part of me knew.

"Listen to me," the witch shoved my shoulder, and I brought my eyes to hers that were the color of sea foam. She stammered but pressed on, "L—look. We can't stay here. We need to *go now*. If you want her to keep living."

My eyes narrowed to slits at her words, her accusation. But they also pulled me further out of my grief, my panic, my rage.

The room was burning.

The whole estate was burning. My queen's brother was impaled on one of the iron supports for the glass wall that was now blown apart. His charred body was still smoldering, and a ripple of satisfaction raced through me. I'd barely been paying attention when I killed him, but seeing the agony melted onto his face, I wished I could do it again.

"The guards are going to be here soon," she seethed beside me, and I looked further out into the burning grounds before us. My fire had caught to one of the servant's quarters, and a cluster of people were running away from the flames with belongings clutched in their arms. When my eyes landed back on the golden witch, I took in the black singes along the ends of her fluffy hair that was so much like my queen's. She was covered in a sheen of sweat, and the dress and tunic she'd worn were darkened by smoke.

My queen's cousin shoved my shoulders again, but my hiss held no heat behind it this time. Shouts in the distance were growing closer, and surely that was the galloping of hooves. "Carry her, and let us *go*. Word will get back to the Council. We need to *get out* of Versillia." The witch stood and tugged on my arm, demanding I stand.

I gingerly nestled my free arm beneath Meline's legs and stood as quickly and gently as possible, whispering apologies and assurances into her unconscious ears.

My queen didn't stir, nor did she make any noise while the three of us walked around pools of fire, crunching on broken glass. None of us spared the charred body stuck into the wall a second glance, and I belatedly realized that the witch was clutching onto the back of my tunic. But I had no idea where we would go. This whole fucking kingdom could burn as far as I was concerned, but we needed to get her somewhere safe sooner rather than later.

We rounded the side of the house that was quickly becoming consumed by my flames, coming upon the stables. The witch jumped and yelped at the sound of something inside the sprawling home collapsing, but I pressed us forward.

The white-haired stableboy was rushing back and forth, releasing the horses from the stables and directing them away from the flames. When he saw us, my queen still limp in my arms, he simply nodded and continued his efforts to save the steeds.

"Can you ride?" I grunted to—Tana, that was her name.

"Yes," she responded in a wobbly tone.

The galloping I'd heard must have been from the stablehands releasing the horses, as there were few left to choose from. We stumbled our way down the rows, and came upon two on the end that were bucking, huffing, and rolling their large eyes in terror. The fire hadn't yet reached here, but it would soon.

I went to the black one on my left, raised the palm I had on Meline's back. "Shh shh, Noxe," I cooed as calmly as I could. The mare stopped bucking, and snorted, perhaps now in more recognition. My footsteps crushed the hay beneath me, but I moved as slowly as I could with urgency pressing on us.

She accepted my touch, though, and I called over my shoulder, "Saddle Bhrila, and we will go." The shuddering of leather signaled Tana doing just as I said, and I made slower but careful work to saddle Noxe. Shaking hands joined me to finish, and I grunted in thanks. I wasn't setting my queen down, but her cousin was right. We needed to go.

With one hand clutching her to me, I hoisted myself onto Noxe. Positioning Meline was a bit more difficult, but I sat her against my chest, and clamped my arm over her waist to hold her to me. The other hand, I held Noxe's reins, then clicked my tongue in command. She started forward, and we picked up speed, heading away from the burning estate. I kept my body rigid but moving with the smooth jumping of Noxe's gallop, and Tana rode beside me, eyes intent on the road before us. We didn't speak but shared a joined purpose.

We pushed the horses harder than we should have, but the mares didn't falter, didn't complain. There was nothing for my queen or her cousin in Versillia anymore. I clutched her tighter to me and gave a soft press of my lips against her temple. She was still warm, still breathing, and I pushed us on.

The sun continued to fall in the sky, and when the blue traded for a deep orange, we flashed past a small house set back in the trees.

We'd been running with no destination, no direction other than *away*. I'd camp in the woods once we were far enough from that evil place, where I was sure no guards, no one from Versillia, would find us.

But something tugged on my mind, and I reeled Noxe to turn and stop. She obeyed, and Tana followed suit beside me.

"What? Should we stop now?" She had dark circles at the top of her cheeks, but she looked alert, ready to follow me wherever I thought best.

I looked down at my queen, still limp but alive in my arms. My hand on her waist trailed lightly with a brush of my fingers, and I commanded Noxe forward, back toward the little, unassuming house.

It wasn't readily apparent from the road, but I'd been there before and recognized its wooden roof and the small garden of herbs and vegetables beside it. Though it was slightly different in the light of the ending day, it looked much the same.

At our approach, a small human woman with dark, short curls opened the front door with knife in hand. A black dog barked wildly at us, but I wasn't deterred by the small weapon or the small beast.

As carefully as possible, I dismounted Noxe and clutched my queen in my arms once again. The woman smelled of fear like she had that night. The knife bobbed in her shaking fist, but she held it tight. Good.

Another human, this one with pale yellow hair, popped her head out of the door. She looked worriedly at the woman with the knife before sweeping to me, standing halfway to her door. Tana remained silent behind me, and when the woman met my eyes, recognition quickly swept her face. She lurched out of the house and towards us, past her wide-eyed companion.

She approached with no fear, and she reached her delicate hand out, as if to touch my queen in my arms. I flinched back, clutching Meline tighter to me, but the woman was not deterred. "What happened?" Worry was etched deep in her face, and she took stock of the rest of my queen's unconscious form.

"I...We are here to call in a debt. I need your help."

44

I hummed softly over her sleeping form, tenderly petted her freshly washed and braided hair. Her breathing was still calm, her heartbeat still strong. But it had been two days. Two days without seeing her enthralling eyes. Two days without hearing that melodic voice.

Mine was hoarse with how much I whispered to her while she slept. But each minute, each day, each hour, her eyes never stirred. Her chest just rose, fell in an unfaltering rhythm.

And I *was* grateful for this. I had asked the Goddesses and the Mother for this. But not one of the witches could tell me why she hadn't woken. They took turns chanting over her under Tana's guidance, and I looked upon it all with wary, watchful eyes. When I did leave her bedside, it was for the briefest of moments that were filled with an anxiety that threatened to choke me outright.

"Elián, you need to eat," Tana spoke softly from the doorway. I just grunted at her, though she was right. My queen's cousin sighed and turned away to give me more time with Meline, to continue my never-ending watch.

She had been the one to braid my queen's hair the first night after washing the smoke and glass and blood from the thick strands. I watched the ritual the first time and joined her when she repeated the bathing this morning.

Krisla seemed so far away, a lifetime ago, but I couldn't help think of the way my queen had *burned* her hair, changed it for that foul king. And she took my disgust of such a thing as dislike, insult, of *her*. If I hadn't felt so helpless, I might have laughed.

Earlier today, my fingers had felt inept, clumsy, but I took my time as I mimicked Tana's deft washing and braiding. She spoke to me all the while, some of it instruction, some more mindless chatter, but I welcomed it all. Her voice was more honeyed than my queen's raspy drawl, but it was similar enough to be... comforting. And she told me stories of her cousin, my—love.

"She's always been a bit broody, you know. Always making you work for it. To pass her assessment before she lets you in."

I'd actually snorted, disbelieving. My voice had felt foreign, mostly unused beside the chanting whispers I'd given these past days, "She was the one to ask me to let *her* in." And the truth of that made my heart ache. Her constant pressing at the time was too much, frightening. When she was supposed to be just another one of the cheap blades for hire, a petty thief who'd stolen Shadow ways for her own use. But then she turned out to be *her*, the queen of legends, and then she was so... *confounding*, and it was bewildering, the effect she was having on me. Until every speck of dislike or rage or *control* I had fell to the wayside.

The night we kissed, the times she had broken my shields, I'd scrambled to construct them even higher. To protect myself and to hold onto the last bit of restraint I had. But when I'd let them fall completely that night in Krisla, I knew that I would never be able to keep myself from her. Even when I tried my best to concentrate on getting her back to Versillia safely, I knew that it was only a matter of time before I crossed into her darkness again.

Because there was only those eyes, that smirk, that bottomless cavern of... solace.

Tana had chuckled heavily beside me as she tied off the end of the thick plait she'd created, "Seems you passed her assessment."

And then we'd dressed her in a soft slip provided by the witches that Meline had saved that first night of our journey. I'd been so *irritated* with her. For endangering her safety, for making *me* save *her*. And then she was upset with me for saving her.

My lips twitched at the memory of her pulling twigs and broken leaves from her hair when we'd gotten back to the inn. She was so fucking stubborn, my queen, but I would give anything now to sit back and let her chastise me, rant at me.

I imagined what she'd say, "*You asshole, I could have gotten myself out of there,"* She would point at me and try to hide her bubbling smile. *"Don't look at me like that! I don't need saving."*

Tana and I took care to pull the slip over her head and thread her arms through the straps. My palm brushed over the wound at her back and cringed at the cool skin where the blade had entered her. The black, curling marks were like the rays of a dark, cruel sun that I could cover completely with my palm.

Through these days, the mark hadn't gone away, and the witches theorized that it may not ever go away. They thought it might be a scar left by the poison, but the feel of it under my fingers—I knew it was part of her gift. What it was doing, I didn't know.

I'd carried her back to the bed that the women gave up for Meline's healing, and after trying to comfort her, perhaps rouse in the way that my mother had when I was a child, I now turned instead to a book on the small table beside the bed.

We'd not taken anything with us when we fled that wretched kingdom, but the curly headed woman who had suffered the most in that Vyrkos attack liked to read romantic tales, too. Admittedly, they were... sweeter than I knew my queen preferred.

I opened to where I left off the night before and began to read to her. I didn't stop until I had exhausted the words of the small book, finishing the story and letting the two of us fall into silence once more. I'd never shied from that lack of chatter before. It was its own comfort, and in my line of work, people often revealed themselves in their discomfort of it.

But the absence of her sound, her voice, was tearing at my heart.

I sat beside her, elbows resting on my thighs, and waited. Waited for the second night in a row for something to happen. And again my mind wandered to my Shadow siblings. I had been in such a state of panic—I hadn't taken in my surroundings like I should have, like what had been ingrained in me. But when I replayed the scene, careful to not think about her blood that had drenched my hand or her last words to me or the bloody smile she gave me—

I swallowed. Jones's burnt body hadn't been among the flames or the rubble, which meant that he'd escaped. Would he go back to the Shadow Well? Had word reached back to the others? Hopefully Noruh had been well on her way back when everything went to absolute shit.

My hands scrubbed my face. I would return to the Shadow Well to sort this out later, and confront Tomás for being stupid enough to get in such a bind that he relayed Shadow techniques to a stranger. I was no longer angry at Meline for utilizing her limited knowledge of our ways, rather impressively, I admitted, but my Shadow brother would have to provide some answers, as would Jones.

We so seldom had traitors in our ranks that the punishment for a betrayal such as Jones's was harsh. My fists clenched in my lap. I was eager to be the one to dole out his sentence. Surely the others would agree.

But that was for another day. I would not leave her side until she was awake and moving and herself again. Then I would go back and sort out things with my siblings, assure that there were no other traitors among us.

I touched my queen's shoulder where it peeked just over the blankets we'd spread over her. I couldn't seem to *stop* touching her now, constantly needing to check that her skin was still warm. That her chest was still truly rising and falling. The pad of my finger circled the individual dots on her skin that were peppered all over.

She would wake up. She would wake, and we would have more time together. And we would fight and laugh and properly spend our days beside one another. There was no alternative. There was no other option that I would accept.

So, I sat back and waited.

45

My back fucking *hurt*.

That was the first thought that swam to the forefront of the endless black. It didn't burn or sting, but it was sore beyond belief. And the feeling went further in, to where I couldn't touch, but also hurt with each breath.

And my mouth was dry. Why was my mouth so damn dry?

I tried to lick my lips, but they felt unreasonably heavy. It felt like my flesh weighed a thousand pounds, but I managed to wet the skin that tasted like remnants of something. Like... an oil or balm. Where the hell was I?

Something warm touched my cheek, but it was familiar. Safe. I leaned into it, and tried to remember. Tried to sort through the murky thoughts, but then there was a rumbling, shaky voice, "My... Meline?"

My lids were so heavy, but after what felt like forever, I managed to pull them apart. There was barely any light, save for that coming from a single candle somewhere in the room, and it allowed me to adjust. It was almost too much as it was, but each slow blink cleared my vision. Goddess, how long had I been asleep?

I was lying down on something soft, and another soft thing was over me, a blanket. Somewhat scratchy, but otherwise warm.

The pillow beneath my head was a bit lumpy, though, and my eyes slowly roved over the ceiling. There was a cobweb in the far corner, but it was otherwise blank. My eyes moved again, and landed on twin, crackling suns.

They were watching me with awe and so much concern, but I relaxed into the safety of them. It felt like my body, my soul, was warming beneath them, and I felt the corners of my dry lips twitch.

That voice was less shaky now, and instead, it cracked into a choked laugh, a cry, and his cheeks pulled back while tears fell.

My arms felt weighed down with stones, but I shot them out from under the scratchy covers. I brought my hands to his face and felt the hair there. My thumbs landed in the shadowed dips on either side of his mouth, and warm tears trailed down my fingers, down my wrists.

It took me a moment to speak, to get my mouth to work, but I was eventually able to croak, "Told you... I'd make you... smile." And then he was grinning even wider at me.

Elián.

Elián was crying and smiling and chuckling over me. Wait—I felt my brow furrow—why was he crying?

When I rasped the question at him, his smile faltered, falling to an uncertain twist of his soft lips. Instead of answering me, he lowered to meet his mouth to where my forehead had wrinkled. The black hair on his jaw tickled my skin, and he curled over me.

My chest expanded, inhaling his musky scent, but my muscles screamed at my too ambitious movement. I hissed in pain, and he stilled, pulling back. He brought his thumb to brush over my nose, my cheek, "Are you in pain?" he whispered.

"My—back. My chest. Just... sore."

He kissed my hair, and I felt another tear splash on my face. He wiped it away, "I am crying because you have been unconscious for a while. I was very worried." But there was more. The torment and *anger* in his voice was clear, even in my fuzzy mind.

I pressed on his chest, giving room between us, and our eyes locked. "Tell me." My fingers stroked the hard lines of his face that were even sharper now. There were dark shadows under his eyes, and even the waves of his inky hair seemed limp.

He swallowed, but I kept staring, kept waiting. There was something that he wasn't sharing, something he was afraid of telling me.

But I needed to know. There was something bad in the murkiness of my mind, and I needed to face it. "Please, El."

He winced and clenched his eyes closed. Two breaths, and he nodded. "You—my queen," he took a deep inhale, "you almost died."

Which, honestly, made sense with the way I was feeling and with what he'd said earlier. But the look on his face... it was worse than that. *Worse* than me almost dying. He had more to tell me, and I waited.

He sighed, broad shoulders sagging, and he bowed his head to meet his brow to my face. His lips moved over mine, just too far to touch, "You were stabbed with your blade. And the poison to your heart almost killed you." But there was more, so I didn't ask any questions, just let my fingers continue to caress his jaw, coax him into speaking more, as if to say, *I am not a soft flower. Tell me.* And he opened his mouth again, "Your—your cousin and I fled and have been caring for you while you've slept."

Tana? She was here? I wanted to ask, but Elián's heart was beating so fast, his breaths coming so quick. What else was there? He didn't want to say what came next. I tried to rub harder at his face, but the muscle at his jaw clenched, as if to keep the words from escaping.

That wouldn't do. I closed the distance between our mouths, and gave him a delicate kiss. Then another. "How—who. Tell me, please, El."

His groan was barely audible, but it was anguished. I kissed him again, and perhaps it was manipulative. I knew that he wouldn't refuse me in this, that my kisses were a reminder that I was here and not going anywhere. When I pulled back from the third press of my lips to his, he swallowed, "Your—your brother."

And my ears started ringing.

My—Mat had. Part of me wanted to wail, to scream that it was a lie. But Elián's words were a spark. The memories were clearing, and with it was the horrible, horrible truth. Mathieu's face was so... awful when he told me those things. Showing how much he'd hated me. How much he hated Maman and—

"I am so, so sorry my queen," he sounded as pained as I felt, and more of his tears plunked onto my cheeks, making it look like I was crying, too.

But there was... emptiness. A resolution that my greatest fears when it came to Mathieu had been true. Not in the exact ways I'd feared, perhaps, with his resentment carrying back to our childhood. When I truly *hadn't* done anything wrong.

But then *Isabella* and *Uncle*, and I choked back a sob.

I clutched my arms around Elián's neck, and he met me, he understood. Despite the burning soreness in my upper body, I nudged him until he lay down and let me curl into his chest. Shoko and Lee had been more casualties of my brother's disdain for me, his need to break me to unwittingly do his bidding. And when I failed, became too big of a problem, he wreaked more havoc.

Lying in Elián's arms, I cycled through crippling despair and utter numbness. It had all been a lie, a ploy for his own selfish, stupid goal. And had every moment with him been a lie, then? The nights of blushed giggling with Tana, the care and consideration he gave me after my birthday—and Goddess, he'd decided to break me on my *birthday*.

My hands clutched even further into Elián's black tunic, the same one I'd last seen him in, and nuzzled my face even closer into his neck. "El?" His soft grunt rumbled against my head, and I sank further into him, "How did you save me?"

At my question, I felt his whole body stiffen, with *fear*. I tasted it deep in my throat, and though I could tell this sense was fading, it was stronger than it had been last time I was awake and, "I... I made you feed from me. While Tana used her magic. She said that my blood burned the poison, rid it from your body. And she healed you." And from the warmth in my bones, the awareness of *him* not just around me but within my veins, I knew it had been a lot. Surely more than he should've given.

"Thank you," I whispered into his chest. There were flashes, glimpses of his face, shouting, and I clutched my eyes closed with the ghosts of pain that rode along with the memories. A searing, agonizing pain that was deeper than I'd ever felt. Only rivaling that was the betrayal that had also strangled my heart. But finding his eyes in the suffering, there'd been... peace.

Before I'd lost consciousness, I'd accepted it. Death. In all ways. My own power wasn't a match against the poison injected directly into my heart, but in his arms, in that moment, it was okay. And I remembered just not wanting him to cry as he was, to scream as he was. So I'd gathered the last whispers of my strength, wheezed through the blood filling my lungs. And tried to make him smile.

"I really have had much fun with you, you know," I spread my hand over his heart, and felt its frantic beating, felt his whole body shudder at my words. What were supposed to be my last words in this realm.

We held each other, breathed in each other's presence for a long time. Elián ran his hands over my hair, kissed my skin, and I did the same to him. There was so much loss, so much destruction, but he was here. I was here, and we had each other. There could be this.

When I twirled a finger around a lock of his hair, he whispered between us, "I have had much fun with you, too, my queen."

My answering grin was genuine, my laugh painful through my chest, but I didn't care, "I *told* you that we would. From the very beginning."

I propped up on my elbow to look at him, and though he looked tired, haggard, the light in his eyes and the utter tenderness with which he looked at me threatened to steal my breath in the best way. Elián opened his mouth to say something, but the door to the small bedroom burst open—I still had no idea where we were—and the intruder came to a screeching halt in the threshold.

"You absolute fucking *prick*." Tana rushed in the room and sank onto the already-crowded bed and glared down at the two of us. Tears were already falling from her eyes, and I belatedly saw that her hair looked windswept, the bottom of her shift caked in mud. "You didn't tell me she woke up!"

She wailed at Elián, but I was smiling at her now. I silently reached my hand out to her, and when she met it with hers, I pulled her toward me. She relented, mud-stained dress and all, and I was then clutched between the two of them, letting their emotions wash over me, cleanse me.

They'd saved me and healed me. And judging from my clean body, neat hair, and soft bed, cared for me. The backs of my eyes tickled while we three lay there, my head fitting into the curve of Elián's neck and Tana clinging to my other side, taking comfort in that I was still here because of them. And in this, I knew that we would be all right. I would be okay.

46

The women I had saved, the *witches* I'd saved on the journey to Rhaestras, were so generous with us those next three days. Reina and Cameryn were their names, and each time I thanked them, waved away their fawning, they huffed and reiterated that they were honored to help me. Indebted to me.

And though they'd suffered such a trauma, they both offered themselves for me to feed from them, to speed my healing, they said. And the aether that flowed though them *was* helping me heal tremendously. The third day we stayed at their little cottage, I was able to properly get out of the bed, to walk the perimeter of the home with Tana and their dog, Speck, at our heels. We talked of her grief for Uncle that burned as true as the betrayal we felt about Mathieu. Not once did she say anything to indicate blame towards me. Though it was hard to believe, to trust, I just let the little voice speak its worries and pass. I was much, much too tired.

Elián hunted game for us, taking down a whole deer with his bare hands that second day and butchering it with a swift precision. All his weapons had burned with my family's home, but he wielded the knives from Reina and Cameryn's kitchen as deftly as his lost twin swords.

He hadn't let me *actually* hunt with him, but perched me on a boulder amongst the dense wood so that I was able to watch. He then directed me on how best to skin it, gut it, and I absently licked the hot, gamey blood from my fingers while I followed his orders. "So, how does a boy from the desert learn to hunt and skin a deer?"

He cleaved the deer's muscles, organized the different cuts and set them in neat piles while we stood over the witch's wide wooden table, "My father was not from the desert, and in his training of Leandro and I, we learned not just Shadow ways, but his family's ways as well." And I learned that Elián was a proficient archer because of this, which, of *course* he was.

While he cleaned our mess, Tana and the witches got to cooking our meal and setting up the rest of the meat to be stored or dried, and when we ate on the floor of the front room with our bowls of deer stew in our laps, it felt like a new start. A new life.

And the next day, the aching in my chest was gone, my lungs being able to fully expand without a single hitch of my muscles.

We'd been at the witch's cottage for nearly a week, and the three of us were already speaking of, preparing ourselves, to go. Reina and Cameryn were inside while Elián, Tana, and I sat outside. Speck barked merrily for Elián to throw his stick again, and when he did, the dog bounded off into the darkness of the forest before coming running back at full speed. He dropped it before Elián's feet, who indulged the pup once more and threw the wood in a different direction but just as far.

"So, where will we go? Back to Nethras?" Tana was especially chipper this evening, as I knew that she was anxious to feel settled. She wrapped yet another bundle of dried sage for Reina and Cameryn. They'd become fast friends, as my cousin was able to do with most anyone. But the shadows under her eyes hadn't fully dissipated.

"Too..." I couldn't find the word for it, but the thought of returning back to that city, where I'd worked so hard to create a new start, to work for the farce of this Lylithan Council, to atone for my sins...

"Much?" Tana supplied, and I nodded. "Somewhere new, then?" Because she was with me, ready to follow wherever I needed. We were all that was left of the Richerre family, but whatever befell Versillia, we'd decided, was up to the people.

Everything about all of that was poisoned, tainted. Ravas, Ajeh, Quen, Edan, the whole fucking *Council*. But it didn't matter, now. It would crumble, as it should.

"Where would you like to go, El?" I called over to him and

watched as he hurled the stick through the air at an impressive speed. Speck went off again, and when my—*he* turned around, his face was… different. It was masked like I hadn't seen it in days. In a way that I'd almost forgotten about in the stark vulnerability we'd shared since leaving Krisla.

He didn't answer, but when he reached his hand down to take the stick from Speck's drooling mouth, I saw a strain to his jaw, a large swallow of his throat. "El?"

He straightened but refused to turn around, the profile of his face almost punishing in how, suddenly, it felt as if he was hiding. Shielding himself from me. My breathing was coming quicker, a knot forming in my chest around my still-healing heart. What was going on?

"I—will follow you anywhere, my queen."

I worriedly glanced at Speck who sat patiently at Elián's feet, then to Tana beside me who was looking just as perplexed, just as worried over her neatly wrapped bundle. My tongue darted out to lick my lips, and I took a deep inhale to push down the bile rising in my throat, "…But?"

And I imagined him turning to me, saying that there was no *but*. That he'd drop everything, *do* anything.

He didn't. His jaw ground and flexed, and his frustrated, lazy flick of the stick away from him even had Speck curious, wary. "I will follow you. But," he turned his shoulders to face me, but his eyes wouldn't meet mine, "I need to return to the Shadow Well, too."

My mouth twisted, my lip curled. "*Why?*" I demanded. With the days of healing, my memories of that day had completely cleared. The way Jones had cut Uncle down right beside me, at *Mathieu*'s silent command. The way Noruh was nowhere to be found to protect my uncle, and Jones held Elián back while my brother stole my blade and tried to kill me. There was nothing for him there if he truly—

Elián's face twisted in misery, his fists clenching, "Because I am a Shadow, Meline. I always will be."

And it was like he'd slapped me. He would always be a Shadow. But surely *none* of that mattered now? "You saw what they did, Elián! They would have killed you like Mathieu tried to do me. There is nothing for me in Versillia, just as there is nothing for you there!" My voice was rising to a screeching pitch, my chest tightening with my hopeful truth. Hoping that he felt the way I did about him, about all of this. I *knew* the way he felt about me.

His eyes looked back at mine, pleading, "But I *am* a Shadow. It is a vow I took, my queen. And I can still come with you, stay with you."

My vision was blurring, my hands trembling, "But it's all—*rubbish*, El. We are *going*. We are leaving all of this behind so that we can start anew, and the Shadows were *helping* Mathieu. They would have cut you down for their goals, just as they did Shoko and Lee and Isabella and Uncle—"

"Not *all*. I cannot believe that. I do not," his voice was gravelly, harsher now. And this was not—it couldn't be.

I stood shakily to my feet and was more unsteady than I'd felt since waking in that bed. But he needed to understand, to choose me, choose *us*. "Look, El, I know that," and my face was wet, my throat choking, "we haven't known each other long. That I can be... difficult and trying, but—"

He looked back at me, horrified, and crossed the distance between us in an instant, but it was too far, too much. His hands grasped my wrists, and brought my palms forward. They were riddled with the black veins, and he kissed my flesh, each finger, "It is not a matter of wanting you. I told you, I will follow you anywhere. I... I am yours," he looked up from his lowered head, "but I am Shadow, too. They are my family."

And I ripped my hands from his. *No.*

He stood still as a statue, molten eyes filled with so much pain, "I am going, Elián. *We*," I thrust a hand at Tana still sitting stunned, "are going. Where no one can follow, can *know* or hurt us. If you still return back there to *them*, they will *know*."

More tears fell from my eyes when he shook his head, fighting my words, my *truth*. Because if he wanted to be with me, to have me as his *queen*, he wouldn't be able to worship at their feet. To bow to them. Tana and I were going far away. I didn't know where this Shadow Well was, but it didn't matter. If he cared for me, none of this should *matter*. He saw how badly I'd been broken, beaten. He'd held me while I *died*, and he was still choosing *them*?

"Meline, this isn't"—he ran shaking hands through his hair —"I am yours *and* a Shadow. I must see to them like I see to you. Noruh —"

And I exploded, wailing, weeping. My tears were like waterfalls down my flaming cheeks, "You are returning to the Shadows for *her?*" The blackness was flowing out of me now, I saw it like the frustration on Elián's face.

"*No*. She may be *dead* or not know what happened, and Jones is still alive, and he must be judged by our siblings for his betrayal, and I have to—"

I felt the coolness of those vines curling around me, but I could not be comforted. I would not. "*Why can you not just come with me?*"

"I *will*. I have never faltered in this, Meline! I have followed and protected and *wept* for you. I—" he choked off what he was about to say. His chest expanded, hollowed, "You do not *understand*. The Shadows are—"

"Your family," my face twisted in sorrow and disgust, and I tasted the onslaught of salt streaming into my mouth. My power didn't move toward him, just wrapped around me, clung to me. Elián scrubbed his large hands over his face, wrung at his hair. But I did understand. He was not choosing me. He would not choose me, in this.

It felt like the blade of my lost dagger was twisting in my heart all over again, but this time, the poison spread fully. When my eyes met Elián's again, all that was echoed was our tears. They were the flames that were truly burning my heart to nothing but ash. My voice was not my own, "Then go. Return to the family, to the *female* you've chosen." And I knew it was a cheap, low cut.

Elián flinched like I'd stabbed *him*, eyes wide and mouth gaping. "My queen—I will come back, I just need to make sure that they are *all right*."

My laugh was cold, mean, "But you will always need to return to them. Again and again. Right?" He clamped his mouth shut at that. Because he *swore a vow*. He would always be one of them, always choose them, and I was nodding at his non-answer that was all too clear, all too confirming. "Then *go*." My voice cracked at my command, but it was done. This was done. No matter how much I felt myself breaking. I had nothing left but myself and the need to find somewhere safe to lick my wounds and rebuild. And I couldn't have a Shadow be part of that. Not after what they'd done.

Elián tried to lurch forward toward me, but I jerked back, bringing my hands forward to bar him from touching me. And now the darkness went toward him. It wrapped around his arms, his chest, and *held him*. But there was no true death in the vines besides that of our end.

We stared at each other for a long, six breaths. And I watched his beautiful face close, his mask slip into place. The skin around his eyes and beneath his stubble smoothed. The curve of his mouth that I had kissed and caressed flattened into a hard line, and he looked down at me over the cutting slope of his nose. "This is what you want?" And there was no emotion in his tone, nothing at all.

My chin trembled beneath my tears, but I held my spine straight despite the sharp pain in my back, "If you cannot choose only me, only *us*, then yes." And I spun on my heel for the door. I already knew his answer, and I couldn't bear the finality of it. The silence was final enough.

Tana's arms around me were distant to my numb skin, now devoid of any warmth. My wet, pathetic cries wracked my body raw, and she held me through it all. The sound of hooves marching away from the house made me turn away from her, and my cousin caught my vomit just in time with an empty basket. I clutched it to me while I retched and cried and felt a pain truly worse than my brother's rage, his detest.

Tana rubbed my back, bore witness to my undoing, and I was too weak to hide it, to run away to hide *myself*. Because he hadn't chosen me. He was *gone*.

My mouth and throat burned with acid, my face a mess of tears and mucous and heartbroken sick as I raised it to the ceiling and wailed.

~

Bhrila snorted and lapped at the cool, twinkling water. She'd seemed troubled with the absence of her sister, but she still pressed on for me, for us. I absently pet her flank and took a hit of the joint that Tana had lit once we'd stopped to let the horse rest. She was carrying both of us, and we didn't want to tire her too quickly.

I passed a hand over my scalp, felt the air and the absence of anything but a few close curls.

My clean, plain clothing that the witches had given me shuddered as I shifted where I stood and handed the joint to my cousin. Aside from our eyes, with our hair now cut as short as could be, it truly was like looking into a mirror. The grief that now haunted her eyes, too, was an echo of my own.

But so was the determination.

Still, I croaked over the babbling of the stream, keeping my eyes on Bhrila's speckled coat, "You don't have to come, you know. I would... understand if you wanted to return to Nethras. Or go on your own."

She coughed a bit as the hash hit her lungs, but once she regained herself, she just snorted and thrust the joint back to me, "Don't be silly. We are going together."

The knot in my chest still hadn't gone away. It was there when *he* left, it was there when we'd said goodbye and thanked Reina and Cameryn, and it was there as I'd cut the braids from my head. Tana and I buried our pasts just beyond the forest, hers golden and mine dark.

This was a new start, a new life. As we mounted Bhrila, me climbing on behind Tana, I looked to the clear sky. The sun was bright, and my cousin chattered companionably while we meandered back to the road. I answered back, injecting my words with lightness, with feeling.

But I was cold. And despite Rhaea's gift living on my skin, my veins were empty. We continued away from Versillia, from Nethras, from Krisla, and from Rhaestras. Tana handled the reins while I clutched her slim waist with one hand and worried at the warm, gold chain and medallion around my neck with the other.

A new life, a new start. A new beginning.

Epilogue

"Are you sure you're feeling up to this?" I called over the grassy space between us. It'd been awhile since we'd last trained, and my weapon felt cool but familiar enough in my grip. Surprisingly, my body hummed with excitement, but I didn't want her to overexert herself.

"I'm fine," she shot me a small, tight smile as she shook out her arms. A soft wind coursed through the forest, and I rolled back my shoulders. The air made a shiver trail down my neck to the rest of my body. We both kept our hair short, and my scalp was still sensitive to everything.

"How about we just start slowly for today?" Worry for my cousin was churning in my stomach, though we'd already warmed up for longer than we'd needed to.

There was just—only so much a person could go through before they broke for good. She always hid it fairly well, but I knew that she didn't share everything with me. That she had far more bad days than she let on.

And it'd only been a few weeks—she needed to be *resting* for Goddess's sake.

She scoffed and walked closer, "I'm *fine*. Please," she took a deep inhale and straightened, "it—it will help me."

I nodded, dropping it for now. Who was I to keep her in the small apartment we were renting? Ralthas was peaceful and uneventful enough, but I knew that the both of us were used to moving around more. Busying ourselves. The itch to go to the next place was getting harder and harder to ignore, and I knew that we'd be picking up soon.

"Ready?" She looked at me with another tilting of her lips, but the smiles never really reached her eyes anymore.

But if this was what she wanted to do to work through the grief, we would do it. I had to admit that it helped me, too. After the shock of fleeing Versillia had settled, training with my cousin, having a few hours outside dedicated to the physical and nothing else, was like a medicine for the both of us.

Still, losing them—all of them—was still a hole blown wide open in my chest. I knew it was the same, *worse*, for her.

I raised my staff, pressing the button that pushed it to expand to its full length. I twirled it between both hands, acclimating again to the feel of it whipping in my grip. Since we'd left everything behind, the two of us had picked up quite a few new things as we bopped around the realm. The staff was a lucky, and expensive, find while passing by a group of nomadic people that had set up their wares on the side of a busy road. As soon as I'd seen it, I knew that I had to have it. The wood was almost the same shade of my skin, and it was carved with beautiful swirls and curling patterns.

We'd stretched and done drills to work our strength back up over the past week or so, but to spar again would hopefully relieve the pressure in my legs, my arms.

"Ready." I then muttered into the air, releasing the words I'd been working on. Eventually, I hoped to do this without having to chant at all.

White light flared in my palms and quickly spread up the carvings in my staff. The laugh that bubbled up my throat was completely involuntary, but I couldn't contain the wonder. All the way extended, my weapon was nearly as tall as me, and at first, it had felt shockingly heavy. But even with these months without training, my muscles supported and wielded it easily.

When I tore my eyes away from the staff, I saw my cousin

stretch her neck from side to side, and my gaze clung to the short covering of leather on both her hands. Black smoke released from her palm, just beneath the hems of the gloves she wore. While some of the darkness curled up her arms and arced over her elbows, the rest solidified in her hands.

Two daggers, dark as the night sky, appeared, and she twirled them familiarly in her grasp. It was easier for her now, but this training was as much for her as it was me. We were both learning to use our abilities in combat scenarios, but she'd been teaching me how to use my body as well.

I wanted to ask her one more time if she felt up to this, physically and mentally, but I knew that she could quickly descend into another dark mood. Where she would refuse to talk, disappearing to sit by the river for hours. Sometimes days.

In those first days afterwards, I sat with her, perched on a boulder and listening to the deafeningly silent wails of our grief. But it became too painful. To sit there and see the shadows on her face, the tears that would only dry for a moment, an hour, before running again.

I focused my energy on mixing my poultices, crafting healing tonics to sell at the local market. There were a few witches in town, but they had been welcoming enough when I'd begun to sell my wares. It gave me something to do with my hands as I processed on my own.

My mother was long gone, but Dad's death made it all seem deeper, more unfair. My cousin was here, and I was so grateful for her. But since he'd died, that deep loneliness never seemed to leave.

Obviously, I'd never tell Leenie that, though. She was going through enough, and her despair made her turn inward more than she already did. I'd indulge her for as long as she was willing to talk, to engage with me.

So, I wasted no more time and lunged forward.

Fighting magic was not my forte, but I was determined to

learn. Her conjured blades collided with my staff in heavy thunks as we let our bodies talk.

The magic I called to my grip made her blows rebound without chipping into the wood. Tendrils of smoke curled each time our weapons collided before dissipating into the air. This close, my cousin's gift felt cool, deadly. Against the electric sparks of aether on my staff, it made for a show of shadow and light.

We circled around each other, and I took each constructive comment from her, adjusting my stance when she slashed at my tunic to emphasize how open I'd left my side. I repeated a strike when she barked encouragingly the first time I'd tried to catch her middle.

After what felt like an eternity of calculating and moving, we were both panting and coated in sweat. The sun was on its way down for the evening, but we still had a few hours left.

We leaned against a giant oak tree and passed her travel mug back and forth. Cool water chilled my throat, and I felt it flow down inside my chest.

"Have you heard anything from Whitley?" I asked while she took another sip. Meline had written a few letters to the caretaker of the children's home in Nethras. After her Shadow had left, she'd told me more of what they encountered. Though she'd initially wanted to leave everything behind forever, I could tell that *he* had changed a lot about the way she viewed things. We never spoke his name, but I knew that it put a lot into perspective for her. It weighed so heavily on the both of us.

She squinted up at the cloudy sky above and sighed, "Yes, but no news." Meline passed an absent hand over her head, roughing the tight waves over her scalp.

I nodded while chewing at my bottom lip. Would now be a good time to ask? To bring up the idea I'd been tossing around for awhile? She seemed in an okay mood today. And she said that this stuff was helping her. Maybe she was ready?

Clenching my eyes shut, I forced out what I'd been considering before… everything had happened.

"Would you want—eventually, maybe—to start taking up contracts again?" She remained silent, but I pressed on, "I c-could help you? I mean, I know I'm not," I took another breath, "at your level or anything. But it might be good? We could earn more money and test out everything I've learned?" I opened one of my eyes, shoulders nearly at my ears.

Her dark, slightly glittering eyes stared back at me, mouth pursed.

"And—and, we could take up looking for F-Francie? Maybe? If you're up for it?" *That* had not been part of my idea, but the words spilled out of me before I could stop them. She'd lamented the disappearance of her old friend enough for me to know that she couldn't heal from all she'd been through with Francie's whereabouts still hanging over her head. With Whitley still taking care of those children without their mate.

Finally, she let out a little huff. Her posture was easy as she leaned against the tree, and she crossed her arms at her chest. The leather of her gloves squeaked on her skin. "You'd be interested in that?"

"Yes!" I cringed at how loud and overly excited I sounded.

Meline looked me up and down and tilted her head from side to side as she considered. Logistically, things had been fine. We had a roof over our heads, money to buy food. But I knew that it wasn't enough anymore.

She seemed to know it, too. My cousin snickered, and it almost—*almost*—reflected in her eyes. My cheeks pulled back in a grin as she said, "All right, witchling. Let's do it."

Pronunciation Guide

- Dyna— DIE-nuh

- Meline— meh-LEEN

- Nethras— NETH-ruhs

- Shoko— SHOW-koh

- Tana— TAH-nuh

- Vyrkos— VEER-kohs

- Lylithan— LIL-ih-thin

- Versillia— ver-SIL-ee-uh

- Mathieu— math-YEW

- Ajeh— ah-JAY

- Ravas— RAH-vahs

- Edan— EE-den

- Elián— el-ee-AHN

- Rhaea— RAY-uh

- Aeras— AIR-ahs

- Zoko— ZOH-koh

- Yeva— YEH-vah

- Bhrila— BREE-lah

- Noxe— NOX-ee

- Hyvan— HI-vahn

- Rhaestras— RAY-strahs

- Erat— EH-raht

- Verot— VEH-roht

- Cera— SEH-ruh

- Jesyn— JES-in

- Roalld— ROH-ahld

- Zonoras— zoh-NO-rahs

- Nâ— nauh

- Vendaco— BEN-dah-koh

- Merro— MEH-row

- Lo pava— low-PAH-vah

- Mé— meh

- Sana— SAH-nah

- Matra— MAH-trah

- Yamita— yah-MIH-tah

- Vitir— vih-TEER

- É— ech

Acknowledgements

Meline and Elián have been in my head for a very long time, and the fact that you picked up my little book means the world to me. So thank you, my dear reader.

I would also be remiss if I didn't take the time to appreciate all of those who have helped make this possible though their love and support and indulgence in my nerding out over this story.

When I began writing, I didn't realize that the bonds of sisterhood would be such a large theme, but with the women in my life, there's no wonder where I gathered my inspiration from.

To my book girlies Darcy and Alexia with whom I've shared so many exciting conversations about all the books we enjoy (and don't). Thank you both so much for reading my first drafts and giving me the feedback and advice I needed to get my first novel to where it is now. To Emma, thank you for reigniting my passion for reading.

To Teri, thank you for your artistic expertise in giving this book its beautiful cover. To Mikki, Linnea, Mary, and Janie, thank you for being my support. And to Allaina, thank you for being my model of sisterhood since the very beginning.

Lastly, I want to thank my husband. For truly showing me what unconditional love is and for providing me the space and support to fulfill this dream of mine. For reading multiple drafts, assuring me that I *could* do this, and being my safe place. I love you.

About

Noelle Upton is an author and lover of fantasy, romance, and dark tales. When she's not writing or reading, Noelle enjoys dancing, chatting with friends over good food, and laughing with her husband. Twin Blades is her debut novel.

Meline and Elián will return in book two, set to be released in 2024.

If you would like to access a sneak peek of the next installment of their story, you can sign up for my newsletter on my website www.noelleupton.com and receive a free download.

You can also find updates on my Instagram @noelleuptonauthor

Milton Keynes UK
Ingram Content Group UK Ltd.
UKHW041152091123
432257UK00001B/15

The Warrior Queen, Protector of Innocents... fights in seedy taverns and picks pockets for hire.

Her people are rebuilding, and after a century of running, Meline returns at the request of the only family she has left. They've built a kingdom from ashes and connected with other leaders to give them all a fresh start, but they are still under attack with perhaps a repeat of the slaughter on the rise.

So to atone for her sins, Meline agrees to travel to faraway lands and persuade more to their cause, even if the agreement demands she take a personal guard. But not all is as it seems, and her Shadow is hiding a secret of his own.

Through homecoming and redemption, Meline finds herself leaning on her companion as they face tense negotiations, assassins, and the mysterious powers of a Goddess. But is it all enough to confront the female she once was and conquer Death? Or will it lead to the ruin of those she loves most and the future of her people?

Cover art by Teri Smithberg

ISBN 979-8-9890779-0-8
51899

9 798989 077908